Simply Mad

a novel

Christina Coryell

Books by Christina Coryell:

The Camdyn Series
A Reason to Run
A Reason to Be Alone
A Reason to Forget
For No Reason

Girls of Wonder Lane
Simply Mad

Facebook: www.facebook.com/AuthorChristinaCoryell
Twitter: @c_tinacoryell
www.christinacoryell.com

Simply Mad

To Karri,

for loving great chick-lit as much as me...

Chapter One

"What do you think of pink? Practically perfect, or pampered princess predictably prowling for a prince like a perfectly-prepared predator?"

Silence meets me on the other end of the phone, and I stare at myself in the full-length mirror with a clothes hanger held precariously close to my face.

"Well?"

"I don't even know how to answer that question," Jess announces. "What's with all the P's, or do I even want to know?"

"Practicing my linguistic gymnastics." Squeezing my neck through the hole between the salmon-hued dress in question and the hanger, I gaze at my reflection carefully in the mirror. "Benjamin is an English teacher, and at night he gives courses in Spanish. He's bound to be well-versed in both languages, so I figure I should warm up my phonological skills, no?"

"Sí. And just in case you think I meant 'yes,' I actually meant, '*See* Benjamin run back to his mother like a frightened puppy.' What happened to Fester?"

"Simmer," I correct, as though it really matters. "He couldn't really bring things to a boil, as it turned out. By the time our second date was finished, I knew I couldn't make it through another."

"You needed a second date to convince you not to be with someone named 'Simmer?'"

"He's a DJ, okay? That's not his real name. Anyway, I'm not snobby enough to judge someone for their name."

"So what was it then?"

Giving myself a guilty grimace in the mirror, I hesitate for a second. "He laughs through his nose."

"And the guy before that? What was his name again?"

Pausing to loop a multicolored scarf around my neck atop the hanger, I place a hand on my hip and pose to the mirror. "Vic? He was weirded out about Josh, so we got in a fight about it. Honestly, though, I was about to cut him loose. One of his ears was higher than the other, and he liked to drink warm milk. So gross. You still haven't answered me about the pink, by the way."

"I'd go with a darker color, and definitely not a dress. You'll look like you're trying too hard. And don't eat that! I saw the dog lick it."

"Excuse me?!"

"Sorry, Maddie, I was talking to Isaiah, not you." Jess has a habit of blurting weird things to her son in the middle of our conversations, so commenting about the dog licking something is actually not that strange. "What about Josh, though? Why would Josh weird him out?"

"It's a long story," I reply simply, prying the hanger away from my neck.

"I'm currently standing in my bedroom wearing my pajama bottoms and my son smells like a toxic waste dump. Please regale me with your tale of woe and allow me to live vicariously through you for a moment. Consider it a courtesy."

Laughing at Jess, I pull a fitted navy T-shirt from the closet. "Okay, so the other day I was Skyping with Josh, no big deal, and I lost track of time. Vic showed up, but instead of knocking, he just opened the door."

"And Vic got mad?"

"Vic? No, Vic didn't care. Josh is the one who got mad. 'Why do you have a guy in my house, Maddie? Specifically, the only thing I asked you not to do was have a guy in my house.'"

"You broke his rules," Jess interrupts in her most motherly scolding voice.

"No, I did not." Pulling out a yellow blazer, I toss it onto the bed next to the T-shirt. "There is a huge difference between a

guy walking into the house to pick me up and 'having a guy in the house.' That's what I told Josh, too."

"Yikes."

"Don't stick up for him, because I'm obeying his ridiculous rule. It's not my fault Vic walked in unannounced." Plucking out a pair of dark-wash jeans, I throw them on top of the blazer. "Josh hasn't talked to me since. It's been six days."

"And what about Vic?"

"He told me that I should tell Josh to stick it, and that he has no say over what I do. I defended him, and we got into an argument. Like I said, though, he was toast anyway. The ears…"

"Of course, the ears." Jess laughs, a tinkling sound that always brightens my spirits. "Don't worry about it. Josh will come around. You're the incessant soft spot in his life, you know."

"As though I care what Josh thinks," I blurt, regretting the words instantly. I do care what Josh thinks. Way too much, if I'm being honest.

"Never touch your doody. Never, never, never." Jess lets out a gasp, and I hear her voice rise a whole octave. "Don't touch me! Bathroom, Isaiah, now!"

Giggling, I tell her I'll talk to her later. Before I hang up the phone, I can hear Jess continue.

…ew…don't you dare… if your dad knew what I deal with every day…

With a slight shudder, I toss the phone onto the bed. My life hasn't been the same since Jess moved to San Diego when her husband Levi got transferred to Naval Base Coronado, although I suppose it began well before that fateful parting.

Josh met Levi when they were together at Recruit Training Command in Great Lakes, Illinois. Jessica Mason and I were enjoying our freshman year of college at the University of Kentucky when Jess went with her parents to graduation at Great Lakes. By the time she came back, it was with her entire future planned out thanks to her instant devotion to the dashing southern boy from Georgia. She married Levi two years later, and subsequently followed him wherever life dictated. Currently, that means the warm days and cool ocean breeze nights of San Diego.

Me? I stayed at the University of Kentucky until I had my degree in marketing and communications, and then planted myself permanently in Louisville when I found a job at the prestigious Cooper Corporate Financial. My adult life officially began without the presence of my lifelong best friend.

Rousing myself from my reminiscing, I glance again at the clothes on the bed. One hour until my date with Benjamin, so I might as well prepare myself.

It's hard to mentally plan for my date while thinking about Josh, though. Truth be told, I don't like the idea of him being angry with me. We became fairly close after Jess walked out of my life. I suppose our relationship began selfishly on my part, connecting with my best friend's brother, but we developed a deep friendship that sustained me through many empty nights. Skyping with Josh became a ritual that I employ about as often as shaving my legs, and I wear a lot of skirts, so that means it's a pretty constant occurrence.

With a year left in his military service, Josh decided to purchase a house in our hometown in the suburbs of Louisville. "The quaintest little home on Wonder Lane," his mother likes to call it. Since he is currently deployed to Camp Patriot on Kuwait Naval Base, the house was sitting empty. That is, until he asked me to move in. He simply wanted someone to keep the place from being unused, he insisted, and he would feel a lot better knowing I was there. "Consider the house yours while I'm gone," he assured. "Use whatever you like, and make yourself at home." He only had one rule: *No guys allowed.*

It's a pretty straightforward rule, isn't it? I thought so, too, but I'm a twenty-five-year-old woman trying to find someone to spend a happily ever after with, and I can't even allow any of my male friends in to use the toilet.

Dressing myself in the jeans and T-shirt, I slip into the blazer and check my appearance in the bathroom mirror. Wrestling with my thick, wavy auburn hair takes quite a bit of time, but eventually I'm satisfied. A bit of mascara and a touch of lip gloss

and I'm ready to go. Smoothing my hair over my shoulders once more, I glance at my watch. Thirty minutes until Benjamin is supposed to pick me up, from the porch, while not stepping one foot inside the actual premises.

So, 6:30 in Louisville—that is 2:30 in Kuwait, I think?

Is it polite to wake Josh in the middle of the night? Maybe not, but six days is a long time.

Leave him alone, Maddie. After the date.

For a split second, I wonder if it's a bad sign that I'm already making plans for after the date. Benjamin is an educated, well-mannered guy. After the date, we could be making arrangements for an elopement.

Unless he likes warm milk. If so, then adios.

"How was the tiramisu?"

Benjamin holds his coffee mug near his lips, gently cupping it between his hands, staring over it with his dark eyes. His tan skin gives him a slightly exotic look, and I feel rather elegant sitting across from him at that small table.

"Oh, delicious," I lie, pushing my fork around on my plate.

I secretly hate coffee. So many people seem to think it's a symbol of sophistication, though, that I force it down and pretend that I'm high society. After struggling to choke down Benjamin's tiramisu, I can't wait to get home and use some serious mouthwash. Bleh.

"I knew you'd enjoy it," he states with a smile. "It's one of my favorites. What's your favorite?"

"My favorite what?"

"Dessert."

Placing his coffee on the table, he offers up an easy smile. His mother is Hispanic, which describes his perpetual tan. It also

explains why being bilingual is second nature for him. So much for the linguistic gymnastics. He isn't a great lover of languages–he just grew up learning and understanding two from the beginning.

"I like sugar cookies," I tell him. "The big, soft, fat ones with the icing piled on top."

"The kind that give you a sugar coma?"

Biting my lip slightly, I look down at my plate. "Yes, but only on very special occasions." Don't want him thinking I sit around stuffing cookies in my mouth, after all. "So, if you're not all about grammar, then why did you go into teaching English?"

"Because I love the written word, and I enjoy sharing literature with those kids. Most of them don't think they're interested in it at first—it's a challenge."

Totally boring first date answer, and I don't buy it any more than I believe my own lie about the tiramisu.

"If you love literature, you must have an extensive reading list. Who are your favorite authors?" I take a second to check the placement of his ears, and they seem to be in the correct position.

"Hemingway. Faulkner. Huxley. How about you? Do you read?"

"Sometimes, sure," I reply with a shrug, trying desperately to think of a book I have read and coming up blank. Then, a name suddenly pops into my head. "Camdyn Taylor. I like her books."

Why is that name so familiar?

"Camdyn Taylor? The one who threw up on television?"

Oh, that's it. I saw her on late night TV. Drat.

"Yeah," I add with a laugh. "Funny, isn't it?"

I should have said I liked Hemingway, too. Would have been way simpler.

"I actually have read a couple of her books, when kids in my class chose to do book reports on them. One was about Martha Washington."

"Uh huh," I agree awkwardly, pulling that dreadful coffee up to my lips.

Note to self: Buy Camdyn Taylor book so I can study up in case Benjamin decides to pursue this conversation at a later date.

"Well, school day tomorrow, so do you think we should go?" He shoves his chair back and stands, so I follow his lead when he pulls my chair away from the table. He is easily a couple inches taller than me in my four-inch heels, which is very appealing. Plus, I've convinced myself that he looks a little like Mario Lopez. Not really, since he doesn't have the dimples and his face is thinner, and I don't really imagine there's much muscle definition hiding under his shirt…

Okay, so he looks nothing like Mario Lopez, but so far I haven't noticed anything perceptibly *wrong* with him.

He places his hand at the small of my back as we walk to his Ford Mustang, and he reaches down to open the door for me to step inside. Attempting to grin up at him, I stop as I notice the coffee taste clinging to my lips like the kiss of death.

The ride home is pleasant, and he behaves as a perfect gentleman, walking me to the door and asking if he can see me again sometime. He bends to place a kiss on my cheek, and then he is on his way. It's not the way I envisioned a first date with the love of my life, but I'm not exactly disappointed as the scent of his citrus-based cologne slowly follows him away from the porch.

Inserting my key into the lock, I push my way inside. The instant the door closes behind me, I can't resist glancing at my watch.

9:30, so that makes it 5:30 in Kuwait, right?

I shouldn't allow myself to call him. He was in the wrong, after all. He's not my dad, and he's not my brother, even if he has grown to act that way over the years. Sure, I'm staying in his house for free, so I acquiesce to following his silly rule, but that's the end of it.

Besides, I just had a lovely date with…

What was his name again?

Oh, yeah, Benjamin. He was wonderful. Maybe he's the one.

Chapter Two

"How are the graphs coming, Maddie?"

Kyle Porter, my boss. He's 6'1", but he still manages to sneak up on me when I least expect it.

"Almost done. I just have to look up a few more numbers."

"Don't forget, we have a deadline of 1:00."

"I know, same as last month." Or should I say every month for the last three years. The Kyles of the world may come and go, but the wheel never stops turning as long as there are hard-working, dedicated employees like myself who do the majority of the work and receive zero credit when the praise rolls in. Not that I'm bitter or anything—it's just an observation.

I glance up to see that Kyle is gone, evidently slipped away as quietly as he arrived. Maybe I shouldn't be too hard on him. It's only his third month here, and he can't have had very many jobs before this one. He's twenty-four-years-old, just one year younger than me, but he's got to be overwhelmed with his job responsibilities. I'm sure I would feel that way if I was suddenly put in a position of authority straight out of a Master's program, with no idea how to manage personnel and only a vague indication of what I was actually expected to do with my time.

On the other hand, I'm sure his salary dwarfs mine, so it's hard to feel too sorry for him.

"You should have that job," Katie whispers from behind me. Katie Green, my confidant. Her transfer to this department two years ago made the workday a lot more bearable. "Maybe next time they'll open it instead of appointing someone."

"Sounds like you don't think Kyle will be around long."

"Poor kid won't know what hit him. Although I do prefer Kyle to you-know-who."

Ah, yes. Bill Davies, or rather "he of whom we no longer speak." Katie and I decided the moment he left that we would never utter his name again, and I haven't said it aloud to this day. Kyle may be a little clueless, but Bill was just plain mean. In fact, I specifically recall one particularly horrible moment from the past…

I was sitting at my desk one afternoon, diligently working on my computer, when I sensed a presence above my shoulder. I turned to see Bill standing above me, face red and straining beneath his white mustache. He was a rather large figure, and with him blocking my view of the office, I felt slightly like a trapped mouse.

"Yes, sir?" I questioned. He exhaled loudly as a sheet of paper slipped from his fingers and floated onto my desk. I leaned forward to view the item just as he brought his fist down like a sledgehammer on the corner of the document. I shuddered and managed to push my chair farther away from him.

"Do you have some problem, Heard, with taking a simple phone message?" His voice was raspy and his neck almost purple above his collar. I hated it when people called me Heard—it reminded me of taunting from grade school.

"No, sir."

"Apparently you do, so let me explain it for you very carefully. First, you take the caller's name and number." He stabbed his index finger in the air as if to punctuate his sentence. "Second, you legibly write that information on a sheet of paper." Stab. "Third, you give this piece of paper to the appropriate party." He crumpled the document in his hand and held it in the air. "Now, is that process painfully clear to you?"

"Perhaps if you just tell me what's wrong with the message—"

"What's wrong?" His voice seemed even louder than before. "I can barely read your scribble. You used the wrong colored paper. You put the message on the wrong corner of my desk!"

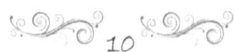

"Sir—"

"Why can't you do things like Shelly?" He stood staring down at me smugly, as though he were the sheriff and I merely a lowly prisoner about to receive an indictment.

"I'm not Shelly."

"No, you certainly are not. THAT is apparent." He stalked out of my line of sight, knocking a stack of papers off my desk as he strode away. I felt tears spring to my eyes, which only served to make me angrier. The last thing I wanted to do was appear weak.

"I'm sorry," I heard a voice behind me whisper. I turned to see petite platinum-blonde Shelly, face white and eyes large.

"It's not your fault," I managed to murmur, probably not sounding very reassuring.

"Yes, it is. I wrote the message."

Ugh, my face is getting hot just thinking about it! Katie is definitely right. Kyle is better than *you know who*.

"So, how do you think 'you know who' is doing in his new job, anyway?" I ask.

Katie shakes her finger at me. "Uh-uh-uh, he of whom we no longer speak. We made a pact, remember?"

"You're right. I don't know *what* I was thinking." I hear Katie giggle faintly as I turn back to my graphs. I've been doing these things so long now that I don't really have to think that much, which seems like a good thing, since I have so many other subjects to occupy my mind. In fact, I should start compiling a list right now, to be sure I don't miss anything.

1. *Choose special outfit for second date with Benjamin.* First impressions are really important, but second impressions are what really hooks a man. This is my theory, anyway, and lately I've been attempting to put it into practice.

2. *Buy book by Camdyn Taylor.*

3. *Actually read a book.* Benji might ~ shudder ~ ask me a question about Martha Washington. Terrifying.

4. *Employ use of the nickname Benji.* I kind of think it's sweet. Mental note—feel it out to see if he likes it.

Why isn't this graph working? My numbers must be off. "Katie, what do you have for the monthly projections?"
She's rustling through the papers on her desk.

Benjamin Westlake.
Benji Westlake.
Madeline Westlake.

"You want to tell me something?" Katie's giving me a stern look. Her numbers must be off, too. Maybe her projections are missing. Well, she must have misplaced them, because I distinctly remember giving them to her early last week. When I handed them to her, she told me that she liked my nail polish, which was funny because I had just been thinking that the color was all wrong for me.

"You don't have the numbers?" I ask. She stares at me blankly, and then begins tapping her finger on my desk. "It's okay, I'll just get them from Kyle." She doesn't say a word, just keeps tapping. Tap, tap, tap. I look down at her finger. Did she get a manicure that I didn't notice? Maybe she got a new ring? Why else would she possibly want me to sit here staring at her finger tapping on my list of things to…

Oh, heavens.

"Benji?" Katie questions.

"Don't tell anybody. I'm just trying it out."

She winks and stops tapping. "Of course not. Number one—the green dress with the drape sleeves. That looks great on you."

"Thanks." That dress does look great on me. Number one accomplished.

Katie hands me the projections and heads back to her chair. I transposed one of my numbers, so I make that quick change and the graphs are done well before the 1:00 deadline.

You're welcome, Kyle.

Settling down at the dinner table later that evening, I help myself to a sleeve of buttery crackers and a scoop of peanut butter. If I'm going to impress Benji, I probably shouldn't eat like this, but I haven't exactly decided that he's worth impressing yet. Just because I can't find something wrong with him doesn't mean there *isn't* something wrong with him, after all.

The urge to talk to Josh is killing me, but I fight it by dialing the number for my parents' house. I almost hit the end button as soon as I hear the first ring, but the other side picks up rather quickly.

"Hello?" There's a weird rumbling noise in the background that I can't place.

"Hi, Dad. I can barely hear you."

"Sorry, the lawnmower's running and I just came in to get a drink. Talk to your mother." I hear the screen door slam, and the noise begins to fade.

"Hello? Mom, are you there?"

"Hello? Oh, Madeline, I'm so glad you called. You will not believe who just called me." Pause. "Oh, come on, you're not even going to guess? It was Brittany. Lance would have called me himself, but he's on a business trip, tying up some loose ends on some deal he's working on."

Lance is my brother, and Brittany is my sister-in-law.

"Brittany kept trying to tell me something, but Marilyn was in the background saying, 'Let me talk to Grandma. Come on, let me tell her. Let me!'"

"Uh huh…" Come on, Mom, get to the point.

"Well, finally Brittany handed the phone over, and Marilyn says, 'Grandma, we're coming to live where you are!' When Brittany finally came back on she said it was true. They're moving back home. They've got a house not five minutes from ours. We'll be able to see them every day! Won't that be terrific?!"

"Yeah, terrific." Like that moment when the creepy music begins in a horror movie.

"It will be so great to have them here when the baby comes. I told her it's about time we have another baby in the family! And they'll be living so close, I'll be able to see this one all the time. Brittany and Lance always have the prettiest babies! I'm so proud!"

Oomph—Mom always has a way of sucking all the air out of me like a deflating balloon.

"I tried to get your dad's attention, but you know how he is about that lawnmower. He's been tinkering with that thing all afternoon, and now that he's finally got it running, he won't let anything deter him. Oh, I wonder what he'll think about all this! Can you believe it's been six years since they moved away? I didn't think they would ever come back, but now they are, and it's going to be so wonderful."

"When are they moving?" I ask, even though I'm not interested. Not in the least.

"Should be about a month from now. They sold their house, so all they have to do is pack up. I told Brittany I don't want her lifting anything in her condition. Wouldn't want anything to harm that precious little one. I am just so excited! But now what did you call about, dear? Did you need something?"

Yes, actually. An interesting life that doesn't pale in comparison to Brittany's.

"No, I was just calling to say hi. I'm expecting my boyfriend to call any minute, so I better go."

"You have a boyfriend?" Mom asks skeptically. "What's his name?"

"Benji Westlake."

"Benji?" she wonders with an audible gasp. "Like a dog? Oh, Brittany's going to love this. I'm going to call her and tell her right now. Do take care, honey, and don't go so long between calls next time."

Click.

Mom?

I can't believe Brittany, always stealing my thunder. Well, my mild rumblings, anyway. I don't usually have much thunder to steal.

She actually got appendicitis during Jess and Levi's wedding. Right in the middle of the lovely ceremony, where I was standing confidently next to Jess in my pale yellow dress, the preacher asked for the rings, and this strange whimpering noise started coming from a few rows back. *Who let a dog in the church?* I thought, only it wasn't a dog. When I turned around, Brittany was on the floor in the aisle clutching her stomach. Who can concentrate on the blushing bride, much less on the beautiful maid of honor, when there's a scene like that? If she had any courtesy, she would have at least gone to the foyer.

Oh, and there was also my college graduation. I looked so distinguished in my gown, sitting in the midst of a sea of flattened caps. The keynote speaker was saying something about changing the world for the better, and I knew that I would. I was thinking about all the important things I wanted to do with my life when I heard a commotion start in the stands behind me. I casually turned my head to see what was happening, and immediately wished I hadn't.

"Madeline!" my mother yelled. "Brittany's water broke. She's having the baby! We're going to the hospital."

My true importance was ultimately revealed in that instant. The notable, stately college graduate, upstaged by amniotic fluid and a slightly inappropriate mother. The worst part was that they hadn't announced our names yet. When they came to me, I heard a rumble of snickers throughout the stands. *That must be the girl,* they were thinking, laughing as they whispered about my inevitable embarrassment.

And I can't forget the time she stole my Mother's Day gift idea. She and Lance hadn't been married very long; in fact, I was still in high school. She happened upon me as I was putting the finishing touches on my gift—an old photo of Lance and me sitting in the garden. Not having much money, I used a simple wooden frame and painted our names on the sides. She looked at the picture thoughtfully and told me she was still trying to choose the perfect gift.

Imagine my surprise when I woke up on Mother's Day to find Mom in the kitchen hanging up a copy of the garden picture that was twice as big as mine and in a classy silver frame. Brittany and Lance were sitting at the table, laughing and drinking orange juice. Mom glanced over at me, standing stupidly in the doorway holding my painted wooden frame.

"Oh, how funny!" she exclaimed. "Madeline gave me the very same picture!"

Brittany only sat smugly at the table, staring at me.

"That is funny," Lance agreed. "Great minds think alike, huh Maddie?"

No, Lance. Great minds have great ideas, and lesser minds steal them.

"I wish we would have known," Brittany cooed. "We would have let you go in on our gift."

I fought back the urge to lunge at her and pull her hair out by the roots.

"I'm surprised you didn't know, since you watched me make the gift."

"Oh, is that what you were doing?" she asked, never skipping a beat. "I was wondering about those finger paints. I thought you were working on a school project."

Mom and Lance chortled, and I stood like a statue in the doorway, silently smoldering.

"I'm going for a walk," I announce to no one in my quaint little house on Wonder Lane.

Correction—Josh's quaint little house.

Managing to get as far as the front step, I lower myself to the concrete and stare at Mrs. Willows across the street watering her flowers. She's a woman on her own, just like me. It occurs to me that I should probably know more about her, but I've never bothered to ask. Was Mrs. Willows once a career girl who had been passed over time and again for promotions? Did she go on countless dates with men who didn't quite measure up to her expectations? Did her family run roughshod over her like she was a doormat?

Will I be in a house alone later in life, watering my flowers while another young woman sits across from me feeling sorry for me?

Shaking myself out of my stupor, I rise and walk undeterred, like a woman on a mission. It has been a long six years, but Brittany is not going to get the better of me. I am going to have my time in the sun, and she can sit in the shadows and sulk. I will persevere. I am determined to take back my thunder.

Or at least make a little.

Chapter Three

I've always thought First Avenue Community Church looked like a page out of history, an old-fashioned little country church somehow misplaced on a city street. In fact, I've often imagined the first parishioners sitting calmly in their pews as the whole building was caught up in a tornado, like in *The Wizard of Oz*, swirling around and around in the air until they were suddenly planted where the church currently rested. They would walk out, survey their surroundings, and someone would inevitably say, "I don't think we're in Kansas anymore."

I never can fully remove the flying cow from my vision, though, which totally ruins the whole picture. And then there's the creepy green lady flying past the window… Well, you get the point.

It's difficult to imagine anything today, however, except a path to the door through the rain coming down in sheets. While I'm debating how to get out of my car and throw open the umbrella in one swift movement, I see someone with their own umbrella quickly approaching.

"You shouldn't be out in the rain," I chide as Hazel Mason holds the umbrella above my car door. She simply smiles. "You look nice today."

"Oh, shush. I look like an old lady next to you." She puts her arm around me and pulls me close.

Since we have been best friends so long, Jessica's parents have taken me under their wings. I got in the habit of going to church with them, and now it's our Sunday morning ritual.

Hazel pauses under the awning to shake the excess water from her umbrella. "Mercy, can you believe this rain? God knows we need it, but it doesn't seem necessary for it to come down with such force!"

"Hi-ya, kiddo," I hear as I receive a pat on the back. I've been around long enough that I'm actually beginning to understand Jessica's father, Tucker. He's a man of few words, but he winks at me before he heads to his seat.

Isn't it funny the way people always seem to sit in the same seats, week after week after week? The first time I came to church with Jess, I started to sit down in the third pew on the right and she said, "No, that's where the Andersons sit." I thought, *wow, the Andersons must be really important.* Turns out they're just your average, ordinary family. The Masons know where the Andersons sit, and the Andersons know where the Carters sit, and the Carters know where the Plineys sit. It's not assigned seats, just assumed seats.

We're in the fifth pew on the left, right behind Lily Jacobs and in front of the Gardwins with their three kids. The Gardwins happen to be neighbors to my own parents. One of those Gardwins "accidentally" pulls my hair all the time, but I just sit there and let it happen. It's hard to talk about such things in church, after all.

Tucker and Hazel slide into the pew next to me, and the music starts, so it saves me from having to talk about Josh. He still hasn't spoken to me, and I don't want to have to explain that to his parents.

Ouch, there goes the hair pulling. It's starting really early today. I should remember to wear my hair up next time so the culprit won't have any ammunition. Never mind, though—I am an adult, and such petty childish things don't bother me.

The congregation launches into a second verse, and behind me I hear Jenny Gardwin singing sweetly. She's probably ten years old, with blue eyes and long blonde hair. Someday maybe I'll have a little girl like her. Except I doubt Benji would have a blonde child, so...

Ouch! Again with the hair! Gardwins, are you people not watching your kids at all? I'm really suffering here! How can I concentrate on praising and all that when I'm being attacked from the rear?

I hear Lily Jacobs in front of me warbling along with the music. Lily never reads the words. She doesn't have to, because she knows every song by heart. She used to come to church with her husband, but since he passed away, she sits by herself.

Ouch! Okay, that was the last time, whichever one of you is pulling my hair...

I turn around and see Billy Gardwin directly behind me.

"What?" he mouths, a smirk on his face. I give him a look of distaste and turn to face the front again. Too bad there isn't some type of activity to keep kids like Billy busy during the service — something constructive, and preferably something that doesn't involve driving me crazy. I'm sure when Josh was a little boy he never pulled anyone's hair in the pew in front of him. Tucker would have knocked him silly.

I never attended a church service before attending with Jess and Josh. My parents aren't really the church-going type. Most Sundays, my mom prepares a very late breakfast and my dad spends most of his time tinkering in his "workshop," which is actually a small storage shed behind the house. I'm not sure what he does in there, because he never manages to permanently fix anything that is broken, and most of his projects go unfinished. Mom's not sure what he does, either, because every time she goes near he tells her she's bothering him.

"There's no rule that says you have to go to church," my mom used to say. "Believe in God, and that's it. It says so in the Bible." Although we had a Bible in our house, I never actually saw anyone pick it up, so I doubt that she ever attempted to see whether her opinion was correct. The only time I ever saw my family step through the doors of a church building was for my grandfather's funeral, which I don't remember very well. I was only six or seven at the time.

The Masons, however, are active members and never miss a service. Tucker acts as the resident handyman, fixing anything that needs repair and taking care of general maintenance on the building, and I'm sure Hazel has made dinner for each family at one time or another. If the least on Earth shall be the greatest in heaven, I'm sure the Masons will wind up on the list. They are humble people, but very revered in this little crowd.

I asked Hazel once why she made a point of getting to know every single member of the congregation. She focused those same gray-green eyes that Josh and Jess possessed on me before answering wisely.

"Even the smallest act of kindness can change a person's life forever. God can do extraordinary things through ordinary people who are willing to trust Him."

I hope she's right, because there's certainly nothing extraordinary about me. In fact, I...

Ouch! Not the hair again.

This could be a very long service.

Sunday afternoon finds me cross-legged on the couch watching a baseball game with a giant pile of nachos resting before me. Sliding a loaded chip into my mouth, I can't help but wonder what Benji would think of my snack. It is fairly disgusting, after all. Nothing like tiramisu and frou-frou flavored coffees.

A very familiar ringtone sounds, and I jerk my smartphone toward me excitedly. Before I press the button to accept, I tell myself to calm down and take a deep breath.

"I was starting to wonder about you," I state nonchalantly, leaving any emotion out of my voice. It's kind of dark, and though I can't fully see his face, I can tell that he's smiling.

"Were you punishing me by not calling, Mad?" He has a teasing tone, and I wish I could see him a little better. He's wearing his glasses, and I can picture his gray-green eyes beneath his arching brown eyebrows rather than actually see them. I know Josh's

face—it's similar to Jessica's, as far as the slight olive-skin coloring. He has a strong jaw and full lips, not that I've noticed or anything. Like I said, it's a familiar face.

"Don't be silly. I've been very busy…and don't call me Mad. I'm not six anymore."

"I know you're not, Mad. Neither am I."

For one month of the year, the three of us are the same age—Jessica is six months older than me and Josh is five months younger. People thought they were twins, because they were always in the same grade together.

"I didn't break your rule, you know."

"It was a slight overreaction," he admits. "It's an odd sensation watching a rather large guy walk uninvited through the door of your house. I'm sorry. How is Vince anyway?"

"His name is Vic, and I have no idea. I cut him loose."

"Poor schmuck. What was wrong with this one?"

"He…just…had an ear problem."

"A hearing issue?"

"No, and it doesn't matter. Can we talk about something else, please?"

"How do you ever manage to talk to me? I'm sure I don't meet your checklist of perfection."

As though Josh is a dating possibility. He's Josh, and I hardly expect him to be perfect. He's seen me and Jess do so many ridiculous things, I'm surprised he can look at me with a straight face anymore.

"There's so much wrong with you, I actually find your quirks endearing," I inform him.

"Thanks for the vote of confidence. Are you watching baseball?" he asks, clearly grinning. "You only watch baseball with me, Mad."

"Well, I technically *am* watching baseball with you, aren't I?" Glancing at the TV, I can't help but smirk. "I don't know, it just made me feel not quite so alone today. And I needed a break from reading my book."

I actually made it to page six of the Camdyn Taylor book before I put it down. Way better than I expected.

"*You're* reading a book? What's his name?"

"His name? It's a book by a woman—Camdyn Taylor."

"No," he counters with a laugh. "I mean, who's the guy you're trying to impress? He likes to read, I take it."

"I'm not that shallow, really." I glance away, but I'm aware that I have a hard time hiding my emotions from Josh. The man practically reads my mind sometimes. "Okay, his name is Benjamin. He's an English teacher."

"Benjamin," he states, trying out the name. "I like your hair all piled up like that."

I self-consciously push a strand away. "I look like a mess. How are things over there?"

"Don't do that, just let me pretend I'm there with you. I want to live vicariously through you for a few minutes."

"You sound like Jess when she wants to hear about my dates."

He chuckles and adjusts the screen closer to his face. "I definitely do not want to hear about your dates."

"Well, I went to church with your parents today."

"That's so awesome. I know how much that means to them, since Jess and I are both gone. You're perfection, you know that?"

"Finally, someone besides me notices," I joke. "One of those Gardwin kids kept pulling my hair. Your mom sent me home with a giant plate of barbecued chicken. I made it into a mess of nachos. It looks gloriously disgusting."

"That sounds fantastic!" He laughs, and I hear his breath hit the phone's speaker. "Explain everything to me, Mad."

"Um…" Josh has a habit of asking me to describe things, and it always catches me off guard. "The sun's filtering through the little window at the top of the door, and hitting the dust particles just right so they're floating in front of me sort of like fairy dust. I actually feel a little bad right now for not cleaning better. Sorry about that."

"Shh…" he whispers. "Back to the dust."

"Okay, it's filtering into the line of the television, where the Braves are currently up three to two on the Dodgers. The guy who's up to bat looks like he's jacked up on steroids. If you were here, you would agree. It's a gorgeous day—it rained earlier, and now it's just kind of mild; not too hot, not too cold. I actually have the window open, and I can hear a couple kids playing down the street."

I can't help but notice that he has his eyes closed, as though he's stepping back into Kentucky as I speak.

"And of course I'm here on the couch, wearing an old T-shirt with my hair piled on my head, eating disgusting nachos."

"Okay, I have to see this mess of nachos."

Smiling slyly, I lift them close to my face. "Like I said, a disgusting, glorious mess. They taste like salty sweet perfection, and right now I smell barbecue sauce mixed with lilac hand lotion."

"I miss that," he mutters.

"Barbecue sauce and lilacs?"

"No," he protests with a laugh. "Normal. Louisville. Baseball and nachos and greasy burgers and Mad, quite frankly. Talking to people at a decent hour. Mom's Sunday dinners."

"Well, we're all here, just like you left us," I tell him quietly.

"If only life could stay the way we want it to, huh?"

I hesitate to answer, because I don't want to leave my life the way it is. I want to make something of myself, and to actually have a career instead of a job, and to find a man for a happily ever after. No, leaving things the way they are doesn't sound good at all.

"You're homesick," I surmise.

"Talking to you feels like home. Don't punish me next time, even if I say something stupid. And don't forget about me when you're with Vince, or Swagger, or this new English teacher guy you're seeing."

"As though I would let a guy get in the way of my friends. And I don't know how you know about that stuff, anyway."

"Jess is a leaky sieve." He seems to visibly slump a bit, and I take a deep breath.

"Hey, listen, you take care of Josh, okay? I don't want to hear about you being depressed and homesick over there. When you get home, I want you to take me to a ball field, or a basketball game, or whatever you decide."

"Is that a promise?"

"As if I can escape you," I tease. "I am in your house, you know."

"Oh, I know," he assures me with a laugh. "It drives me crazy every minute."

"Relax, I'm not going to tear the place down."

Rather than acknowledge my comment, he simply smiles. "I better turn in. Tell me goodnight? I know it's not night there, but just humor me."

"Goodnight, Josh," I offer with a smile.

"Goodnight, Mad."

Chapter Four

It's a little past 3:00 Monday when I get back to the office from a trip to my physician for an annual physical, and Katie is sitting at my desk, rifling through papers, her brown curly hair bobbing back and forth as she searches furtively.

"What's going on?" I ask.

She jerks back, startled, and then breathes a sigh of relief. "I'm so glad you're back. Kyle is looking for that spreadsheet he gave you Friday. He said it was urgent. I hope you don't mind that I was looking through your things."

"Of course not," I say, dropping my purse on the floor by my desk. "I think I put that in the top drawer." I pull it open and fish out a stack of papers. Flipping through, I find the right one and hand it to her.

"Aha! Thank you, Maddie." Katie takes the paper and heads to Kyle's office.

Urgent? Why didn't he save that spreadsheet on his computer, if it was so urgent? He should have left poor Katie alone. He's been here long enough to know that she's not good under pressure. She's probably seconds away from a nervous breakdown right now.

As if to demonstrate my point, Katie returns very quickly, eyes wide and hands clenched in front of her abdomen.

"What's so urgent?" I ask.

Katie shakes her head, sitting in her chair and taking a sip of her iced coffee. "I have no idea. Cooper's been calling him ever since you left."

"Cooper?" Now that is a big surprise. Cooper is the owner of the company. Since he works on one of the upper floors, I think

I've only seen him once or twice. I've certainly never spoken to him. He doesn't make time for the "little people." Why would he be calling Kyle?

"How was the doctor?" Katie wonders.

"The woman at the receptionist desk wasn't very nice to me."

Katie has a shocked expression on her face. Wonderful Katie—I can always count on her for some sympathy.

"What did she say to you, Maddie?"

Now that I have to put it into words, it seems rather silly. I shouldn't have brought it up. "Oh, you know, just emphasizing words like you would with a three-year-old, all because I couldn't find my driver's license. She was acting like I was a fraud or something, and kept telling me that she needed to verify my identity."

Katie's giggling now, her hand clamped over her mouth to muffle the sound. "That *is* mean," she whispers when she catches her breath. "What did you do to set her off?"

"I didn't *do* anything," I retort. "She didn't like me from the minute I walked in there. How was I *not* supposed to notice that her bangs were cut crookedly? And perhaps I should have just kept my mouth shut, but giving her a stylist suggestion was simply a common courtesy. Besides, she was very frumpy, and one of the other people in there told me she is hard to get along with."

"Being frumpy is not a reason someone is mean," Katie lectures. She adds in an eye roll and shakes her head.

"No, not a reason in itself, but if you're generally unhappy with your appearance, it probably takes a toll on your attitude."

She giggles again, like I am a small child who just said the cutest, silliest thing. *Oh, little Maddie thinks all people who dress nice are happy. Isn't that sweet!*

Honestly, I think my observation is spot-on this time. Some people find themselves in a bad mood just from having a bad hair day, after all.

"Besides, you didn't say anything about giving blood when you had *your* physical," I interject, interrupting her giggles. "What

a nightmare." I have a notoriously weak stomach. I'll spare the gory details, but in some circles, I am still widely talked about to this day.

"You're right. I should have warned you about that."

Katie thinks I'm a wimp. I'm about to tell her that I can't control my stomach, but my telephone begins to ring and I turn to see that the caller ID reads D. Hamilton.

Kyle's boss? Why is he calling me?

"Madeline Heard," I say into the receiver as I hear a commotion on the other end of the line. "Hello?"

"Heard, Doug Hamilton. I need you to gather your department members and report to my office."

Click.

I'm gone all of two hours, and the world has flipped on its head. Doug Hamilton has never called me to his office before, let alone the whole department. Poor Katie will hyperventilate. I turn around to look at her, arms still crossed on her desk, waiting to continue our conversation.

"We need to go to Hamilton's office," I say. I can actually see a white pallor spreading across her face. Funny, Katie can handle all that blood-letting at the physical but can't handle a little office meeting.

"Why?"

"I don't know, but it's okay. We're all going together. Where are Justin and Shelly?"

"They're on break. I can go get them."

I nod, and she starts off toward the end of the hall while I look up just in time to see Kyle headed down the hall as well.

"Kyle!" I call. He completely ignores me and walks right by without so much as a sideways glance. Maybe Hamilton called him, too, and he's on his way to his office right now. It was still pretty rude to ignore me. I'll be sure to mention that to him later, after all the drama subsides.

I make my way to the hallway outside Hamilton's office, where I plan to wait for the others. The first thing I notice is that Kyle's not in there, and he seems to have disappeared.

"Come in, Heard," Hamilton barks. I cast a backward glance into the hallway, wishing that Katie would hurry, and then creep into the office. Hamilton is not an especially big man, but he has a large, deep voice, which makes him seem slightly intimidating. I haven't had much contact with him over the years – normally he just passes information on through whoever my supervisor happens to be at the time. When he has spoken to me, he hasn't ever really been impolite, but his attitude makes him seem as though he could be.

I watch silently as he picks up a stack of paper from his desk and drops it with a thud. He rummages through a mess behind his chair as though he's looking for something in particular, and then tosses a few items onto the floor. Katie, Shelly and Justin appear behind me, all three sporting deer-in-the-headlights looks as they face me with inquisitive expressions, but all I can do is shrug my shoulders.

"Alright, gang, come on in and have a seat," Hamilton instructs. By this time, it definitely appears as though he's lost something. His desk is beginning to look like the aftermath of a tornado.

I glance over at Katie, whose fingernails are now digging into the cushion of her chair. Patting her hand for reassurance seems like it would be comforting, but I decide against it. Who knows what Hamilton would think of such a gesture?

"Okay, tough day, but we're all going to get through it if we work together." Hamilton stops sifting through the ruins that once resembled a desk and sinks into his oversized leather chair. "The numbers Mr. Porter has been sending to me are not the same numbers he's been sending up to Mr. Cooper. Apparently there's been some manipulation to, let's say, paint a better picture—do some airbrushing, if you will."

He pauses, takes a breath, and drums his fingers against the desk. I sneak a quick peek at Katie, who is still sitting upright and appears to be breathing. Good signs.

"Needless to say, Mr. Cooper is furious about the whole situation; however, we are both convinced, from our interrogation

of Mr. Porter and from your respective histories with the company, that this was a solo operation. That being said, if I discover any information that indicates the opposite, there will definitely be consequences."

I can hear Katie's shallow breathing beside me. Where's a paper bag when you need one?

"At this point, Mr. Porter's employment has been terminated, and he has been instructed to leave the building immediately. Cooper is going to be keeping a watchful eye on the information coming from the department to be certain this problem corrects itself, so we all need to be very careful to do our jobs in a precise and timely manner. Heard, I want you to assume Mr. Porter's duties for the present time, until a replacement is named. I'll be working closely with you to try to rectify the problems and bring everything back in line. The rest of you will report to Heard the same way you reported to Mr. Porter. Any questions?"

Um, yeah. Why is Kyle "Mr. Porter" and I'm just Heard? Ugh.

No one says a word, not that I really expect them to. Hamilton just looks from one of us to the next, silently drilling us down. Surely he doesn't think that one of us had anything to do with this? He didn't say anything to implicate anyone, but the look in his eye speaks volumes.

"Okay, that will be all."

I've never seen my colleagues so eager to escape from a situation. They practically turn and sprint, leaving me with Hamilton amidst the rubble. He begins sifting through papers again, and I can't help feeling a bit shell-shocked.

This is certainly not the way I would have envisioned receiving a promotion, and Hamilton absolutely did not bill it as such, but I suddenly feel that this could finally be my chance to prove myself. I've paid my dues, after all. I've worked for people who knew much less than I did. I've been paid half as much as my supervisors to do twice the work. I've come in early and stayed late, all so someone else could earn the praise.

Oh, and let's not forget the agony of working for Bill...ahem, he of whom we no longer speak. I deserve a merit badge for that. A purple heart. A Nobel peace prize. I suppose even a little monetary compensation would suffice.

Speaking of compensation, if I'm going to clean up Kyle's mess, I really should be entitled to some of his salary. That's only fair, after all, although it might not be an ideal topic for the present circumstances. Hamilton looks like he's up to his ears in something. Whatever he's looking for, it must be terribly important. I'll just leave the salary conversation for another time.

Probably best to really show him how well I can do the job first. That shouldn't be a problem. I've practically been doing all the work ever since Kyle showed up. Well, everything except the extracurricular stuff. I had *absolutely* no part in that, just so we're clear.

If Cooper is going to be paying close attention, maybe I can impress him, too. Forget Hamilton—I'll just go straight to the top dog himself. It won't take any time at all and he will realize what a valuable asset Madeline Heard is to this company.

Why do we have Ms. Heard in her present position? She could be doing so many great things for us. We have to move her up, increase her salary, give her more benefits.

I'll be an office legend. A superstar.

"Heard," Hamilton mumbles with a heavy sigh.

"Yes, sir?"

"First things first: Bring me the numbers for the past few months." He waves his hand above the mess, gesturing at the stacks of paper. "Apparently my desk has eaten them."

I stopped to pick up some cookies on the way home. It wasn't hard to convince myself I deserved some, considering the type of day I had. Settling down on the couch and attempting to read my book once again, I manage to shovel in far too many of those sugary rounds—probably at least ten before I realize what I'm doing. Seeing the familiar face of Jess on my cellphone's caller ID, I force the cookies behind a pillow. Why I feel guilty about eating cookies and want to hide them from Jess is a bit perplexing, but not enough so that I retrieve them.

"Hey! How are things going with Benjamin?"

Jess. She is always more interested in my love life than I am. Well, almost.

"Oh, I guess okay. I'm supposed to go out with him Friday. We talked a bit yesterday."

"He's not knocking down the door to take you out already?"

"Hello, that's desperate, and he isn't. Anyway, I wouldn't be good company tonight. I had a very trying day."

"Spill."

"First of all, I had a physical at the doctor's office, and I had to get blood drawn."

"Who did they call to come get you?" she jokes. "Did they strap you to the table before you passed out? Did they use the smelling salts?"

"Very funny! For your information, it didn't hurt a bit, and I wasn't the least bit woozy afterwards."

"That's surprising. I wish I had seen your face when they told you they wanted your blood. That's the kind of moment you can never have back. Once gone, it's gone forever."

"Ha ha, you crack me up," I add with a shake of my head. "So, guess what happened at work today?"

Why is that such a popular phrase? *Guess what... Guess who...* It's really rather silly, when you think about it, unless the person you're speaking with has ESP.

"Let's see... Your boss got fired."

Perhaps Jess does have ESP. She could be reading my mind right now, which is a most terrifying thought. I try to force the cookies from my memory.

Cough if you can hear me, Jess.

Cough.

Go on—cough.

"How did you know that?" I ask, convinced that she's not going to make any hacking noises.

"You told me last week that his days were numbered. It was just a lucky guess."

A lucky guess! I can breathe much easier knowing that. Unless she knows I'm onto her mind reading ability and is just trying to divert my attention. That is such a clever tactic!

"That's not all," I explain. "I also got a promotion."

"Really? The same day your boss got fired? That's a strange coincidence."

"Well, I guess it wasn't a promotion, actually. I'm going to be doing Kyle's job for a while. After a few months, I think I'll definitely be up for an advancement."

"I hope you're right. You deserve it. If you put that in your mouth, I swear I will never kiss you again. I mean it."

I really hope that last bit was directed at Isaiah.

As far as deserving it, though—I do believe she's correct. I'm ready for a change of pace. If all goes well, this could turn out to be quite an exciting year. The only things I don't want to change are Jess and Josh, and I don't think I need to worry about that. Jess is like a steady anchor—my solid rock. And Josh balances me, like a brick tied onto the end of a balloon. I start fluttering in the wind, and he holds fast.

The rest, though… I feel the glorious day coming.

It's my year to rumble a little thunder for a change.

Chapter Five

"Mom," I call through the screen door. "You home?"

I know she's here—her car is in the driveway. I'm not the kind of person who likes to go barging into places unannounced, though. I'd rather make my presence known and be invited in. Not that she would ever *not* invite me in. Well, she hasn't yet, anyway.

The flowerbed that circles the front porch catches my eye with its lovely blooms. I would have a hard time guessing the number of hours she puts into her plants, but she has plenty of time for that now that she's not working. If I remember correctly, it was last November that she decided twenty years at the same job were more than enough. She had been wanting to stay home for a long time, and Dad finally relented.

Poor Dad—I bet she's driving him crazy. No wonder he's working late tonight.

"Mom," I call again. I can hear her moving around in the kitchen, banging pots and pans. As a last resort, I ring the doorbell and watch as she comes around the corner.

"Maddie!" She offers an exasperated sigh. "I thought somebody was here."

"Somebody *is* here," I retort.

She shakes her head rapidly, her blonde wavy hair swinging back and forth. "Oh, you know what I meant."

I pull open the screen door and head into the house, which smells like a mixture of cheap rose potpourri and tomato sauce, neither of which make sense. The house usually smells like a combination of motor oil from all Dad's contraptions and Mom's peppermint-scented ointment that she uses for her sinuses.

"Are you making dinner?" I ask as she heads toward the kitchen. She seems to be a little blonder than usual tonight, which means she must have been to the salon recently. She's been dying her hair now for…gosh, I can't even think back that far.

When I was a little girl, I had light golden hair, and when Mom would take me somewhere, people would comment about the beautiful color. One morning, I was nonchalantly playing with my dolls, and Mom snuck up behind me and grabbed the left side of my head. When I turned around, she had a huge chuck of golden-blonde in her hand. I sat there, nearly in tears, while she explained that she wanted the same color I had, but Freida could never get it right. This time she was taking the hair to her, and if she still couldn't get the color correct, she was changing beauticians.

Needless to say, I had to get my hair cut after that, too, since Mom had given me the hack job. What a sad turn of events. At the time, Hazel used to babysit me after school, and Jess begged her mom to let her cut her hair like mine. It was a great show of solidarity from my friend, and we have been inseparable ever since. My hair also grew significantly darker from that point forward, and while I can't exactly blame it on my mother, I have my suspicions that her hair robbery destroyed the golden innocence of my youth.

"I'm making spaghetti," Mom calls from the kitchen. "I probably don't have enough. I wish you had told me you were coming."

"I really didn't come for dinner. I just thought I'd drop by for a few minutes on my way home from work."

"Oh? Well, that's nice. Your father won't be home for another half-hour or so."

Rounding the corner, I witness Mom standing in front of the stove, spice jars and cans spread out around her.

"You're making your sauce from scratch?" I'm slightly stunned as I watch her stir.

"Uh-huh. I've been watching that Italian lady on the food channel. You really should watch her sometime. She has lots of helpful tips, and sometimes she does specials on easy cooking— that could be right up your alley, sweetheart."

"Thanks, I think."

She lifts the wooden spoon from the pot, holds it under her nose for a moment, and then goes back to stirring. It's a little strange, seeing Mom so busy in the kitchen. She never was what you would call a domestic diva, not that I blame her. I know what it's like to come home from work, physically and mentally drained, and have to worry about what's for dinner. That's probably why I've never bothered to learn how to cook properly. Who has the time, really?

"Was your appointment at the clinic this week?" she asks, wiping her hands on a towel. I notice her apron, which reads: *You Want Dinner on Time? Stop Kissing the Cook.* Mom in an apron—not a mental picture I could have easily conjured up before now.

"Yes, boring tests and blood work."

"Did you ask them why you're so skinny? Enjoy it while you're young, because you'll never get your body back."

Thanks for the encouragement.

Mom is constantly chiding me for being skinny, even though I'm really more on the average side. I'm skinnier than her, but that's about it. That's too thin in her book.

"It's just from eating nutritiously," I feel the need to say. That's mostly true, if you don't count the cookies I bought on my way home the other day. How many did I end up eating, anyway? Eight? Twelve?

"Did you call Brittany? I know she wanted to talk to you."

Already with Brittany? Honestly, Mom, can't we have a conversation without talking about her?

"No, I haven't called her."

"Well, you're going to call, aren't you?"

"If I thought Lance would answer the phone, I would."

"So you're not calling."

"No."

"You're going to have to grow up a little eventually, Maddie. The whole world doesn't revolve around you, you know."

Ha! As if I could actually think so at the moment.

"How is Dad doing? Is he still tinkering as much as ever?"

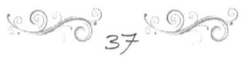

Mom stops stirring and begins fiddling with the knobs on the oven. Underneath the tomato sauce, I think I detect the scent of homemade bread. She must really be watching a lot of those cooking channels.

"Yes, of course, but don't change the subject. Brittany's been calling me a lot lately, and the last thing she needs is unnecessary stress."

"I don't know what you're talking about. Why would not calling Brittany make her life stressful? It should actually rid her of an unwanted burden, since I'm so self-absorbed."

Mom cuts me a stern look before she opens the oven door. "Don't talk in circles around me. She told me you practically hung up on her the other day, and she was just trying to be friendly and give you some advice about your love life."

How do you express complete indignation when the other person in the conversation has her head in the oven?

"First of all, I did not hang up on her. Secondly, she wasn't offering any friendly advice. The only reason she called was to be judgmental and hurl insults at me."

"Don't you think you might have misunderstood?" Mom asks, pulling the bread out of the oven and placing it on the stovetop. She drops her fists to her hips and stares at me, her round face slightly flushed from the heat.

Is it possible I misunderstood Brittany? Could she have been calling just to offer me friendly advice?

"You know, Maddie, I've always thought you should go out with that Rob who lives down the street from your parents. He's just your type."

Sure, except for the fact that he's fourteen years older than me, lives in his mother's basement, and spends his time collecting playing cards that he discusses online with other grown men who live in their parents' basements.

No way did I misunderstand *that*.

"I don't know," I relent with a sigh. She doesn't look pleased with my answer, but at least she turns back to her cooking.

"Well, we can't fix what's already done. Just try to make more of an effort next time."

"Yeah," I mutter, although I secretly hope there's not a next time. If Brittany calls again, I can run some water and pretend that I'm in the middle of taking a shower. I can bang some pots and pans around and pretend that I'm in the middle of cooking dinner. Anything to avoid talking to Brittany. *I* don't need any unnecessary stress, either.

Mom takes the "fancy" tablecloth out of a drawer and drapes it across the table. The cooking channels must have really gone to her head. I wonder how Dad feels about all this fuss for a weeknight meal. Surely she hasn't been doing this every night!

She crosses to the hutch and removes some of the good china, which she doesn't even use at Christmas. I was beginning to wonder if it was built in—one of those displays for show only, with no functionality. I would open the door and pull out a plate one day, expecting it to be quite heavy and fragile, and instead would find it was plastic with a lot of paint on the front. We would have a good laugh about her hoax, and she would ask me to keep her secret, which of course I would.

No need to worry about keeping secrets now, though, because the plates are out and on the table. Four of them, to be exact.

"You planning on eating for two?" I ask jokingly as she begins digging through the silverware drawer with a chuckle.

"No, dear, the Hubers are coming over for dinner. I'd ask you to stay, but like I said before, there just isn't enough food."

The Hubers—Brittany's parents. I can just imagine the conversation at the dinner table:

"So, when's the last time you talked to Brittany?" Mom will ask.

"I spoke with her this morning," Mrs. Huber will say.

"Ha! I win! I spoke with her this afternoon," Mom will chirp.

Mrs. Huber will sit there dejected while Mom heaps spaghetti onto her plate.

"Eat up, Cathy, there's plenty of food, since Maddie didn't stay."

"Who's Maddie?" Mr. Huber will ask.

"Oh, Maddie is my daughter, remember? She was at Brittany's wedding—the completely self-absorbed bridesmaid on the end."

"Oh, yes, I remember her," Cathy will chime in. "Wasn't she the one who made the terrible fuss about her dress being two sizes too big?"

"Yes, that was her. It still seems highly unlikely that the tailor would have made such a huge mistake after Brittany took the measurements in herself. If you ask me, I think she did one of those crash diets for a few weeks right before just so she'd have something to complain about."

"That certainly sounds like her," Cathy will say, and they all will laugh, except Dad, who of course does not agree. Why don't you speak up, Dad? Defend me a little.

Mr. Huber will sit there and watch the exchange, while Dad rolls his eyes and dips into the spaghetti again.

Yikes. I need to get out of here, just in case they arrive while I'm still in the general vicinity. Maybe I should call Dad, have him fake a flat tire. Surely he will want to avoid this atrocity, too.

"I really couldn't stay anyway, Mom," I inform her, sounding a little more self-important than I anticipated. "I have a million things to do tonight. Like I said before, I just dropped by for a few minutes to say hello."

"Well, come back when you can stay longer. You never have time for us anymore."

Okay, I'm just going to ignore that comment.

I walk back through the living room and can't help but notice a large stack of cookbooks on the coffee table, visual confirmation that Mom is taking this new hobby seriously. And when did Mom and Dad get a new couch? I guess I didn't notice it when I came in. She's purchased new drapes and wall hangings, too. Mom being home all day could send Dad into bankruptcy.

The sweet smell of blooming flowers greets me as I open the screen door. Wouldn't it be great to have time to work in the garden? Josh and I only have a few potted plants around our house

(I mean his house, of course) and those have never even been transferred into better soil. I'm much too lazy by the end of the workday to be a gardener.

Looking up, I see Dad shuffling up the front walk.

"Hi, Dad," I say gently as he moves closer. "I was about to call you and have you fake a flat tire."

He leans down and kisses me on the cheek. "Hi, hon. I know, the Hubers." He wrinkles his nose in mock disgust. "You're not staying?"

"I'm sorry, but you'll have to face this one alone. Mom informed me that there simply isn't enough food."

"Nothing like coming home from a hard day's work to a peaceful, relaxing evening," Dad groans softly. The lines in his face seem deeper than the last time I saw him. I wish Mom would let him take it easy. He deserves a little rest—maybe a vacation.

"Well, if you need to fake an emergency to escape, you can always come over to my house," I inform him. The edges of his mouth turn into a slight smile.

"I just might do that. Tell Josh I said hello."

"I will. Please give the Hubers my love." The temptation to give him a wink overcomes me, and I drop one eyelid mischievously.

Dad wraps his arms around me in a tight hug, chuckling as he squeezes my shoulders.

"My little Maddie—ornery as ever."

By the time I get back to the house, the spaghetti smell in the car is driving me half insane. No, Mom didn't relent and give me a to-go box. I stopped at an Italian carry-out on the way home. Smelling the spaghetti at Mom and Dad's made me hungry, and I don't have time for sauce from scratch and homemade bread. Honestly, when I was finished I probably wouldn't want to eat what

I made anyway. I haven't been watching cooking shows all day, after all.

The answering machine light is blinking when I walk through the door, showing three messages, so I hit the play button.

"Good afternoon, Mr. Mason. This is Charles seeing if you would like to order your tickets for the annual Policeman's Ball."

It seems to me that Charles should utilize his time by chasing criminals or rescuing people or something, but a ball could be interesting. I save the message so I can pass it to Benjamin later, if the opportunity presents itself.

"Oh, she's not picking up," I hear Brittany's voice on the second message. "Obviously she's screening her calls. Why do you think? Because she can't find a steady man in her life, and she's embarrassed. I could tell that the last time I talked to her." Click.

Brittany.

That's all I've got. It's like on Seinfeld, when Jerry would lift his fist in the air, and you knew it was coming: *Newman.*

Brittany has become my Newman, fist in the air and everything.

I'm trying to unclench my Brittany fist when I hear the third message:

"This message is for Madeline Heard. This is Gayle at Dr. Harper's office. There was a problem with the sample we took the other day and it might have been tainted, so we request that you come in again for a redraw. Thank you."

Redraw? What does that—

The blood.

Dread washes over me as I realize this unlikely turn of events is probably due to an unfortunate bang trimming and my notice of that sad mistake, since that receptionist saw how I reacted to the blood drawing the first time.

Mom watches cooking shows and manages to make impressive dinners, while I watch makeover shows and manage to work my way into an appearance-related catastrophe.

This might be the first time I wish all the messages had been from Brittany.

Chapter Six

The doctor's office beckoned, but I managed to put it off all day, and I stayed at work as long as I could. After all, I am trying to make a good impression and doing my best to really astound the people upstairs. Funny, aside from Cooper, I don't even know who the people upstairs are, but I'm sure they will be in awe of me nonetheless.

There aren't many people in the waiting area today. One of those cable news channels is playing on the television in the corner, and a well-dressed man is sitting in front of it reading a newspaper. An elderly couple sit in the opposite corner, the woman being in a wheelchair. The receptionist who had a distaste for me the other day is nowhere to be found. Maybe I should ring the bell for service. I wonder who came up with that idea? It seems a little demeaning to have to come when people ring a bell, like a dog reacting to a whistle. If it *is* the same receptionist who tried to belittle me, though, I don't feel too badly about getting her attention in this fashion.

Smacking my palm loudly on the bell, I wait for her to appear. Hmm…wonder what she'll do when she sees me. She shouldn't have enough reaction time to come up with a very detailed scheme. Unless Gayle told her I was coming, and they sat there together thinking of a way to get the better of me. She's probably back there right now making notes and writing out her script.

If she doesn't come in a few seconds, I'm going to ring the bell again. Terribly spiteful, I know. I'm really going to have to work on controlling those types of actions in the future if I'm going to be an executive.

Yes, I said executive.

After ringing the bell for a third time, someone finally emerges through one of the doors – an older woman with curly, white hair and a red smock.

"Can I help you?" she asks respectfully. I feel a little relieved, but also somewhat cheated. I had fully prepared myself for a confrontation with the smug, horrid receptionist, and instead I'm faced with a lady who reminds me of Mrs. Santa Claus.

"Hi, I'm Madeline Heard, and I'm supposed to have a blood test."

"You're Dr. Harper's patient?"

"Yes, ma'am," I reply politely.

"Okay, someone will be right out for you."

"If it could be Lisa, that would be great. We really connected the other day."

In other words, I didn't faint and she didn't maim me.

Sister Claus clucks her tongue, shaking her head. "Lisa's not here today. I'll send someone else. It should only be a few minutes."

I watch as she disappears behind the door, wondering if I've given her a reason to dislike me too.

You won't believe the girl out there, ringing that bell like I'm her servant and requesting special technicians like she's the Queen of Sheba! No wonder they marked her as a difficult patient. I'm going to add demanding and impossible to the list.

Locating a chair halfway between the businessman and the elderly couple, I somehow manage to earn smiles from both as I walk by.

"Do you need something to drink?" I overhear the elderly man ask his wife. She shakes her head, and he pats her hand lovingly. When we've been together that long, I wonder how Benjamin will treat me. I can't imagine him looking any older. In fact, I can't imagine him much at all, come to think of it. I'm sure that will change after Friday.

The only man I can imagine myself next to like that is Josh. He'd push my wheelchair in front of the television and turn on a baseball game, and I'd probably be cantankerous and talk to him the whole time, just because I know it drives him crazy. That's just silly, though, because of course some undeserving little looker will convince Josh to be with her, and it will be her sitting in that wheelchair.

Oh, who am I kidding? She won't need a wheelchair, because she'll probably be a cheerleader or something. Ugh, she so doesn't deserve him.

"Madeline Heard," a deep voice bellows behind me. Turning, I see a giant standing in the doorway. As I rise slowly and walk towards him, I surmise that this must have been how David felt when he approached Goliath. Except David wasn't a girl.

"How are you today?" he asks. I indicate that I'm okay as I look up into his face. He's probably 6'8", which seems pretty tall next to my 5'6" frame. He's fairly stocky, too, which makes me feel like a small child walking beside him.

A child happens to pass me on the right, holding his mother's hand, looking slightly disgruntled and holding a lollipop.

"Where's Lisa?" I inquire, not that I don't believe Sister Claus about her being gone, but you never know.

"She has the day off," he explains, not looking up from what he's doing.

"Have you been here very long?" Trying to be friendly seems like the best approach, since I'm slightly terrified.

"Three months."

"Where did you work before this?"

"A video game store."

Sister Claus sent me off with a big burly giant who quit his job at the video game store three months ago? Isn't there some sort of requirement for how long a person has to practice before they're unleashed on the public?

"So you've only been doing this for three months?" I ask cautiously.

"Yeah, but I went to school before that. That's why I worked at the game store."

I'm going to assume he's talking about some type of medical school for people who draw blood and not (gasp!) high school. That would be just my luck! Friendly Sister Claus would send in an enormous kid right out of high school to draw my blood. *It would serve the diva right.*

"Are you scared?" he whispers in a low, deep voice. "You should be."

I was right! He's here to do me bodily harm. I should scream right now so someone comes to my rescue. I can't just sit here staring at his cold, dark eyes, but my body is not cooperating with my brain. What am I going to do?

Scream, Maddie.

Scream.

He begins to laugh, shaking his head and pulling a bandage out of a drawer.

"I'm just kidding. You seemed too tense."

"I knew you were kidding," I blurt, trying to sound convincing, "and I'm not tense. I just expected Lisa to be here, and she's not, that's all. She's usually the one who takes care of me."

"Okay," he says with a chuckle. He doesn't believe me, and I don't blame him. I wouldn't believe me, either. My story didn't sound very credible, even in my own ears.

He starts poking around on my arm and rubbing it down with alcohol. I'm fairly convinced now that he's not going to try to hurt me purposely, so I guess I can calm down. This part doesn't hurt – I know that from the other day. Maybe I'll even look this time.

"Here comes the needle," he says. On second thought, I definitely can't look. I'll just wait a few seconds, and then the needle will be in and the test will be almost over, and—

Ouch! Oh my goodness! It's an arm, not a piece of chicken! You didn't have to stab me! I'm afraid to look—half my arm might be gone.

"Looks like I'm going to have to find the vein," he mutters. Glancing at my arm, I immediately wish I hadn't as a wave of nausea

passes over me. He's moving the needle back and forth, left to right under my skin. The end of the needle is visible beneath my flesh.

You big brute! Just hurry up already! How hard is it to find a vein, really? And now I'm bleeding. Not into the tube, but down my arm. I'm bleeding to death!

Sure enough, like clockwork, I begin to grow woozy.

Removing the needle, he places a large piece of cotton over my arm.

"Bend your elbow for a second to stop the bleeding."

Doing what he says, I can't help but stare in disbelief. What in the world just happened here? He *is* a ringer! That's the only explanation, isn't it? Surely this isn't common practice.

"Sorry about that," he adds with a sigh. "Maybe I'll try the other arm."

The words come tumbling out before I can even try to stop them.

"If you must, but when I'm finished, I better get a lollipop for this."

"Heard!" Hamilton barks. I look up to see him standing in the middle of the hall, coffee cup in hand. "Cooper was impressed with that extra report you created. Keep up the good work."

Score! A small victory in the hunt for a promotion. It must have been the awesome color-coded graph I included. No, I'm sure it was the witty sentence I used at the end. Either way, it doesn't really matter. Cooper was impressed! I'm on my way to the top, baby. I should see the payoff roll in any day now.

"Did you hear that?!" Katie exclaims as soon as Hamilton is out of earshot. "You impressed the invisible man! That is quite an accomplishment."

When Hamilton told us Cooper would be keeping a watchful eye on us, we all assumed he would be popping into the department from time to time. This has not been the case. In fact, I have not seen him one single time since I began doing Kyle's job. He calls Hamilton with his requests, I compile the information, and Hamilton forwards it upstairs. Katie has concluded that Cooper is not a real person, but is in fact Hamilton's imaginary friend. Thus, Cooper has earned the nickname "invisible man" within our department.

"Not really," I reply with an exaggerated shrug. "I actually impress him all the time, but he has no way of telling anyone, being invisible and all."

"You're so kooky."

"I know. It's all part of my charm."

Self-consciously, I tug at the wrist of my jacket. It's not one of the ones I wear often—it's a little itchy and it pulls funny around my shoulders. I had every intention of taking it off once I reached my desk this morning, but as I prepared to do so I remembered about my arm. The lab giant left an enormous green bruise, and I really don't feel like fielding a host of questions about what happened. (Stabbing, nausea, wooziness, ultimately having to lie on the cold floor with a wet cloth on my face...)

Needless to say, here I sit, still wearing the jacket, uncomfortable as can be.

"Why don't you go ahead and take your jacket off, Maddie? It's not that big a deal. If someone sees your arm, you can just tell them you mashed it in a door or something."

"Or they might assume I'm a junkie!" No, the jacket definitely stays on. I'll probably have to wear long sleeves tomorrow, too, despite the fact that it's summer and hot enough to fry an egg on the sidewalk. As a matter of fact, I'll probably roast in the car on the way home, all because that lab technician should have never left his job at the video store.

Oh well. Maybe my car will act like a sauna, and I'll sweat off some of that gross food I've been eating. My pants are feeling a little snug today, and I'm sure it's the oatmeal cookies I polished off, or the spaghetti I had the other night. Or possibly the ice cream I ate last night right before bed. Or the snack cakes I had for breakfast yesterday. Ew, I think I had pizza for lunch yesterday, too. A day for the record books. Wish I had a do-over on that one!

New to-do list, beginning today: No more junk food. It's all nutritious from here on out.

Except I already had a donut for breakfast. In fact, there's still a piece of it sitting on my desk. I should throw it away, what with starting fresh and everything. No more giving in to temptation, starting now.

That would be terribly wasteful though, wouldn't it? It's such a small piece of donut, after all, and one tiny bite probably won't hurt anything. So...

Yeah, shameless, I know.

Okay, it's gone.

Starting now.

Chapter Seven

Benji and I are no longer an item.

And I know you can't officially break up with someone after only one date, but I did have the beginnings of a future formulating in my mind. When he called to verify what time he was picking me up Friday night, we got to chatting a bit, and I casually mentioned that I was highly involved in the Camdyn Taylor book I was reading. He said, and I quote, "Meh, she's okay if you're into that kind of thing."

There would have probably been a better way to have reacted, and I'm sure I could think of one now given the separation from the moment, but I full-out excoriated him. Camdyn Taylor breaks into your heart and takes residence, I said. She is a bright light amid a dreary sea of Hemingways and Faulkners, I added.

Looking back, I might have overdone it just a tad.

Seriously, though, this book…

Last night, I really wished I could go back in time and smack Willa's father or something. How could he keep her from leaving with Robert? He was the love of her life, couldn't he see that? But instead she had to marry Adlai. Ugh, my heart is breaking again just thinking about it.

So even after all that effort, Benji thought we just didn't connect, and he canceled our second date. I *knew* there had to be something wrong with him. First of all, he was definitely no Mario Lopez. Second, he obviously didn't know a good thing when he saw it. *That* is a fatal flaw.

Benji is just a tiny chapter in my life, though, and I'm ready to move full-steam ahead. That's what Jess cemented in my brain last night when I gave her the details. It's also what I was told this morning, when I woke up to a lovely text from Josh: *He obviously didn't deserve Mad.*

No, he most definitely did not.

I've got to dwell in the present, though, which currently means going through all the paperwork in Kyle's desk. Hamilton is under the impression that the company is going to hire someone soon, so I want to make sure that person (me) has a fresh start. I've already got plans for the office, including how I want the furniture arranged and which prints I want on the wall. I'm going to get a nameplate for the door, too, because I've always wanted one.

The first thing I'm going to do, when I get the job, is redistribute the workload. Shelly is really underutilized—a product of the reign of him of whom we do not speak. I'm not sure what his fascination was with Shelly, but he always seemed to think that she was overworked, which meant that Katie and I took on a lot of her responsibilities. Now Shelly spends half her day on personal phone calls and the rest of the day slowly plodding through her duties to make them last as long as possible. I've even seen her giving herself a manicure at her desk. Don't get me wrong, I'm all for looking your personal best, but she can do her primping and grooming on her own time like the rest of us.

I also plan on letting the other members of the department have input into the way things work around this joint. Everyone I've worked for here has acted as though they were the boss and no one else's opinions mattered. Well, that is going to change. Everyone who works for me will know that I value what they think and what they have to say. Of course, Hamilton will notice that our department functions differently than the others, and he will ask how to emulate our success. I could bring about positive change for everyone who works here. The entire company is going to thank me in time.

Yes, I believe things are starting to look up around here. That light fixture is terrible, though. I'll definitely have to do something about *that.*

"Psst…" I hear behind me and look towards the door. Katie is standing there, arm stretched across the doorway.

"Something wrong?" I ask, and she shakes her head.

"What are you doing, taking measurements?"

"Just cleaning things up, as a courtesy for whoever gets the job."

"Yeah, I get it. You're just preparing a place for yourself." She removes her arm and steps away from the door. "You might want to check your desk soon. You've got some interesting items in your mailbox."

Intriguing. Following Katie back out into the hallway, I veer towards my desk and check my inbox. I'm not seeing anything interesting, but I pick up the papers and begin leafing through them. Fall projections, blah blah blah. Get your timesheets in early this week – no problem. A reminder about the dress code. Do we really need a reminder? Evidently someone does.

Ah, what is this? A memo from the Human Resources Department...the one I've been waiting for.

There is currently an opening in the Marketing Department for Marketing Account Leader. Anyone interested in this position should submit a résumé to the Human Resources Department.

Instead of going outside like they have every single time the position has come open, they opened it internally. It must have been for me! I can almost imagine the conversation Cooper and Hamilton had when they were discussing the opening.

"How do you want to approach this position?" Hamilton would have asked.

"I've already made up my mind. The only person who could truly make that department shine is Madeline Heard. We should offer the job to her, with a double in salary and full management benefits."

"That is my thinking exactly. Should we go ahead and post the position to everyone, just as a formality?"

"Yes, I suppose that would be necessary, but don't even bother setting up any interviews. Madeline is the one we want, and I don't want to waste my time on anyone else."

"I agree with you wholeheartedly. So we will hire her for the job and double her salary."

"No, wait," Cooper would have said. "Triple her salary, and get her a company car. Not one of those cheap little numbers some people have to drive, either; get her something flashy. People need to know what happens when we have a star performer like that one. Get her some new office furniture, and bump her up to four weeks of vacation instead of two. Oh, and an annual bonus. I think she should get at least twenty thousand, don't you?"

"Absolutely. I will have Human Resources begin working on it immediately."

Yes! If they sent the information out now, I bet they will make an announcement sometime in the next two weeks. Before the month is out, that office will be mine, and all the perks associated with it. No more thanklessly pouring out my best efforts while someone else takes the credit. From now on I will create my own destiny in this company. I'll start with this marketing position, and I'll diligently work my way into being an executive.

"Hey, Maddie," Katie says, drawing me back to the present. "I take it you saw the mail I mentioned."

"Yes, I did," I casually respond, pretending not to be interested. "It was the thing about the dress code, right?"

"Yeah, that was the one," Katie replies with a laugh. "I guess you better get to organizing that office pretty thoroughly. Sounds like it won't be long until it has a new permanent resident."

"Well, it will just have to wait. I've got something more important to do."

"More important than setting up your new humble abode? I'm terribly worried about you. What could you possibly consider more important?"

"If you really must know," I reply, twisting in my chair so I can look directly into her face, "I have a résumé to write."

"Of course! This is so exciting. Just remember the little people while you're on your way to the top."

"How could I forget you, Katie? I'll even let you in on a little secret: When I move into my new office, I'm giving you my stapler."

Tonight marks my inaugural jog—my first foray into the world of exercise and physical fitness. I'm trying to forget about that darn Benji and the fact that he turned out to be such a disappointment. If I can't forget, I figure it will be a great motivator as I try to make myself healthier. The more upset I get, the more physical I will become, which will help me go farther and faster than I normally could.

Besides, I purchased some specialized running gear. The shorts have a special panel to increase air flow and reduce perspiration, and my shirt is completely breathable. The salesman at the fitness store highly recommended them. They were a little pricey, but I'm sure they will be totally worth it in the long run. The shoes are specially designed for people who do a lot of running, so they will cushion my feet at just the appropriate places, making my jog a lot like running on air.

With my water bottle hanging around my waist and my running app open on my phone, I head out the front door, pausing only long enough to notice Mrs. Willows pulling weeds from her flowerbed. She turns and looks at me, and I wave with a winning smile. *Don't I look smart in my running outfit, Mrs. Willows? I'll probably be doing marathons soon enough!* She gives a slight wave and returns to her work.

I'm feeling pretty good as I head down Wonder Lane. My feet have already found a rhythm, and I'm pounding the pavement in perfect time. Proper planning might have included music, but I doubt I need it today. I'm going to enjoy looking at the scenery and I feel pretty cool in my outfit, despite the heat of the day. Yeah, jogging could definitely become my new hobby.

Rounding the corner at the end of the block, I peer casually into the neighbors' yards. The house just past the corner is impeccably groomed and belongs to someone named Martin, which

I know because they have a wooden plaque hanging by the door. They have a couple weeping willow trees and a big wooden bench on the porch, along with flowers in a built-in box on top of their mail receptacle. Naturally, I presume their house is as clean on the inside as it is on the outside.

Whew, I am really feeling the oxygen going into my lungs now. I must have gone quite a long way. I'll just check my app and see my progress...

Two-tenths? That can't be right. Let's see, if I was in my car and I made that one left turn, I would have gone...

I guess it is right. Sure didn't expect to be winded after only two-tenths of a mile. How am I ever going to jog the five miles I anticipated?

Never mind, maybe I am about to get my second wind. I hear runners talk about that sometimes on television; just when you think you can't go any farther, you suddenly get a second wind and it's like starting over fresh. I'm not sure these shoes are doing their job properly, though. It doesn't feel much like I'm running on air—running through sand is more like it. It's like the soles of my shoes are covered with chewing gum and it's an effort to simply pick up my feet.

Power through. I can do this, it's just going to take a little extra motivation.

Something begins clicking behind me, and I turn slightly to see a little boy riding his bicycle down the street. He's got training wheels, and he doesn't look to be much older than a kindergartner. Expecting to see his mother or father, I look around and see no one.

Never mind the kid. Just keep running. He's not my responsibility.

Focusing on the ground in front of me, I realize that I need to set some goals to push myself. If I just try to jog to the mailbox up the street, that seems like an attainable goal. Of course, walking for a moment to check my jogging app is important, and it's not like *that* constitutes giving up.

Three-tenths of a mile? Seriously? I'm going to die. They will have to pick me up with a spatula and get a body bag ready. Who's going to come rescue me, though? Nobody even knows I'm

running, except Mrs. Willows and now this bike kid, and I doubt either of them is going to send a patrol out looking for me.

The clicking noise returns again, this time from my left. The little boy is riding directly beside me, glancing at me now and then.

"Can I help you?" I ask the kid. My voice sounds funny—like I'm panting. It's fairly pathetic.

"I'm just riding my bike," he says, not bothering to look at me. His peddling perfectly matches my strides, which are getting shorter by the minute.

"Do you think you could ride it somewhere else?" I complain breathlessly. A little oxygen might be necessary soon.

"You don't own the road."

Well, I guess he's right about that. I can't *force* him to get away from me. Maybe I should try to make him nervous.

"Where are your parents?" Gasp. I reach for my water.

"Working."

"Who's watching you?" I'm not sure I've ever ingested half a bottle of water in two gulps before. Maybe I'll improve, now that I'm fully hydrated.

"My grandma."

"Where's your grandma?" My calves are starting to cramp. Honestly, I wish this kid would go away so I could walk for a moment without feeling like a complete loser.

"Over there," he informs me, not motioning to anywhere in particular. When we reach the end of the block, I turn off the road, hoping he won't follow. He keeps going, not bothering to look and see where I went.

Once that kid is completely out of sight, I slow down to a steady walk. Drinking all that water probably wasn't such a great idea. It's sloshing around my stomach now, with a "whoosh, whoosh" every time I take a step. Forcing the thought out of my head, I continue on the downhill stretch and head for home.

As I round the last turn in the road, a small white dog begins barreling toward me, running as fast as his little legs will go. When he gets closer, he begins to release a high-pitched yap.

Picking up my speed, I attempt to outrun him. No such luck, as he is almost immediately at my heels.

Looking at the houses nearby, I don't see anyone outside. Determined to ignore him, I simply continue past a man mowing his lawn. He looks at me inquisitively, no doubt alarmed to see a woman running with a half-crazed dog yipping at her heels. Instead of reacting, I simply wave as though my situation is perfectly normal.

Alright, you little nightmare. I know you can't keep this up all day.

I decide to take off in a sprint, hoping he won't be able to keep up and will instead watch in bewilderment from the center of the road. As it turns out, sprinting is not easy when you're not used to jogging and you're already winded and have the water sloshing in your stomach. Where did that dog go, anyway?

Yap, yap…

Ouch!

Stopping dead in my tracks, I glare down at that dog where he cowers in the road. Inspection of my ankle reveals two large scratches.

"You bit me! I can't believe you actually bit me!"

"Spark!" a voice calls. "Sparky, get back here this instant." The dog turns at the sound of that voice, so I believe it must be his owner. "There you are, Spark." His owner is a middle-aged woman who is slightly overweight and red-faced. From all appearances, she was having about as much fun chasing Sparky as I was running away from him. The little dog wags his tail, yaps a couple more times, and then spins around her excitedly. She responds by scooping him up and cradling him in her arms like he's an infant.

"What did you do to him?" she asks accusingly, stroking his back.

"You might want to watch your dog more closely," I tell her. "He bit me."

"Oh, not my Sparky-poo," she coos, rubbing his nose with her finger. He makes a low noise that sounds almost like purring, licking her hand. "He wouldn't hurt a fly."

"Well," I begin, attempting to catch my breath from the sprint, "I don't know about any flies, but I do know that he bit me. Just look at my ankle, if you don't believe it."

"I'm certain that my Sparky didn't do that!" She continues to pet her dog, staring down at him lovingly. He just sits in her arms, letting her caress him smugly.

"I'm jogging down the road, minding my own business, and your little yapping dog is chasing at my heels. How exactly do you propose I got the marks on my ankle? I don't see any other obstacles in my way."

"I don't know, maybe your shoe caught against your ankle as you were running and it left a scratch."

Is she kidding?

"You know, I did forget to take the razor blades out before I started jogging tonight, so you're probably right." She puffs up with that little dog and tries to glare at me. At least I think that's what she's trying to do—the sweat is clouding my vision a bit.

"Well, I'm sorry you got blood on your fancy little socks, but you don't have to be snooty about it. Sparky was just having a little fun."

Snooty? Me, snooty? But they are fancy little socks—at least she noticed that.

Fancy little socks with blood on them. A wave of nausea overtakes my abdomen, and I begin gagging from the sight of the blood coupled with the splashing water in my stomach. Giving that woman a piece of my mind is really tempting, but I'm incapable at the moment.

Turning away from Sparky and his half-crazy owner, I walk to the corner and see my humble abode in the distance. I never thought that jogging one little mile would be so difficult. If you're out of shape, you're out of shape.

Picking it up to a slow trot again, the sound of a honking car jolts me from my thoughts and I move over a tad. A black BMW slowly rolls by, and I glance over at the driver, who happens to be a beautiful young woman wearing dark shades and heading down my very own Wonder Lane. In fact, she looks a lot like that news reporter that's always on Channel Six…Harley something-or-other. Naturally, I pick up my pace to see where she's headed.

Just a few houses down from Josh's quaint little number, that Harley look-alike pulls that Beemer up at the large stately two-story at the end of the cul-de-sac, proceeding to walk up the steps and through the front door like she owns the place. Which she probably does.

She doesn't need to jog—practically perfect news reporter. If she did, she surely wouldn't be out of breath and about to collapse. The waistband of her shorts wouldn't be all wet with perspiration, even though they were supposed to have the special air flow and breathable fabric. And she definitely wouldn't have been bitten by that little snarling Sparky, who probably has rabies.

No, I can't even think about that again.

Of course, to add insult to injury, my app on my phone indicates that I've only gone nine-tenths of a mile. Pathetic.

One thing has certainly been accomplished on my jog, though. Josh doesn't need to worry about me having any guys come near the house anymore. Not since I know Harley is in the neighborhood.

Chapter Eight

Normally I would be really nervous about a job interview; however, interviewing with Doug Hamilton really isn't intimidating. I've been working closely with him ever since I took on Kyle's job responsibilities, so I feel like he knows my abilities quite well. Besides, there haven't even been any rumblings about anyone else interviewing, so it seems like I may be the only qualified candidate. If that's true, I was spot-on in my thinking before: Hamilton and Cooper opened the position internally just for me.

Even though I really have nothing to worry about, I still wore my most impeccable suit today. No sense leaving him with anything less than the best possible impression. I even skipped lunch simply to avoid spilling anything on myself. Plus, I have minty fresh breath, which is always an advantage. Hunger might currently serve as my enemy, but I'll power through. It's not like I haven't been hungry every day over the last couple weeks anyway, since I started trying to watch what I eat. It really is difficult to cut your calories with your stomach putting up a staunch fight.

According to everything I've read lately, I should begin seeing the results of my hard work within the next two weeks. With my emphasis on healthy food combined with exercising every single day, I'm eager to see what happens. I have officially succeeded in jogging a whole mile without stopping, and I am pushing myself for two miles now.

Katie's been in an especially good mood lately, too, ever since I found out about the interview. She said it just reinforced the fact that I was actually going to get the job. Until then, she was still afraid they might hire another Kyle and we would just show up one day and someone would be in the office – *my office.* It's spotless now, and everything's arranged just the way I want it. It should be no problem to pick up my paperwork and personal effects and move on in.

When the clock on the wall shows 1:45, I begin to get a bit fidgety. The 2:00 interview is looming ahead of me, and I can hardly wait. What could he possibly have to ask me? He knows I'm completely capable of doing the job. I've been here three years, after all. If he doesn't realize my potential, he must not have been paying any attention.

When I hear my phone begin to ring, I hastily grab the receiver. "Madeline speaking," I chirp, probably a little more brightly than usual. I can't help it—I'm on top of the clouds right now.

"Heard, it's Doug Hamilton."

Calling to remind me about the interview? Don't worry—I won't miss it.

"There's been a slight change in plans regarding your interview."

Change in plans? I don't like the sound of that.

"Kent Cooper has decided that he would like to handle the interview himself. He would like to see you in his office at 2:00. Okay?"

Huh? Not okay!

"Yes, thank you," I answer instead, completely betraying myself.

Cooper wants to interview me? No—I was prepared for Hamilton. He knows about the department, knows what I do, knows my capabilities. Cooper doesn't know anything about me! He'll probably ask me all types of questions, trying to test my knowledge. I'm not ready for that type of inquisition!

What if he doesn't trust Hamilton to do the interview?

Or, yikes, what if Hamilton really wants me to have the job, and Cooper isn't sure?

This is not good—not good at all.

"Katie," I hiss. She looks up from her computer, inquisitively eyeing me through her curls.

"Hey, it's almost time," she informs me with a smile. "Are you excited?"

"No. I just found out I have to interview with Cooper."

Katie's eyes grow a couple sizes, and her face suddenly looks a little pale. "Cooper? What happened?"

"I don't know. There's been a change in plans. What do you think that means?"

"I'm sure it's a good thing. At least he's taking it seriously. Don't worry, everything will be fine."

That's easy for Katie to say. She doesn't have to go to the top floor and face Cooper in his big office with the big chairs and big doors. The place is practically built for giants. I'm going to look like a tiny bug.

Well, so I've heard. I've never actually been in Cooper's office myself, or even on the top floor, so I'm just basing this on hearsay. This is not good—not good at all. (I know, I said that already.) Now I feel very nervous, and it's starting to feel stiflingly hot in here. What if I begin to feel sick?

"You better go, if you have to make it to the top floor in time." She's right, I know, but I'm not prepared. What if he doesn't like me? What if I'm nervous and come across as scatterbrained or unprofessional? What if my weak stomach rejects the fact that I want this promotion and I throw up on his rug?

Still, I guess I have to face the music, and there's no getting around it. I have to go.

Scratch that…I *want* to go, because I want this job. The job is mine, and I deserve it.

That's it! I'll just keep reminding myself of that fact, and I'm sure I will be assertive and impressive in the interview.

The job is mine, and I deserve it.

Pushing the button for the elevator, I prepare to wait for the doors to open, but they slide apart almost immediately, as though they were awaiting my arrival. Hmmm… I was hoping for a moment to stand here and calm my nerves, but it looks like it's not happening.

The elevator jerks upward in its ascent to the top floor. What if Cooper doesn't come out of his office to greet me? How am I going to approach him? Should I go up to his desk and shake his hand, or should I just politely sit in one of the chairs? What if the desk is so enormous that I can't reach across it to shake his hand, and I wind up doing a belly flop on its surface, and he is appalled and thinks I'm crazy, sprawled out across his desk with my arms extended toward him?

Breathe. The job is mine, and I deserve it.

The doors to the elevator open, and I step through. This is it—the top floor. Definitely nicer than my floor, but I don't see anything giant yet. Hardwood flooring adds a touch of elegance, and the plants are real, unlike those fake things we have in our department. Even though there are several offices, all the doors are closed. People up here must like their privacy, or maybe Cooper makes them keep the doors shut so the place always looks neat and tidy. Looking at the nameplates until I find the correct office seems like the only option.

At the end of the hall, I finally locate Kent Cooper, but I can't decide what to do. Should I knock and go in? That doesn't seem like a good idea. I should check with his assistant, but where is that office? The door beside his is marked "Dina Barlow—Secretary," so that seems like a safe bet. Knocking on the door, I wait patiently for a response.

"Yes?" comes the muffled reply, and I open the door.

"Excuse me, but I have a 2:00 appointment with Mr. Cooper. Should I wait outside?"

Dina looks a little skeptical about me, giving me the stink-eye over her reading glasses. She looks to be maybe fifty-five, with her blonde hair piled into an old-fashioned beehive hairdo. The dramatic red shade of her reading frames matches her lipstick perfectly, which I have to admit is mighty impressive.

"And you are?" she asks, pinching the corner of her glasses as she continues to look over them.

"My name is Madeline Heard."

She nods and begins dialing the phone, holding it up gingerly as though she's afraid it might burn the side of her head, or alternately get caught in the hive.

"Mr. Cooper, there's a Madeline Heard here to see you."

Dina's office really isn't that nice. It's nicer than where I have to sit, for certain, but not nearly as nice as the hallway would suggest. She does have a window, though, which would be lovely on those long, dreary days when a person simply gets tired of staring at the blank walls.

"He will see you now," she states as she places the phone in its cradle. Attempting to smile, I back out into the hallway and close the door. It certainly is quiet up here, and a little chilly. Back on my floor, there are people everywhere, coming out of the woodwork like ants.

Forcing a deep breath, I knock on Cooper's door and carefully crack it open.

"Come in," I hear a loud voice call. The large space is at least three times the size of Dina's, with thick, dark blue plush carpet and light blue leather chairs. The desk *is* rather massive—someone was definitely right about that. It's polished to a high shine, and behind it sits another tall blue leather chair. The other furniture is not really *that* big—I don't know who started that rumor. Aside from the desk, everything looks fairly normal.

Cooper stands to the right of his desk as he awaits my entrance, probably about two inches taller than me, and in his late forties or early fifties by my guess. His skin is tan, most likely from visits to a tanning bed rather than natural coloring, and his dark brown hair is parted to one side and held there with quite a lot of hair product. When he smiles at my approach, it's hard to miss the fact that his teeth are startling white—unnaturally, really, to the point that I find myself wanting to look away.

"So this is Madeline Heard," he bellows, extending his hand. If this is his only volume level, it's certainly going to take some getting used to.

"Yes, sir," I say, taking his hand and forcing myself to look at his face despite the blinding smile. He squeezes my hand and then motions to a chair.

"Sit, sit. Make yourself comfortable. Would you like something to drink?"

"No, thank you." I lower myself into one of the leather chairs, and suddenly I realize why people think the office is odd. The desk is built on a podium or something so Cooper towers over his guests. I *am* like a tiny bug in this chair.

"I don't believe we've had the pleasure of meeting before now," he says, continuing to grin. "I'm sure I would have remembered."

"That's correct, sir, we've never met." I didn't notice his cologne at first, but now it's starting to become overwhelming. Is it possible for cologne to give you a buzz? I think my mind is starting to get fuzzy.

"So, Marketing Account Leader—you think that's the right job for you?"

That's certainly a strange way of posing a question.

The job is mine, and I deserve it.

"Yes, sir. I've been in the department for three years now, so I'm very knowledgeable about the policies and procedures that go into the daily responsibilities. I've also been performing in the position for the past several weeks, while we corrected the discrepancies caused by a former employee, and all of my coworkers have thrived in that time, going above and beyond what was expected."

"I don't like any of that 'sir' stuff. You can just call me Kent."

Yeah, right.

"Thank you. With my work experience here and my educational background, I could easily be integrated into the position with practically no effort on behalf of any of the other staff members. I'm sure you've noticed the strides we've made in the past few weeks."

"Yes, indeed I have," he says, stroking his chin. His gold ring flashes every once in a while, when it catches the overhead light in just the right way.

"Perhaps you'd like to hear some of my ideas for the department?" I ask. He purses his lips for a second.

"In a moment. First I'd like to know a little more about you."

"Absolutely. I have a B.S. in Marketing and Communications from—"

"No, no, no. I don't want to hear about your education or job skills. I want to know about *you*."

Okay, I'm completely confused. Doesn't he want to hear my great ideas? I've been practicing them for my interview with Hamilton. What does he want me to say?

"I'm not sure what type of information you're referencing," I admit. My stomach churns and lets out a loud growl. *Naturally, perfect timing for that.*

"Are you hungry? I can have something sent up for you."

"No, I'm fine. It was nothing."

"Nonsense, I'll get you something. What do you like? Salad? You look like a salad girl." He picks up his receiver and pushes a button. "Dina, get Miss Heard one of those chef salads. Just have them send it up. Yes, right now." He hangs up and looks at me again.

"Thank you," I offer, not knowing how to respond. I certainly don't want a salad right now. I want my job, and I deserve it.

"Now, for instance, tell me about your hobbies. What do you like to do after work?"

Hobbies? That isn't a very interview-ish question. What does that have to do with anything?

"Oh, I exercise, and I cook. Sometimes I watch the baseball games on television, or read a book." I admit, they're not exactly hobbies, but they are things I do after work. It doesn't matter if I particularly like doing them or not. I can't very well tell him I like to watch makeover programs on television and go on dates.

"What type of exercise do you do?" He's leaning over his desk, hands folded in front of him. He actually seems interested in this nonsense. Why isn't he asking me about the department, or the job duties?

"Jogging, mostly, around my neighborhood. I find it very relaxing."

Yeah, I know, I don't really think there's anything relaxing about it, but I can't act like I find it to be a chore, now that I named it as one of my hobbies.

"Yes, I can see it. You look like the jogging type. I'm actually an athlete myself. I play tennis quite a bit. Do you like to play tennis?"

No. I feel like an ant and I just want to get out of here. Can't you just ask me the questions you need for the interview and let me be on my way?

"Actually, I've never really played tennis properly, so I'm not sure whether I like it or not."

He claps his hands together in front of his face. "That is just not acceptable. We have to get you playing tennis. I'll set you up with my trainer for lessons or something. You'll be a pro in no time."

"Thank you, but that's not necessary."

"Nonsense, you're going to enjoy it, and I'm going to see to it."

He scribbles a note on a paper beside his arm and then folds his hands together while he stares at me again.

"Tell me, Madeline, what do you think of those new tennis shoes with the tree frog on the side? They're supposed to be excellent for running, I've heard."

Tennis shoes with tree frogs? Wasn't this supposed to be an interview?

"I'm afraid I'm not familiar with those."

He starts scribbling again, his lips moving as he writes. "What size shoes does a woman like you wear, anyway?"

What size shoes? A woman like me? This has to be a joke.

"I don't know about a 'woman like me', but I generally wear a seven."

"Yes, that sounds about right. I can see that. Now, what kind of shoes do you use for running?" He reaches up and strokes his hair, and then puts his hand back on his desk. He needn't have worried—I really doubt that hair is going anywhere.

"I don't have any shoes that I would endorse. I purchased some that were highly recommended at the fitness store, but they don't perform in the manner described."

"You can't run in them?" he asks, his dark green eyes boring into my skull. These questions are beginning to make me mega uncomfortable.

"Of course I can run in them, but it feels nothing like I would imagine running on air would feel, and that's what the promise was…the manufacturer's guarantee."

He begins to laugh—a deep, bellowing laugh—and I just sit silently twirling my fingers around each other.

"That is false advertising, I guarantee it!" He laughs for another moment, and then clears his throat and gets back to business. "You're very well spoken for a young lady your age."

Great. He thinks I'm a child. Why can't I be well spoken for any age, not just *my* age?

"Thank you," I respond carefully.

Cooper sits silently and continues to stare at me, passing his pen back and forth between his hands. Am I supposed to say something? Speak, Cooper, speak! Please, just get to the point of the interview and put me out of my misery.

"You remind me of a girl I knew when I was in college," he states. "Her name was Elise Harrill. Any relation?"

What?

"I don't believe so."

"She was a nice girl, and very smart. Didn't date very much, but she did go out with me a couple times, of course."

Of course, because who wouldn't want to go out with a weirdo egomaniac who's obsessed with his hair and peoples' shoes?

"I saw her a few years ago, and she immediately knew who I was. It's actually very strange, but I never seem to age. I look just like I did when I was in college."

He must have looked fifty in college. That's sad, really.

"Do you take vitamins?" he continues.

"Yes, I do."

"That's very good. Very good. I take my vitamins faithfully every day. It helps to keep me from becoming ill. Plus, it keeps me physically in tip-top shape, which I'm sure you can tell is very important to me."

"Uh, yes." What the blazes is he talking about? He doesn't look to be in physically tip-top shape. He's a little thick about the waistband—I noticed that when I walked into the office.

"Tell me, Madeline, are you much of a night owl?"

"No."

"That's good. It leads to an early grave. I personally try to get up at the crack of dawn, get an early start to the day. I usually have a couple raw eggs for breakfast. Have you ever eaten a raw egg?"

Somebody get me out of here. Set off the fire alarm or something. I can't take it anymore. This guy is out of his mind.

"No, I've never eaten a raw egg."

"You don't know what you're missing. It's the best protein drink you can find, and gives you lots of energy."

It could also give you salmonella.

He leans back in his chair and lifts his head slightly, as though he's silently assessing my appearance. He begins drumming his fingers on the desk, still staring at me, tapping out a rhythm. After a moment he stops, makes some notes on his paper, and then leans back again.

"You have a big future at this company," he suddenly bellows, arms spreading wide. "Big! Very big! Mark my words."

"Thank you," I say again. *You got the job. Just tell me I got the job, and let me go.*

"I guess that will be all for now." He stands up and moves to the right, extending his hand again.

That's it? We're done, just like that? No particulars about the position or my qualifications?

Standing up, I shake his hand and head to the door, pulling it open and emerging into the hallway.

"I'm serious about the tennis!" he yells. "I'm calling my guy!"

The door closes behind me as I wonder if he's crazy. That wasn't an interview. That was more like a truly horrible blind date. He didn't ask me about my ideas or suggestions for the department at all. I have to admit, I am very disappointed.

My goal is to slide past Dina's office unnoticed, since she has the door open now. She looks up as I walk by and calls out to me.

"Miss Heard!" Stopping, I pause in her doorway. "Don't forget your salad." She hands me a green mound in a plastic container and swings the door to a close just inches from my face.

Wow, it is so nice to have received such a lovely reception on my first visit to the top floor. I don't know about it being built for giants, but giant personalities...most definitely.

It's impossible not to replay that awkward conversation in my mind as I stand in the elevator. Hamilton would have never asked me such bizarre questions. I would have been able to impress him with my ideas, and Cooper didn't even seem to be interested. Why do things like this always happen to me?

The door opens and I walk slowly back to my desk, the plastic container full of salad swinging back and forth at the end of my arm like a pathetic souvenir from my trip to the top. "I interviewed with Cooper, and all I got was this stupid salad." Not exactly a winning slogan.

Katie smiles when she sees me coming, her face bright with anticipation.

"Well? Did you get the job?" She hurries over to my desk, plopping her backside on its surface as she looks at me. "How did it go?"

"I have no idea," I mutter, setting the salad down on the desktop.

"What's that?"

"Parting gift. Chef salad. He decided I was hungry."

"Why did he decide that?" she asks. It's impossible for me to tell whether she's about to laugh or simply anticipating good news.

"It probably has something to do with the fact that my stomach growled like a trapped bear."

"No, it didn't!" Okay, she's definitely laughing now. "I told you to eat lunch!"

"You were right, I admit."

When she's finished laughing, she leans a little closer. "Do you feel like it went well? What sort of questions did he ask you?"

"Let's see...he told me about tree frogs, shoes, vitamins, raw eggs, girls he knew in college. Pretty much just your basic interview questions."

"That's strange. What was going wrong?"

"He's insane, that's what. He needs a serious evaluation."

Katie begins to laugh again. "He can't be that bad! What's that smell?"

"I think his cologne followed me into the elevator. It was a life form in itself. I really think it was giving me a buzz."

"There you go," Katie surmises. "The cologne has affected his brain."

"You're probably right," I agree with a sigh. I can't help feeling let down. I hope Hamilton calls me soon to give me the verdict. In the meantime, at least I can say that I've finally been to the top floor, and I think I know why everyone keeps their doors closed:

They're all hiding from Cooper.

Chapter Nine

It's the day after the interview, and I'm feeling much better about my chances. After all, he did say I had a big future with the company. What else could he have been referring to, if he wasn't going to give me the job?

Besides, after talking to Josh about it last night, he convinced me that Cooper might have simply been trying to get to know me, to see if he wanted me on his team, so to speak. If he did have big plans for me, he might have been assessing my personality. I'm sure he's right—Cooper seemed to like me, after all. If not, he probably would have made no mention about my future.

Of course, Josh also told me that if Cooper didn't give me the job, it was his loss and I deserved better.

I sort of wish I could bottle Josh and take a shot of that optimism whenever I need a pick-me-up.

Anyway, the job is mine, and I deserve it. It's only a matter of time.

Stepping out of the elevator onto my familiar floor, the people bustling about give me a renewed sense of normalcy as they retrieve coffee and talk about their prior evenings. I head toward my own desk, curiously eyeing a box sitting in my chair. When I get closer, I realize it's a shoebox with tiny green tree frogs on the side.

Maybe it's not what it looks like. Maybe it's just a box, and there's a stack of paperwork waiting for me on the inside. Yes, I'm sure that's it.

Except I know that's not it. They're tree frog running shoes, size seven. There's no note, but there's only one person who could have done this.

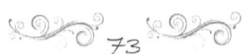

Great, now what am I going to do? I can't pay for these shoes. I just bought the other running shoes less than a month ago. Picking up the phone, I dial the number for the directory. Maybe if I explain the situation to Dina, she will tell me how to handle it. She didn't seem like the friendliest person when we met yesterday, but she is human, after all.

"Dina speaking."

Wow, I didn't expect her to answer so fast.

"Hi, Dina, this is Madeline Heard. We met yesterday, remember?"

"Yes, I remember," she replies in her husky voice. "The chef salad girl."

I manage a small chuckle. "Yes, that was me. The thing is, I have sort of a strange question, and I'm hoping you can help me. I'm calling about some shoes."

"Yes, size seven. Is there a problem with the fit?"

Good! She knows about the shoes!

"Oh, I don't know, I didn't try them on. The thing is, I simply can't afford them, and I was wondering how I should go about returning them. Maybe if you tell me what store they came from, I can just pop by and—"

"The shoes were from Mr. Cooper."

Okay, don't just point out the obvious. Help me out here!

"Yes, I suspected that was the case. He did recommend the shoes to me yesterday, but perhaps he isn't fully aware of my financial situation."

"The shoes are a gift, Miss Heard, and I certainly don't need to hear about your financial situation."

I see she's still sporting the charming personality she greeted me with yesterday.

"A gift? I'm a little uncomfortable accepting such a costly gift."

"Well, then I suggest you call Mr. Cooper yourself and explain the problem, because I don't intend to go into his office and tell him you refused his gift."

"Okay, thanks for your help," I say sarcastically.

She hangs up, which is just as well. I decided yesterday she wasn't very nice, but this really puts the icing on the cake. Now what am I going to do with these shoes? I definitely don't feel comfortable calling Cooper and complaining about them. This is a real dilemma.

Suddenly, a hand grabs my upper arm and yanks me behind a filing cabinet. I turn to see Katie, wild eyed and clawing at me.

"Good grief, Katie. You could have dislocated my shoulder!"

"Keep your voice down," she whispers. "I can't believe you were just standing there, calmly talking on the phone, on this, the worst day of our lives."

"Seriously, Katie, what is wrong with you? Are you on something?"

"You didn't see him? Oh my gosh, you didn't see him! Maddie, what are we going to do? This is the mother of all nightmares."

"Would you calm yourself and just tell me what's going on?"

Katie backs away a little bit, looks at the floor, and takes a deep breath as I peer past the file cabinet to make sure no one is watching this unbelievable display. She must be out of her mind.

"He...of whom...we do not...speak," she explains, punctuating her words as she stands there crazy-eyed and waiting for reassurance.

"What about him, Katie? What did he do to..." I stop short, because I happen to glance around the file cabinet and see what caused Katie's reaction. There he is, bigger than life, standing right there in front of me, hanging up an ugly motivational print in the office—*my office*. Bill Davies? No, no, no.

No!

"What is he doing here?" I mutter, not taking my eyes off him.

"Oh, Maddie, I don't know. When I walked in this morning, there he was." Katie's eyes well up with tears as she gazes into my face.

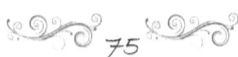

"But he moved to the third floor. He has nothing to do with us anymore. There's no reason for him to be in there unless..."

No, they wouldn't dare. There is no way Cooper could have made such a mockery of my interview yesterday and then given the job to Bill Davies! What a patronizing, condescending, utterly demeaning, cowardly way to behave! I should go up there and give that crackpot a piece of my mind!

"Maddie? Are you okay? You're scaring me."

"I'm going to Hamilton."

"Hamilton? What are you going to do, Maddie? There's nothing we can do."

"I can tell him what I think about this."

"Don't do that," she begs, grabbing my arm. "What if you get fired?"

"He'll just save me the trouble of quitting, because I'm not working for that joker again."

I move away from the cabinet and head down the hall, leaving Katie practically crying in the corner.

It was nothing but a big game—the questions about the hobbies, the raw eggs, the vitamins. He was only toying with me, because he had no intention of giving me the job. That's why he didn't ask me any serious questions! And Hamilton...that weasel let him do it. He didn't stand up for me, after all I've done the last few weeks. Did Cooper really think those stupid tree frog shoes were going to appease me after this? I don't think so!

Hamilton is sitting at his desk when I walk in and slam the door shut behind me. He jerks and looks up, his chair moving back a few inches.

"Good grief, Heard, you startled me."

"You want to tell me what's going on?" I demand. He sighs and leans back in his chair, his hands spread on the desk in front of him.

"Okay, now, before you jump to conclusions, just let me—"

"Why is Bill Davies on this floor? Why is he in *my* department, hanging his ugly prints in the office that should belong to *me*?"

Hamilton pauses for a moment and takes a deep breath. "Cooper gave him the job."

"And you just sat back and let that happen, knowing the kind of supervisor Davies has been in the past? How could you think for one moment that we would ever agree to work for—"

"Now hold on a second, Heard. If you'll just let me explain things, I'm sure you'll understand."

"Understand a blatant, gross injustice? Try your best to explain *that*."

I stand resolutely in front of the door, silently drilling him with my eyes, daring him to give me a lame excuse. He clears his throat and tugs at his tie.

"I was all set to go with you. I mean, there's no doubt you earned the job, and I had every intention of giving it to you. The interview was just going to be a formality." He clears his throat again, which makes me slightly concerned that he's not being honest. "Yesterday, at about 1:00, Cooper called me and told me he was really pleased with the way we turned things around. He asked who was responsible for that, and I told him you had a lot to do with it. When I told him I was getting ready to give you the job, he said that he would like to interview you himself, since he had never met you. Naturally, I assumed he would agree with my decision."

"And then he made a mockery of my interview. I still don't understand."

Hamilton looks confused as he pushes around some papers on his desk, searching for something.

"Your interview? Sorry, I don't know about that. Cooper had his secretary bring me a note yesterday afternoon...aha, here it is. It says this: Madeline Heard is an impressive young woman, and I think she can be better utilized in some other facet of the company. Please return Bill Davies to his former job duties for the

time being." He stops and drops the paper on his desk. "That's all I know."

"So what am I supposed to do, just sit around and wait to see what that cryptic note means?"

"Look, I'm not happy about this either. You know what it means, that you can be better utilized somewhere else? It means you won't be working for me anymore, and you're one of the best employees I have. You would have been great in that position, and instead I'm going to lose you altogether."

Pulling up a chair, I slump down and put my head in my hands. "I'm not working for Bill Davies," I murmur.

"I don't blame you for feeling that way, but what am I to do?"

What can he do? Nothing. That was my job, I deserved it, and now I have to sit around waiting for Cooper to tell me in which "facet" he wants me to be involved. What if it's cleaning toilets or washing cars? What if he wants me to write his dating memoirs?

"I want the day off," I verbalize without thinking it through.

"Okay."

"With pay."

Sigh. "With pay."

"Katie, too."

"Come on, Heard, that's a little—"

"Katie, too, or I ask for a week."

"Okay, okay. Katie, too."

Standing up, I head for the door.

"You know, Heard, you're a lot fiercer than I would have imagined. You're like a little bulldog."

Woof.

"Thanks for wanting to give me the job. It's nice to know that you think I deserve it."

He nods and smiles sadly as I turn the knob and pull the door open.

"What am I supposed to tell Cooper, if he calls looking for you?"

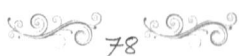

"Just tell him that I'm running in tree frogs and eating raw eggs."

"Sorry?"

"Tell him I took the day off."

Chapter Ten

It's been a rough week, more because I feel sorry for Katie than anything else. Even though I'm not sure where I'm going or what I'll be doing, at least I know I'm getting out. All Katie has to look forward to is an undetermined amount of time with Bill Davies. Oh, the horror.

Bill has been really quiet since he came back, barely speaking to any of us. He's probably just biding his time until I'm gone, thinking no one will try to stand up to him when he revamps the department. He will strip Shelly of all her duties, so she can fully devote her attention to beautifying herself and writing out grocery lists. Before the month is out, he'll probably have Katie shining Shelly's shoes and picking up her dry cleaning. Poor Katie—I should do something to help her.

Well, I would if I could.

The phone rings, pulling me away from my thoughts.

"Madeline Heard."

"Hi, Madeline, this is Max Kimball from the Big Cedar Tennis Club, calling to schedule your tennis instruction."

Tennis instruction? I didn't order any...

Oh, good grief!

"I'm sorry, but there's been a mistake. I didn't order any lessons–besides, tennis instruction isn't in my budget right now."

"No need to worry, ma'am, the cost of the instruction has already been covered. What day of the week would you prefer?"

Why do I get the feeling lately that I'm not in charge of my own life?

"Actually, I work Monday through Friday, so there's really no time to—"

"You're in luck, because we also have instruction on Saturday. Do you prefer morning or afternoon? Morning is sometimes more tolerable in the heat of the summer."

This guy has an answer for everything.

"That sounds great," I offer. "The thing is, I'm pretty much booked every Saturday for the next month. Maybe I should just call you when I'm ready to schedule something."

"No need for that, ma'am. I'll just schedule you for the first Saturday in September."

"Oh, that won't work. I'm having a family get-together that day, so I wouldn't be able to make it."

That at least is true—Mom's Labor Day picnic.

"Okay, then the second Saturday in September. I'll put you down for 10:00."

Surely I can come up with a reason to cancel. I could probably come up with a good reason within the next five minutes if I thought hard enough.

"See you then!" he states cheerfully, right before the line goes dead.

I cannot believe this! What exactly is it that Cooper wants me to do at this company, begin a fitness program? First the running shoes, and now the tennis instruction. If I walk in next Monday and find a glass full of raw eggs, I'm going to scream.

I immediately contacted Josh on the day I left work early, indignant about the job and hoping he would validate my feelings. When he called me back later, he was sympathetic until I happened to bring up the shoes, and then he laughed. He told me I should give them a try, so I acquiesced and they actually did feel more comfortable than the air-walking shoes I purchased earlier. I didn't admit that to Josh, though. I e-mailed him later and told him it was like running with bricks strapped to my feet. He didn't believe me.

"We've got to do something, Katie," I whisper, turning to her.

She looks up from her paperwork. "What, run away?"

Wow, I've never seen her so depressed. "Maybe we can stage a coup."

"That's not funny," she replies with a sigh, looking back down at her desk. She is definitely not her usual, cheerful self.

"Tell me how to help, Katie. I'll do anything."

Katie glances over at Bill Davies, who is typing away at his computer. She closes her eyes for a moment and then shakes her head in disgust.

"You can't do anything. I just have to get used to the fact that I am going to be working for *him* again, and hope that things get better. What else can I do? I need this job."

It's so unfair. If Cooper would have given me the promotion, Katie would have been happy and things would have continued on the way they were. Instead, he made a big mistake, and we all have to live with the consequences.

Why did Cooper even have to get involved at all? If he would have left things up to Hamilton like he should have, I would be sitting in that office right now, not Bill Davies.

This is all Cooper's fault.

"I'm going to Cooper."

I am vaguely concerned that the voice that just blurted that sounded like mine, and I am quite certain that is not something I want to do under any circumstance.

Katie's eyes grow a little larger as she leans forward across her desk. "Are you insane?"

Am I insane? No, Cooper is insane, and going back up to his office is insane, but I am *not* insane. I have to help my friend.

"What are you going to do, Maddie, beg him for the job? You already said he's a little crazy. What if he fires you on the spot?"

"Then that means everything Hamilton told me was a lie, in which case I wouldn't want to stay here anyway."

"Don't do it," she pleads as I push my chair away from my desk resolutely. I know in that instant I've sealed my fate, and I have no choice.

Stepping toward the elevator, I pause to push the up button, completely regretting my move. Sensing Katie's eyes boring into my back, I'm painfully aware that I can't chicken out.

My palms start to get sweaty as the elevator doors open and I step inside.

The knowledge that I can't just go up to Cooper's office unannounced and demand that he makes things right for Katie engulfs me. I wouldn't even know how to begin. She's staring at me as the doors close, though, and I attempt to smile.

Oh, why am I so impulsive? I should have just sat there and kept my trap shut.

Maybe he's not in the office. Why would he be, on a Friday afternoon? I'm sure none of those executives on the top floor even bother to come in on Fridays. I'll just go up, see that all the lights for the top floor are shut off, and come straight back down. At least Katie will know that I made an attempt.

The elevator doors open to the top floor. All the lights are on, unfortunately, and Dina is sitting at a desk in the hall. To my dismay, she saw me and is glaring at me over those red glasses.

Wait a minute, Dina's sitting in the hall?

Never mind that now. How am I going to get out of this? I can't just turn around and head back down in the elevator—she's watching me. Oh, dear God, what do I do?

"Can I help you?" Dina responds with a scowl.

Someone must not have told her it's Friday, and it's okay to be happy on Fridays. Maybe Cooper is tired of her attitude and sat her in the hall as a time-out.

"I would like to see Mr. Cooper," I manage, voice cracking.

"Of course you would," she snaps, snatching up her receiver and continuing to squint at me over those red frames. "Mr. Cooper, Miss Heard is here to see you."

She places her phone back on her desk and begins writing on a notepad in front of her. After a moment, she glances up at me.

"Well, don't just stand here staring at me. Go in, if you're going."

No, that's okay. I changed my mind. You can just tell him it was a mistake. Katie won't be too awfully disappointed.

Oh, drat.

Opening the door gingerly, I peek inside.

"Madeline Heard, if this isn't a surprise!" Wow, I forgot how loud he is. He stands up as I shut the door behind me, and I can't help but notice his bright pink polo shirt. I'm not certain that's a great color for a lot of men—especially not him. "I don't have things quite ready yet, but I'm glad you came up."

Don't have things ready? What is he talking about?

"I'm glad...that you're glad, I mean. I actually want to talk to you about something, sir, that's been—"

"I thought we settled all this 'sir' business the other day. Just call me Kent."

I can see nothing has changed. I'm never going to get anywhere with this conversation.

"Well, what I want to talk to you about is—"

"I'm sure it can wait," he interrupts. "Let me show you what I've been doing."

There is no denying that I'm filled with dread, half afraid he's going to show me his bicep and go into another fitness monologue. Instead, he walks to the far side of his office and opens a door.

"Come on, come on," he instructs as I walk toward him. The door opens to join Dina's office, which has been newly remodeled with fresh carpeting, new furniture, and window dressings.

"Well, what do you think?" he asks, grinning at me.

"I'm sure Dina will love it," I reply, listening as he chuckles.

"Oh, no. This isn't for Dina. This is your office."

Come again?

"My office?"

"Yes, absolutely. You're going to have to be close by so we can really collaborate on all my ideas."

"I'm sorry, I guess I don't know what you're talking about. Exactly what is it that you want me to do?"

"You're going to be my assistant."

Oh, no. No, no, no.

"But Dina's your assistant."

"Oh, forget about Dina," he states with a wave of his hand. "She's my secretary. She's great with paperwork and all that stuff, but you are going to be my right hand man. Or woman, I should say. I've got all kinds of ideas, and you're going to help me see them through."

"I really don't want to take Dina's office. That doesn't seem fair."

"Dina doesn't care. Besides, with her sitting in the hallway, she'll be better able to greet my guests. It will all work out for the best."

No wonder Dina was so hateful. I don't blame her, being relegated to the hallway to make room for new blood.

"Oh, I almost forgot the best part," he says eagerly, practically jumping. "Wait right here!" He steps out of the doorway and into his own office.

I don't want to be Cooper's assistant. I cannot imagine having to work with this lunatic day in and day out. After a year or so, I will probably have to check myself into an institution!

Ding-dong.

What was that, a doorbell? I didn't see a doorbell outside Cooper's office.

Ding-dong.

"Did you hear it?" he calls.

"Yes," I acknowledge, moving into the doorway so I can see him. "It's a doorbell."

He claps his hands together loudly. "Technically correct, but it's so much more than that. You see, I had this doorbell installed in your office, and the other end is installed right here under my desk. Every time I need you, I'll just ring the bell."

It's worse than I thought. Cooper doesn't want an assistant. He wants a lap dog.

"It's pretty ingenious, isn't it?" he wonders, his eyes twinkling. Against my better judgment, I nod slightly, desperately wishing to get away. Why did I even come up here in the first place?

"How did you like the tree frogs?" he bellows, plopping down in his chair.

"They're nice," I say as he nods vigorously.

"Yes, I suspected as much. Monday morning, you just come straight up here. There are a lot of things I want to get done, so we'll get started right away. Now, there was something you wanted to talk to me about, wasn't there?"

Oh, yeah, Katie. I almost forgot.

"Actually, yes." How do I word this? "My coworker in the marketing department, Katie Green–I think she might be better utilized elsewhere in the company."

"Marketing is not her forte, eh?"

"No, it's not that. She does a very good job. I just believe she'd have a lot more potential in another setting. I was hoping maybe someone could look over her résumé and see if there was a better fit for her qualifications."

He strokes his chin for a moment, staring down at his desk, then reaches down and begins flipping through a brown leather book. "I'll just make a call," he explains as he begins dialing the number. I hear the phone ringing through the speaker.

"This is Nora," a voice says on the other end of the line.

"Nora, this is Kent Cooper. What openings do we have right now?"

"Openings? Uh, let's see... We have an opening for a computer programmer."

He looks at me expectantly, and I shake my head.

"No, that's no good. What else?"

"Outside maintenance."

"No, no, no," he says. "That's all you have?" He drums his fingers on the desk impatiently.

"Yes, sir, for the time being. I'll have another opening soon—next Friday is Ariel's last day with us; she's a Human Resources Assistant."

"That's the ticket!" he states emphatically. "As of right now, that job is filled by..." He looks at me and begins rolling his hand in the air.

"Katie Green," I whisper.

"Katie Green, from Marketing. Make it happen."

"I will, sir."

"Oh, and do you have all the paperwork ready for Madeline Heard?"

"Yes, sir."

"I'll send her over."

Cooper sits back in his chair and grins, looking quite pleased with himself.

"Thank you," I manage.

"No problem," he roars. "We are going to be a great team. I'm looking forward to it. By the way, did my tennis guy call you?"

"Yes, he did."

"When's your first lesson?"

"September."

"September? No, that won't do."

"I'm extremely busy on the weekends," I offer, although it doesn't deter him as he begins dialing his phone again and motions me to silence with his hand.

"Max, it's Kent Cooper calling about Madeline Heard. I know, that's no good. Reschedule it. How about Tuesday? Sounds good. Book it." He sets the phone down and looks at me contentedly. "You're all set for Tuesday at 1:00."

"I don't have enough vacation time to—"

"Who said anything about vacation time? This is important to your job responsibilities. Plan on Tuesdays at 1:00 from this point forward."

"Okay," I mutter.

Talking to this man feels like being run over by a truck. I just can't work for him. I can't!

"Don't forget to stop by Human Resources and see Nora," he calls as I walk to the door. *Ding-dong.* The noise makes me turn and look at him. "See you Monday!"

That is *so* not funny. Is life playing some sick joke on me?

Closing the door quietly behind me, I glance over at Dina, who is staring down at her desk. I really should say something to her, shouldn't I? I feel so horrible, but what can I do?

"I'm sorry, Dina," I whisper. "I didn't know." She sits up straight and pulls her glasses off, placing them gently on top of her paperwork. Taking a deep breath, she looks me in the eye.

"Let me tell you something, missy," she says quietly. "I've been at this company for twenty-three years. Twenty-three! You bring your opportunistic little self up here one time—one time!— in your pretty little suit and parade around, and suddenly I'm out in the hallway, buying you shoes, setting up tennis lessons. You don't even have the decency to try to take my job. No, you just take my office, so you can sit in there on your pretty little can and do nothing while I sit in the hallway doing all the work. And you want to tell me you're sorry? Believe it or not, I really don't want to hear it right now."

She stares at me defiantly for a few more seconds, then puts on her glasses and looks back down at her work. Backing slowly away, I turn to walk toward the elevator.

If it makes you feel any better, I want to say, *at least you don't have to waltz in his office when he rings a bell.*

Instead, I just step into the elevator and watch her bent form as the doors close in front of me. I really do empathize with her, but it's not my fault. I didn't ask for any of this—who in their right mind would? I don't want to be Cooper's right hand woman.

Maybe I won't. Maybe I'll just go home at the end of the day and never come back.

I press button five for Human Resources. If I don't stop, Nora will probably call Cooper, and he'll start hunting me down. Maybe I should just take the elevator back to my desk, pack up my things and leave. Surely Josh wouldn't be too angry at me for mooching off him for a bit while I found another job. I could look at the postings tonight and be headed in a new direction by Monday morning.

But if I walk, will they take care of Katie?

The elevator doors open, and I step out onto the fifth floor.

"Excuse me," I say to a nearby gentleman, "I'm looking for Nora."

"At the back to the left," he answers, not bothering to look up as I meander towards the back of the hall.

"Nora?" I wonder as I greet a middle-aged woman with short dark hair. "I'm Madeline Heard."

"Of course. Come on in." She fiddles with some papers on her desk as she glances at me curiously. "Madeline Heard. Do you know how fortunate you are? Some people work here for thirty years and never even see the top floor."

"Yeah, it's great," I mutter half-heartedly. She motions for me to sit as she pulls out a file stuffed with paperwork.

"Let's see, I've got your new employment sheet here somewhere. Ah, here it is. This shows your new job title and your updated salary. You can just sign and date it on the bottom."

Taking the sheet from her, I begin reading: Assistant to the Chief Executive Officer. Job responsibilities to be provided at a later date. Salary of...

"Are you sure this is right?" I wonder aloud.

"Yes, it's correct."

Wow, Cooper's paying me about twice what I make now. He must really have something important in mind if he's willing to pay me this much! Maybe it won't be so bad. I mean, I will have to put up with Cooper, but if I have some really important responsibilities to handle, my days might be tolerable. Perhaps I should stick it out for a couple weeks and see how things go.

"And here are the keys to your Chevy Tahoe," she adds.

"I'm sorry, my what?"

"The Tahoe, your company vehicle. Mr. Cooper insisted that you will need adequate transportation in your new position. Your parking spot will be number 6."

I get to park in the lot? I don't have to park in the garage across the street and risk life and limb at the crosswalk anymore? It can't be true!

"I think that's all," she says, "unless you have any questions for me."

"Can I call you later if I think of anything?"

"Sure, that's fine. Congratulations again!"

Walking back to the elevator, I suddenly feel different about today's turn of events. The huge salary increase, and the company vehicle... Maybe this move won't be so bad after all. There's still the problem of Dina to worry about, but perhaps I can find a way to make it up to her later. If we just got to know one another, it might be possible to work together harmoniously.

Okay, I doubt it, but it's still worth a try.

Riding back down to my own floor, I'm now aware that this is my last afternoon in my current job. I'm really going to miss Katie. Sure, I'll be able to call her all the time, but it won't be the same as turning around and seeing her face.

As if reading my mind, the moment I step out of the elevator, she begins waving her arms frantically, motioning me to hurry.

"What is it?" I ask, rushing to her desk.

"How did you do it?" she wonders, beaming. "You got me out!"

"It was nothing," I say, dismissing her with a wave of the hand while she laughs.

"You hadn't been gone ten minutes when they called to tell me I was moving. I hope you'll be as happy about where you're going as I am!"

"Yeah, me too," I mumble as she hugs me.

I really hope I will. It's bound to be a big step up for me. Imagine, my ideas being put to work in the running of the company. I will finally get the respect I deserve!

So why do I feel like I just sold my soul to the devil?

Chapter Eleven

"You don't think it's weird?"

"Of course it's weird," Josh replies. "Sounds like the guy is half crazy, but if someone wanted to pay me that much to take tennis lessons, I would laugh all the way to the bank."

I manage to pick up my stride a little, although I'm not jogging as fast as normal since I'm trying to carry on a conversation with my long-distance friend. He called while I was mid-run, and I don't pass up the limited opportunities we have to converse.

"So you think I should take the job?" I ask breathlessly. The talking while running game is definitely not easy.

"Do what you think is best, of course, but it doesn't seem like there's any harm in waiting a while to see how things go."

He's probably right. Cooper definitely seems eccentric, but maybe after I get to know him I'll find out he's not that bad. Only time will tell.

As I near the driveway, I slow down a bit and try to calm my breathing pattern.

"How far have you been running?" he wants to know.

"Two miles," I admit. And, thanks to Josh's interruption, I've finally gone the entire two miles without walking. Woohoo!

Sitting down on the step, I place my arm on my knees and stare across the road at the rosebushes in the adjacent yard. My eyes naturally slide down the street and toward the two-story at the end of the cul-de-sac.

"Do you know any of the neighbors?" I casually remark, feeling Josh out.

"No, not yet. Why? Anyone interesting?"

Yeah, super beautiful news lady. No big deal.

"Interesting?" I repeat. "I couldn't say."

"It's Friday night. Who's your hot date?"

"Really, Josh, you act like I constantly have a guy on my arm. I haven't even been on a date since I broke up with Benjamin."

Or did he break up with me? I can't even remember anymore.

"Which was why again?"

Glancing down at my shoes, I twist my right foot slightly so I can view the little green amphibians on the side. "He was a fraud. He was supposed to be this great lover of literature, but he wouldn't know a good story if it bit him in the behind."

"Oh, yeah, because you're suddenly a voracious reader."

"It was such a beautiful thing," I protest, rising to my feet. "She follows Robert all the way to Tennessee, and then, when she finally catches up with him, and she's standing there with her heart on her sleeve…" Sighing, I press my hand to my chest.

"You've pulled me in," he states with a laugh. "Come on, she's got her heart on her sleeve, so what happens?"

"He just looked at her like he had expected her to show up, and he said, 'My heart never stopped waiting for you.' Isn't that beautiful? Camdyn Taylor is my new favorite."

"You like that sappy romance stuff?"

"Naturally *you* would think it's sappy for a man to love a woman so much that his heart pines for her," I complain, stepping into the house. Pulling a bottle of water from the fridge, I twist the cap and take a huge gulp. "What would you know about it, anyway? You don't read."

"I read all of your e-mails."

"Literary masterpieces," I sass, smirking at my own little joke.

"The world's best known wordsmiths couldn't hold my attention better than you can, Mad."

If he wasn't Josh, that comment might have made me swoon.

"Who needs a hot date when I have you?" I joke. "Some random guy would definitely not say something so sweet."

"Definitely not," he agrees, growing silent for a second. When I'm about to try to break the quiet, he finally speaks again. "What does Jess think about your job offer?"

Untangling my hair from the knot atop my head, I allow it to smack in a damp mess across my arm. "I haven't had time to call her yet. I had to have Katie follow me home so we could pick up the Tahoe."

"It seems to me that you've already decided, if you picked up the vehicle," he says with a laugh. "What are you doing tonight?"

"Maybe reading," I state, stopping to gaze at a portrait of Josh on the table that his mother left right after he bought the house. Without even thinking, I pick it up and hold it in front of my face. "I bought another Camdyn Taylor book—well, a C.W. Oliver book, but that's the same thing since she had the pen name."

"That Benjamin's an idiot. Something's wrong with him, you know that, right?"

"Of course, that's why I broke up with him." I think?

"If I was home, I'd take you out tonight to celebrate your newfound success."

"Where would we go?" It's an innocent question, at least until I start thinking about the man in that photograph actually walking up to the door and grinning at me from the other side. He's wearing a V-neck T-shirt the same mocha color as Benjamin's disgusting latte on our first date. His gray-green eyes dance playfully behind his glasses, and his dark eyebrows rise a bit when he sees me. He always gets two little wrinkles across his forehead when that happens, right under that fabulous head of chestnut hair that he likes to keep messy in the front. It's part of his alluring, scholarly look, because without the glasses and the messy hair, he might just look like another handsome frat boy type with the dashing good looks and the muscular arms and the full lips that always seem to be inviting something…

"You still there, Mad?"

"Huh? Oh, yeah, just thinking." Thinking completely ridiculous thoughts. Josh's hair wouldn't look messy right now in his current profession, of course.

"It would have to be something completely great," he informs me quickly. "Let's see. I would take you to Hampton's Drive-In and we'd get double-swiss burgers with grilled onions and curly fries, and we'd follow them up with chocolate malts. After that, I'd take you to that field on the outskirts of town where we caught all the lightning bugs that time. Remember that?"

"Your idea of a great celebration is a drive-in and lightning bugs?" Suddenly the alluring man on the other side of the door has his baseball cap on backwards and he's pulling my hair and calling me names. Of course Josh still sees me as kindergarten Maddie who his mother used to babysit after school. Like a foster sister, really. An after-school foster sister.

"My idea of a great anything is just what reminds me of home, I guess," he admits with a slight sigh. "I suppose you'd like me to say that I'd take you to Ruth's Chris Steak House and then we'd dance the night away at some hoity-toity club."

"You really think I'm that shallow?"

Even though I want him to say no, I think I already know the answer.

"I guess I hope not." He clears his throat and I'm not sure how to respond.

"I would eat double-swiss burgers and curly fries with you, Josh, just so you know. Well, not right now, because I'm trying to be healthy and everything, but in theory I would. And I'd even catch lightning bugs with you, if you could manage to find some, but I'd rather go to that old water tower where we drove after prom."

"You'd want to go back there? As I recall, that wasn't a very good memory."

"It was a good memory for me," I insist. "Yet another instance where I had bad luck with dating, right? Who would have ever thought that Ricky Buchanan would leave me standing there on the dance floor while he went off into the night with Heather

Atchison? And don't say anything, because I know in hindsight I should have realized that Ricky was a sleazy two-timing backstabber when he dumped Caitlin Soward to ask me in the first place, but I thought he was just madly in love with me and couldn't think straight." Hmm... Maybe I *am* self-centered and ridiculous. "Anyway, you rescued me like a true hero, Joshua Mason. You drove me to the water tower so I wouldn't have to face my mother while I was crying, and you let me sob all over your tuxedo. You were my knight in shining armor."

"So Ricky Buchanan dumping you is a good memory?"

"No, silly," I tell him while I shake my head, although I realize he can't witness the action. "You're the good memory, don't you see? We were sitting on the back of your car underneath that water tower, and I was feeling pretty unlovable because of that slime ball Ricky, and you told me that I was worthy of better. You said, 'Mad, if a guy is not willing to throw his heart on the line and give you the entire world, he doesn't deserve you.'"

"I said that?"

"Yes," I respond, tears inadvertently filling my eyes at the sweet memory. "I said that I thought Ricky loved me, and you said, 'Love isn't so easily pushed aside. It's long-suffering and patient and steadfast.'"

"That doesn't sound like me."

"It was definitely you," I assure him with a short laugh. "Trust me, Josh—it's permanently on my heart like it's stamped there, and I'll never forget it. The front of your shirt had a smear on it from my mascara. I'm sure your mother scrubbed and scrubbed trying to get it out."

"Probably," he agrees, joining my laughter. "Your dress had that sheer lace stuff over the front, and my button got caught in it. I remember because while I was trying to get loose, you leaned against me, and you smelled like vanilla and peaches. You had glitter in your hair, and by the time I got home, it was all over me."

"So you remember, too," I say wistfully.

"It's pretty difficult to forget. The first of many broken hearts I've nursed."

"I know, me and the broken hearts. You'd think I'd grow up after all this time."

"You didn't wound me too badly. I'm still alive, anyway."

Usually my conversations with Josh leave me feeling pleased and uplifted, but this one is making me emotional and depressed. And apparently Josh considered dealing with my broken heart that night some sort of punishment, which is news to me and slightly disheartening. All this time I've considered his actions that night gallant and sweet; could he have been annoyed with me the entire time? Ouch.

"I'm sorry, Mad," he continues, letting out an extremely exaggerated sigh. "I'm tired and I'm afraid I'm not being good company. Besides, it's late and I should be getting some sleep. I better turn in."

"Goodnight, then," I tell him. "Sweet dreams." Hearing the click on the other end of the line, I hit the end button on my phone and then stare down at the screen still bearing his likeness.

"Hurry home," I whisper into the stillness.

Chapter Twelve

Big Cedar Tennis Club—right where Cooper said it would be. I've driven this stretch of road many times and never noticed it before, probably because it's down a long drive and nestled in a valley full of trees. Cooper insisted that I leave more than thirty minutes early so I could go to the pro shop and be outfitted. I had to endure Dina's icy stare on my back the entire way to the elevator. Managing to quietly slip into the office yesterday morning, I thought I might escape her notice, but she glanced up to glare in my direction and then immediately look back down at her desk.

Never mind her now, though. Since I have to be out here learning how to play tennis, even though I am definitely not crazy about the idea, I might as well make the most of it. If nothing else, I can enjoy the sunshine and time away from the office.

Does a person simply walk into the pro shop and *ask* to be outfitted? I'm not even completely sure what that means. I assumed when he mentioned it that Cooper wanted me to get one of those tennis skirts like the women wear on television, and maybe a polo top or something, although I can't see what difference it makes what I wear to take tennis lessons. Besides, I am definitely not wearing those silly little sweatbands on my wrists, no matter how hot it is outside.

Stepping out of the Tahoe, I grab my gym bag and head into the pro shop. As I open the door, I am greeted by a wall of cold air, which probably feels wonderful *after* a tennis lesson, but definitely feels less than comfortable right now, forcing me to shiver in the entrance as I wait for someone to appear at the desk.

Really, I'm not certain I can wear one of those outfits. They practically look like spandex. I *have* lost a little weight lately, but would definitely be uncomfortable in spandex. In fact, I think most people should avoid spandex. Scratch that—all people, except maybe Olympic sprinters.

"Can I help you, miss?" A tall, thin man clad in a blue polo shirt and khaki shorts suddenly appears from around the corner.

Yes, can you outfit me? No, I can't say it.

"I have a tennis lesson today, and I'm not sure where to go."

"If you know your instructor's name, I can just make a call and have them meet you here."

"I believe the lesson is with Max Kimball." He immediately reaches behind the desk to pick up a phone.

Walking to a wall of visors, I spy a pink one and give it a once-over. Do people really wear these things? Why don't they just wear sunglasses? As I glance at the price tag, I put the visor back immediately. Honestly, how can they charge so much for half a hat? I could buy a cheap one somewhere else and cut the top off. It would be basically the same thing. It might not look quite as pretty, but I'm sure it would be worth the price difference. Except that Cooper has just doubled my salary, so in reality this is the first time I actually might be able to afford a frou-frou half-hat.

"Max is just finishing up a lesson, but when he's done someone will tell him you're here," the clerk states.

"Thank you." Any more time in this icebox is too long! I'm considering going outside when the clerk begins toward me.

"Have you ever played tennis before?"

"Not really, just fiddled around," I try to fib. To be frank, I've never played tennis at all, but I've played table tennis, and I would assume they are somewhat similar.

"So you don't have any equipment, then?"

"No—do I have to provide my own paddle, or is that part of the lesson?"

He clears his throat as he walks across the store.

"A paddle won't be necessary," he states with a hint of sarcasm, "unless you brought your canoe. We carry a wide selection of *rackets*, if you'd like to take a look. You don't need one for your lesson, but if you're planning on continuing, you'll probably want your own."

Of course they're not paddles—they're rackets. The silly tennis newbie didn't know what to call the equipment…absolutely hilarious!

"Oh, pardon me," I attempt to explain. "I'm used to the table version of the sport." There—maybe he'll think I'm a table tennis pro and have never bothered with this lesser version of the game.

"You're referring to table tennis?" he asks, a smile playing about his lips. "I suppose they both do involve sending a ball over a net."

That's it—I'm finished. There's no use going into a battle of wits unarmed, and I definitely don't have any ammunition on this topic.

"This racket looks like it would be a perfect fit for you," he mentions as he brings me a yellow racket with a black stripe. I look it over for a minute, but I can't agree. The color is all wrong.

"Actually, I'm thinking maybe something in a light green, to match my tree frogs." Unzipping my gym bag, I pull one out so he can be sure what color I'm referencing.

"Ah, yes, of course. Something to match the tree frogs."

By this time I'm well aware that he's patronizing me, but I could not care less. If I have to buy the equipment, it might as well match, shouldn't it? I don't want to go out there clashing with tree frog shoes and a bumblebee tennis paddle…er, racket.

He finally locates a light shade of green and places it in my hands. It is a lovely color, and I believe it matches perfectly.

"How does it feel?" he asks.

What does he mean, how does it feel? It feels wonderful to find the right match, of course. Why does he suddenly care about my feelings?

"Great," I respond halfheartedly.

"The fit feels right? It's not too heavy?"

Oh, how does it *feel*! I don't know...it feels like a long handle with a round part on the end. How is it supposed to feel?

"Seems fine to me," I attempt to state confidently. He walks over to the desk and begins to log the sale into his computer. "Oh, you can just put it on Kent Cooper's account."

"Mr. Cooper? Very well." He continues typing on his computer as I go back to the visors and pull down a light green variety. If Cooper's picking up the tab, I might as well have one to complete the look. It is his idea that I'm down here, completely uninformed and being laughed at in the pro shop. Since I have done my best to outfit myself, he should at least be pleased with that, even if my tennis winds up being lousy.

I walk up to the counter with the visor and see another man standing by the clerk. This one looks about my age, with shoulder-length ebony-colored hair and striking blue eyes hovering above a thin, shapely nose and a trim-shaved goatee. He's also wearing a light pink polo shirt, so there apparently is a man who can pull it off after all. Of course, I'm also betting he could wear a potato sack well.

"Just sign this slip, and we're all done," the clerk states. I sign somewhere near the line, but I'm finding it difficult to concentrate as he points to that man beside him. "This is Max, your trainer."

Max doesn't have to speak, because he's already practically shouting, "*Look at me, shouldn't I be on a Calvin Klein billboard?*"

"Nice to meet you," I manage to squeak out as he takes my hand. His grip is strong, which is probably from playing all that tennis.

Taking my racket from my hand, he points to a side door. "The lockers are through the door to your right. When you're done, come meet me on the courts. I'll hang onto your racket for you."

His velvety voice is still swimming around me as I enter the locker room, where I'm quickly met by a middle-aged woman who sits red-faced and wiping sweat from her forehead.

"You training with Max?" she asks, and I nod. "He's a slave driver!"

Great. Not only do I end up with the male supermodel of tennis, but he's also apparently going to be trying to kill me and will make me look gross and sweaty. This is not good at all.

As a result of my newly acquired information, my attempts to look presentable to visit the courts are pretty ridiculous. Admittedly, I brush lip gloss across my pout, adjust my ponytail underneath that visor, and glance at myself in the mirror a few too many times.

Spotting Max upon my arrival at the courts isn't difficult, considering the fact that he's wearing a pink shirt and I could probably pick him out of a crowd of millions. He's fiddling with a machine full of tennis balls when I walk up.

"I'm all ready," I state cheerfully, hoping he won't be too hard on me. He looks up from the machine and assesses my appearance without any clear signs of love at first sight. I should have bought a white shirt or something, because in retrospect my blue shirt looks weird with all the green I'm sporting now. Plus, he's probably wondering why I'm not wearing the silly spandex skirt instead of jogging shorts.

"Have you ever played before?" he asks, squinting slightly against the sun's glare.

"No."

"So it's tennis 101, then. Good, because I could use a slowdown for a while."

Maybe he won't kill me after all.

"If you really want to relax, we could skip this altogether and I'll just pretend I had a lesson. Cooper will never know." I doubt he'll take me up on it, but I might as well offer. The temptation to offer to run away with him to a distant land also presents itself, but I am too mature to blurt it out loud.

"So you're not Mr. Cooper's daughter?"

Ew—no way would I ever run away with a man who thought I was Cooper's daughter!

"Goodness, no! What made you think that?"

"Just a guess," he says with a shrug. "He's always talking about his daughter when he comes in here, and how he wants her to learn to play tennis, so I just assumed when he set up the lessons that she finally gave in."

"Well, I'm no relation—just his assistant." As though I could be related to Cooper...ick.

"That's good. I wasn't really looking forward to working with his daughter." Max stands up and wipes his hands on his shorts.

"I didn't even know he had a daughter." He's never said anything about her to me, although I suppose I haven't known him that long, really. Still, you would think he might have mentioned his children in passing.

"Yeah, but judging by the rest of the family, I'd say she's probably a spoiled brat." Max sits down on a bench in the shade and takes a long drink from a Gatorade bottle. Standing beside him, I rock back and forth on my tree frogs.

"So most of Cooper's family comes here?" I wonder. Maybe it will help to find out a little about the eccentric nut, just so I know how to deal with him. Besides, the longer I can keep Max talking, the less time I have to play tennis and the more time I can stand here shamelessly staring at him.

"His brother is here all the time. Kent's wife has only been a few times lately, but I don't think he cares for playing tennis with her. She basically just stands in one place and hits the ball when it comes to her. Kent's pretty competitive, so something like that drives him crazy." Max puts the Gatorade bottle on the ground and begins messing with a towel on the bench. Doesn't look like he's too eager to play tennis today, either.

"So, you've met his wife?"

"Faith? Sure, I've met her. She's as spoiled as they come. You can tell he gives her basically whatever she wants. She comes to the court perfectly manicured, every hair in place. She has no intention of doing anything that would make her look less than her best, and tennis is a pretty tough sport."

I've seen Mrs. Cooper's picture in the office. If I didn't know better, I would think it was a picture of one of those big

Barbie heads they sell at the department store with all the things to adorn her hair. She looks practically plastic.

"So what is his brother like?" I prod further. Max leans back on the bench and looks up at me as though he's posing for a professional photo shoot. I secretly hope my admiration of him is not evident on my face.

"They're a lot alike, really, Kent and Brent. Brent is a couple years younger, I think. They're both competitive and extremely demanding. From what I've heard, they've been coming here to the club for years. Their wives were practically best friends, and they would have competitive tennis matches between the husband and wife teams. Back then, things were pretty well evenly matched. Brent's wife was a lot like Kent's, so the men did all the work while the women stood there and looked pretty, relatively speaking."

"So what happened? Why aren't they evenly matched anymore?"

"Brent doesn't have the same wife. About a year ago, he divorced her and married his assistant. The two of them are here constantly, always practicing."

"She's a lot more competitive than Kent's wife, then?"

Max gives me a lopsided grin that turns my stomach upside down. "Even if she wasn't, her age would probably help her out a bit. Word around here is that wife number two, Kelli, went to high school with Brent's son. I don't know if that's true or not, but it wouldn't surprise me. She's in her twenties, and he's got to be in his fifties."

"So when they play with Kent and his wife, they probably beat them."

"They probably would, only that never happens," Max explains, tossing his empty Gatorade bottle in the air. "Faith won't have anything to do with Kelli, so Kent doesn't even have a partner. Your ultra-competitive boss comes here and listens to taunts from his brother, and he can't even try to beat him on the court, because his wife refuses to show up."

"Maybe the obsession is starting to make sense," I mutter. Max looks up at me inquisitively. "I'm sorry, I didn't mean to say that out loud."

"You said you're Kent's assistant?" he asks, standing up and stretching his arms while I try not to gawk at him.

"Yes."

"Kind of funny, him sending his assistant for tennis lessons. You know, Brent sent Kelli for tennis lessons, too, once upon a time."

Two brothers so intense in their love for tennis that they would force all those around them to get lessons? That's not funny—it's pathetic.

"It almost seems like Kent is trying to pull a fast one on Brent," he continues.

"How so? You think there's something else going on behind him sending me for these lessons?" I place one hand on my hip in a clear attempt to posture myself more attractively, consciously sucking in my stomach.

"Think about it," he says, giving me a sly wink. "Kent would never leave his wife—he completely dotes on that woman. He couldn't bring anyone else onto the court to face Brent and Kelli, because Brent would know that he was just trying to beat him. He has to have a perfect partner for the match."

"But I'm confused...how exactly do I fit into that equation?"

He looks thoroughly amused, wrapping the towel around his wrist and unwrapping it again.

"Oh, come on, don't you see? What is Kelli to Brent? She's his wife, of course, but what else is she?" He smiles over at me as though he's waiting for an answer. "She's his assistant. Kent can't bring his wife, so the only other person he can bring to the court is..."

"...his assistant. You're right!" Ugh, I can't believe that man actually had the audacity to infer that he needed my help in running his company!

"It's really pretty clever, if you think about it."

Very clever, indeed. I'm onto you, Kent Cooper, and you better believe I'm going to make this worth my while.

"So you're a ringer!" Max exclaims with a laugh. "How does it feel?"

"I don't know how much of a ringer I can be, if I can't even *play* tennis."

"That's where I come in," he states, heading toward the court. "Come on gorgeous, we'll have you playing an 'A' game in no time."

The fact that he just called me gorgeous is not lost on me—not by a long shot.

"What if I don't have an 'A' game?" I wonder aloud, hesitantly following Max onto the court.

He simply shrugs his shoulders and offers me a smile. "My guess is, the longer it takes you to learn, the more Kent is going to send you over here. If he wants to beat his brother, he'll do whatever it takes."

"Sounds reasonable."

"So, if you happen to be a really slow learner, you and I might be spending a lot of time together."

I hear the faint sounds of angels singing, and I'm pretty sure a giant ray of light just descended upon us.

"I'm afraid I might prove to be a very, very slow learner."

"We better get started then," he answers with a smile.

Maybe this means I'll be over here every day. Kent Cooper will do whatever it takes? Well, I'll do whatever it takes to use the situation to my advantage. Whether that means getting even with Cooper, or spending time with Max, this looks like a win-win.

Approximately two hours later I'm headed upwards in the elevator to my new office. No, the tennis lesson didn't take that

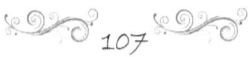

long, but I've spent some time unwinding from my first unbelievable Max encounter and mulling over my options. My first impulse was to storm back here and tell Cooper exactly what I thought of his little scheme, but then I thought better of it. I need to really think this over and come up with a marvelous plan. There's no reason I can't use this to my advantage for a long, long period of time.

By that, naturally I mean a "long enough to convince Max that I'm the right girl to spend forever with" kind of time.

As I step out of the elevator, Dina looks up at me over her red frames. Honestly, I'm getting tired of her glaring at me. My desire to say something to her has been tempered so far by the fact that I have taken her office, and I've tried to put myself in her shoes. I'm sure I wouldn't be enamored with me if I was her, but she should at least place the blame where it belongs—solidly with Cooper. I haven't noticed her acting strangely toward him at all, and he was the one who put her in the hall in the first place.

"Back so soon?" Dina asks with a snort, rolling her eyes. Gliding past her, I'm determined not to respond to her nastiness. I'm in no sort of mood right now to deal with the poorly directed attitude. "Were you anxious to get back over here to tell Mr. Cooper how much fun you had at your little lesson? I'm sure he'd love to hear all about it!"

I push open the door to my office and pretend I didn't hear her. Everything is just as I left it, with no new work on my desk. If Cooper insists on needing an assistant, the least he could do is provide something on which he needs assistance.

"I wish I knew what it was like not to have to work for a living," Dina jabs as I start to shut the door.

And that proves to be the snapping point, where I decide I've been nice long enough. I can't take her constant barbs. We both have to work on the same floor, after all.

"Where is Cooper, anyway?" I ask her, stepping back into the hall.

She adjusts her glasses on her face to better glare over them.

"*Mister* Cooper is out."

"That's good, because I have something to say to you," I begin. She snarls her nose and crosses her arms across her chest defiantly. "You don't like me. I get it, loud and clear. In fact, you don't have to keep going out of your way to express your disgust, because I can feel it in the air every time I step into the hallway."

"Is that all?" she asks smugly.

Walking up to her desk, I stand directly in front of her. "No, that's not all. I heard you out the other day, and now you'll hear me out. You say you've been here twenty-odd years and now you're stuck in the hall? I'm sorry about that, whether you want me to be or not."

"So what?"

"So what? Now we both know your side of the story, and you're going to hear mine. I've been here three years. No, three is not the same as twenty, but it's something. I've worked hard every day I've been with this company, trying to advance my career. I finally had an opening for a position I wanted and deserved, and my boss was prepared to give it to me. Instead, I had a surprise interview with Cooper and found out I was moving upstairs. To do what, you might ask. Turns out Cooper wants me to be his assistant, only there's a small problem: He doesn't want me to actually do any work. He wants me to be his assistant in title only. Now, why do you think he would do that?"

"I have no idea," Dina states, shifting uncomfortably in her chair and clearing her throat.

"Neither did I, until today. Turns out *Mister* Cooper promoted me so I could learn how to play tennis. Does he merely want to promote physical fitness in the company? Oh, no. He wants me to learn how to play so he can involve himself in some sort of grudge match with his brother. Why me, you might ask. Maybe I was just in the wrong place at the wrong time—I may never know, but the next time you're thinking about the raw deal you were handed, I want you to think about this: I could be sitting downstairs right now as Marketing Account Leader, with my good friends around me, enjoying my career and making a mark in the world.

Instead, I'm sitting up here in this friendless office with nothing to do but learn how to play tennis while a grown man plans his childish revenge. I'm a pawn. You're out in the hallway, and I'm a pawn. Deal with it."

Stepping into my office, I shut the door behind me. This is one of those times when I wish Katie was right here. It's just not the same calling her from a distance. Besides, the last couple times I tried she was busy, and by the time she calls me back, I usually forget what I wanted in the first place.

Never mind, though, because I have very important things to think about. Exactly how am I going to deal with this situation? I believe I'm in a very unique position. As long as Cooper thinks I'm becoming a pro at tennis, he'll probably do anything to make me happy and keep me working for him. After all, if I was to decide to leave, it would take him that much longer to find another girl and start the process of lessons all over again. If he's truly as competitive as Max indicated, he is going to want to schedule this big match as quickly as possible.

Coincidentally, that big match brings up another set of problems. It seems to me that I need to postpone that event as long as humanly possible. What are the odds that I'm going to become good enough at tennis to beat Kelli? Max seemed to think she was a pretty tough competitor. If the big match actually happens, and Cooper loses because of me, what will the consequences be? It's too big a risk.

In the meantime, I should make sure to provide myself with plenty of experience so I can find a better job, if that problem arises. It shouldn't really be too difficult. Cooper's bound to let me run with any of the ideas I present for the company, because he isn't going to want to cause conflict. If I just sit around a while and think of things that will look good on my résumé, I'm sure I can come up with some programs to run by him. As long as they don't interfere with tennis time, we should be in business.

Hearing a light rap on my door, I look up just in time to see Dina's beehive poke around the corner. Undoubtedly she's been sitting out there thinking of a retort, and now I'm going to get

it. She closes the door to my office and stands demurely in front of me, her hands folded together. Clearing her throat, she stares at me calmly.

"Madeline, I have heard your remarks, and I apologize for the way I've treated you. I understand your situation."

I'm so stunned, I can't think of a single word to say. I nod and expect her to turn and exit, but she stays put, staring into my eyes. After a moment, she bends down, places her palms on my desk, and leans toward me. Her voice is lowered to a whisper, but I clearly hear what she says.

"Now, let's take him down."

Chapter Thirteen

I am absolutely dreading this Labor Day picnic. Josh thinks I'm crazy, but I have a bad feeling about the whole affair. Call it woman's intuition, or just a general bad vibe, or blame it on the fact that I've been to these family get-togethers before. Any way you slice it, no good can come out of this event.

Things will most likely be better than anticipated if I'm simply determined to make the best of it, and I desperately want to believe that. I even made a cake for the occasion (it's what Mom suggested when I asked—chocolate with chocolate frosting). I am certainly not a baker, which gives me an added bonus, because there won't be any temptation for me to eat this cake and break my diet, since I made it myself. There's a high probability that it's slightly burnt, undercooked, or absolutely tastes like dirt.

"Don't leave me alone," I request to Katie as we step out of the car.

Yes, I brought Katie along to soften the inevitable blow.

"Come on, Maddie," she complains. "It's your family."

"Yes, it is, so I'm completely aware that it's a hostile environment. Please, Katie." I give her puppy dog eyes and bat my eyelashes, to which she smirks and shakes her head.

"Okay, I'll do my best."

That's all I can expect, I suppose.

Katie follows me down the walk and up the steps to the house. The smell of barbecue is drifting in from the backyard, and my stomach is already growling. Eating a better breakfast probably would have been wise. That's one of the big things that hurts your dieting habits, isn't it? Going to an event while hungry?

I wait on the porch for Katie to open the door, partly because I'm carrying the cake and partly because I want to make sure she's still right behind me. The scent of apple pie wafts through the air. Mom must be baking, too. So strange to think of my mother watching Martha Stewart-types and actually trying to emulate them. My mother, whose idea of a good dinner was stopping to grab a bucket of chicken on her way home from work. Then again, she probably thinks the same about me baking a cake.

"Hi, Mom," I call when I see her in the kitchen. She's leaning over the oven door pulling the apple pie free, but she looks up and nods.

"Maddie, there you are. I've been wondering about you."

Walking fully into the kitchen, I set my cake on the table next to...three other chocolate cakes with chocolate frosting.

"What's with all the cake?" I wonder aloud.

Mom glances at the table but continues fussing with her pie. "Oh, Brittany wanted to bring cake, and I told her that was fine. Those grandkids of mine do love chocolate cake!"

Of course. Could I have expected a different answer? Brittany even piped little flowers onto the top of her cakes in yellow and white icing. Mine looks like a big chocolate blob next to the others.

"Madeline Jane Heard, what in the dickens is wrong with you?"

My head snaps up, quite startled. I haven't heard my full name like that in years. She's standing there with her hands on her hips, and I glance at Katie, who is trying not to laugh. I'll have to ask later what she finds so amusing.

"Nothing," I reply.

She narrows her eyes and scrutinizes my face closely.

"Are you sick?"

"No."

"Have you been sick?"

"No."

"Then why are you so skinny?"

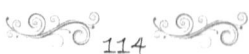

"Oh, that," I reply, laughing with relief. "I've been jogging at night, that's all. I'm becoming physically fit."

"Hmm…" she mutters, lifting her chin. "Well, stop it. You look positively ill."

"I think she looks great," Katie offers.

"Who is this?" Mom blurts, pointing at Katie while she stares at me. Nice question from a woman who thinks me being physically fit is revolting.

"This is my friend Katie, from work," I state carefully, trying not to allow my head to explode.

"Well, Katie, be a dear and take this potato salad out to the back yard," Mom continues sweetly, smiling at Katie. Surprisingly, Katie does her bidding without a word. Naturally, I attempt to follow her out the door, to no avail. "Now just hold on a minute, Maddie, I need you in here."

Katie shoots me a quickly mouthed "sorry" before she makes her escape. I've been defeated by potato salad and an overbearing mother. Awaiting the inevitable like a prisoner before a firing squad, I hesitate until Katie is out of sight and Mom looks me squarely in the eye.

"You're involved in that anorexia, aren't you?" She waves a wooden spoon under my nose to try to press her point somehow.

"No, Mom, absolutely not!" Talk about a ridiculous assumption!

"What is it then, the vomiting? Madeline, I did not raise you that way!" I grab the wooden spoon, now an inch from my face, and place it out of her reach on the table.

"For the last time, Mom, I've been jogging. That's it! I've been eating healthy and jogging. I'm not sick, and I'm certainly not bulimic!"

Mom continues to stand in front of me and stare deeply into my eyes for a moment before she retrieves the wooden spoon and goes back to the stove. As she stirs her concoction slowly, something inside me fizzles a bit.

Why can't she simply be happy that I've done something good for myself? Instead, I'm always being measured by this

impossible invisible standard that I can't achieve. Most of the time I can't reach high enough, but today somehow I'm overreaching. It's quite exasperating.

"I've got my eye on you," Mom states with her back to me. "If you go out there and eat something, don't you dare come back in here to the restroom. I'm onto you."

Oh, honestly! Is it too early to call it a day and go home?

Opening the back door, I walk out to search for Katie, who I immediately realize is next to my brother, Lance, near the food table. The yard is decked out in red, white, and blue banners, and Mom even has a centerpiece of blue flowers with red streamers shooting up in the middle. This Martha Stewart stuff is obviously going to her head.

Upon reaching the bottom of the steps, I'm greeted by a screech.

"Aahhh! Maddie! It's been so long since I've seen you." I turn to see my cousin Sonya, about three years my elder, approaching from the side of the house. She's right—it's been a long time. The last time I saw her was probably Lance and Brittany's wedding, but she hasn't changed much. Exact same haircut.

"Hi, Sonya," I say quietly. "It has been a long time."

"Too long, but look at you! You look incredible! How did you do it so quickly?"

Um, what exactly does that mean? I could have looked like this for the last few years, for all she knows.

"Nothing complicated. I've been jogging and watching what I eat."

"Well, I must say that I'm impressed!" she exclaims, scanning the yard like she's searching for someone. "Now, where is the little one?"

Surely she's not so confused that she believes Lance is my *little* brother. "Little one?"

"The baby? Where is the baby? Your mom told me a while back that you were pregnant."

My cousin thinks I was pregnant and have lost some baby weight. Very nice turn of events.

Two children choose that moment to dart in between us, almost knocking Sonya over. Taking her arm, I pull her toward the corner of the house where no one will overhear.

"You think I was pregnant?" I attempt to clarify.

"Your mom said her daughter was pregnant," she states, suddenly looking concerned. "I'm sorry, was it supposed to be a secret?"

"No, there's no secret. I am not, nor have I ever been, pregnant. You've got some wrong information."

"Sorry, Maddie," she says, making a hasty exit.

Without even thinking, I head back up the steps and into the kitchen. Mom has her head stuck in the refrigerator, but she glances up as I swing the door closed behind me. I must have failed to notice earlier that she's wearing a shirt with red, white and blue stripes. Perhaps Martha Stewart recommended matching the wardrobe with the décor.

On second thought, I'm guessing Martha would give that a big N-O.

"Mom, did you tell people I was going to have a baby?"

She pulls her head out of the refrigerator only long enough to give me a puzzled look, and then dives back in.

"Good grief, Maddie, why would I do that?"

"You didn't tell people that your daughter was pregnant?"

Mom shuts the refrigerator door and heads to the counter, placing the condiment bottles on a tray and arranging them neatly from smallest to largest.

"My daughter *is* pregnant," she insists. "Brittany. Now be a dear and help me out with this."

"You didn't stop to think that people might assume you were talking about me? Sonya thought I had a baby."

"And that's my problem, you're saying? Well, don't worry, I'll take care of it!" she exclaims with a sigh as I hold the door open with my arm. "Why do I always have to do everything around here?"

This has been a dreadfully long day, and we've been here, what…ten minutes? How am I ever going to make it?

Katie is still talking to Lance, so I head in their direction. No Brittany in sight yet—at least that's one silver lining. Lance sees me approaching and offers a huge smile. He looks so much more relaxed since the last time I saw him. The move must have done him some good, at least. His sandy brown hair is cut shorter than normal, which makes him look older somehow. As I come closer, he opens his arms for a hug.

"Hi, big brother," I say as I embrace him.

"Don't you eat?" Lance remarks as he hugs me, and I swat him on the arm. Honestly, do I look that different? Why do people keep commenting on my appearance?

"I eat plenty, thank you very much. Looks like you've been doing a little of that, too."

Lance pulls back and pats himself on the belly. "It's sympathy weight. I'm sure it will fall right off in a few months. How you doing, Maddie? You okay?" The concerned look in his eyes makes me smile.

Sure, if you don't count the fact that everyone here thinks I have a child and my mother is convinced that I'm bulimic. Everything is a-okay.

"Good grief, Maddie, you look positively anorexic."

Perhaps I spoke too soon.

"Hi, Brittany," I mutter, turning to watch her approach. The pregnancy is not wearing well on her—her face and arms look really swollen, like she's been stung by a swarm of bees. Her face is blotchy from the heat underneath a thick swath of molasses-tinted hair. Mentioning that fact is tempting, since she just threw in the anorexic comment, but I choose to take the high road.

"Seriously, you need to put some weight on," Brittany says, wrapping her arm protectively around Lance. "I would swear I was talking to a twig. Am I right, Lance?"

"She looks fine," Lance comments with a sigh.

Brittany pulls away as though he violated their sacred agreement. *Whatever I say, always agree with me.*

"Well, *I* think she looks like a twig. Will you get me some lemonade?" she asks Lance, who dutifully takes the few steps to a clear pitcher full of the yellow liquid and grabs a plastic cup. "It's so dreadful being pregnant through the hot part of summer. Your mom really should have thought ahead before she invited us over, so everyone wouldn't have to be miserable."

Watching that softball hang in the air in front of me is pretty painful, but I decline to comment. It would be too easy.

"I'm sure no one would mind if you had to go inside for a while to cool off," Lance offers.

"Why should I have to go inside and sit by myself? I wouldn't be able to talk to anyone!"

Um…

"Your lemonade," Lance announces, handing the cup to Brittany. She takes a drink and runs the back of her hand along her temple, pulling it away to determine whether she's perspiring.

"I'm sure you never get hot," Brittany states, peering at me. "You're like one of those scrawny hairless dogs. You'll probably just stand out here and shiver all day." She turns her glare in Lance's direction. "Where's my cake? Why didn't your mom put my cake out?"

"I don't know—go ask her," Lance says in a defeated fashion. The three of us watch as Brittany slowly crosses the yard.

Poor Lance. I wish there was some way I could rescue him, but I don't suppose there is anything I can do to assist him with that particular problem. Plus, I'm pretty sure she just called me a dog, and I'm most certainly not hairless. I have a huge mess of hair. Huge.

"Don't mind her," he explains. "This pregnancy is making her more than a little irritable. I've been looking forward to the picnic, just so I could spend a few minutes away from her. She's starting to drive me crazy."

"Well, we didn't even notice, right Maddie?" Katie asks cheerfully. Katie is such a little saint.

"No, I didn't notice." Besides, Brittany is *always* that irritable. Lance shouldn't blame it on the pregnancy.

I hear a slight commotion and look over to see Mom standing on a chair. Yet another fashion statement I didn't notice before jumps out at me as I realize one of her flip-flops is red and one is blue. Martha Stewart would positively cringe on that one!

"Can I get everyone's attention, please?" she calls. "The food is ready, but before we eat, I just wanted to say a few things. First of all, thank you everyone for coming to our home. I hope this will be the beginning of many gatherings in the future."

Dad emerges from the side of the house and steps in line next to me, face red and hair plastered to his forehead. Looks like he's been slaving away in the heat next to the grill for quite a while.

"Also, there is plenty of food, so don't be bashful. I don't want to have anything left over when we're finished, so feel free to stuff yourselves."

That sounds mighty healthy.

"Oh, and one more thing: For those of you who think my daughter Maddie was pregnant—she does not have a baby. She's not in a relationship and isn't pregnant, because she can't find herself a man. Eat up!"

Mom claps her hands loudly and jumps down from the chair, ushering people towards the table. I'm vaguely aware of several looking in my direction, some of them whispering.

"Let's go," I whisper to Katie, who shakes her head.

"Just wait a few minutes and things will die down. You don't want to storm out."

Oh, yes I do. I want to slam every door between me and the Tahoe and then peel out of the driveway, throwing gravel everywhere.

Well, maybe not spewing gravel, because Mom would just make Dad pick up the mess, but the slamming is a definite must.

"What are you working on in your workshop these days?" Lance asks Dad.

"Oh, I've got this old lawnmower I've been trying to get working…"

Sliding away from my family, I offer Katie an apology and make a silent retreat to the back of the yard. I've never been able

to figure out why Mom is always at odds with me. She certainly doesn't treat Lance the same way. Maybe it's because I'm a girl, and she wants me to do things exactly like she would? Dad always treated me like a princess, except during the times Mom berated him for doing so.

The thing I can never quite grasp is why Mom seems to adore Brittany. For years I thought Mom just liked her for Lance's sake, but now it seems like she does truly care for her more than me. I've never heard Mom talk to Brittany the way she speaks to me, and she always seems to take her side in an argument. Maybe she *expects* me to be the bigger person, being her flesh and blood, but it still seems odd.

Unless it's because they're kind of the same? Mom and Brittany? I mean, they do have some traits in common, and that would explain why I can't make any headway with either of them. Maybe that's the whole thing with a man marrying a woman who is like his mother...

"Hey, sis," Lance interrupts my thoughts, startling me.

"Hey."

"What are you doing back here?"

"Not finding myself a man, in case you were worried about that. Oh, and pondering why Mom keeps trying to ruin my life."

Lance sighs and leans against the wooden privacy fence. "I don't think it's intentional, if it's any consolation."

"Not really, no."

"Mom just doesn't know how to be tactful."

"You don't have to defend her, Lance," I say, pulling a weed from the grass and twirling it between my fingers. Dad's lawnmower obviously isn't quite working up to par.

"I know, and I'm not, but take my advice and ignore her. By the way, when is Josh coming home?"

"He says he still doesn't know," I inform him with a sigh.

"I always thought you and Josh..."

Laughter comes out of my throat before I can stop it. "Josh is every bit as brotherly to me as you are, Lance. He still calls me Mad and everything, just like when we were kids."

"Mad," he repeats, laughing along with me. "That's hilarious. That kid always did follow you around wherever you went. It makes sense that he'd want you in his house, so you couldn't get too far away."

"Very funny," I say, throwing the weed at him.

"Come on," he states, pulling me by the hand. "Let's get some food and fatten you up a bit. I have a very jealous pregnant wife who just can't stand you looking skinnier than her, so we have to do something about that."

Lance and I walk back toward the food, and his pep talk has shone a slightly brighter light on the day. Very slight, like the difference between 2:00 p.m. and 2:15 p.m.

Standing in line by the food, I mentally prepare my healthy lunch strategy by locating grilled chicken, salad, a vegetable tray before I feel someone grab my arm. Aunt Maria cuts in line behind me, her gray bob swinging in the breeze.

"There you are, kiddo," she says. "I was wondering where you disappeared to."

"Well, you found me," I reply as we fill our plates and slowly move through the line.

"So sad about you not finding a man, sweetie," she adds, taking a spoonful of potato salad. "Did you know Serena got married?"

As I'm hunting down a lawn chair, my eyes find their way to my cousin, Serena.

"Yes, I heard. Congratulations."

"Thank you," Serena states as I settle myself into the chair and begin cutting up my chicken. Serena is fifteen years older than me, so I guess Aunt Maria is trying to convince me that it's never too late. Not really helpful, because spending the next fifteen years alone is not exactly a pleasant prospect at the moment.

"Serena met her husband in an internet chat room," Aunt Maria continues. "Maybe she could give you the website."

Serena appears to be only slightly less uncomfortable than me, so I smile as a reassurance that I will most certainly *not* be asking her for any websites.

"Or, maybe she can give you the names of some of her husband's friends," Aunt Maria suggests, glancing at Serena. "They have an online gaming club."

"Oh, no, I forgot my lemonade," I quickly say, removing myself from their presence. Poor Serena. It's bad enough that I have to endure this insanity! There shouldn't be any innocent victims in the wake.

Helping myself to the lemonade, I notice Brittany sitting by herself in the shade. She looks lonely, and for a split second I almost feel sorry for her. I know, I must be out of my mind.

"Hey, Brittany." As I sit down beside her, she looks over at me and simply raises her eyebrows. "Feeling any better?"

"It's still hot out here, if that's what you mean," she replies.

Hmm... I can see it's going to take a lot to bring down the emotional wall of distaste.

"How do you like being back home?" I ask, taking a bite of my chicken.

"Oh, it's got its ups and downs. I definitely miss my friends."

"But Lance is home a lot more now. That must be nice."

"It is nice, when he helps me out a little. Most of the time he just sits around expecting me to wait on him, like he's the king of the castle or something. Being married isn't that great, Maddie. You should just stay single."

I might be able to brush off that comment if she wasn't talking about my brother, who just finished saying some nice things to me. Unable to keep up my nice veneer, I mutter something about needing to find Katie as I take my leave.

As it turns out, Katie is being held captive by my father as he relays information about old lawnmowers, so I spot a small area set up for the kids along the side of the yard and make my way in that direction. One or two of them are eating, and the rest are running around in circles. That looks like the ticket, because they surely won't question my love life.

Settling next to a little girl and boy who are politely eating their food, I begin to eat my chicken again.

"You're Maddie, right?" the little girl asks. I nod, mouth full of chicken, and realize that I've placed myself in the middle of the Gardwin clan. "I heard somebody say you can't find a man. Why not? They're everywhere."

"That's just something silly that grown-ups say," I explain. "It doesn't really mean anything."

"Sure it does," Billy Gardwin states. "She fell off her wagon."

"Fell off her wagon?" Jenny questions. "Do you have a wagon?"

"No, I don't have a wagon."

"It's not really a wagon, silly," Billy directs to Jenny. "That's what they always say on TV when people get drunk. They can't find a man, and they fell off the wagon."

"You get drunk?" Jenny asks incredulously.

"No, I don't get drunk," I state very sharply, making sure I glare at Billy.

"That's what they always say on TV, too," he answers very succinctly.

Shaking my head, I go about eating my chicken. He apparently didn't like me glaring at him, because he's concocting a plan in his head. The reason I'm aware of that is that I've seen that look in his eyes before at church when he's jerking me bald.

"I wonder what would happen if I put my hot dog in this mustard, and then put it in my pudding," he expresses.

Ugh, for goodness sake, don't let him try it.

Silently chewing, I watch as he does the very thing he was pondering. Still, I know there's no way he's going to…

Oh, he ate it. Be still, my stomach. He's laughing now, with his mouth open and everything.

"That can make you very sick," I try to tell him. "You shouldn't do that."

"Maybe it can make *you* very sick!" he exclaims. "Did that gross you out? What should I do next?"

"Please don't do anything else," I request, but he just laughs and sticks his hot dog in the mustard and pudding again. My

attempts to look away are fruitless, since he is trying desperately to get my attention.

"Let's see, what can I do now?" he asks, chuckling to himself. That has to be making him ill—it's making me queasy just thinking about it.

"I know!" he shouts. "I'll mix my potato salad with my pudding, and add a little mustard, and then mix that with my chocolate cake. Should I eat it?"

Jenny is goading him on, even as I am shaking my head, emphatically begging him not to eat that mess. He just sits there staring at me, laughing as he holds the trembling fork in front of his mouth.

"Do you dare me?"

"No."

"Do you dare me?"

"No."

"Do you dare me?" he tempts a third time.

"Yes, do it!" Jenny shrieks. He shoves the fork into his mouth.

And that's it—I'm going to be sick. I've always been cursed with a weak stomach, and once it starts, there's no stopping. Tossing down my chicken, I go running for the house, taking the stairs two at a time. I don't even bother to see whether the back door closes behind me as I quickly make my way into the bathroom and lock myself inside, hitting the floor hard.

I had a sneaking suspicion that the Labor Day picnic at my parents' house would be a nightmare, but I couldn't have predicted sitting in the bathroom with my head hanging over the toilet. Nothing—I mean absolutely nothing—could make this day worse.

Standing up to wash my face, I turn on the water but jump when I hear someone banging on the door.

"Maddie? Maddie, are you in there?"

Mom. Perfect.

"Yes, Mom, it's me."

"Maddie, you get out of there this instant. You think I don't know what you're doing? I'm onto you, young lady."

I can't help but laugh in disgust as I drop my head into my hands.

"Maddie!" she yells again, banging even louder. "I mean it! Being skinny is not worth it. You need professional help."

Humph. Maybe we all do.

Chapter Fourteen

Ding-dong.

Cooper and that stupid bell! I wish I knew how to put a short in it.

Opening the door between our offices, I stick my head inside to peek at him.

"You rang?"

"Ha ha, yes, I did! You rang! I like that." He sits there smiling with those blindingly white teeth, clearly amused at himself.

"Can I help you with something?" I prod.

He clears his throat and leans back in his chair. "I just wanted to tell you that I'm leaving. I'll be gone the rest of the day."

"Okay, thanks." I begin to shut the door, and then realize he isn't finished.

"You're still going to your tennis lesson this afternoon?"

"Of course, just like every Tuesday."

"How is that coming along?"

"I still have a lot to learn, but I'm progressing slowly." Actually, Max says I'm a natural, but Cooper doesn't need to know that. Not yet, anyway.

"Well, I'm sure you'll be a pro in no time. If you need more practice, I can set up an extra set of lessons with Max."

"Maybe I'll take you up on that," I state breezily. No, I don't need any extra lessons, but I wouldn't pass up a little more time with Max if it was presented to me.

"Very well," he says, rising from his chair. "I'll have my cell phone if there's an emergency."

"Is there anything you'd like me to do while you're gone?" I ask. It really is starting to become dreadfully boring up here, with Dina doing all the work and me basically doing nothing but playing tennis and running an occasional errand.

"Did you return that yellow shirt?"

"I did it yesterday."

"What about that specialty coffee?"

"It's on order."

"Well, then...just sit there and look pretty."

Of course—just sit there and look pretty. Forget you have a brain. Forget that you could have been settled comfortably into your new marketing position by now. You're in the big times, sister—just sit and look pretty.

That's it. I've had it. Project Cooper begins today.

"Psst...Dina," I whisper, sticking my head out the door. "We need a brainstorm session."

Dina looks around for a moment before she meanders toward my office. Things have gotten a little better up here, since Dina doesn't exactly despise me anymore. I wouldn't say we're friends, but we share a common goal, and that counts for something.

As soon as Dina's inside my office, I close the door. I'm not sure why everyone around here is so secretive, but if that's the way things play out on the top floor, then I will keep the door closed. She sits down in my chair meant for visitors, smoothing her skirt with her palms. Always so prim and proper, with her up-do and her wool suits. I definitely can't imagine her chasing balls on the tennis court.

"Don't chase the ball," Max always says. "Anticipate it." Easier said than done, especially when I can't force myself to

concentrate on much of anything other than chasing Max. That's beside the point, though.

"You've thought of a plan?" Dina asks. She's like one of those ladies in *Arsenic and Old Lace*.

"No, but I think we need to. He's getting out of control."

"I heard the doorbell this morning. What was that about?" Dina pushes her glasses up on her nose and crosses her legs, hands folded in her lap.

"Nothing, really. He was just telling me he was leaving."

"That seems harmless enough."

"And then I asked him what I should do today, and he told me to sit here and look pretty."

"Sit and look pretty?" she gasps, whipping the glasses off her face. I'm sure I've never seen Dina so animated. "He told you to sit and look pretty, after he gave me that huge pile of work this morning? That little weasel!"

"Exactly. So what are we going to do about it?"

Dina and I sit and watch each other for a moment, each silently trying to come up with the best possible scheme. She's definitely angry, I can see it on her face.

There's nothing I'd rather do most days than march straight into Cooper's office and give him a piece of my mind, but what is that really going to accomplish in the long run? He can buy and sell a dozen of me in a minute, so I have no choice but to keep my cool and maintain the status quo. He has to believe I'm invaluable to him for any of this to work, so I have to keep acting as though I love this job. Poor Dina does, too, even though she's obviously being treated much worse than me.

"Got anything?" I ask.

"No."

"There has to be something we can do," I complain. "Is there anything he absolutely despises? Or something that drives him completely crazy?"

"I don't know," Dina states, relaxing a little and placing her elbow on my desk. "He's already completely crazy."

"Yeah, that's obvious."

"He hates going to the doctor," she offers with a shrug of her shoulders.

"That's good, but how could we use that?"

"Maybe we could convince him that he's sick."

"As many vitamins as he takes, that might be harder than it sounds. What does he hate about the doctor?"

"You name it, he doesn't like it…the testing, the poking, the prodding. When it's time for an appointment, you would swear he was a child getting ready to have a tooth pulled."

Well, one can hardly blame him for not liking to go to the doctor, especially for testing. Like when I went to have my blood drawn and got that creepy giant who abused my arm like a giant piece of meat.

"Wait a minute!" I exclaim as I reach a sudden epiphany. "What about blood?"

"I don't think physical harm is a good solution," Dina is quick to inform me. She emphasizes her point by sliding her glasses further onto her face and eyeing me strangely.

"No, no, that's not what I meant. How does he feel about blood? Is he squeamish?"

"I suppose so, yes," she says cautiously, still looking at me as though I'm going off the deep end.

"And blood tests?"

"With needles and the whole bit? I would say that ranks pretty high on his list of things he wouldn't want to do."

"Then it's settled," I conclude, slapping my hand on the desk. "I have the perfect plan."

It was raining when I got to the tennis club today. I ran from the Tahoe to the clubhouse, and I still managed to get drenched. No tennis outside today, I'm afraid, not that there isn't

plenty to do if the inside courts are crowded. I'm sure Max will have some off-the-wall chore he wants me to accomplish in the next hour…no doubt something that will prove more difficult than the game itself.

I went straight to the locker room to change clothes, and then came back out to look for my instructor. Working with Max has been lovely. He's very patient, even though he is fairly demanding. Plus, we always have in-depth conversations while I'm learning, which makes the time go faster.

"You looking for Max?" another trainer, Jill, calls across the room. I've been here enough times that most everyone knows me, at least as Max's student.

"Yes, time for my weekly session," I reply.

She smiles as though she knows why I'm excited about my tennis lesson, and she's probably correct. "I think he's in the equipment room."

As I walk through the door to the equipment room, Max looks up. "There's my favorite protégé!" he exclaims. We have developed quite a rapport since my first day here. He says I'm his most unpretentious client, and he's impressed that I still don't have the clingy tennis skirt. And I won't get one anytime soon—I'm standing my ground.

"Looks like the weather isn't going to permit a lesson today," I say, pretending to be sad.

He takes one look at my face and laughs heartily. "Oh, don't worry. I've got plenty in store for you."

"I was actually afraid of that," I complain with a sigh. He stoops down to adjust some of the buttons on one of the machines.

"I can't have any slacking," he explains, "especially since Kent called me today."

Oh, no.

"He called you?" I ask weakly. That is not a good sign.

"Yeah, a couple hours ago. He said he just wanted to know how you were coming along."

"What did you say?" I wonder, suddenly nervous. Inside I hope that he said the right thing, even though I'm not quite sure what that is at this point.

"I told him the truth–that you're really starting to get quite good, and that you seem like a natural."

"Why did you have to tell him that?" I whine, plopping down on a piece of equipment. He looks up for a moment (to make sure I didn't break anything, probably) and then continues what he's doing.

"Why shouldn't I tell him that?"

"Because I need more time. If he thinks I'm good, he's going to schedule a match, and I'm not ready."

"You could hold your own in a match," he states, standing up and placing his hands on his hips. "I've trained you well, little grasshopper."

"Of course you have," I agree, rolling my eyes, "but can I beat Kelli?"

"Hmm... I'd say that would be a close call."

"Well, until I can beat Kelli, I'm not ready." Max points to the door and I follow him onto one of the indoor courts, my tree frogs making a squeaking noise with every step I take. Thinking they probably sound a bit like *actual* tree frogs right now, I grind my toe into the floor to get a longer squeak at the end, until Max notices what I'm doing and begins shaking his head.

"I had no idea you were so competitive, Maddie," he states, grabbing a racket and balancing a ball on the end.

"It has nothing to do with me being competitive," I argue. "I'm worried about Cooper. If he'd go to all this trouble just to try to defeat his brother, what's going to happen if we don't win? What if I lose my job?"

"He wouldn't do that, would he?" he asks, grabbing the ball and tossing it to me.

"I don't know."

Max hops the net and heads to the opposite end of the court while I stand where I am and wait for instructions.

"Well, you won't have to worry about it for a while yet," he states. "Let me see your serve."

Throwing the ball into the air, I swing the racket hard, connecting and sending the ball in his direction. He catches the ball in his hand and tosses it back to me.

"What makes you think that?" I wonder, throwing the ball up again and sending it whirling over the net. This time, he taps the ball back over the net with his racket and I catch it in my hand.

"I overheard him talking to Brent this weekend, when they were both here."

"Well, what did they say?" I demand, standing with the tip of the racket brushing against the ground.

"No information without a serve," he commands, while I obligingly throw the ball into the air again. "Kent told Brent he wanted to challenge him to a match." He pauses to grab the ball. "Bend your arm a little more this time."

"And?" I prod, catching the ball after Max flings it over the net.

"Basically, Brent laughed at him."

"Really? He laughed?" I throw the ball in the air, concentrating on bending my arm as I bring the racket forward.

"Nice. Much better," he comments, tossing the ball back over the net. "Brent said he would take him on anytime, anyplace."

"So, what is the time and place?" Imitating my last serve is my goal, but Max has to move to the left a little to catch the ball.

"Okay, return my serve now. By next spring, is what Kent said. No later than next spring." He sends the ball flying over the net, and I move to the left about one second too late to connect with the ball. "Don't react—anticipate." Picking the ball up near the wall, I toss it back to him.

"Next spring, that's plenty of time," I decide as the ball comes back over the net, whirling toward my head. I move instinctively and connect, sending it back to Max.

"Good return!" he states. "By next spring, you'll probably be a pro."

Chapter Fifteen

I left work a little earlier than usual today. When I got back from the tennis lesson, I basically just sat at my desk with nothing to do. Unless you count looking pretty, that is.

Ugh—insufferable.

Dina and I talked about our plans for a few minutes, but there's only so much we can do before we talk to Cooper. Before *I* talk to Cooper, I should say. Dina wants to be a silent partner, and I agreed. She probably has a lot more to lose than I do, being at the company for twenty-some years. Besides, who knows how stable my job is, with Cooper being such a lunatic. He could come in one morning, decide he hates tennis, and send me on my way.

Without any pressing plans, I think I'll head out to jog a couple miles and then come back to cook dinner. I have some impressive plans for a sautéed mushroom grilled panini. (Sounds fancy, huh? Move over, Martha—here comes Maddie.)

I'll probably have these tree frogs worn out before too long, with all the jogging *and* the tennis. I never did get them to squeak like actual frogs, no matter how hard I tried. I even stood in the rain for a minute on my way out of the tennis club and tried to make the right noise, to no avail. All I got was extremely soaked. When I went back to the office, Dina said I looked like a drowned rat.

Well, it's definitely not raining now, and the downpour we had cooled the temperature off, so this should be a great time for a run. I'll probably just go two miles tonight and won't push myself too hard. No need after the tennis lesson. Max always runs me ragged chasing his serves.

I'm just about to head out the door when I hear a car pull into the driveway, so I peek through the blinds to see who would have stopped by.

Mom? What is she doing here? She never comes over. And who is that on the other…Brittany?

Brittany!

Mom gestures wildly with her hands as she plods toward the front door with Brittany, and then they both stop suddenly on the walk. Mom turns to face Brittany and begins smacking the side of her hand down on her palm, emphasizing whatever she is saying. Brittany stands there nodding her head, occasionally glancing at the house and shifting uncomfortably.

What is this, I wonder, *some sort of ambush?*

I hurriedly withdraw from the blinds as Mom starts up the walk again, and wait patiently until she rings the doorbell. Should I pretend I'm not here? The car is in the garage, so she'll never know. I'm usually not home quite this early, so I'd have a good excuse. She doesn't know the Tahoe is mine.

It takes me a good moment standing in front of the door to ponder whether or not to allow them in before I see Mom cup her hands and press her face to the glass. Unfortunately, I can't tell if she saw me. Bleh.

"Hi, Mom," I express with a sigh as I open the door. "Brittany."

"Hello, Maddie," Mom begins soberly, stepping up into the house while Brittany follows silently. "We've just come for a friendly visit."

Then why do you look like you're going to a wake?

I sit down on the couch and Brittany and Mom sit close by, leaning forward toward me. There is an impending sense that I'm about to be attacked.

"What's going on?" I wonder, glancing back and forth between them. Mom's mouth is in a grim line, and Brittany's eyes look a little wider than normal.

"Maddie," Mom states solemnly, "this is an intervention."

Ha!

"An intervention?" I repeat, giggling. "What type of intervention?"

"For your bulimia, of course," Brittany adds. "This is a very serious matter." She shakes her head slowly, as though I've just been handed a death sentence but I'm too ignorant to understand. I turn my head and look at Mom.

"How many times do I have to tell you that I'm not bulimic?!"

"Denial," Brittany assesses. "That's the first sign."

"Don't bother trying to deny it, Maddie," Mom says. "I have all the evidence I need."

"I already told you, that kid in the yard made me sick." I lower my head to my hands to try to keep from laughing. It is beyond my comprehension that they are taking this so seriously.

"I know what you said, Maddie, but I'm intelligent enough to see past your excuses to the real problem."

"There is no problem."

"Look at you, Maddie," Brittany states. "How can you explain your appearance?"

"My running shorts? I got them at the fitness store. This is one of those breathable tank tops, and of course tree frog jogging shoes. You should try them, they're extremely comfortable."

"I'm not talking about your clothes," Brittany interjects. "Why is your hair so limp?"

"I got caught in the rain today. Any other questions?"

"You can't go through life acting as though everything is a joke," Brittany replies, her eyes steely.

"I'm sorry, Brittany, but this *is* a joke. Do you two even know anything about bulimia?"

Mom and Brittany exchange glances with one another.

"Of course I know about bulimia," Mom blurts. "I certainly know enough to recognize the signs."

"Really? Bulimia is all about binging and purging. In order to binge, you have to eat a lot of food. Go look in my cupboards or my refrigerator. There's nothing unhealthy in there...no potato chips, no ice cream, no chocolate cake, no cookies. Look at my credit card statement, in my trash, on the floorboard of my car."

"I'm not the kind of person who goes snooping around someone else's house," Mom says, acting offended. "Besides, it seems to me you would hide the evidence."

"Is that so?" I ask. "Then what makes you think I would throw up in your bathroom, when I knew you were going to see me? Why would I run up the steps and fling the door open when I could have snuck around to the front yard and no one would have been the wiser? How do you explain that?"

"Well, it seems like you have given this a lot more thought than I have. That would mean you have the explaining to do, wouldn't it?"

"Okay," I interject, rising to my feet. "You know what? I've had enough. Don't come over here with your accusations when you don't even know what you're talking about. I was just heading out for a jog. Would you care to follow me around with your car to make sure that's what I'm really doing?"

Sliding between them, I walk to the front door and swing it open wide. Brittany and Mom rise from the couch, both of their mouths in angry lines. I stand to the side as they exit and head down the walk.

I don't even bother to wait for them to get to the car before making a beeline for the street to start jogging. They can sit in the driveway all night, for all I care. The nerve, coming over to *my* house for an intervention! Of all the ridiculous things the two of them have ever done, this has to take the cake. The real kicker is, I am absolutely positive that I am not anorexic-looking. I will be the first to brag about my improved physical fitness, but I am definitely not teetering at the low end of my healthy weight scale.

About one block into my jog, I hear the car's engine coming up behind me, and I glance over to see Brittany rolling down her window.

"I tried my best, Maddie!" Mom shouts. "If you die, don't come running to me."

"That's not even physically possible!" I retort. Brittany jerks the window up and Mom speeds away, pulling farther and farther from my view. Finally they fade completely, and I take a deep breath before I chuckle to myself at the sheer ridiculousness of the whole situation.

Ding-dong.

Ugh, I have to find that wire and disconnect it somehow. The doorbell is driving me crazy.

Okay, deep breath. This is my chance to talk to Cooper. If I spin this the right way, he has to agree.

"Maddie, are you in there?" Cooper roars.

If I could find a way to shut *that* off, we'd be in business.

Opening the door, I step into Cooper's office. He's wearing a canary yellow shirt today with a shiny blue tie, which makes me wonder if he dressed in the dark.

"You wanted to see me?" I ask politely. He clears his throat and motions for me to sit, so I take one of the pint-sized chairs and look up at him on his monstrous throne.

"I talked to Max yesterday," he begins. "He thinks you're coming along quite well."

"Well, we've been working hard."

"I appreciate you taking this so seriously. It really means a lot to me." He pauses for a second and then starts waving his hand back and forth in the air. "Your physical fitness and health and all that, of course."

"Of course."

Liar.

Cooper pulls a garment bag from the side of his desk and passes it over to me.

"I need you to take this shirt back again. The new one they gave me still doesn't fit."

"Certainly."

"Well," he says with a sigh, leaning back in his chair, "I guess that's all."

It's now or never.

"Actually, while I'm in here, there was something I wanted to discuss with you."

Cooper leans forward in his chair, clearly intrigued. He probably thinks I want to ask him about my backhand. Choosing my words carefully, I drape the garment bag across my lap.

"When you hired me for this job, you said you wanted us to really collaborate on some new ideas. Well, I've been contemplating a new idea that I think you're simply going to love."

"Go on," he instructs, placing his chin on his hand. At the least, I have his full attention.

"This company could really use a facelift in the community, something that tells people that we're not here simply to make money, but also to make a difference in the world."

"Uh-huh, I'm very interested. Please continue."

"Well, what better way to do that than to contribute to the health and wellbeing of the entire city?"

"It's a very nice thought, but how do you intend to pull that off?"

"It's very simple, actually," I reply, leaning forward in my chair. (I decided earlier that appearing animated about the topic would peak his interest, so I'm giving it a shot.) "Picture this: In October, we host a community-wide blood drive. As long as we do it during that month, we can tie in a Halloween-based theme. You know how people are—they eat up the gimmicky, themed events. I believe we can get a large number of people in the community involved, and the more involved the community becomes, the more likely the media is to cover the event. The television networks love these types of events, too, so I can't foresee any reason why they wouldn't turn out in full force."

Cooper tips back his chair, folds his arms across his chest, and gazes out the office windows. The view of the city from this office is really amazing; it's possible to see for miles, overlooking corporate buildings, parks, and houses. I wonder if he's imagining all this territory, thousands of people, showing up for an event at his company.

Sitting back in my chair, I let everything I proposed sink in. I've never really had a serious conversation with Cooper before. Every time I talk to him, he turns the conversation to tennis or what vitamins he is taking or what he ate last night. I do know, however, that this entire project hinges completely on whether or not I can convince him to trust *me* to oversee it. Not only do I have to sell the concept, but I have to sell myself as the project planner. That might be easier said than done.

"So the entire community would be coming to an event that we host," Cooper says dreamily, still gazing out the window.

"No question about it."

"And you're sure it will generate positive publicity?" he asks, bringing his hand up and rubbing the back of his neck. Viewing this behavior, one would think he never made a single decision about the running of his own company.

"Absolutely. In the media's eyes, you'll be hosting the event and getting nothing in return. However, you and I are both aware of the kind of windfall that can come from a good name in the community. It's a win-win situation for everyone involved."

Cooper rises and walks to the window, placing one hand on the wall and staring down at the street below. For a moment I'm afraid he'll turn around and shake his head, ushering me out of his office. Instead, he turns around and slams his fist on his desk.

"I love it! It's fantastic!" He sits at his desk and pulls out his brown leather book. "I'll just make a few calls and—"

"If you don't mind, sir, I have another suggestion." *This is it—everything rides on this tiny detail.*

"Kent," he states, looking up from the book.

"I'm sorry, Kent." *Deep breath.* "I would like to handle the blood drive myself."

Cooper taps his finger on his desk for a moment. "The entire thing, yourself?" he questions, one eyebrow raised quizzically.

"From beginning to end."

"I just don't know," he begins, rubbing his forehead. "What about the—"

"I've already considered all the details. There's no doubt that I have plenty of time to take care of the planning, and of course it won't take any time away from my tennis lessons. Besides, with my marketing background, I have a lot of connections. I'm certain you wouldn't want anyone else internally to take time out of their busy schedules, so it would appear that I'm the perfect candidate."

He folds his brown leather book and puts both hands on top of it.

"You're certain it won't interfere with…anything else you already do?"

"I'm certain." How could it interfere with doing nothing?

Cooper leans back again, assessing me and thinking about the situation. I think I've got him—how can he say no? This is going to be so much fun! Besides, just think how great it will look on my résumé.

"Okay, then. Full speed ahead. All systems go."

Good grief, who does he think he is, Captain Kirk?

Standing up, I head toward my own office door, swinging the garment bag in my hand, mentally preparing for all the things I'll need to do in the next few weeks.

"That means yes, by the way," Cooper calls.

"I know," I reply, turning in the doorway.

He nods his head up and down a few times, smiling. "I knew you had potential. You'll do big things here, mark my words!"

If I thought those big things didn't involve sitting around looking pretty or perfecting my serve, I might be inclined to agree.

Chapter Sixteen

It has been a month, and Mom still hasn't spoken to me. Why is she the one pouting and sulking and refusing to converse with me when I am the one who should be angry over her false accusations? I mean, coming over to my house and staging that ridiculous intervention—and with Brittany, no less, who is apparently not even capable of having a short, polite conversation with me. How could she possibly expect me to take that kind of nonsense seriously?

I'll tell you who I really feel sorry for, and that is poor Dad. I wish there was something I could do for him. He has been calling me on the sly, waiting until Mom is out of the house or on an errand. He says he goes out to his workshop whenever possible, especially on the nights when she's acting particularly loony. He also told me that Brittany spends most of her time there during the day while Lance is at work. I can only imagine the crazy schemes the two of them could come up with while no one else is around to talk sense into them. No wonder they accosted me like they did.

When I came home from my jog the night they came over, I immediately shot an email to Josh, completely indignant with their behavior, and he responded by telling me that it was pretty darn hilarious. Not helpful in the least!

I have only had compliments about my appearance, so I'm absolutely certain their comments about me looking sick are unfounded. Besides, if I did have anorexia or bulimia, I'm pretty sure the way Mom and Brittany handled their concern would not have been effective.

Strangely enough, it all follows the general pattern of the way things work in my life. Every time something good happens, there is an equal dose of the unpleasant to balance it out. I make twice as much money as before, but I have to work with Cooper. I make strides towards becoming physically fit, but now my job hinges on my athletic ability. I am a little closer to wearing Max down in the quest to make him fall in love with me, but now Mom isn't speaking to me. It's as though I can't have the good without inviting the bad somehow.

My car practically drives itself into the parking lot of that little church with the country ambiance. As I exit the vehicle, I see Hazel walking towards me. She smiles as she comes near, and the thought that she's been waiting for me fills me with happiness. No matter how weird my life becomes, at least I have the wonderful Mason family in my corner.

"Hi, Maddie," she states as she folds me into a hug. "Are things going better with your mom?"

"Not really," I breathe as she links her arm in mine. We usually see eye to eye, Hazel and me, mostly because we're the same height. She's a very thin woman, just like Jess always has been, and her light ash-brown hair reaches halfway down her back and straight as a board. I can't remember it ever being styled differently through the years. Looking into her face, I see a bit of my reflection in her glasses.

"I'm sorry," she says simply. "Listen, I have something I wanted to ask you. Josh said you really like that author Camdyn Taylor?"

"Yes, I love her books!" She stops walking, and I face her expectantly.

"Well, she's going to be here in Louisville in a couple weeks for a conference, and Josh was able to get some tickets. He asked if you would want to go see her with me. Of course, if you'd rather take one of your friends—"

"No, Hazel, I would absolutely love to go to the conference with you. Thank you so much! You just made my day."

"It was all Josh's idea," she insists. "Good, I'm looking forward to it!"

Two of the Gardwin kids brush past me at that moment, making vomiting noises.

"I'll tell you what I'm not looking forward to: having my hair pulled during church," I mutter, giving Hazel a weak smile.

"Boys," she jokes. "That's how they tell a girl they like her, when they're that age. Don't you remember Josh pulling your hair all the time?"

"Did he?" I wonder with a laugh.

"Did he?!" she repeats, shaking her head. "Honey, sometimes I think he still is."

When I arrive at work Monday morning, the first thing I see as I step off the elevator is Dina motioning subtly at me. She seems to hear all and see all from the hallway, so she often has some interesting tidbit to offer for Project Cooper. I sidle up to her desk and lean down.

"What is it today?" I whisper. She glances over at Cooper's office and then slides her glasses down on her nose.

"Possible kink in the plans," she murmurs. "There's a new body on the floor."

"A new VP?" I wonder distractedly. "Not another assistant, I hope."

"Even worse. Another Cooper."

One of the doors behind me opens, and I quickly move towards my office. What does she mean, another Cooper? How could there be another Cooper? One Cooper is bad enough.

Surely she doesn't mean Cooper's brother, Brent. No, it can't be. He has his own law firm or something across town. Maybe she is referring to someone as off-the-wall as Cooper. That doesn't seem likely, either. Not even possible, really. I wonder how long

I'll have to wait until I can sneak back out there. I wish she hadn't even said a word!

Swinging open the door to my office, I step into blood drive central. There are design schematics resting all over the office for ad layouts and press materials. Sketches for backdrops and fliers are scattered across those. Then, of course, there are the stacks of paperwork showing who I've contacted, who I need to contact, who has committed, and who I need to convince to commit. It's been more work than I thought it would be, but it will all be worth it in the end.

Ding-dong.

Oh, come on, are you kidding? It's way too early in the morning for that already!

"Maddie," Cooper belts a song through the door. "Maddie Heard, are you in there?"

Why is he in such a good mood? It's Monday morning, for crying out loud.

"You rang?" I ask, poking my head through the connecting door. He laughs, just as he does every time I say that. As wealthy as he is, you would think he would have a more sophisticated sense of humor.

"Yes, I did. Come in, I've got something to tell you."

I hesitantly step into his office, wondering what it is this time. Shirt collar a bit too tight, so he wants me to return it? Socks don't quite match, so he wants me to scour the city looking for the right color? Maybe wants me to run across town to pick up one of those special cinnamon rolls he likes so much?

He stands up and begins pacing as I sit in front of his desk.

"We've got a new employee today," he states. *Yes, so I've heard.* "I want her to work directly with you. She can help you on this project you're working on, and then you can figure out which direction she needs to go...what she needs to do within the company."

"Okay," I reply uneasily. This doesn't sound very appealing.

"She is going to be working out of Bentley's old office. We went ahead and moved him down a floor."

This does sound like another assistant. Maybe he found someone who might be good at golf this time.

"When should we get started?" I ask.

He pauses and sits back in his chair. "Right away. You should go get her first thing this morning. She probably doesn't know much about the type of project you're doing, but she should be able to make some calls for you, do some basic clerical-type work."

Well, I know for certain that I, for one, do *not* need an assistant. This is a nightmare.

Rising from my seat, I walk toward the door, pausing as I push it open.

"What's her name?" I question.

He looks up from his desk and smiles. "Audrey," he replies. "Audrey Cooper."

Audrey Cooper? So there is another Cooper on the floor, Dina was right about that. I wonder what the story is with this woman.

Stepping out into the hall, I immediately notice that Dina is on the phone, so it's impossible to ask her about the situation and prepare myself. The office Cooper referenced is the third one on the left, so I might as well dive in like a super sleuth and solve the mystery right off the bat.

I stop short in front of the office and look back at Dina, who bulges her eyes and shrugs her shoulders. She knows what's going on, because she knows everything. Ugh, I wish she wasn't on the phone, because I'm dying to find out who is behind that door.

I should just call Katie—she is in Human Resources now, after all. She should know who the new employee is. What if she's busy, though? If she says she'll have to call me back, it could be an hour or more before I find out about Audrey Cooper. No, I'll simply have to see for myself.

Knocking on the door, I wait for a moment before I hear a muffled voice tell me to come in. As I push the door open and step

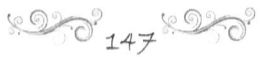

inside, I see a young woman chatting on her cell phone. She motions that she will only be a minute, so I stand waiting, using the opportunity to assess her appearance.

I'm guessing her to be close to my age, slightly heavier than me, with plump cheeks and entirely too much blush. Her bleach-blonde tousled hair is showing about a half-inch of dark roots, and she's wearing a raspberry shade of lip gloss. As she leans back in her chair, I notice that she is wearing Capri pants and flip flops.

Honestly, flip flops on a Monday morning in the office. Didn't anyone tell her about the dress code? Has she no sense of propriety?

"Well, I guess I need to go. There's someone in my office," she groans into her tiny phone.

From all appearances, I can safely surmise that Cooper did not hire her for anything related to a sport. She looks like she would have a hard time keeping up on a long walk, much less in a tennis match. At least my job would seem to be safe, for the time being.

She places the phone gingerly on her desk. It occurs to me that she looks completely out of place in the office, the way those teenagers look when they come here to shadow people in their jobs. She begins combing through her purse until she finds a hair pick, and then carefully brushes her hair to the side before turning to look at me.

"Hi, I'm Maddie Heard," I say, ignoring her rudeness. "Mr. Cooper said we would be working together, so I just wanted to stop by and say hello."

"Yeah, okay," she mumbles, turning her attention back to her purse. I watch in silence as she pulls out a compact, flips it open and checks her reflection, rotating her head slowly back and forth so she can see every angle. She purses her lips a couple of times and then inspects her teeth.

What are you, anyway? Some kind of beauty queen wannabe? Can't you even be polite for one minute?

She glances up at me over her compact.

"You're still here?" she wonders, looking at herself in the mirror once again.

Well, you certainly aren't Miss Congeniality either. I hope you have something really special in store for the talent competition.

"Your name is Audrey, right? Audrey Cooper?"

"Yeah," she states, not bothering to look at me. She flips her compact shut and begins looking through her purse again. It's a nice handbag, too, and much more expensive than anything I own.

"Well, Mr. Cooper said you would be working with me on a big project we have coming up, so whenever you get some time, I'm just up the hallway. I'll be glad to get you started."

"Okay, whatever," she says, throwing me a look that is all but screaming for me to get out of her personal space. I twist the doorknob and start to step out, but then turn back to her.

"Cooper," I casually mention. "Any relation to Kent Cooper?"

"Yeah," she says, eyes narrowing. "He's my dad."

"Oh...I see," I reply, practically stammering.

So it *is* bring your daughter to work day, after all! I certainly didn't expect that response, especially after seeing her. She looks nothing like Cooper or his wife. I wouldn't have even pegged her as a relative, if I had been guessing.

"If I have some time, I'll stop by your office," she states, giving me a clear signal to leave her alone. Simply nodding, I close the door.

Dina's desk is currently vacant, which is unfortunate, because I'm dying to tell her about my discovery. Well, not really a discovery, because she probably already knew Audrey was Cooper's daughter. I actually want to tell her that I know, too, so we can be on the same page. She was right, this could throw a kink in our plans. I don't want to work closely with Audrey Cooper, beauty queen aspirant and major cheerfulness inhibitor. What if she doesn't agree with the way I'm handling Project Cooper and she complains to her father? Everything I've accomplished so far could go right down the drain.

I slink into my office and close the door, picking up the phone and dialing Katie's number. Maybe she'll have some insight into the situation. If nothing else, I would just like to hear a friendly voice.

"This is Katie Green," she calls cheerily. Apparently no one informed Katie that it was Monday morning, either.

"Katie, it's me," I say quietly into the phone, not wanting Cooper to overhear my conversation.

"Maddie, how are things on the top floor? I hope you had a good weekend."

"Yeah, it was fine."

"Mine too. Not much going on, but it's always nice to relax, right?"

Yeah, yeah, cut the chit chat. I need information and I need it now, lady!

"Uh-huh. Hey, what's the story with Audrey Cooper?" I listen for a second to be sure I still hear Cooper's voice conversing with Dina.

"Audrey Cooper? Oh, the new girl upstairs. I don't know much about her. Nora took care of that one herself. She was in here the other day, but I didn't get to talk to her."

"Well, you're not missing much," I whisper. "Did you know she's Cooper's daughter?"

"No she's not!" Katie exclaims. I can almost envision her mouth hanging open.

"I assure you that she is."

"That grouchy girl with the bad dye job? We must be talking about two different people here."

"Chubby cheeks, too much makeup, completely inappropriate clothing. That sound like her?"

"Yes, that's her, but she can't be Cooper's daughter."

"She can, and she is. What is she doing here? Cooper says that she's going to be working directly with me."

"I'm sorry, Maddie, but I really don't know. I'm as astonished as you are."

This is not good—not good at all.

"Well, I'll let you know when I find out," I whisper, placing the phone down.

Great! Things have gone from bad to worse. Not only do I have to work for that insane Cooper, but now I'm going to have to babysit his spoiled grown daughter. What did I do to deserve this? If it's true that hard work pays off, I will gladly give a refund for this type of payment.

Ding-dong.

Oh, how I hate that contraption!

"Maddie!" Cooper calls out, not waiting for me to come to the door.

"Yes?" I reply.

"Why don't you run across town and get me one of those cinnamon rolls with the icing on top?"

So I'm a babysitter and a gofer. What's next, the laundry? Perhaps his house needs to be painted?

"Oh, and a mocha double latte with extra foam!"

What a way to start the week.

Grabbing the keys to the Tahoe, I prepare to head out the door. I'll go get Cooper his breakfast, and then I'll come back here and work like mad on the blood drive before Audrey gets involved. Who knows what kind of mess she'll make when she starts adding her two cents.

"Maddie, one more thing!" Cooper blurts as I pause just inside the door. "Why don't you take Audrey with you? It will be a good chance to get to know one another."

Drat.

Chapter Seventeen

There are probably worse things than spending a morning trapped in a vehicle with Audrey Cooper, but none are coming to mind at the present moment. To say that the girl is difficult could be the understatement of the century. Carrying on a conversation with someone who doesn't even want to be with you, much less have to speak to you, is not an easy task. I tried all the tricks the experts recommend, and was very careful to only ask questions that had to have an explanation for a response rather than a simple yes or no. She still managed to answer most of them with a grunt, much to my dismay. I really hope Cooper doesn't try to ask me anything about her later, because I've got nothing, quite literally.

Well, I take that back. There was one topic she was happy to discuss, and that was her fiancé, Derrick. She even dug a picture out of her purse to show me, as well as several taken on her cellphone. To be perfectly honest, I was a little surprised when I saw him. Given her appearance and attitude, admittedly I had a certain impression about the type of guy who would be attracted to her. This fiancé of hers is actually very good looking, and a successful businessman from what she told me.

Oh, and dogs. She wouldn't stop talking about dogs. Apparently she loves them above all else.

Maybe there is something to Audrey Cooper that I haven't quite seen yet, hidden beneath the surface and the prickly shell. I'll keep my fingers crossed, but after our adventure this morning, I have my doubts.

You would think a trip across town to get a cinnamon roll and a latte would be an easy task, but not with Audrey in tow. After we picked up the items for her father, she insisted that we stop at a convenience store so she could get a snack. I waited in the Tahoe for what seemed like ten minutes, and she finally emerged with nothing but a large bag of cheesy puffs. When she got in the vehicle, she started complaining because that particular store did not have any frozen diet cola. There was no satisfying daddy's little princess until we drove even further across town to a place that she *knew* had frozen diet cola. It seemed like it took forever to get back to the office, and I'm sure Cooper's latte was disgusting by that time. I'm surprised he didn't mention it, now that I think of it.

In any case, I really have managed to get a lot done today, and Audrey never has stopped by to help me on the blood drive. I'm fairly certain she has nothing else to do, so she must simply be sitting in her office, looking in her mirror and talking on the cellphone. Maybe she's playing on the Internet or something. Whatever she's doing, it must be more appealing than spending any more time with me.

Ding-dong.

I've got nothing else to say about the bell. Every time I hear it, I just drop my head and mutter a prayer to find the strength not to tear the little box from the wall as I walk by.

"Yes?" I ask, poking my head in the doorway. He puts both his hands up and plasters a surprised look on his face.

"You're not going to say it?" he whines. Some days I would swear I work for a six-year-old.

"You rang?" I say halfheartedly. Cooper doesn't seem to mind. He smiles and motions for me to come in.

"How are things going with Audrey?"

Wonderful—the very conversation I was dreading.

"Fine," I reply.

"Has she been very helpful with your project?"

What am I supposed to say? No, I think she's more interested in the consistency of her lip gloss?

"Actually, I haven't seen her since our outing this morning." An unfamiliar expression crosses his face...disappointment, maybe? I can't place it.

"You told her that she was to work with you?" His voice is quieter than I have ever heard it—still not as quiet as some people, but definitely subdued for the loud, boisterous Cooper.

"Yes, I did."

Cooper stands up and pulls on the bottom of his jacket, as though he's trying to make himself appear taller, and then marches out of the office.

Great. Now Audrey's in trouble, and I'm the snitch. She's going to be a real joy to be around after her daddy yells at her.

I go back to my office and try to busy myself with the newspaper ad I've been writing. The blood drive is drawing ever closer, and everything seems to be going well. I've been able to get several other businesses involved, and the city has been very cooperative. Plus, I've got these ad spots going into the newspapers, and the local media outlets have agreed to provide airtime for the cause. If everything goes as planned, the event will be a huge hit. I will have something great to put on my résumé, and Dina and I will have successfully staged the first portion of Project Cooper.

A graphic on my computer screen is holding my interest when my door suddenly swings open. Audrey stands in the doorway, cheeks red and neck a bright shade of pink. I can see Dina directly behind her, eyes wide and shaking her head. Looks like she's here to help at last. Lucky me!

"Hi, Audrey," I say as she walks in and shuts the door. It's only after she comes closer to me that I notice that her fingers are bright orange with cheesy puff dust. Daddy must have interrupted her afternoon snack.

"Well, what is it you want me to do?" she growls as she sits down next to my desk.

What is it that I want you to do? Nothing. I want you to turn around and leave my office and never come back. In fact, keep walking to the elevator and just exit the building entirely.

"Maybe I should start by briefing you on what I'm working on," I suggest. She drops her head a bit and glares at me.

"Why don't you just give me something to do and then I'll go back to my office, and we won't have to sit here and stare at each other."

That's a great idea. Get out.

If only it were that easy. Besides, if anyone is getting a raw deal here, it's me!

"I wish it were that simple, but there are some things I would have to tell you first, before I just sent you away with something to do."

"What's this?" she wonders, picking up an ad layout I've been preparing. She looks at it for a second and then tosses it back to my desk, bright orange cheesy puff dust now adorning the edges. She begins tapping her cheese-stained fingers along the corner of my desk.

"Actually," I say, watching her disgusting fingers and fighting the urge to lunge at her, "that's an ad layout for the blood drive, which is the project you'll be helping me with."

"Blood drive? That sounds lame." The little orange spiders are reaching for another ad layout when I snap.

"Look, Audrey," I blurt, snatching up all the papers on my desk and protectively placing them behind me, "I'm sure you're working here for a reason. Whatever the problem is, that is between you and your dad. The last thing I need right now is for you to take it out on me. I have a lot of work to do on this project, so you can either stop fighting me or I can go tell Cooper you're not cooperating. It's up to you."

Her eyes widen and her nostrils start to flare, but she just sits silently, not saying a word. After a minute, she leans back in her chair and looks at the floor. Obviously she doesn't want me to go talk to her father. At least she's not mouthing off anymore, which is a start.

"Why don't you go to the restroom and wash your hands, and when you come back I'll brief you on the project," I suggest. She pauses a couple of seconds and then stands up, walking toward the door. Right before she turns the doorknob, she flips her hands over and stares at them in disbelief.

Honestly, you're a grown woman, Audrey. A short supply of cleanliness is certainly in order.

I fight the urge to beat my fist against the desk after she shuts the door, angry that I'm going to have to redo that ad layout simply because of those cheesy puffs. If Cooper ever sends me out with her on an errand again, she is *not* getting a snack. Absolutely no puffed cheese of any kind, and no frozen diet cola either. Good grief!

Now, what am I going to have her do? This has been a one-woman show. I haven't shown anybody the things I've been working on. Cooper just seems to take it in stride that I know what I'm doing, and I really don't want her to mess anything up. If only Cooper gave me some normal, day-to-day work, I might be able to pass that off on her. How can *I*, having nothing to do, keep someone else busy?

Audrey returns, opening the door slowly and stalking to her chair before sitting down. I casually glance over at her fingers, which are now clean, thankfully. Sorting through a few papers, I ponder where to begin.

"My dad hates me, you know," she says quietly, staring at the floor. My eyes fly up to her face, but I can see that she's not joking.

"I'm sure that's not true," I offer. She shakes her head slowly, intertwining her fingers and rubbing them together.

"No, it's true. He hates me."

I'm not sure why, but at this precise moment I'm reminded of Nancy Olsen from *Little House on the Prairie*, always telling people that everyone hates her. Her mother always believed her. Sometimes others believed her, too, even though they knew deep down she was lying.

I admit that I feel a little twinge of sadness right now looking at Audrey, but I also get the strong sensation that she might be playing my emotions to her advantage.

"Come on now," I reply, "why would your dad hate you?"

"Because I'm not perfect," she states, eyes welling up with tears. "Everything around him is perfect. My mom is perfect.

Derrick is perfect. This office is perfect. You're perfect. Even my dogs are perfect."

I watch her for a moment as she swipes at her eyes with the back of her hand. It's not hard to imagine Cooper demanding perfection from those around him. He's certainly competitive enough to cause him to lean in that direction.

"Nothing you mentioned is perfect," I counter. "Look at your mom, for instance. My trainer at the tennis club said that she's not the best player he's ever seen."

"That's true, I guess," she agrees with a sniff.

"And what about Derrick? There's got to be something about him that is less than perfect."

"Well, he does get really irritated when his hair is out of place. Oh, and he can't say probably. He always says probly."

"See? So he's not perfect either. And this office...well, it echoes in the hallway if you talk too loud, and sometimes the elevator sticks."

"Yeah, and you're not perfect either. You snapped at me earlier."

"No need to throw sticks and stones."

"But what about the dogs?" she asks.

"Oh, come on, they're dogs. They eat their own poop. What's so perfect about that?"

She stifles a giggle and looks at the door to her dad's office.

"So, no more nonsense," I suggest. "We've got work to do, so you just have to cheer up and forget about it."

"I'll try," she sighs.

You better, because I'm not a psychiatrist and I don't feel like offering any counseling today.

"Okay," I relent, gathering my papers and setting them in front of her. "What I'm working on is the Halloween Bloodfest."

"Bloodfest?"

"Bloodfest."

"That sounds disgusting," she says, wrinkling up her nose.

"Yeah, that's kind of the point. See, if we hold it around Halloween and have a gimmicky theme like this, people are more

likely to remember it. Basically, it's just going to be an enormous blood drive with our company as the main sponsor. One of the major medical centers has signed on to help us, and we've also got several companies around town that are going to provide food, drinks, door prizes, and games for the kids."

"Sounds like a big deal," she states, leafing through the papers.

"It will be. The whole community will be involved. What I'm working on now is the advertising. These are the print ads. I still have to write something up for the radio ads, as well as the television spots."

"We get to be on TV?" she asks incredulously, her eyes brightening.

"Well, not us exactly, but our words will be, so it's very important that everything is just right."

"I can't believe that my dad would trust me with this type of important job!" she exclaims. I nod my head and begin going through the print ads one by one, showing her what I've done so far. She is finally starting to loosen up when the unthinkable happens.

Ding-dong.

"What was that?" Audrey asks as I fight the urge to roll my eyes.

"That's just your dad," I respond, walking over to the door.

"What does he think you are, a dog?"

Apparently, yes.

"You rang?" Yeah, that's getting really old by now, but if I don't say it, he'll just torment me until I do.

"Everything going okay?" he asks.

I nod and begin to shut the door, but Audrey closes in behind me.

"The bell is a little over the top, don't you think?" she wonders aloud to her father.

He jerks a little in his chair like he's taken aback, but then he laughs.

"Why, that's nonsense. This method works very well for us. You like the bell, don't you, Maddie?" He stares at me from behind his monstrous desk, and Audrey looks inquisitively into my face.

Of course I don't like the bell. Audrey's right, I'm not a dog. I wonder how you would like to answer to a bell, like a little kid at recess responding to a whistle. That bell is an embarrassment to me, to you, and to your company. Frankly, Cooper, it's downright insulting.

Instead, I force myself to offer a shrug. "It's just a bell."

That thing flying out the window? Yeah, that's a little bit of my dignity.

Chapter Eighteen

It is completely fangirling and decidedly uncool, but I am so excited to see Camdyn Taylor tonight, I might even pee my pants. Okay, not really, but I am jittery and nervous like I'm going on a blind date or something. She has provided stories that made my heart swell and reaffirmed my belief in true love, and I can't wait to hear what she has to say this evening.

Hazel wanted to pick me up, so she's coming around at 5:30. I've dressed myself in a new pair of jeans that fit me perfectly, and I'm wearing a navy blue top with purple jewels sewn into the neckline. I opted for flats so I wouldn't tower over Hazel, and I'm convinced that Camdyn will think me fashionably cute if she does happen to lock eyes on me.

Like I said, decidedly uncool.

The phone rings, and I immediately know exactly who is calling. Smiling to myself, I pull the phone up to my ear.

"This better be important. I have a hot date tonight."

"With my mother," he quips with a laugh.

"Thank you for the tickets, Josh. I'm really excited. Stupidly excited."

"I can tell. I can hear it in your voice." He pauses and I use the opportunity to cross to the window and peek out the blinds to see if Hazel has arrived yet. "I wish I was there. I'd take you myself."

"Yes, well, I'm sure you'd find it incredibly boring, with all the gushy mushy romantic stuff and everything."

"Probably," he admits. "I did read the book you loved, though...*Crossing Heartbreak.* I wanted to see what was so great about the main character that would make the hero 'pine away' for her all that time, as you so poetically stated."

"Please don't tell me you hated it. I'll have to boot you just like that teacher guy, whatever-his-name-was."

"No, don't boot me," he begs with a laugh. "It was a good story, but she was just a fairly ordinary girl."

"Well, yeah, that's kind of the point," I say, plopping down on the couch. "It's not a story about incredible people—it's a story about ordinary people who share an incredible love. That's what I'm hoping for myself, eventually. Goodness knows I'm about as ordinary as they come."

"You're not looking for someone ordinary," he counters, a hint of sarcasm creeping into his voice. "Sure, maybe you'll give a guy the time of day, if he's exactly the right height, laughs properly, has the same taste as you in reading materials, doesn't eat any food you think is gross, his facial structure is perfectly symmetrical…"

"Hey, what is this, another ambush? You're worried about my stellar dating strategies? Your mom's not coming over here to stage another intervention, is she?"

"No, forget it," he breathes with a sigh of exasperation—a sound that makes my heart drop in my chest a couple inches. "How is the pirate, anyway?"

Pulling my knees up against my chest on the couch, I fiddle with the hem on my jeans as I listen to the quiet sound of him breathing on the other end of the line.

"Pirate? I have no idea what you're talking about."

"Your tennis instructor, with the long flowing hair and the goatee. He looks like the guy from that pirate movie."

Oh, whatever, he really doesn't look like…

Well, on second thought, I guess he might resemble him a little.

"He's nothing like a pirate."

"I never said he acted like a pirate, I simply said he looks like a pirate. But now that you're protesting, I think maybe I spoke too hastily. Arr, Maddie, be ye here to learn the art of tennis this fine day? Just let me remove ye olde hook and replace it with ye olde tennis racket. Aha! Shiver me timbers, but don't make me run too far, on account of me olde peg leg."

"Very funny, Josh, but there's nothing going on between me and Max." Not yet, anyway. "Besides, how do you even know about him? I didn't mention him to you."

"Jess."

"What did Jess say about him? This is a little annoying! Don't you people know the meaning of privacy?"

"You're interested in him, that's all. I'm surprised you didn't bother to mention it to me, but I get it. Is there anything to this one other than the fact that he's good looking?"

"Of course not, just a handsome pirate," I quip, shaking my head. "Honestly, Josh, sometimes I think you must believe I'm the shallowest person in the world. Max is funny and intelligent, and we have lengthy conversations about lots of things. He hopes to travel to Barbados soon—that's where his father lives. He has a shipping business there."

"So the guy who's definitely not a pirate has a ship in Barbados?"

"Sometimes you're on a ship. Does that make you a pirate?"

"I'm in the Navy," he counters quickly.

There are days when I can almost forget what Josh is really doing with his life, and then he makes statements like that and his words sort of smack me about the head.

Hearing a door slam, I rise again and check the window, but all I see is a moving van parked next door. Peering around the blinds, I wait to see if I catch some movement.

"Are you still there?" Josh wants to know.

"Yeah, sorry, a moving van just pulled up next door and I got distracted. And there's your mom pulling in now, so I better go."

"Okay, well, I hope you have a great time. And I wish you lots of happiness with the pirate."

"As I wish you joy in your delusions, crazy man." I blow his words off with a shake of my head. "Goodnight, Joshua."

"Mad," he says right before the phone goes silent.

"Hey!" I announce, opening the door right as Hazel is set to knock on it, hand still lifted precariously in midair. "Are we ready? I just got off the phone with Josh, and he hopes we have fun."

"I'm sure we will," she answers with a smile. "Looks like you're getting new neighbors. Do you know who they are?"

Stepping out onto the porch, I look to my left at the moving van. "No, I didn't even realize the house was empty, to be honest. I guess I…"

My speech is suddenly cut short, because at that precise moment a man walks around the front of that van, and Lord have mercy, he is spectacular. He has short acorn-brown tinted hair that's a little longer near the front, and a swagger that quickly informs me that he's sure of himself. For an instant he catches my eye and nods with a smile, just long enough for me to note the dimple in his cheek.

"What were you saying, Maddie?" Hazel interrupts my thoughts.

"Oh, I have no idea," I mutter, trying to pull my eyes away from him. He grabs his wallet off the dash of the van and shoves it into his back pocket right as a little girl streams out of the house and runs directly to him.

So the handsome guy has a kid…big deal. I could handle a kid, right? I'm sure I'd be a really stellar stepmother. Not like the one Cinderella had.

"Bailey?!" I hear a female voice yell, and I glance over at the house to see a woman strolling toward them, dressed in a football jersey with a baseball cap perched atop her head.

So the handsome guy has a kid *and* a woman…big deal. I could handle…

No, definitely not. Total deal breaker. Sorry, handsome guy. This ship has sailed.

Besides, what am I even thinking? It's Max, right? My focus should be on Max.

He could definitely be the one.

Camdyn Taylor is really nothing like I thought she would be. Don't get me wrong, she's great. I suppose I just expected…

Well, to be honest, I had two very different pictures in my head. First, there was this stodgy kind of history lady who knew all the ins and outs of pioneer life and early American politics. She was naturally full of facts and unknown tidbits, and mildly fascinating.

The second picture was of the woman I saw on television, barfing into a plant and being proposed to by everyone she met. I expected this woman to be almost like a stand-up comedienne, and to entertain us with one-liners about the publishing world and her big Hollywood friends.

Instead, she's just kind of…normal.

When she was talking about how she met her husband, getting lost in the middle of nowhere, I swear I was on the edge of my seat. What I wouldn't give for a great meeting like that! What am I going to tell my kids some day? *Yeah, sweetie, I met your dad when Cooper sent me over to Big Cedar to take tennis lessons.* It's not very romantic. Of course, there is still time for him to sweep me off my feet and take me to Barbados, so the story isn't exactly written in stone.

Then, she talked about reconciling with her mother, who basically abandoned her when she was four years old. I have to admit, the guilt was weighing on me pretty heavily right about that time. Sure, my mom is obnoxious on occasion, but she never flat-out left me, so perhaps I should cut her some slack. Camdyn saw things in her life as being orchestrated by God, and I wondered if I thought about it hard enough, could I make that apply to my own life? Although it's hard to understand why God would want my mother to think I was bulimic.

In any case, the speech was really good, and afterwards she allowed people to ask questions, which many did. Then, her drop-dead gorgeous husband had to come out and practically propose to her all over again, of course, just to rub it in all of our faces. If it had been any other situation it would have been annoying, but since she had just been talking about their wonderful love story, it just made it all the more swoon-worthy. I was practically in tears in those high-up seats, staring down at the little ants on the stage.

When everything was over, people started milling about, and I noticed that Camdyn didn't leave. There was a line of people pressing toward her, and she stood there, smiling and shaking hands and signing autographs. Hazel seemed to understand my intent, because she simply walked with me, staying by my side.

An hour and a half we have waited in line to get close to her, and by this time I'm only three people away, so naturally my palms begin to get sweaty. I hastily wipe them against my thighs and pull my copy of *Crossing Heartbreak* out of my purse, hugging it to my chest. Another person takes their leave, and my heart starts pounding uncontrollably. I suppose inside I know it is stupid to have such a reaction, but my body is not cooperating. Besides, it would probably be easier to be calm if her hunk of a husband wasn't standing next to her. I'd probably blush while talking to him even if I ran into him in the grocery store or something.

Then, that pretty blonde-haired authoress is standing right in front of me.

"Hi," she tells me with a smile, her happy blue eyes locking directly on mine. My mouth momentarily feels like it's stuffed full of cotton.

"Hi," I manage to force out, holding the book out a bit. "I loved your book. Really, really loved it. I even broke up with a guy because he told me it was 'just okay.'"

"That is some hardcore book love," she states, offering up a soft laugh. She's wearing black suede platform heels, so she looks down at me a bit even though I suspect I am actually just a smidge taller than her.

"Oh, I do love it, trust me," I reiterate. "I even convinced Josh to read it, just because I went on and on about Robert and Willa's love story."

"They have a great story," she adds, pausing a second. "What's your name?"

"Maddie," I answer quickly. "I also loved what you said about your mom. I have a mom, too. I mean, of course I have a mom. What I meant to say was that my mom can be sort of annoying. She's not speaking to me right now. The last time I saw her... Well, I've been jogging, so I lost a little weight, and she asked me if I had an eating disorder. Just a little while later, this kid at her picnic was doing all these gross things with his food, and I wound up throwing up. Of course now she's convinced that I actually *do* have an eating disorder. She tried to have an intervention."

"That sounds like something you would do," the stunning husband laughs, smiling over at her. I'm really glad he didn't smile at me, because I might have died. Seriously.

"Of course, because everything goofy sounds like something I would do," Camdyn adds with an eye roll for my benefit. Instantaneously I am completely convinced that we would be best friends in the right circumstances. Because of course she wants someone in her life who will not be able to talk properly when she's nearby. I am such an idiot.

"Thank you," I mutter as she hands me the book. Now that I'm close to her, her blazer is a cream color instead of the light pink it looked on the screen, and her ratty black Poison T-shirt has a tiny hole near the bottom of the seam. Having heard the story of the T-shirt earlier, though, I know she wouldn't care.

"Thank you for coming," she tells me, and then she reaches out and gives me a hug. Me. Maddie Heard. I am in the middle of convincing myself not to hyperventilate when she whispers something in my ear. "Work it out with your mother."

Her blonde curls are brushing against the side of my face, and as I lean back she gives me a quick wink before she turns to focus her attention on the next person. I sweep my eyes over her husband's face as I turn, but naturally he's looking at his beautiful wife and isn't concerned about her crazed uber-fan. Sighing to myself, I head over to where Hazel is waiting.

"It went well?" Hazel wants to know.

"She's so great," I say, grinning from ear to ear. "She signed my book and talked to me about my mom and even gave me a hug. I can't wait to tell Josh thank you again."

"Well, let me see your book," Hazel requests, and I hand it to her gladly. She pauses in our pursuit of the exit and stands in the aisle, looking down at the signature. "Did you ask her to write that?"

"Write what?" I want to know. She hands the book back to me, and I glance down at the title page.

To Maddie and Josh, for connecting with a great love story.

I don't need a mirror to tell me that my face is turning red, because the heat in the room just went up by about fifty degrees. Hazel's going to think I was standing up there blubbering about Josh, and then she'll naturally assume that I have a thing for her son. She's going to be planning our wedding in her mind, and then she'll say something to Josh about my undying devotion to him.

Ugh, I can see it now! She'll ask him when we're getting married, and he'll say, "*You can't be serious! Me and Mad? Mom, come on, she's like an extra bratty sister.*"

And then he'll call Jess and they'll laugh about the prospect of their mother thinking he would honestly be interested in me—goofy Mad. The next time he calls me it's going to be so weird, because he'll think I have feelings for him, and how do I tell him that I don't when I'm not supposed to know that he knows? Because Hazel won't have said anything to me, only to Josh.

This is a catastrophe. A full-blown, four-alarm, extra Maddie-sized catastrophe.

No, scratch that. This isn't my fault. Camdyn just stood up there for a couple hours explaining how she always makes messes of things, getting herself lost, running into stuff, stumbling around, finding herself locked in weird places. Well, look what she's done! It's all completely, utterly true.

This day will forever live in infamy as the day I met one of the really great storytellers, Camdyn Taylor, who consequently proceeded to destroy one of my life's greatest friendships.

Chapter Nineteen

It's B-day. Bloodfest, that is. The show begins at 10:00 a.m. I thought for a little while about wearing a costume, but I decided to look corporate today. Probably a better move for the old résumé in the long run. Besides, I'll just leave the costumes for the characters in my little drama.

Ha, ha, ha.

Okay, that was my best Dracula laugh, but it was really weak. So I'm not sinister—that's a good thing, right?

All the planning has gone wonderfully, despite the fact that I had to deal with Audrey the entire time. She has been much easier to work with, although she's fairly clueless and not much help. In fact, most of the time she just sits around and watches me work. She's almost like a little lost puppy dog, following me around all the time. She even wants us to go to lunch together every day. Some days I bring something from home, and others I try to come up with an excuse, but I have had to take her out several times. Cooper doesn't mind if we come back late or even if we're gone for hours. I think he wants the two of us to become friends, although I'm not sure why. Most days I wish he would find something else for her to do so I could have some peace. As it is, the only time I have alone is Tuesday tennis lessons, and I'm sure it will only be a matter of time before she manages to infiltrate those, too.

I'm not going to worry about Audrey right now, though. I'm sure she'll locate me soon enough. I've been maneuvering in and out of all the booths in the center of the excitement, making sure things are going smoothly. So far, so good. The blood-letters are already here, apparently ready to go into full swing the minute the clock strikes 10:00. At least, that's what their director assured me. I told her several times that the timing was imperative, since I would have media people here for the beginning of the day. It's funny, but any time I've mentioned the media, people have voluntarily cooperated with whatever I've asked. That seems like a good card to keep up my sleeve in the future.

The games are already here for the kids, too, including a large blow-up bounce house with a few slides set up in one area. We also have a magician, a puppet show, and a few carnival games, and everyone donated their time to the event. People find it difficult to say no to a good cause, I found, which is also good to keep in mind for the future.

The food smells delicious, and if I wasn't watching what I eat, I would be very tempted. There are freshly baked cookies from the bakery down the street, and a neighboring coffeehouse has their cappuccino-maker set up and ready to serve. We've also got food from a pizzeria, a delicatessen, and an oriental restaurant. Plus, I've convinced some of the employees at Cooper Corporate Financial to grill hamburgers and hot dogs. The best part is, it's all free in an attempt to get people to donate blood. Truly a win-win situation, if I do say so myself. I'm quite proud that I came up with the idea.

I've got to admit—even though this started out simply as a way to get back at Cooper, it has really turned into an amazing thing. Imagine, one little idea leading to this huge event that is eventually going to help so many in our community. Who would have thought that I, the humble Madeline Heard, could ever coordinate this type of massive effort? I have surprised even myself.

The lead-up to this day has been a month of anxious anticipation. Some of the details required a lot of convincing, but in the end everything went exactly as I hoped. Cooper won't even know what hit him until it's too late. He has no idea that he will be the first donor of the day. I've already told the people taking the blood, and the media has wind of it, but I'm waiting to spring it on the man himself until the last minute. He'll be here for the start of the blood drive, and the cameras will be in the vicinity, and when we announce that he will be the first donor, there's no way he'll be able to back out. No thinking about it in advance, no trying to come up with an excuse. He'll be stuck, and he will have to agree to go under the needle.

Thinking about who will be taking his blood sort of makes me want to giggle like a schoolgirl. Of course I told everyone we needed a rather large gentleman for the first draw of the day, because it was important that he be in character for the media coverage. Naturally, I was only too happy to suggest an individual that I believed I had seen in the lab on occasion—a rather burly, tall fellow who, if I was not mistaken, until recently worked at a video game store. They knew just to whom I was referring, and he agreed to my requests.

Just imagine when Cooper sits down to have his blood drawn, already a little jumpy simply because of the process itself, when suddenly there appears an enormous version of Frankenstein equipped with a needle and one of those stretchy rubber arm bands. That should make his artificial tan skin turn white! Plus, there is the added bonus that the lab giant will make Cooper look like a shrimp, which will absolutely drive him crazy, since he is so overly fond of looking down at people from his throne.

If that isn't enough, I also got the lab giant (who answers to his last name, Luca, by the way) to agree to recite a little script, simply for effect. Nothing too fancy, just enough to put Cooper a little off guard, so he won't know what to say. In the end, when Luca is finished with him, the Bride of Frankenstein will appear to ask him if he wants a cookie. It's going to be simply beautiful!

I plan on donating myself, later in the day and definitely not with Luca. I still remember what he did to my arm the last time. Ouch!

"There you are, Maddie!" I hear Audrey call my name from across the street.

Admittedly, I'm slightly annoyed that she found me, but nothing is going to ruin my day.

"Hey, Audrey," I respond. She is wearing pants that look a little like scrubs and an oversized sweatshirt. She clearly thought the blood drive was an opportunity to dress down. Trotting across

the street, she pulls up right beside me with a grin on her face. Returning her smile briefly, I begin going through a checklist I made up earlier this morning.

"This is really something," she says, popping her gum.

"Yeah, it turned out well, didn't it?" I ask, not bothering to look up from my checklist.

"Too bad Dad isn't going to see it. He doesn't know what he's missing."

Jerking my head up, I gawk at Audrey, who is carelessly blowing a big pink bubble with her gum and gazing off at the food stands.

"What do you mean, he's not going to see it?" I question her as my stomach drops a few inches. She simply shrugs her shoulders.

"He told me something came up this morning." Audrey casually looks around her at the scenery, unaware of the shattering blow she just threw my way.

"What came up?" I prod, fighting the scream rising in my throat.

"I don't know, just something."

Whipping my phone out of my pocket, I begin frantically dialing. This can't be—absolutely can't be. Cooper has to be here. If he is somewhere else, he simply needs to make his way here right this instant. The whole thing completely hinges on him. If he doesn't show, there is no...show.

"Kent Cooper," I hear through static on the other end of the line.

"It's Maddie. Audrey said something about you not coming to the blood drive," I begin, but the static cuts me off. "Mr. Cooper?"

I hear nothing.

No, no, no, no. Say something, Cooper. It's just a misunderstanding, right?

"Maddie, I'm losing you...I'll have...call back...minute."

And then my phone goes dead.

Okay, I'm not going to lose my cool. The crowd is arriving, but I'm going to stay calm. Cooper called me back, and once I explained that he was going to be an integral part of the media coverage, he assured me he would try to make it.

Try to make it. As if that's even remotely adequate.

Like I said, I'm not going to lose my head over this. So what if it's 9:45 and there's still no sign of him? I'm sure he'll be here any minute. He's probably here now, in fact, and there are simply too many people to catch a glimpse of him. Yes, I'm sure that's it.

Grabbing my cell phone out of my pocket, I dial the numbers, attempting to walk casually while doing so. Wouldn't want anyone to think I was becoming frantic, after all.

Come on, Cooper! Pick up the phone!

Luca looks great in his Frankenstein costume. I saw him a few moments ago, and he looks amazingly spooky, being such a big guy and all. The look on Cooper's face when he sees him will be priceless.

Pick up, Cooper. Pick up!!

I sent Audrey out to look for her dad, and Dina's keeping an eye out, too. They'll probably both be headed back soon, though, given the fact that it's almost 10:00. I'd go try to find him myself if I didn't have to oversee the beginning of the event. Of all days to split on me, why did Cooper have to choose this one?

A few seconds are spent staring at the phone, wishing it could save me from the possibility of a Cooper no-show. I promised that he would be here. What if the media turn on me like a pack of hyenas? What if I become a laughingstock and no one comes to the blood drive, and the entire city starts talking about what a fool I was to try to plan such a big event? Everywhere I go, people will say, "*Look, there's Maddie Heard. Remember, she's the one who botched that great idea for a community-wide blood drive?*"

"Can't find him," Audrey calls from behind me. The fact that she has managed to find an ice cream cone while on her hunt for dear old dad does not escape me, nor does the fact that it is already half-eaten. Apparently "look for dad" sounds more like "find a snack" to Audrey.

My phone begins vibrating, and I whip it out of my pocket anxiously.

"Hello?"

"Still no sign of him," Dina states, "but I'll keep watching."

I'm not going to freak out. This is not the end of the world. There are worse things that could happen.

Although I currently can't imagine anything worse than Cooper irresponsibility skipping out on my big day and ruining the entire event. Or anything worse than Cooper possibly removing any chance I have at a future career, past the obviously perfect job of tennis playing assistant. Once the word gets out, I will be completely undesirable as an employee. What will I do for the rest of my life?

Cooper!

He has officially earned his own spot in the clenched fist hall of fame, right alongside Brittany and Newman.

"Maybe now is the time to come up with a backup plan," Audrey states through a mouth full of ice cream.

She's right, of course. Why don't I have a backup plan? Why didn't I think ahead and at least consider the possibility that Cooper might be a no-show?

I wonder if anyone would notice if I sat down right in the middle of the street and cried.

Chapter Twenty

"It's that time, Ms. Heard," a guy with a camera tells me. He's standing fairly close to Harley Laine, the reporter from Channel Six. The media turned out in full force.

Perfect.

I've decided that I'm going to be honest, and if they bury me right here in the street, then so be it. It's 10:00 and still no Cooper, so what else can I do?

Maybe I can ask them to be patient and wait a little while. It has to be worth a try.

"Excuse me," I begin, but no one pays any attention. "Excuse me!" I try again with a louder voice, causing people to stop and look in my direction. "I'm afraid we have a bit of a delay. Kent Cooper is running late and isn't here presently. If we could postpone the interviews for a little while, that would—"

"We can't postpone anything," Harley pipes up. "We're on a tight schedule here."

"I'm sure he'll only be a few more minutes. Surely mere minutes wouldn't—"

"Get somebody else then," Harley suggests, brushing her waving dark locks away from her face. "Just make it snappy." Beautiful Wonder Lane neighbor news reporter. She looks perfect at close proximity, too, which is beyond annoying.

"Well, let me think for a minute, and I'll try to come up with someone," I suggest, scanning the crowd. Maybe another executive would work, if I can locate one nearby.

"Maddie's the project coordinator!" Audrey shouts. "She should do the interview."

Audrey is beaming as though she thinks she did me a favor, and I really wish she would just go hide under a rock or something.

"That's a great idea," Harley agrees. "People would rather watch you than Kent Cooper, anyway."

I can't really express what I'm thinking at the moment, other than the fact that I don't want to be on television and I am definitely not a public speaker. This is going to ruin everything.

Harley ushers me towards the front of the crowd, and I'm propelled by a sense of the entire experience being out of my control. She could try to push me off a cliff, and I might actually simply walk off the edge.

Just a few words, if I have to, and then I'll manage to slink away. Climbing up on the makeshift podium, I scan the crowd, hoping to catch a glimpse of Cooper coming to the rescue. Rather than Cooper, I see what seem to be a million faces staring back at me, waiting patiently.

"Good morning," I say into the microphone, which lets out a high-pitched squeal. Backing away for a moment, I hesitantly begin again. "Good morning. Welcome to the Cooper Corporate Financial Halloween Bloodfest, a community-wide blood drive. First of all, I'd like to thank all the companies who have co-sponsored this event. Your heartfelt commitment to the community is evidenced by your presence here today."

Taking a short pause for the sporadic claps going through the crowd, I try to settle my nerves. That cameraman is pointing his big flashing red light directly at me. For a split second, I worry that I might throw up. (Wouldn't Mom love that? In front of the whole city on television, no less.)

"The object of this event is to provide a service to the community. I want to thank everyone who came out to donate today, and I hope you'll encourage others to come out as well. Tell your neighbors and your friends, your coworkers, and people you just met on the street, because we'd like to make this a banner day for our life-saving friends here and the people of this city." Forcing a deep breath, I focus on a tree a few hundred yards in front of me, trying not to faint. "As you can see, we have games for the kids and the young at heart, as well as a wide variety of food and drinks. You are more than welcome to partake of all these things completely free. Once again, thank you so much for your presence, and I hope we can make this event a success."

Stepping down from the platform, I'm aware only of the fact that I'm anxious to get away from the spotlight. My stomach feels funny and my legs feel like they're about to give out. Seeing a break in the crowd, I begin to bolt towards the back.

"Okay, just a few words, if we may," Harley states, suddenly in front of me. "Your name, please?"

"Madeline Heard," I blurt, slightly frightened of her. She certainly doesn't seem this pushy on television. Maybe I should tell her I don't feel well and ask her to speak for me instead, but I don't think she's going to give me the opportunity.

"We are speaking with Madeline Heard, project coordinator for the Cooper Corporate Financial Halloween Bloodfest. Tell me, Madeline, why is Cooper Corporate Financial hosting this event?" She places one arm across her stomach and holds the microphone out in front of me expectantly.

Deep breath—sound professional and speak clearly. Surely I can do at least that much.

"Cooper Corporate Financial was looking for a way to support the community that supports them, and we thought there would be no better way than to make a contribution to the health and wellbeing of the community's citizens."

"Why Halloween?"

Oh, come on, Barbara Walters! It's a blood drive. Just take some pictures of people donating blood and leave me alone!

"That's a valid question," I lie with a chuckle. "We were hoping to entice people with the idea that this is a fun event for adults and children alike, and a Halloween theme played into that nicely."

"It must have been a tremendous undertaking, coordinating such an event," Harley states, pushing the microphone in front of me yet again. I would agree, but complaining about hard work on the evening news doesn't sound like a great idea.

"If we can help change one life with what we're doing here today, then it's worth any amount of effort," I state with a smile.

"For those at home, what would you like to tell them about this event?"

"I would say, what are you waiting for? We're having a blast out here, and we sincerely hope you'll join us. Free games, free food…what's not to like? Show your support for your community, your neighbors, and a worthy cause. We'll be here until 6:00 this evening."

"Thank you," she adds, turning to her left and facing the camera. "Harley Laine reporting from Cooper Corporate Financial with a great opportunity to support your community and your fellow citizens."

Harley hands the microphone to her cameraman and offers me her hand.

"Nicely done," she offers. "Kent Cooper would do well to make you the new spokesperson for the company, instead of those old bald guys he usually uses. Might give the company a friendlier image. Next time I'm called here to report on something, I think I'll just ask for you."

"Thank you," I mumble, "but I actually don't—"

"Come on, let's get rolling!" she shouts to her cameraman, swinging open the door to the Channel Six van.

"Hey, not so fast, we have to get the shots of the first donor," the cameraman states. "I've got orders."

"Oh, very well," Harley grunts, looking in the rear view mirror and smoothing her hair. "Just make it snappy. I want to be back at the studio in time to redo my hair before we go live. This wind is absolutely horrible."

She steps away from the van, practically perfect and with her hair looking very much in place as she stalks over to the blood drawing station and waits at the steps.

"Where's the first donor?" she calls. The cameraman looks at me expectantly, and I shake my head.

"It was supposed to be Kent Cooper, but since he's a no-show, just take the first person in line."

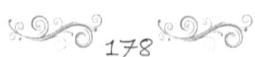

"Send Madeline up here," Harley declares. "She's the company spokesperson. Besides, I have a feeling the camera likes her. She should be the first one."

No, not the first one. Second or third or fourth or two-hundred fifty-sixth, but not the first!

"All these people have been waiting," I suggest. "Just let them go ahead and go in."

"That doesn't make sense," she complains, marching over to grab my arm. "You're the project coordinator, as well as the face of Cooper Corporate Financial, so you should go first. When you're finished, you'll be able to coordinate, or whatever it is you do, for the rest of the day."

Glancing back, I search for a friendly face, but the only person I recognize close by is Audrey, who is waving and grinning from ear to ear. I should make her be the guinea pig and face Frankenstein. If it can't be Cooper, it would at least be a member of his immediate family. I'm fairly certain, however, that Harley would not think the camera loves Audrey in her scrubs and ice cream-stained sweatshirt. That girl never seems to stay clean.

Before I know it, I am being ushered into the hot seat. It's a picture perfect photo op, and the newspaper photographers are standing by, ready to grab the first moments. Outwardly I try to appear cheerful, though I'm inwardly cringing. I know who is preparing to come around that corner, in his Frankenstein suit with his big needle, and it doesn't seem so funny anymore.

Within a matter of seconds, Luca emerges looking every bit Frankenstein, with the bolts coming out of his neck and his enormous shoes. He gives me a wide-open gaze to express surprise at my presence in the chair rather than Cooper, but then shrugs his shoulders and straightens to his full stature. He lurches slowly toward my chair, not bending his legs at all as his arms are outstretched in front of him. Apparently he is determined to take his role seriously.

"Are you scared?" he asks in a deep voice.

Drat. I forgot about the script. Maybe he didn't memorize the entire thing.

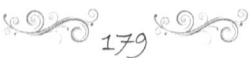

"No," I protest with a slight forced laugh, conscious of the cameras focusing on me.

Of course I'm scared, you big ogre. I remember what you did to me last time, jamming the needle back and forth like you were sewing a sweater.

"Well, you should be," he growls, bending down to tie the rubber around my arm. I'm vaguely cognizant of a camera flash behind him, and I lean close to his ear to get his attention.

"Luca," I whisper, "forget the script."

"Really?" he wonders softly, staring at my eyes. "But I memorized it and everything."

"And I appreciate that, I really do, but it's not necessary anymore."

"You told me this would happen," he adds with a hint of a smile, as though a light bulb is going off in his head.

Um, yeah, technically true. I told him that Cooper might protest, but I am decidedly not Cooper.

"Do not worry, lady. I have never killed a mortal before lunch time."

Panic. Total panic. Think fast.

"Foul creature, I shall not permit you to maim me. I demand that you return from whence you came and locate a more genteel monster."

"Nice ad lib," he whispers, glancing behind him. I'm ever cognizant of the fact that there are cameras on me, and as I shift slightly in my seat to see if they're filming, my rump slides a little too close to the edge of the chair.

Oomph—the sound of my deflating ego as my backside hits the floor and I rest there, propped up on my elbows as I stare at the giant green man in front of me with the bolts protruding from his neck.

"You should not try to flee," he says mechanically in a monotone. Like a scene from my own mental horror movie, he bends down to retrieve me.

"I refuse to allow you to lay a hand on me, you grotesque beast." Obviously not catching my drift, he slides his arm underneath my knees and hoists me into the air as though I'm a child. "Unhand me at once, vulgar brute."

"Me no leave until have blood. Dracula's orders." Lowering me into the chair, he slaps the rubber band around my arm and begins poking around for a vein. I'm having nightmarish flashbacks, but he strangely seems pleased with himself.

Please, God, don't let me flinch in front of all these people. Or faint. Or drop dead.

"Any advice on preparing to donate blood, Madeline?" someone calls from the back. A newspaper person, I imagine, since Harley is standing so close to me.

"Not much preparation needed," I answer. "It's relatively painless."

Luca jabs the needle into my arm without giving me a warning, and I fight the urge to jump back. A burning sensation rips up my arm, like a raging forest fire headed straight for my face.

It's okay, Maddie, just remain calm. It will all be over in a minute, and life will go on as usual. Surely I can put up with a little pain for a good cause. Besides, with all these people watching, I have to make this look as though it's the best experience I've ever had. I certainly don't want to dissuade all these blurry, faceless people from giving blood today.

"How long does it take to donate blood?" someone else calls as Luca digs around under my flesh looking for a vein. I unclench my teeth only long enough to respond.

"That sounds like a good question for my friend Luca," I reply, trying to erase the fuzziness from my brain as he pokes around under my skin. It occurs to me seconds too late that distracting him with answering a question while he's trying to find my vein might not be the smartest thing I've ever done.

Ouch! Oh, Luca, why do you despise me so? Can't you do one simple blood draw without turning my arm into ground beef?

And Cooper, where are you? This was supposed to be you in here, not me. It's like you can't seem to avoid making my life miserable!

Turning, I force a smile at the multiple cameras, hoping they don't manage to catch me grimacing or squinting. That wouldn't be a pretty image to represent this event, which I've been promoting as happy and fun. Instead of kids playing games and people enjoying a free lunch, there's a photo of a grown woman crying.

Luca finally manages to get the needle maneuvered correctly and blood starts to fill the bag. I manage to take a deep breath, knowing that I can relax for a moment without worrying about him stabbing at me any longer. Some of the newspaper people express an interest in taking a picture of us together. Luca seems eager to fulfill the request—apparently he likes the attention. He kneels down next to me as I smile toward the cameras.

"No," a man with one of the larger cameras complains, "I want to get one of Frankenstein leaning over her, with her looking frightened. It is Halloween, after all."

A couple of the other camera wielders express their agreement. Luca leans down over me and stares somberly into my eyes while I bring my hand over my mouth in mock fright. Well, mock fright at this point. If they had captured me a moment before it would have been hellish and all-to-real.

Seriously, how did I get roped into this ignorance? I can only imagine the captions under that picture in the paper tomorrow: *Blood Drive Turns Into a Fright Fest. Woman Faints After Frankenstein Takes Her Blood.*

"I think we have what we need," Harley states to her cameraman. The red light on his camera blinks off and he pulls it down to his shoulder. Several of the other onlookers prepare to head to the door.

"Thanks for coming, everyone," I offer. A few smiles and nods are passed in my direction, while Harley leads her processional back out into the sunshine. Just like that, the frenzy is over as quickly as it began, and I'm a little relieved. Now I can sit here and try to be calm instead of faking happiness at the prospect of becoming a blood drive voodoo doll.

Other volunteers begin spilling into the room, and I notice Audrey among them, rolling up the sleeve of her stained sweatshirt.

She waves eagerly as she catches my eye. Of all the people who could have wanted me to be their friend, what are the odds that I would wind up with Cooper's daughter as my eternal shadow? Sure, I feel sorry for her—it's hard not to sometimes. She must not have very many friends at all, the way she chases after me like I'm going to get away from her. I sometimes wonder if she behaves that way toward her fiancé as well.

"You doing okay?" Luca asks, apparently finished with his ridiculous role-playing. He pats me on the shoulder and heads off to mutilate someone else. Unleashing Luca on the community was not exactly a service, was it? I try not to watch the blood dripping into the bag while I order my stomach to remain calm.

What I should do is force myself to relax and try to enjoy the day. Instead of being cooped up in the office with Audrey, I get to spend all my time outside in the sun, meeting people and watching kids play. I can sample some of the cuisine and have some cappuccino. Best of all, I can avoid Cooper, his stupid doorbell, and his nutty requests.

Will you take these shoes over to have them shined?

Will you go to the supermarket and get me some fresh shrimp?

Will you go to the coffee shop and have them grind some of those dark roast Colombian beans for me?

Last week, the man even asked me to take his teeth to the dentist. I know that sounds like a joke, but I am definitely not kidding. He said his teeth needed to be adjusted. I didn't even know the man wore false teeth until that moment, when suddenly he thrust out the little plastic case and said those dreadful words. Never in a million years would I have imagined myself holding a grown man's chompers in my hands, yet the situation arose and I sadly could not refuse. I never took my eye off that case on the way to the dentist's office, almost afraid the teeth were going to jump out and start nibbling at me. I even wrapped the case in several paper towels before I took it into the dentist's office, and before I left I must have washed my hands about a hundred times. That still didn't stop me from dry heaving every time I thought about the chore.

It would seem to me that a man who cared that much about his appearance would be a little hesitant to hand someone his teeth. Honestly, is he really *that* busy, that he can't make one simple trip to the dentist on his own?

Luca returns and checks the tube going from the needle, picking up the bag and looking at it.

"Guess you're finished," he states, pulling out some cotton and a bandage. "Too bad we didn't get to use the entire script. I thought it was great."

"Thank you," I mutter.

"I bet those camera people would have really eaten it up, too."

"Probably."

"Maybe I should use it on some of the people who come in here throughout the day," he suggests, pressing his big fingers down over the bandage to hold it firmly in place.

"Just don't scare people too much. We wouldn't want to send everyone running for the hills."

"Don't worry, I won't," he says in his spookiest voice, using his eyes to drill a hole in my skull. "Have a nice day."

I'm about to stand up when the Bride of Frankenstein walks to the foot of my chair, holding out a tray. "You look a little woozy," she states solemnly. "Perhaps you would like a cookie."

I suppose one cookie won't hurt. I can't believe how long it's been since I had a cookie, actually. A couple months, I'm guessing. Mistakenly believing she was just reciting her lines about being woozy, I stand and immediately have to settle myself back in the chair.

"Maddie?" a male voice above me swims to my left.

"Isha nom…" I try, blinking slowly. "Ert?"

Apparently I have more than earned a cookie today. Waking up on the floor of a bloodmobile with Frankenstein and his wife hovering over me is not likely to make it onto the highlight reel of my life. To make matters worse, as I was flat on the floor being nursed back to my senses by that duo, the man of the hour decided to show up and laughed heartily at my discomfort through those shiny white fake teeth. Afterwards, he commented about how well things seemed to be going, grabbed something to eat, and disappeared. He didn't even bother to donate any blood.

To be clear, I never expected him to do so on his own, that's why I prepared the ambush. Of course the story of my life would dictate that I actually ambushed myself. I should have known better, really. Has anything ever gone the way I planned?

Nevertheless, I was able to hone up on my public speaking abilities and appeared on the Channel 6 news. Not bad for one day's work.

Audrey followed me out of the bloodmobile like a groundhog chasing a shadow, but after a couple hours I was finally able to ditch her. Her dad called a little while ago and asked her to run an errand. She wanted me to go with her, of course, but Cooper told her I was too busy. The first good thing Cooper has ever done for me, giving me a little extra time to enjoy myself today. He certainly didn't do it intentionally, though.

There were also the tree frogs, which I like tremendously, but those were just some kind of weird bribe. And I guess in truth he was responsible for introducing me to that delightful hunk Max...

Okay, I reluctantly admit that knowing Cooper has had a couple slight perks.

We've had a steady stream of people all day, which indicates to me that the event has been a success. We'll have a meeting after the event to find out the results, but having a large crowd is certainly a positive sign. As for me, I've been a jack of all trades. I assisted the magician for a while and helped grill some hamburgers early in the afternoon. There were a couple slight incidents to deal with, but none of them turned into full-blown problems. All in all, I would say I've had a fun afternoon.

Right now, I'm volunteering next to the donor sign-in area, watching people walk by. A few have come in full costume, which has been interesting. One guy was dressed as a giant baby, and two girls came dressed as Little Bo Peep and her sheep. Some of the little kids wore funny headbands with ears or antennae on them.

"Look, Mommy," a little girl sporting brown pigtails says, pointing up at me. "It's the lady from TV."

"Yes, it is," her mom agrees with a smile, heading into the donor area. The little girl chances another peek over her shoulder, and I wave.

"Maddie!" I hear someone yell. "Maddie, there you are. I've been looking all over for you!"

Ugh, Mom? What is she doing here?

"Sweetheart, I had no idea you were involved in all this until I saw you on Channel Six today!" she exclaims breathlessly, hair swept back with a tortoiseshell comb and wearing more makeup than usual.

"You broke the silence just to come down and tell me that?" I ask frankly.

She plasters a smile on her face and looks at the people standing nearby. "That's my Maddie, always joking around. Of course I came here to donate. Why else would I have come?"

Why indeed? Isn't that the million dollar question?

"Why didn't you tell me you were in charge of this blood drive they've been advertising in the paper?" she asks, clearly not interested in donating as the line passes her by.

"I might have, Mom, if you would have bothered to speak to me one time in the last month and a half."

"Now, honey, you know that I've been very busy lately, with Marilyn and Jordan coming over fairly often."

It's nearly impossible to keep the scowl off my face. "They're in school, Mom."

"And I've been helping Brittany take care of things after the move and all."

"She's a grown woman. Surely she can take care of herself."

"Then there's your father. He's always wanting me to do things for him, you know."

"Dad?" I ask, letting out a short laugh. "The man who hides in the closet to call me because he doesn't want you to catch him? Give me a break."

"Please don't do that, sweetie," she pleads, grabbing me by the arm, right above where the bandage rests on the cotton ball. "I only came here to do the right thing."

"The right thing for whom?" I wonder, looking earnestly into her face. "The right thing for you?"

For a split second, she looks a bit stunned as she allows her hand to drop off my arm. "The right thing for the community, of course. You said it on TV—for the health and wellbeing of my fellow citizens."

"Well, while you're here, you might as well warn the medical technicians over there about my eating disorder. I'm sure they'll want to know."

"Oh, poo," she states, waving her hand in the air, "that was all just a big misunderstanding. Surely you can see how it must have looked to us, things happening the way they did."

The premise of her silently asking me to forget something she won't even admit doing causes me to fume a bit inside.

"Well, if you're here to donate, you might as well go ahead," I finally say.

"I was so surprised to see you on TV," she says, unmoving as the wind whips her hair sideways behind the comb.

"That makes two of us."

"You spoke so well, and you looked so pretty," she comments, giving me a weak smile.

This is worse than being followed around by Audrey. Does she honestly think I'm buying this act?

"Thank you," I reply, brushing past her. "Listen, I've got to make sure everything is going smoothly. Just go over to that area and sign in, and then they'll tell you what to do."

"I want the same person who helped you earlier!" she exclaims hurriedly, attempting to stop me from walking away. "He looked like he was doing such a good job, I want to make sure I get him, too."

Whirling around, I face her silently for a second, pondering her request. "Just take whoever's available, and it'll be fine."

"No, it won't. I want that Frankenstein fellow, the one that you had."

Yikes, Mom, you have no idea what you're asking.

"You know, someone else in there could probably do a better job," I press, trying to dissuade her. "Are you absolutely sure you want Frankenstein?"

"Of course I'm sure," she states, standing defiantly in front of me like a child bent on having her way regardless of the cost.

Alright, but just remember that I'm following your wishes.

"In that case, when you get inside, just ask for Luca."

"You're sure they'll listen to me?" she wonders, grabbing my arm again.

Without bothering to answer, I walk up the steps and poke my head inside. "Hey, Luca," I call, and he looks up. "This is my mom. I want you to take good care of her, okay?"

I only feel like a bad person for about half a second as he looks at my mom and gives her a wink. "You betcha."

Chapter Twenty-One

A beautiful, crisp Sunday morning, and the Gardwins aren't at church today. That means no pulled hair, no stuck-out tongues, and no getting kicked beneath the pew. Oh, and no worrying about that Billy Gardwin putting his gum on me. He acted like he was going to do it last week, but his dad finally caught his eye and gave him a pretty stern warning look.

Without having to worry about those Gardwins, I'm free to concentrate on Reverend Shell's sermon, but I'm also tracing the pattern of the carpet with my eyes. Sometimes I feel a little strange when I watch him preach, because he looks out at the crowd when he says something and I feel as though he's directing his comments specifically to me. He probably isn't because he doesn't know me very well, but it still makes me uncomfortable. As a defensive measure, each week I find a specific item on which to concentrate. Sometimes it's the wood grain of the pew in front of me, or the way the paint is speckled on the walls. Today it happens to be the pattern of the carpet.

"Maybe God allows us to have enemies not because He wants us to hate, but because He's teaching us to love." Meh, that doesn't really make sense, Reverend Shell. Nice try. "There may be someone in your life right now who has deliberately tried to hurt you, and you have a hard time forgiving them. Perhaps it's someone who has done something unkind to you, and you have difficulty letting go of your anger. You may have wanted God to do something about your hurt and anger, even if you didn't say the words aloud."

Okay, maybe with an ordinary enemy he might have a point, but not the ones I have. Look at Cooper, for instance. He gives the job I deserve to a total goon and then creates a phony position for me, all because he wants me to help him exact some silly revenge on his brother for being better at tennis. Or my mom, who won't speak to me for a month and a half and then suddenly shows up just because she saw me on television. What was she doing there, anyway? Did she hope that the cameras might still be there and she might make the evening news simply for being related to me?

"But God doesn't respond to your prayer by doing harm to your enemies or sending you weapons to use against them. He responds to your prayer by giving you situations in which to love them."

Um, bleh? Love Cooper? I don't think so.

"If you ask God to help you rid yourself of an enemy, do you really expect Him to send an angel along to smite them?"

Maybe not smite them exactly, but a good scare might be helpful.

"Wouldn't it be more characteristic of God to help you rid yourself of an enemy by making it possible for them to become your friend?"

I totally see where he's going with this. Too bad Cooper and my mom can't be here to hear it. Or even those Gardwins, in fact. They could have used this information.

Reverend Shell continues reading some scripture about loving your enemies, blessing those who curse you, and so on and so forth. It really seems unfair that I should be expected to be extra nice to Cooper *because* he is taking advantage of me.

"Once again, if you pray that God will help you rid yourself of an enemy, I am here to tell you that God is not going to send you weapons for destruction. He's not going to send you a tailor-made plot for revenge. He's not going to send you a permission slip for the cessation of forgiveness."

Man, why did I stop looking at the carpet? That guy is staring right at me.

"God is going to send you an opportunity to be loving, to be forgiving, to be more like Him. Are you going to step up to the challenge?"

Wow, I wish those eyes would stop boring into me. It's like he's calling me out or something.

"Watch for the opportunity." Okay, he can start looking at someone else now. I get it—keep my eyes open. "Watch for an opportunity."

"Maddie, I was so surprised when I saw you on television the other day," Hazel says. "I wish I had known about it earlier, so I could have recorded it. Are you sure you don't want any pie?"

"No thank you, I'm stuffed. I didn't know I was going to be on the news. It was a last-minute change of plans." I watch as Hazel passes a large slice of chocolate cream pie to Tucker. It does look really good. *Willpower, Maddie.*

"You can't expect your plans to go smoothly when no one knows about them but you," Josh states. Hazel was pretty thrilled that Josh made arrangements to Skype with us during lunch, although it's kind of strange for him to be here remotely. Plus, I'm still feeling a bit leery about the whole "Maddie and Josh" thing in the Camdyn Taylor book. Hazel hasn't brought it up again—to me, at least.

"Well, I did cut your picture out of the paper," Hazel states. "It was so funny, with that big Frankenstein hulking over you. Tucker thought you looked like a frightened little mouse in that chair, didn't you, Tucker?"

Tucker grunts and nods, seemingly determined not to talk with his mouth full.

"Where did you find that big guy to wear that costume, anyway?" Hazel continues. "You couldn't have found a better person."

Instinctively I glance at Josh on that screen, making sure he's not going to make any snide comments. "Actually, I met him at a doctor's appointment. When I was setting things up, I thought of him right away."

"It's so nice that your company is trying to give back to the community," Hazel adds. "Do you have anything else planned in the near future?"

"We're going to be helping with a food drive for the Thanksgiving holiday. It's still in the planning stages, but I got the company's okay to proceed."

"It's so unusual to see a big company like that doing things to help charities." Hazel stands up to begin clearing the table, so I hand her my plate.

"I thought the same thing when Maddie told me she got a raise," Josh teases with a laugh.

Tucker snickers for a second and then clears his throat, glancing over at me.

"Did you hear that, Hazel?" I ask. "Your son thinks I'm a charity case."

She makes a clucking noise in her throat at Josh as she turns to leave the room. It's unusual for the Masons to have a Sunday dinner with no guests—either they are tired of company, or people must have had plans today. Maybe there's something going around, because the church pews seemed a little emptier than usual this morning. I know the two Gardwin boys have the flu, because Hazel told me that earlier.

"So, what did you think of the sermon today?" Hazel presses, sitting back at the table.

"It was okay," I say, watching my words carefully. "I really wish he wouldn't look at me so much, though. It makes me uncomfortable."

"Hmm… I didn't notice him looking in our direction very much this morning."

"Well, he was," I counter, feeling Josh's scrutiny from that lifeless screen. "Every time I looked up he seemed to be staring right at me."

"You know," Hazel says, rising from the table again and heading to the sink, "I've felt that way too, like he's staring at me while he's preaching. Usually, when I look back, I see that those are the times when God is trying to get something through my thick head."

"I always assumed you had a direct line to God, Hazel," I offer jokingly. Somewhat jokingly, anyway. I'm positive her line is a lot more direct than mine.

"Oh, heavens no," she insists with a laugh. "He has to pound things into my head sometimes, and it still takes me a while to accept them. I'm sure He gets tired of my stubbornness."

Hazel stubborn? Those are two words I can't quite place together. Besides, I'm pretty sure God wasn't trying to get anything into my head today. It was only that Reverend Shell trying to bore a hole into my skull with his eyes.

"Maybe you should get Camdyn Taylor to preach the sermons over there, Mom," Josh interjects. "Then Maddie wouldn't mind being stared at."

"Josh, really, I don't know why you're so obsessed with that writer," I complain. "If I didn't know better, I would think you have a crush on her."

"You can act all nonchalant about it, but Mom told me you waited for almost two hours just to get her to sign your book. Was it worth it?"

Fighting the urge to blush, I try to convince myself that he doesn't know what she wrote in that book. It still embarrasses me every time I think about it. "Yes, of course it was worth it. She was really nice. She hugged me and everything. I'm thinking about becoming the de facto president of her fan club."

"That's a pretty big commitment," Josh informs me with a smirk, his forehead getting those two familiar wrinkles as he raises his eyebrows. "It would probably last more than two weeks, so I'm not sure you're the person for the job."

"Very funny," I counter, shaking my head. "I didn't notice anything perceptibly wrong with her, so it shouldn't be a problem."

"Do you think I'm shallow?"

I pose the question to Jess as I'm standing in front of the full-length mirror in my bedroom, gazing at my appearance in my yoga pants and jacket. She called me right after my run, which was absolutely necessary today following Hazel's lunch. Even though I managed to avoid the pie, I still wound up eating a lot more than I have been lately.

"In what aspect?"

"In what aspect? Um, every aspect, I guess. Good grief, the mere fact that you had to quantify it tells me that you think I am."

"Of course not," she answers. "You know I love you, Maddie. Don't put words in my mouth."

"Josh has just been on my case lately about guys, making fun of me for being so particular. Don't I deserve to be particular? Why should I have to settle for someone who isn't right for me? If there's something about the guy that annoys me, shouldn't I have the right to abandon pursuit of a relationship?"

"That's a pretty dumb question," she mutters. "You do have a tendency to find things wrong with every man you meet, though. Even you have to admit that."

"Because they have things wrong with them," I say, staring deeply into my own eyes in my reflection. "And that's not even true. Look at Max. I haven't found anything about him that I don't like yet."

"Have you been on a date with him?"

Nervously, I pick at the waistband of my pants. "I'm still working on it, but eventually we'll get there."

"Then Max doesn't count. As soon as you go out with him, you'll discover something. It's inevitable. You don't really want to fall for anybody."

"That's preposterous," I huff, unzipping my jacket. "Why wouldn't I want to fall for anybody?"

"Because you're in love with Josh."

Heat floods my veins as I toss the jacket on my bed and stand frozen in my place.

"Jess, that's not true."

"Geez, Maddie, I thought you realized it. Iron Man doesn't belong in your pants."

Furrowing my brow, I hesitate for a second.

"Sorry, Iron Man what?"

"Isaiah had Iron Man… Never mind, what were we talking about again?"

"Nothing," I toss out. "Absolutely nothing."

"Right, you not being in love with Josh. If you're worried about my feelings, please don't be. I've had a couple years to reconcile myself to the idea, after all. Quite frankly, I'm getting a little tired of pussyfooting around the issue. You're never going to be happy with any man who's not Josh, and Iron Man never talks about doody—it's not polite."

"Actually, I can totally see Iron Man talking about doody." It's a blatant attempt to change the subject, because I am unbelievably uncomfortable, and I can't believe how totally wrong Jess is about this topic.

"Okay, if you insist," she agrees with a laugh. "Forget I said anything, and you and Max can ride off into the sunset together, and I hope you'll be happy."

"Maybe we will," I tell her confidently.

I don't feel confident, though. In all honesty, I feel anything but. Jess has just thrown the biggest of kinks into our friendship, and I'm not sure how I'm going to look past her beliefs when I speak to her again. Accusing me of wanting to be with her brother is a pretty huge hurdle, isn't it? Even if I was in love with Josh, which I'm not, there's still the obstacle of him looking at me like his sister.

Or, at the very least, his sister's annoying friend who he has to chastise constantly because she can't find a man.

And so what if I can't find a man? I shouldn't have to settle simply because the right one hasn't come along yet. He doesn't have to be perfect, either. I'm not looking for perfection, to be absolutely frank about the matter.

No, truth be told, I'm just looking for a guy like J...

Oh.

Chapter Twenty-Two

Another Monday morning, and I've been here fifteen minutes already without seeing Cooper. I also haven't seen Audrey, which is unusual. She normally pokes her head into the office first thing to begin telling me about her weekend. Maybe this means it will be a good day.

I know, I know, but I can be hopeful, can't I?

The good news is, Cooper was so pleased with the positive publicity we received from the blood drive that he accepted my idea for the food drive with basically no explanation. This one won't take as much effort, either, because we're partnering with a local charity that has already put things in the planning stages. When I contacted them to see if they wanted a corporate partner, they were so excited, I could practically hear them jumping up and down on the other end of the phone.

If the point of all this was simply to make my résumé more enticing, I think I've succeeded. Project coordinator for community-wide blood drive: check. Coordinating partner on Thanksgiving food drive: check. Coupled with my marketing experience and my added expertise in communications, I think I've made myself a very desirable candidate. I guess that's one small blessing that this nightmare with Cooper has unintentionally presented.

Preparing myself is key, because who knows how much longer I have before the day of truth arrives? Or, to state it more succinctly, before Cooper finally challenges his brother to a tennis match. I've become fairly certain over the last month or so that my time as Cooper's assistant will end after that match. If we lose, then Cooper will probably fire me out of anger for not defeating his brother in his revenge plot. If we win, Cooper will no longer have a use for me. That is, assuming his brother isn't silly enough to want rematch after rematch after rematch. In that case, this thing could go on forever.

"Maddie!" I hear Cooper call through the door.

What, no doorbell today? Perhaps things are looking up after all.

Rising from my chair, I walk to the door between our offices. Since it's Monday morning, he likely has a lot of things he thought of over the weekend. Pick up his dry cleaning? Get the tires rotated on his car? Maybe he wants me to return the movie he made me buy Friday afternoon. (Why he wanted a movie about Babe the pig, I will never know.)

I swing the door open and step inside onto the plush blue carpet, surprised to see that Audrey is residing in one of the chairs. She grins widely at me as I shut the door and walk towards the second chair cautiously.

Another babysitting adventure, it would appear.

"Maddie," Cooper begins, "Audrey and I were discussing the blood drive over the weekend, and I just wanted to mention again that you did a fantastic job organizing that whole event."

Not what I expected. Much more pleasant, actually.

"Thank you," I reply quietly.

Audrey is eyeing Cooper expectantly, which is still making me nervous.

"Audrey and I also happened to be discussing another event that is coming up soon, and she was very insistent that I consider you as the event planner." In response, Audrey leans toward me from her chair and claps a few times very softly, smiling like she's practicing for a toothpaste ad. "Now, the planning could be slightly difficult because of the time frame. What is the date again, Audrey?"

"February 24th."

"Yes, February 24th. So you can see that gives us only about three months to plan, which is not a very significant amount of time when you're insistent that only the best will do. Of course that is one of Audrey's stipulations, naturally."

What is he talking about? It almost sounds like I'm working for Audrey here, not the other way around.

"You can do it, Maddie. It's going to be great, I just know it!" Audrey is practically beaming at me, which scares me out of my wits.

"I'm sorry," I pipe up, "but I guess I'm not sure what you're talking about."

Audrey giggles as though I just blurted the silliest thing in the world. "My wedding, of course. I want you to plan my wedding, and Dad has agreed."

Maddie Heard, wedding planner? No good can come of this.

"Wouldn't you rather have someone in your family help you, Audrey?" I ask, turning towards her. She shakes her head rapidly back and forth. "Well, what about someone in your bridal party? Surely one of your friends would be able to help you with this better than I could."

"Who could help me better than my best friend?" Audrey asks with a smile. "Besides, you *are* in my bridal party. You're going to be my maid of honor."

Somehow I manage to remain silent while inwardly I'm imagining my eyes doing that cartoon thing where they fly forward out of my head. Best friend? I believe it's time to admit that this has gotten out of hand.

"Are you certain about this?" I press, posing my question more to Cooper than Audrey. Somebody has to be the voice of reason in this room.

Cooper drums his fingers on his massive desktop and leans back in his oversized chair as Audrey and I look anxiously at him. "Audrey says you're the maid and her best friend, so who better to do the job?"

Perhaps I should have known better than to trust Cooper as the voice of reason.

"But I'm not exactly…" I pause, glancing over at Audrey. How am I supposed to tell Cooper that she's not really my friend when she's gazing at me like that? Besides, what if he thought I had said or done something to cause his daughter to believe she *was* my best friend? Maybe that is a stone best left unturned.

"Of course," I agree with reluctance, exhaling slowly. "If Audrey really wants me to, I will help her with her wedding. I just wonder if hiring a professional wouldn't be more helpful, since this is the biggest and most important day of her life."

"It *is* the biggest and most important day of my life," Audrey repeats, giggling slightly. "That's why you have to do it, Maddie. We can work together on every little detail—the food, the music, the dresses. You have such good taste, and you're always so classy. Dad, you shouldn't make her work on anything else while she's helping with my wedding, so she doesn't get overly stressed out."

"Maybe she's right," Cooper barks. "You can just hand off this charity project you're working on to someone else so you can devote yourself to Audrey full-time. I'm sure Dina can pick up any slack if you run out of time to do things during the day."

That sounds like a death sentence...devote yourself to Audrey full-time. Besides, I'm pretty sure Dina would kill me.

"I'm sure I can keep up with both things, so that won't be necessary."

Cooper looks at me discerningly for a moment and strokes his chin with his thumb and forefinger. "Well, okay, but if Audrey thinks things aren't going as well as she hoped, we'll have to do something about the charity. Audrey comes first for the time being."

Naïve Cooper. He doesn't realize that, to me, Audrey *is* the charity.

I'm already having nightmare visions of myself in pink taffeta with puffy sleeves. We're standing in a side room, where Audrey insisted that I do her hair personally. Of course she had someone else do *my* hair, and I look like I belong to an '80's heavy metal band. I even have a scrunchy holding some of the hair up in the back.

Audrey is crying on my shoulder and staining my dress with a mix of raspberry lip gloss and black mascara. Oh, and cheesy

puffs, because she insisted on the way to the church that we stop to get a snack. Now her fingers are orange and her face is all puffy from the crying, and she doesn't know what she's going to do.

Mrs. Cooper is standing in the corner, looking plastic as usual. Wait a minute…maybe that's a mannequin. No, I saw her blink—definitely Mrs. Cooper.

"Audrey," I say, "you have to snap out of it. Today is your big day."

"Oh, Maddie," she sobs, "you're the best friend I ever had." Then she throws up cheesy puffs in my lap, and of course I throw up too, because of the whole weak stomach issue.

I practically have to drag her into the church, where her dad is waiting for her, but she thinks her dad hates her again, so that sends her into another bout of tears. Being Kent Cooper, he starts berating her in front of the entire crowd for acting like a baby. He probably doesn't mean to be so loud, but as I well know, he only has one volume level.

I finally manage to console her enough that she's ready to walk down the aisle, and I meet up with my escort, who of course is about four feet tall.

"You stink," he says, wrinkling up his nose.

"Thanks a lot."

Oh, dear God, what am I going to do?

"Go ahead, you two," Cooper insists, dragging me to the present conversation, "and have your fun. Maddie, I'll have the bank set up a wedding account and give you all the information later on today. Whatever Audrey wants, make it happen. Within reason, naturally. I don't want puppies running around everywhere or clowns at the reception. You know what a proper wedding should include."

"Okay," I mumble as I stand up to leave the room, sinking a little in the plush carpet. Audrey is clapping her hands in that fast, quiet way again, walking behind me. I wish I could step through the door to my office and slam it behind me—maybe lock her in there with Cooper. Where would I go, though? It's not like I could run away or hide.

"Oh, Maddie," she whispers breathlessly, "I am so excited. We finally set the date over the weekend, and the first thing I thought was that I had to have you plan everything. You're so good at setting things up, and with the way you dress and do your makeup I just know everything is going to be perfect."

"We'll figure something out," I manage to say.

"Who would have thought when Dad made me come to work here that I would find a best friend like you?"

Enough with the best friend business! I am not your best friend, got it? Never have been, never will be.

Audrey plops down in the chair beside my desk and begins tapping her feet on the carpet in a rhythmic pattern, and then begins moving them from side to side slightly, as though she's practicing a dance routine. She blows a bubble with her pink chewing gum, pops it loudly, and then smiles at me.

"So, what do you think?" she wonders. "Are you excited?"

"Yeah, it's great," I reply, rearranging some papers on my desk. When Audrey is nearby, it's like a tornado is in the room. I wouldn't want to lose anything important.

"We should start right away, don't you think?"

"Sure. Why don't you go think about exactly what you want, and then make a list?" That seems harmless enough, and it will get her out of my hair for a little while.

"Don't be silly," she giggles. "I need you to help me—that's why I wanted you to do this. I have no idea how to go about planning a wedding."

"You don't know what colors you want, what type of dress you want, what flavor cake you want? Nothing?"

"If I knew all that, I wouldn't need your help, would I?" She begins humming a little tune, tapping her fingers on the armrests, and I watch her silently for a moment.

She is quite possibly as wacky as her dad—an entire family of nut jobs. From my humble little marketing job, somehow I wound up being the Cooper family servant. Tomorrow Mrs. Cooper will probably call, wanting me to walk her dog or

something. Maybe she'll ask me to come by and clean the house, or to drive her to the mall.

Audrey's still humming and tap, tap, tapping. Her giddiness is driving me a little crazy.

"Okay, this is what I want you to do: You're going to go to your office and start thinking about things you like. What's your favorite color? What's your favorite kind of music? Your favorite food? I want you to start writing those things down so we'll have a place to begin. I can't help you plan anything until I know what you like."

"Favorite things, got it." She stands up and opens the door.

"And don't come back here until you have a list of at least ten things, alright?"

"That seems like a lot of—"

"No less than ten things."

She lets out a deep sigh and her shoulders sink a little. "Okay, ten."

Standing up to shut the door, I watch her back as she crosses the hallway and enters her own office. Dina is peering over her glasses as she raises her eyebrows inquisitively, wondering what's going on.

"Don't ask," I mumble, shaking my head.

It was bound to happen, and the day has finally come: Audrey is accompanying me on my trip to Big Cedar. She brought her list of ten favorite things to me about an hour ago (yes, it actually took her more than one day). I insisted that I would spend some time with her when I got back, but she was adamant that she had wasted too much time on the list and she really needed to talk to me during the tennis lesson. When I informed her that she would have to practice tennis right along with me, I was absolutely certain

that would dissuade her, but she came back a little while later with her gym bag and told me she was ready to go.

That's how we wound up where we are now—with me maneuvering through afternoon traffic and Audrey sitting in the passenger seat, going on and on about how she wants her wedding to be the event of the century. Personally, I think there's no chance of pulling that off, but I'm simply nodding and letting her have her moment. As we pull into the driveway for the club, I glance at the time. We still have fifteen minutes left, and I really don't want to have to introduce her to everyone inside, so maybe it's best if we wait in the Tahoe.

Drawing up to the front of the building, I park the vehicle and stop the engine. Audrey reaches for her bag as I drop the keys into my purse.

"Wait—there's no need to go in yet. It's too early," I explain.

She leans back in her seat and drops her shoulders a bit. "I'm going to look so stupid playing tennis. You've been taking lessons all this time, and I don't know what I'm doing."

"Well, you won't look any sillier than I did the first time I came here. Besides, it's not like people stand around watching you. It's just you and the trainer."

Audrey begins rifling through her bag and pulls out a package of bubble gum. I didn't realize that she had nothing in her mouth, but I should have noticed. The girl constantly has *something* she's chewing on.

"While we're sitting here, I'll look at your list," I offer.

She gladly pulls the pink sheet out of her bag and hands it to me, and it's hard not to notice that she has drawn little hearts at the top and bottom of the paper.

1. Favorite color: Pink, of course. *Naturally.*
2. Favorite music: Rap. *What is your dad going to think about that?*
3. Favorite food: Cheesy puffs. *Obviously someone missed the point of the list.*

4. Favorite drink: Diet cola. *The beverage of choice for every upscale wedding.*
5. Favorite cake: Chocolate. *Finally, something I can use.*
6. Favorite dress: The ones with the big, puffy bottoms. *A possibility, I suppose.*
7. Favorite shoes: Flip flops. *I can already hear her flipping down the aisle.*
8. Favorite book: Harry Potter. *Irrelevant and completely off topic. Are you nuts?*
9. Favorite movie: Harry Potter. *Yes, clearly nuts.*
10. Favorite dog: Cocker Spaniel. *Favorite dog? Seriously, favorite dog? I guess I shouldn't expect less, though, when dogs are her obsession.*

"Okay," I sigh, wrinkling my nose a touch. "At least it's a start."

"You don't like it," she says with a pout. "I can tell by the way you look right now."

When I imagined Cooper's spoiled daughter, I pictured a young woman with too many cars and a different outfit every day—no repeats. I never pictured a whining three-year-old who pouts when she doesn't get her own way. I wonder what Max is going to think of Audrey.

"It's not that I don't like it. It's just not very…wedding related, I guess."

"What do you mean?" she asks, folding her arms across her chest.

"Harry Potter and cocker spaniels? What am I supposed to do with that?"

"You said you wanted a list of my favorite things. Those are my favorite things. I had a hard time coming up with the last few, but you said I had to have ten before you would talk to me about it."

"And these are the ten you came up with?"

"What do you think took me so long? I was trying to think of topics. You try to think up topics on the spot like that. It's not easy."

Sighing, I rest my head against the back of the seat. "So, based on your list, the guests at your wedding are going to show up to a boy wizard greeting them with a cocker spaniel as his sidekick. You will walk down the aisle in a puffy dress with flip flops while carrying pink flowers to a fine selection of rap music. At the reception, your guests will dine on chocolate cake, cheesy puffs, and diet cola."

Audrey just stares silently at me for a moment, her eyes looking slightly confused. Maybe she doesn't understand the point I'm making. I should have simply started planning this whole thing by myself, without even involving her in the fiasco.

Suddenly, she begins giggling. "Well, when you put it that way, it sounds ridiculous, although it would still be better than some weddings I've been to."

Okay, I give up.

"Let's go in," I order, grabbing my bag and opening the door to the Tahoe. She follows suit as I shut the door and use my remote to lock the vehicle. As I walk with her right at my heels, I realize that my occasional shadow is now going to be pretty constant. How long can I possibly stand to spend every waking moment with Audrey Cooper?

"Why don't you go ahead into the locker room and change, and I'll be there in a moment," I suggest, pointing her in the right direction. She looks a little leery of leaving me, but I simply have to warn Max. This isn't the kind of thing you spring on an unsuspecting person, after all.

Walking through the corridor, I glimpse one of the other trainers filling out some paperwork.

"Hi," I call. "Is Max around?"

"Equipment room," he states, not bothering to look up.

"You looking for me?" I hear Max's voice behind me. "What gives? You're not dressed yet."

"I know," I say quietly, turning toward him. He has his hair in a ponytail, so he really does look a little like that dashing pirate, and I nearly forget why I was looking for him in the first place. Other than obvious heart-fluttering reasons. *Oh, Audrey.* "I came out here to warn you."

"About what?" he asks, giving an appealing grin. He doesn't appear overly concerned.

"I've got a guest with me—Audrey Cooper. Kent's daughter."

"Aha," he says, a disappointed look crossing his face.

"I'm sorry, she insisted on coming with me. Since Cooper is paying for the lesson, why don't you go ahead and give her some pointers today, and I'll just practice for a while?"

"If you're sure that's what you want," he says with a shrug of his shoulders.

"Trust me, you're going to want to keep this girl occupied. Besides, maybe you can wear her out so she'll have to go home early."

"I knew there was an ulterior motive," he whispers, looking behind me as though we're being sneaky. "Shall I try to break a leg while we're at it?"

That would be scary if I didn't know he was joking.

"No, not today," I protest with a laugh. "Maybe next time."

"I can't pretend that I'm not a little disappointed," he adds, placing his hand on my arm. My skin shivers a bit, and I freeze in place as I look at his face.

"Why is that?" I manage to squeeze out of my throat.

"I enjoy my time with you, Maddie." He pulls himself close to me, so he can speak directly in my ear, and I can no longer see his face. "If I can't get my Maddie fix today, I'm going to have to get it sometime. Friday night?"

My head nods up and down right before he plants a soft, breathy kiss on my cheek. With a parting smile, he turns and walks back to the equipment room, leaving me feeling breathless and confused behind him.

Max has finally asked me out—which is precisely what I wanted.

It is, isn't it?

Stepping towards the locker room to change clothes, I witness Audrey standing in the middle of the large space, gym bag still over her shoulder.

"What are you doing?" I wonder.

She looks at me quickly as though I startled her. "I can't get changed in here," she whines. "It's all out in the open. What if somebody sees me?"

"Um, just use the restroom?" She looks behind her at the open doors and I can practically see the light bulb going on over her head.

"Oh, okay."

Sure, because it never occurred to her that she could just go in there and shut the door. How does she get dressed in the morning without someone picking out her clothes? Never mind— someone probably does pick out her clothes. I forgot for a second who her dad was.

On second thought, if someone does pick them out, they should be fired, because they do a terrible job every single day.

I'm finished changing when Audrey finally emerges from the restroom wearing loose shorts and a T-shirt. As she begins walking toward me, I hear a distinct sound that I was absolutely not expecting.

Flip flops? She can't be serious. She brought flip flops for a tennis lesson.

"Don't you have any tennis shoes in your bag?"

She looks at me as though I've just asked her for a million dollars. "I don't really like them."

Of course, she doesn't really like them.

"Come on," I tell her with a sigh, "let's go to the pro shop."

"What for?"

"You can't play tennis in flip flops, Audrey, no matter how much you like them. I am not going to be the one to explain to your dad that you broke your leg trying to play tennis in flip flops."

"What's the big deal, anyway? We're just hitting a ball back and forth."

Yeah, naïve girl. You are in for a rude awakening. Max is going to eat you alive.

Max—my Max.

Yeah, totally what I wanted.

Chapter Twenty-Three

Audrey wants to go dress shopping today. Normally you breathe the word "shopping" and I'm there, but spending a whole day trying to please Audrey is the last thing I want to do right now. She has been breathing down my neck ever since Cooper agreed to grant her wishes, and I haven't had a moment's peace. Last night she got my cellphone number somehow, and she called me at 7:00 p.m. to ask if I could help her choose some stationery. I asked her why she needed stationery now, since we haven't ordered the wedding invitations yet. Turns out she just needed it to write some letters and it had absolutely nothing to do with the wedding. After that, caller ID became my best friend.

Yesterday she brought me an armload of bridal magazines that she bought at a bookstore the night before. She had bent back the corners of several pages with dresses that she liked so I could inspect them. Obligingly I began flipping through one of the magazines, and the first folded page contained a very slender woman in a form-fitting dress made of what appeared to be some type of crocheted material. The very bottom of the dress flared out into a bell shape.

"That one would be hard to walk in, let alone dance," I told her, avoiding the obvious objection that it absolutely would not work with her figure. She seemed to accept the explanation, so I began flipping to the next bent page. This one was of a knee-length dress with a pencil skirt on the front and a long train in the back. The first thought that came to mind was '80's rocker chick, which does not exactly mesh with the wedding theme I have planted in my mind.

"This one probably wouldn't match the décor," I explain. "Besides, I thought you wanted a puffy dress." She nodded and seemed okay with my disapproval, so I kept thumbing through the pages. Nearly every picture she marked was of a form-fitting dress, nothing like the "favorite dress" she described to me earlier.

"Which one do you like the most?" I finally asked, hoping that she had just picked some of the dresses as filler. She immediately grabbed up one of the magazines and began flipping until she found the correct page.

"Here—this one."

I looked down to see a picture of a tall, thin blonde in what appeared to be some type of silk or satin. It was very simple, with a modest neckline and one solid piece of fabric from head to toe. It wasn't as clingy as some of the dresses she had shown me, although it was still a little too form-fitting.

"What is it you like about it?" I asked, slightly confused. I never really pegged Audrey as someone who would go with clean, simple lines. Big and gaudy and completely over the top seemed more her style.

"I like the back the most," she stated. The back of the dress was on the following page, so I flipped it over. When I saw that dress—good gracious, I almost choked. There was no back! There were a couple scraps of fabric around the arms to hold the dress up, and the rest was…well, nonexistent. The front of the dress wrapped around to a V-shape exactly where it needed to in the back, barely covering the model's behind, and then followed to a short train.

"What do you like about it?" I attempted to clarify, immediately dreading the impending answer.

"The butterflies," was her simple reply. It was only after she mentioned it that I realized there were embroidered butterflies that floated across the V and all the way to the floor.

"Yeah, those are pretty," I agreed.

She sat down in the chair next to my desk and folded her arms across her chest, tears springing to her eyes. "It doesn't matter, anyway. None of those dresses cures ugly."

"I'm sure we'll find a lovely dress, Audrey," I assured her, attempting to be soothing. *The girl has more meltdowns than an ice cream parlor on a hot summer day.*

"I'm not worried about the dress," she cried, a tear sliding down her cheek. "It's me—I'm ugly."

Observing her quietly for a moment, I surmised that her eyes and nose were noticeably red under her two-tone hair—an effect that was not improved by the excessive blush. *What that girl needs is an attentive mother to help her with these kinds of issues, really. I'm not a therapist.*

"You're not ugly," I told her, really hoping that would resolve the problem.

"Yes, I am," she insisted with a sniff. "Besides, no one cares about me."

So we're back to this again. It seems like I have to put out this fire once a week at least.

"That's just silly. Your dad must care about you a great deal to go through all this time and expense to give you exactly what you want on your big day."

My expectation was that she would calm down as she normally did, but instead she began to sob. "Throwing money at someone doesn't mean you love them."

Of course she was right, so how was I to argue with that?

"Well, what about your mom? Don't the two of you do things together?"

"No," she blurted between sniffs. "I'm not...good enough...for her."

"Listen, Audrey, I need you to calm down. Take a few deep breaths, because I don't want you to hyperventilate in my office. Do you understand?"

She nodded and began breathing deeply, her head bobbing up and down with each labored breath. Staring at the wall, I wondered what I was going to tell that girl. *I've seen how Cooper treats her—he's definitely not the greatest father figure I've ever witnessed. If her mother is anything like he is...well, Audrey doesn't really stand a chance.*

"You better now?" I asked, and she nodded carefully. "Okay, what makes you think you're not good enough for your mom?"

"She…told me so," she explained, words interrupted by short gasps of breath.

"What did she tell you, exactly?"

"She said…that I'm too fat…and I dress like a hobo…and she won't go out…in public with me…until I do something about it."

Yikes. My mom can be a pain sometimes, that is certain, but Audrey's mom makes her look like a saint. I can't imagine having someone be so critical of me.

"Let me ask you a question," I begin hesitantly. "The way your mom looks, is it, you know, organic?"

Audrey swiped at her eyes with the back of her hand, leaving a black mascara trail across her cheek.

"I don't know what you mean."

"Okay, let me put it another way. Is your mom's beauty…you know, all hers?"

"You mean has she had plastic surgery?" she asked, and I nodded. "Duh, a ton of it."

Hmm… No wonder she looks like a Barbie.

"Don't you see what that means? Even your mom isn't good enough for your mom."

We sat silently as I let my words sink in. I imagined Audrey as a little girl, her mother constantly chiding her for not doing things exactly right. Then again, her mother might not have been there at all. If she feels the way she does about her daughter now, she might have had a nanny raise her all along.

"I guess that's true," she agreed, sitting a little straighter in her chair.

"So what are you going to do about it?"

"I don't know," she muttered, her forehead wrinkling a bit. "Tell her she's stupid?"

Tell her she's stupid? I should definitely not be a therapist, since I am obviously not good at this.

"No, you're not going to tell her she's stupid. What did your mom look like before she changed her appearance?"

"A little bit like me, I guess."

"Well, then why don't you show her what her natural beauty looks like? You've got to start by loving yourself and accepting yourself as you are."

"But I don't really want to accept myself as I am," she groaned. "There are things I want to change."

"We all want to change things about ourselves, but if you're not happy with who Audrey is on the inside, none of that will matter in the end."

She nodded her head a couple times and squared her shoulders. "I just have to be okay on the inside?"

"You have to start with the inside," I clarified. "If you don't, then you'll never be happy with anything else you change. Look at your mom. Do you think she's really content with herself, despite all the improvements she's made over the years?"

"No way," she said with a chuckle.

"Then don't make those same mistakes."

For a second I thought she might burst into tears again as I sat looking at her, her eyes welling up and bottom lip quivering. Then, suddenly, her arms shot forward and wrapped around me, her face mashed against my sweater.

"I'm so glad you're my best friend," she whispered. "You're the only person I can count on."

And that is how the shopping excursion was set for today. I agreed to go partly because I was just trying to get her out of my office, and partly because I was ready to scream and didn't want to hurt her feelings. You see, for years I have wanted really nice cashmere sweaters, but I never could justify the cost. I finally went out and got myself one, and I was so proud of it…until yesterday. When Audrey stopped hugging me, I glanced down at my beautiful blue cashmere, which was sadly smudged with black mascara. I felt sorry for her and all, but she's a very wealthy girl—couldn't she spring for some waterproof mascara? If you know you're going to be sobbing at least once a week, it would seem like a wise investment.

When I asked the cleaners, they seemed a little unsure about removing the stain. My sweater is probably ruined, all because I was trying to do something nice for someone. I should just go buy another one and put it on the Cooper wedding account. It was a wedding-related incident, after all. If Audrey keeps up the waterworks, I may need a whole new wardrobe before this thing is over.

"How about this one?" Audrey wonders, pulling out an extremely long dress covered with lace. The girl has no discernable pattern. One second she'll choose a dress that is entirely too revealing, and the next second she goes all Laura Ingalls Wilder on me. I don't believe I will ever understand her.

"It doesn't really say 'Audrey' does it?" I try, hoping she will say no. She shakes her head solemnly and puts it back on the rack.

"Can I help you ladies?" a saleswoman interrupts as she approaches. She is probably in her forties, with light brown shoulder length hair and hazel eyes.

"That would be wonderful," I state. "We're here looking for a wedding dress."

"Well, I can certainly help you with that. Which one of you is getting ready for the big day?"

"Me!" Audrey belts, raising her hand. She has two speeds—crying and giddy. Apparently at this outing we are beginning with giddy.

"Okay," the saleswoman begins, walking over to the counter. "I'm going to start by getting a little information. What's your name?"

"Audrey Cooper," she replies, running her hand across the dresses on the nearest rack.

"How about an address?"

"You should have that already," I offer. "It will be under her father's name, Kent Cooper."

"Oh, so you're Kent's daughter? Well, let's get started then. What are we looking for?"

Audrey shrugs her shoulders and continues to gaze at the dresses. The saleswoman looks questioningly at me, presumably awaiting instructions.

"What's your name?" I wonder.

"Jane."

"Nice to meet you, Jane. I'm Maddie, the wedding planner." And that sounds completely ridiculous, even to me.

"Oh, I'm sorry. I thought I had met most of the wedding planners in town."

"Well, I'm new." Brand spanking new. "What we're thinking for Audrey is maybe something with a little detailing on the top, but with nice clean lines—nothing too revealing. Perhaps something with an empire waist and an A-line skirt. Do you have anything like that?"

"I'm sure we can find something," Jane agrees with a smile. I can't help but notice that she is acting a little differently toward me, now that she knows I'm the wedding planner.

Yeah, it still sounds ridiculous.

"This line might be close to what you have in mind," Jane says, pointing to a rack of gowns. "What size do you think you are, Audrey?" Audrey takes a moment to glance between me and Jane, as though she's been asked a question to which she doesn't know how to respond.

"I think maybe a size four," she finally replies.

I have no idea what size Audrey really wears, but I am positive it is not a size four. Jane knows better too, and she's looking at me as though wondering what to do. I wave my hand dismissively, implying that she should do what Audrey wants. For

once she could have made things easy by giving us her true size instead of playing a guessing game.

Jane pulls a couple dresses off the rack and calls to a younger salesgirl in the back to set up a fitting room.

"Eliza will help you," she tells Audrey, who looks at me for reassurance.

"Go ahead. If you need anything, have her come and get me," I say. She nods and heads to the back.

"Looks like you have your hands full with that one," Jane informs me, going back to the counter. "How many weddings have you done?"

"This is my second." Well, it's partly true—I was at the fitting when Jess picked a dress. Surely that counts.

"Trial by fire, isn't that what they say? I can't imagine putting on a wedding for Kent and Faith Cooper."

"You know them, then?"

"Only enough to know that I don't want to. Faith comes in here from time to time for formal gowns. She always leaves with something, but she makes it a point to tell us before she walks out the door that all our dresses are trash and nothing here is good enough for someone like her. Funny, though, that she always winds up wearing them to her banquets and fundraising events. I've seen her in the paper dressed in them several times."

"Yeah, that sounds about right."

"I hope you won't have to work with her too much on the wedding," Jane continues, continuing to gaze in my direction.

"She hasn't taken an interest so far."

She nods her head as though she understands and begins writing in her book as Eliza reappears from the back and begins going through the rack of dresses. I know exactly what she's doing—there is no way Audrey was even close to fitting into a size four.

"Is there a problem, Eliza?" Jane asks, glancing at me.

"No problem, Miss Cooper just needs a different size."

"Well, tell me which size you need and I'll help you find it," Jane suggests, walking over to the rack. Eliza glances at me quickly before returning her attention to Jane.

"The thing is," she whispers, "Miss Cooper doesn't want her wedding planner to know her size."

It's like the seventh grade all over again. As if I really care what size Audrey is. If I really wanted to know, I would just look at the back of her shirt during one of the many times she's crying on my shoulder.

"Just take her what she needs," I insist with a laugh. "As long as you know what size she requires, I don't really care."

An understanding smile crosses Jane's face. She probably deals with bridezillas all the time. In fact, I'm absolutely certain that Audrey is easygoing compared to some of the girls that come in here.

Sitting down in the waiting area, I begin looking through a bridal magazine. Within a few pages, I come across an article on the cost of the average wedding. The price for the dress is totally unrealistic, unless you're someone like Audrey and your dad says anything goes. The food is ridiculous, like serving a full three-course meal to 200 people…which I guess we will probably be doing for Audrey. And the flowers—who could possibly use that many flowers?

On second thought, Audrey will probably want all those flowers, too. It's nearly tragic that the average wedding costs more than my car. To think that people spend all that money for one single party almost makes me sick.

Thank goodness Max and I will probably elope to Barbados when the time comes.

"I think we're finally on the right track," Jane says quietly, stepping up to me. "Were you looking at bridal party attire today, as well?"

"I hadn't thought about it, but since we're here, we might as well."

"What sort of color palette are we looking for?"

"I think we've settled on rose and pale yellow, so we could probably start with anything you have in those shades."

Jane heads off in search of the dresses, and I hear someone call my name from the back. It must have been Eliza—I would have recognized Audrey's screech.

The fitting area is set up to look like the front of a church. There are candelabras and ivy in front of a huge mirror, presumably so the bride-to-be can see herself in an appropriate setting. Audrey is standing to one side in a dress that Jane previously showed her.

"What do you think?" I wonder.

"It's pretty," she offers, but shrugs her shoulders.

I step around her to get a better look. "You're right, it is pretty, but I don't think it quite works around the waist. It's a little too long in the cut. Why don't you try another one?"

"Okay," she agrees cheerfully, trotting back to her dressing room. For the moment she's having fun and not crying. It could be so much worse.

This is every girl's dream—isn't that what they say? Trying on dresses for the big day and being treated like a princess? I'm certain I could probably spend an entire day in here trying on dresses and twirling in front of the mirror. If this were my wedding, I would settle on one of the draping, flowing gowns, and I would wear my hair partially up with ringlets swirling down my back. When I walk down the aisle, I would hear, "Is that you, Maddie? I thought you were an angel."

Naturally, I would laugh at that. "Of course it's me, Josh."

I mean, Max.

"Do you like this one?" Audrey interrupts my blush-filled daydream. Turning around, I see an almost identical copy of the dress I had in mind to be perfect for her. It's simple, with the empire waist and an A-line skirt that slims her figure. It really suits her perfectly.

"I think it's wonderful," I state. "What do you think?"

"It makes me look really good," she agrees with a smile.

"You look like Audrey at her best."

"Audrey at her best," she says dreamily. "I like that. How do you know all this stuff, anyway, like what type of clothes are going to look good?"

"Just something I picked up," I mumble. Actually, it's something my cable provider picks up: it's called a makeover show. They're really quite helpful, and I would recommend one to Audrey if I wasn't worried about hurting her feelings.

Jane comes around the corner carrying a couple of dresses in roses and pale yellows. None of them look like bridesmaid dresses, thank goodness. At least Audrey won't be able to pick something that is absolutely nauseating.

"Here we go," Jane sings. "I think I've found the perfect hues, and we had some styles that closely resembled the wedding dresses you chose."

"They're all lovely," I insist, and Audrey nods her head in agreement.

"Well, if you would like to choose one today, I can write down the number, and the members of your bridal party can come in for fittings at their convenience."

"Oh, there's no need for that," Audrey states. "Maddie can try it on today, since we're already here. In fact, she should try on both colors to see which one looks best."

"I wasn't aware you were also the bridal party," Jane says, looking at me curiously.

All I can do is smile sheepishly in return. "Yes," I whisper. "It's a long story."

"Of course it is," she quietly tells me, and then turns to Audrey. "Did we find a wedding gown we like? Why, that one is very flattering on you!"

Yes, I made a truly wise choice. I am the wedding planner extraordinaire.

No, it still sounds stupid.

"Do you really think so?" Audrey wonders, twirling around and smiling. And to think I was worried that today would be miserable, full of complaints about being fat, tears rolling and mascara running all over the place.

"Would you like to try a veil with the dress?" Jane hangs the bridesmaid dresses on a nearby hook. "We have a wide variety to your left, hanging on the wall."

"Yes!" Audrey squeals, bolting toward the veil display. Within a few seconds, she returns with the biggest, fullest veil she can find. It's all she can do to gather it up in her arms without dragging it along the floor. Jane glances at me as I shake my head with an exasperated smile. Poor Audrey—she just doesn't get it. I wonder who would be helping her now if her dad hadn't pegged me to do it. Her mom, maybe? No, that would require going out in public together. I'm sure he would have hired a professional wedding planner.

"How do I put it on?" Audrey asks, fiddling with the hair comb. Jane pushes part of the veil aside and helps Audrey place it on her head. She looks in the mirror, fluffing the veil out around her face and then around her arms. She sways back and forth a little for some unknown reason, and I sincerely hope she's not planning to do that on her wedding day.

"What do you think, Maddie?" She turns her head to ensure that I'm looking.

"You look like the ghost of wedding present," I assess, shaking my head. "I can't even see your face. You don't want to hide on your wedding day, do you?"

"Maybe." A ghost of a frown adorned her face.

Oh, no. Don't do the Audrey flip-flop on me. Where is giddy Audrey? Come on, bring her back. I don't feel like dealing with tears right now.

"Of course you don't want to hide," I say, walking toward the veil display. "You're going to look beautiful and you want everyone to see you. Here, try this one. It's just going to sit on the back of your head so you can actually see Derrick, and most importantly, you can see where you're going. You wouldn't want such a large veil that you wind up tripping down the aisle."

"I hadn't thought about that," she mumbles as Jane helps her place the second veil on her head, then steps back to look thoughtfully at Audrey's silhouette in the mirror.

"Yes, that looks lovely, don't you think?" Jane directs the question at me. I nod, and Audrey continues to stare at the mirror. "Actually, I have a similar veil in the back that matches the stitching on the dress. I'll just be a minute."

Audrey continues to stare at the mirror, and I can't help but wonder what she's thinking. She doesn't move or twirl or twist to see the back of the veil. She just gazes silently into her own eyes, as though she's studying something deep within.

"Do you think my dad will like it?" she finally manages.

Who cares what your dad thinks? How can you please a man who takes no interest in anyone but himself?

"Sure he will," I attempt to reassure her.

She swallows and continues staring. "What about Derrick? Do you think he'll like it?"

"Of course he'll like it. He loves you, doesn't he? He would like any dress you picked out, and wouldn't even care if you wore your pajamas."

Audrey turns to me and grins. "I don't think he'd be crazy about my pajamas."

"Maybe not, but you get the point."

Jane emerges with the new veil and places it on Audrey's head, standing back to admire her potential sale. "It's very similar, but it matches perfectly with the dress, don't you think?" Jane fluffs the back of the veil a little and studies Audrey's face in the mirror.

"I like it," Audrey finally agrees.

"Okay then. I'll just have one of the girls come back and do some measurements so we can make sure the dress fits you perfectly."

"Don't forget about Maddie!" Audrey calls as Jane walks away. "She still has to try her dresses, too."

"Oh, yes, I almost forgot. What size should I pull for you?"

"I can't tell you my size," I suggest slyly, glancing over at the bride-to-be in her attire. "Not in front of Audrey."

Chapter Twenty-Four

Naturally, I've received a bit of teasing the last couple of days because I'm finally going out with the "pirate" after all this time. It was with a great deal of hesitation that I admitted the fact to Josh or Jess at all. I told Jess because I wanted to dispel the notion that I was after her brother, because it still felt like a really weird wall that had been placed between us. I told Josh because…

Well, I guess I told Josh to see what his reaction would be. He laughed at my persistence, and then told me to call him when I found something wrong with the guy.

When I insisted that Max was pretty great, he said:

"Arr, Maddie, call me from the pirate ship in Barbados, then."

Exasperating.

Not that it matters, because tonight isn't about Josh—it's about weeks of anticipation of what it would actually be like to date Max, and tonight I'm going to find out.

Jess once told me not to wear a dress on a first date because it would look like I was trying too hard. Tonight, I don't care. Putting my best foot forward is essential, because it's Max. He's pretty fantastic, and I want him to know that I'm trying without looking like I'm trying, if that makes sense.

It's a perfect opportunity for a little black dress, which I've paired with a simple pair of black stilettos. My hair has been straightened and polished until it shines, and it's hanging like a cascade of strawberry molasses down my back. I've probably never looked better, I must admit, as I sit and wait for Max to arrive.

When the doorbell rings, I take a deep breath before opening the door, finding him leaning casually against the door jam.

His lilac-colored button down shirt is tucked into a pair of dark-gray jeans, and even though the night is slightly chilly, he holds his sports coat in his fist. His blue eyes sparkle from beneath his dark eyebrows as he offers up an easy smile.

"Maddie," he breathes as he gazes at me. "Wow, you look incredible."

"Thanks, you do too," I answer quietly, openly gawking at him. He looks pretty fantastic at the tennis club, but tonight, he looks even better. I can't help believing that I have totally hit the jackpot.

"I'm kind of surprised by your little house. I figured you as a city girl through and through, yet here you are in the suburbs."

"You are looking at the quaintest little home on Wonder Lane," I assure him, gesturing to the house as though I'm Vanna White flipping a letter.

"Quaint is a perfect word. Not for you, though. I'm thinking stunning, gorgeous…"

"Do go on, I could listen to you for hours," I tease.

He holds out his arm, allowing me to latch my hand onto his elbow. "Come on, my funny lady. The night is young."

Max took me to a fantastic restaurant with jazz piano playing in the corner, where the atmosphere was quiet and romantic. We have shared easy conversation the entire night, and it's the type of first date I've dreamed about for a long time. Sheer, absolute perfection, practically. I haven't found a single thing wrong with Max yet, and not in the "settling" kind of way that I haven't found anything wrong with other dates in the past. Beyond not being at all disgusted by Max, I am finding myself completely drawn to him.

After dinner, we went to dance at a piano bar, where he held me against him and whispered his dreams and aspirations into my ear. Being with Max was easy, and it was delightful. I was almost sorry to feel the night coming to a close, but I'm also filled with anticipation.

We're pulling onto Wonder Lane right now, and that handsome fellow with the black flowing hair keeps glancing over at me. I've been on enough first dates to tell when I'm clicking with someone, and wow, are we ever clicking. He places his car in park as we arrive in the driveway, and then turns off the engine.

"You actually have a pretty cool little neighborhood here," he states, smiling over at me.

"Oh, I know. Harley Laine lives at the end of the street down there."

"The news reporter, no kidding?" he wonders, giving a crooked grin. Opening the car door, he crosses to my side and takes my hand to pull me out of the car.

"We should have done this a long time ago," I sigh, walking toward the door.

"Yeah, that's a fact," he agrees. "I don't usually like to date people from Big Cedar—too much potential to cause problems, you know?"

"Absolutely." I step up onto the porch and fiddle with my keys just a bit. He pauses to wrap his coat gently across my shoulders, his fingers grazing my skin and causing a sharp intake of breath on my part, which he definitely notices. He gives me one of those signature lopsided grins, lowering his face a bit, and I tilt my head up expectantly. His lips meet mine gently at first, and then more firmly, as the edges of his goatee scratch my cheek. Wrapping my arm around his neck, I hold him solidly against me as he breaks for a second, but then tilts his head the other way and kisses me again.

"Should we go inside for a minute?" he whispers against my ear. "I don't want you to get cold."

Going inside is really tempting—I mean really, really tempting. Max's lips taste like peppermint, and his breath is warm

against my neck, and I don't want the evening to stop. In my mind, though, all I can see is Josh's face staring at me, his brow wrinkled in two places, regarding me sternly over his glasses.

"Sorry, Max, but I can't," I tell him quietly. "My friend who lets me live here...well, he has a rule about having boyfriends over."

"Whoa, hold up," Max says with a laugh, recoiling slightly. "Where did this boyfriend stuff come from? It was just a date."

"That's not what I meant, really," I insist, feeling him pull away from me. "I just meant that he doesn't like me having guys over, that's all."

"I had no idea you lived with some guy." His tone indicates that he's teasing, but his smile is telling me a more sordid story.

"I don't. I'm just using my friend's house while he's overseas..."

"Gotcha," he says, straightening himself. "It's okay, I really should turn in early, anyway. Thanks for the nice evening, Maddie."

"I'll see you Tuesday?" I offer, trying to lighten the mood.

"Sure," he responds with a shrug, turning to walk away. He takes only two steps before he turns around. "Hey, let's not make this weird at the club, okay? You're a great girl—funny, beautiful—I'm just not at that place right now where I'm ready to give the time it takes for serial dating, you know?"

"Oh, yeah, I get it," I assure him with an uneasy laugh. "I'm so there myself."

"Good. That makes me feel better." He smiles once more. "See you Tuesday, pretty girl."

Fumbling with the key in the lock, I twist it three times before I manage to let myself in the house, where I instantly drop my purse to the ground and stare at the door, aware of the headlights pulling away from the driveway. So much for a future with Max. He *is* totally a pirate, simply out to enjoy life's pleasures. *I'm not ready to give the time it takes for serial dating.* Seriously, who even says something like that?

Suddenly, Josh's words from that long-ago prom flood back to my mind: *If a guy isn't willing to throw his heart on the line and give you the world, he doesn't deserve you.*

Lowering myself to the floor, I allow the disappointment to flood over me.

Goodbye, Barbados.

Oh, who am I kidding? Forget Barbados—goodbye happily ever after, or Christmas with a boyfriend, or even next Friday night's date. I had thrown so much hope on my pursuit of Max, to my own detriment, because as it turns out, he definitely has a massive, blatant, truly fatal flaw:

He's not Joshua Mason.

Chapter Twenty-Five

Mom has called three times this week, and I haven't called her back yet. I've just been so aggravated by the way she treated me leading up to the blood drive, I don't know what I'd say to her. If I knew what precipitated the sudden change in her behavior, I might be a little better prepared. I'm pretty sure I know what brought her to the blood drive—if it wasn't to get close to me for the purpose of possibly getting herself on television, then it was to be able to tell all the people nearby that I was her daughter, since I *had* been on television that day. I wouldn't have thought much about it after the fact, but she has been calling me ever since and leaving phone messages.

Maddie, it's Mom. I just want to talk to you. I miss you.

Maddie, this is Mom. I was thinking about you and thought I'd call.

Maddie, Mom again! Just called to tell you I love you.

It's nice, isn't it? The problem is, she never talks to me that way. Why is she suddenly being so affectionate? Is there some other gain she is hoping to take away from that thirty seconds of television? If so, I can't imagine what that would possibly be. Does she finally consider me a success, and now wants to make up for lost time? Maybe she truly feels bad about the bulimic intervention and is simply trying to apologize, in her own backwards way.

I've considered calling Dad several times to find out what's going on, but the fear that she might answer the phone always stops me in my tracks. It's silly, really, that I should be afraid of my mom caring about me. The problem is, that's not it exactly. I think I'm afraid that my mom is pretending to care about me, and I don't want to know how I'll feel when that is proven. It's one thing to believe someone is lying and making you into a fool, but it's quite another to discover that it is, in fact, true.

Sometimes I wish my mom was more like Hazel. I never have to worry about whether Hazel cares for me, because she shows me. She doesn't have to call me every five minutes and leave me messages telling me she loves me or misses me. She always takes the time to listen to my problems and never makes me feel stupid or silly or insignificant. Her actions resemble what I imagine a mother should be.

Still, I should just call my mother, shouldn't I? It does seem pretty cowardly, sitting here acting frightened about calling my own parent. I'm a twenty-five-year-old woman with a wonderfully advancing career (well, sort of) and a very happy life. I almost sound like Audrey, seeking my mom's approval and knowing I won't get it, so in turn trying to avoid the situation.

Eww, I do sound *just* like Audrey. Well, without the crying and whining and certainly not as rich, but I do. I sound exactly like Audrey.

That's it! I'm definitely calling.

The phone rings two times before I hear a voice come across the other end of the line, muffled and distant.

"Mom?" I ask.

"Oh, Maddie, is that you?" she says, louder than before. "I'm sorry—I was just pulling something out of the oven."

"Well, if you're cooking dinner, I can call back later."

"Don't be silly! Dinner can wait. It's been so long since I talked to you."

"It can't have been more than two weeks," I say, counting back in my mind to the blood drive.

"Well, two weeks is forever, isn't it? Two weeks—almost an eternity!"

Except I distinctly recall you not speaking to me for over a month, and you brushed that off when I mentioned it.

"I'm just returning your call," I state, waiting for her response.

"Good, so you did get my messages. I was afraid your phone was broken or something."

"Yeah, I got them," I assure her with a sigh.

"Oh, I wanted to tell you that I recorded that segment you did on the news. I made a bunch of copies and sent them to all our relatives. Of course I gave one to Lance and Brittany, too. Everyone was so proud of you!"

"Really?" I ask doubtfully. "What did Brittany say, exactly?"

"Just something about how great it was, I can't really remember. I don't want to talk about Brittany—I want to talk about you. How is your job going?"

"My job? It's fine."

That's a first. Mom has never asked me about my job before.

"Are you working on any more big projects I should know about? I can tell everybody to watch you in advance, so they will set their DVRs."

"That was just a one-time thing. I won't be on the news anymore."

"Well, that's a pity, because you were so good at it. You should go to the TV station and get one of those anchor jobs. I know they would hire you."

She thinks I'm famous. Or maybe she just wants me to be famous. Either way, I don't think I like it.

"It's not that easy, Mom. First of all, I don't have a background in broadcast journalism. Second, I'm really not interested in that type of career."

"That's a shame, Maddie. I know you would be an excellent newswoman."

"Thank you, I guess."

"Well, if you're not going to be on the news, then what are you working on now? What is the next big project for my little coordinator?"

Living vicariously through me, maybe? I don't get it.

Well, let's see. I'm planning a grandiose wedding for my boss's daughter. That doesn't sound like a job, though; it sounds like a movie plot. What else?

"We're going to be helping with a food drive for Thanksgiving," I offer. "We've teamed up with a project already in process to be a co-sponsor. I'm going to be at a homeless shelter the day before Thanksgiving, helping to prepare all the food."

"That is so heroic of you! My little Maddie, volunteering to help the homeless. I'm so proud of you."

She has officially gone off her rocker.

"Why don't you come, too?" I suggest. "They need as many volunteers as they can get."

That ought to shut her up. There is no way Mom would spend her day volunteering at a homeless shelter. I don't think she has volunteered for anything in her life, with the exception of the blood drive, and that was just for attention.

"Let's see, the day before Thanksgiving?" she repeats, pausing for a second.

Go ahead—take your time and come up with an appropriate excuse. Brittany is coming over that day, perhaps? The kids might be out of school on account of the holiday?

"Okay, I've got it marked on my calendar. This is so exciting! Just imagine, you and me, side by side, volunteering for the homeless. I can't wait to tell your father!"

What? Who are you, and what have you done with my mother?

"Um…alright. I'll send you the details the next time I'm at the office."

"You go ahead and do that, dear. That sounds great. Listen, I wanted to ask you another question. What are you doing for Thanksgiving? Your dad and I really hope you'll come over. We do so want to see you."

She does *so* want to see me? She's been watching old westerns or something, obviously.

"Actually, I already promised Josh's parents I would go over there. I hate to leave them by themselves on Thanksgiving."

"Oh," she says with a sigh.

Wow, she actually sounds disappointed. Something must be wrong with me, because I feel the stirring of a feeling like sympathy in the pit of my stomach. I should just leave it alone, ignore it. Tamp it down like a brush fire that is getting out of control.

"Listen, I have an idea. Why don't you come over here? I'm sure Josh's parents wouldn't mind coming over to the house instead."

"Oh, Maddie, what a wonderful idea! We'd be delighted to come. Of course, you did mean Lance and Brittany, too?"

Drat. I forgot about them living here now. Can I take back my offer without being a jerk?

"Sure, Lance and Brittany, too."

"Hooray! This is so exciting. Imagine me going to my little Maddie's house for Thanksgiving. I can't believe you're so grown up now."

I'm twenty-five years old. Did you miss the last ten years or something?

"Okay, well, it's all settled then. I've got some stuff I need to do, so I'm going to go..."

"It's been great talking to you, Maddie! I'll see you the day before Thanksgiving!"

"Bye," I mutter, hanging up the phone.

Unless I'm mistaken, I just offered to have Thanksgiving dinner at my house. I don't know anything about cooking turkey. I've never even bought a turkey before in my life.

Perhaps I could ask Hazel, but do I really want her to know I can't cook? I guess I have to tell her about the change in plans, so I might as well bring it up in casual conversation. *Oh, by the way, how do you usually cook your turkey? I want to make sure I do it in the best possible fashion, and you're such a great cook, after all. No, don't be modest, Hazel, you know it's true. So you grab the bird from the frozen food section, and then what?*

I am so out of my league.

Chapter Twenty-Six

We just made it to the homeless shelter to help with preparing Thanksgiving dinner. Yes, I did say we—my constant companion and "best friend" insisted on coming with me. At least I'll be sure she actually does some work today, because there won't be any loafing as a volunteer.

Removing myself from her sight has become absolutely impossible. She has gone to every tennis lesson with me, and I've forced her to take the lessons once we get there. I'm not sure Max is crazy about the situation, but I'm not going to have her sitting there watching me. Besides, it actually helps to have a little distraction with Max, since I now know without a doubt that I was only ever that to him—a distraction.

To be honest, I'm not even attracted to him anymore. I'm not sure what I saw in him in the first place, other than the obvious dashing pirate good looks.

While Max couldn't get away from me fast enough, Audrey believes she has to be by my side every waking hour of the day in order to properly plan her wedding. I'm running out of things to talk to her about—there is only so much planning a person can do, after all. At some point, you just have to step back and let the plans take shape.

She wanted me to take her shoe shopping tomorrow. I had to inform her politely that it was Thanksgiving and I would not be leaving my home. I'm sure we'll just postpone it until Friday, although I wish we could push it back until next week. We have already been shoe shopping three times, and Audrey can never find anything to suit her. She's obsessed with flip flops, so I almost get the feeling that she's looking for a dressy white pair, which I will absolutely refuse to allow. I cannot imagine what her parents would think if she showed up in that beautiful, expensive gown and wore flip flops underneath.

"Doug!" I call, seeing the director of the shelter, a tall slender man with a full, dark beard. He looks to his left to check on one of the volunteers and then comes toward me.

"Maddie, it's nice to see you again. Have you brought help today?"

"Yes, actually. This is Audrey." I watch as Doug extends his hand to Audrey and she takes it firmly. "We came prepared to work," I state, following him into the shelter. "Just tell us where you want us."

"Would you ladies prefer setup and layout, or food preparation?" he asks, pointing to two different areas of the busy room. I can't help but notice my mother in the food preparation area, who is smiling and waving like a lunatic.

"I think setup would probably be a safe bet," I say. My cooking skills are definitely limited, and I'm fairly certain that Audrey has never cooked in her life.

"You'll just be over there, then, with Sue," Doug replies, pointing to an older woman with short graying black hair. She is wearing an orange shirt bearing the name of the shelter, as is Doug.

"Who is that waving at you?" Audrey whispers as we move towards Sue. I look over to see Mom still trying desperately to get my attention.

"That's my mom," I say nonchalantly. "She wanted to volunteer today, too."

"That's nice of her," Audrey finishes just as we arrive at Sue's station.

"Uh-huh," I mumble. It is nice—and I still want to know why she's doing it.

"Hi, ladies," Sue greets us cheerfully. "You're here to help, I hope?"

"Absolutely!" I agree.

"We certainly have a lot of new faces around here today. Did you two hear about this on the radio?"

"Actually, no. We're from Cooper Corporate Financial."

"Fantastic! It's so nice what Cooper has done for us this year. We've never seen the kind of donations we have, and it's all because of the advertising and promoting your company handled. We'll actually have more food than we can use this year, which is something we've never faced before."

"That's great news," I state sincerely. "You should call anytime you do something like this. I'm sure the company would be happy to help again."

"You know, that's what's so strange about all this. Every year we call on the community to help, and Cooper is one of the companies that always turns us down. When we found out that they actually wanted to help this year, we were completely flabbergasted."

Why doesn't that surprise me? Cooper would never bother himself with caring about this type of operation. If it hadn't been for me exploring the opportunity, this never would have happened.

"Well, enough jibber-jabber. What are your names, ladies?" Sue asks, sorting through some canned goods.

"I'm Maddie, and this is Audrey."

"Maddie and Audrey," she repeats. "Well, I've got signs put up to show what goes where, so just find a box over there and start unpacking."

Unpacking...that certainly sounds like something we can't screw up.

There are boxes upon boxes stacked against the wall, and several are open on the floor. The first box I pull open is full of cans of green beans. Glancing behind me, I see where Sue hung a sign that has green beans spelled out in large green letters, so our job seems simple enough.

Audrey and I work diligently and unpack several boxes. I'm sure she's never done this type of work before in her life. She never talks about having a job before coming to work for her dad, and *that* job is definitely not a job at all. While some people might call following me around all day a job, I don't think it's worthy of a paid position at the company. If her dad really wanted to do her a favor, he would make her earn a living. That could be the best possible scenario for Audrey, because she would have to work to get what she wanted, and she wouldn't be running to dear old dad every few minutes. It might even give her a little self-esteem to know she could actually do something by herself.

"You'll be really busy tomorrow," I remark to Sue as I stand beside her and sort through some corn.

"Yes, it's a busy day, but it's worth it to see the looks on peoples' faces when they get a hot meal for the holiday."

"How long have you been volunteering here?"

"Let's see…this will mark my fourteenth year, I believe."

"Wow," I say admiringly. "That's really remarkable."

"Well, like I said, it's worth it," Sue replies, looking a little embarrassed by my praise. "Do you have big Thanksgiving Day plans?"

Boy, do I ever.

"Yes, actually. Thanksgiving dinner will be at my house this year for the first time. I'm a little nervous."

"I remember the first Thanksgiving," Sue says with a chuckle. "It does seem like quite an undertaking that initial time."

"And if you knew me, you would understand. I am definitely not the best cook."

Sue begins counting the cans in front of her and pauses for a moment, adding some numbers in her head. She then goes back to sorting and stacking.

"Well, the hardest part is the turkey," she finally continues. "Once you've got that under control, everything else falls in line. Do you think you have a pretty good grasp on that?"

"I do, but only because I asked someone at work for directions."

Sue stops stacking and places a hand on her hip. "So you're all set and ready with your turkey for tomorrow, then?"

"Actually, it's cooking right now."

"Right now?" she asks, narrowing her eyes. "Are you having the dinner tonight?"

"No, it's tomorrow."

"And you're already cooking the turkey? I've never heard of that before."

"I thought it was a little strange, too, but those are the directions the lady gave me. Thaw the turkey for 6 hours, and then cook for 36."

"Oh my," Sue spits out, biting her lip and glancing over at me. "I'm just going to go into the back for a minute. Maddie, can you hold the fort down for me?"

"Absolutely," I agree as she hurries into the kitchen.

What was with the face? She acted like I'd done something wrong. I knew I shouldn't have left the oven on all day. She's probably afraid I'm going to burn my house down. Well, she doesn't have to worry about that. I was careful to...

Actually, why didn't I think of that before? I probably *will* burn the house down! I'm sure it's too late already. I can practically hear the fire trucks in my mind, sirens blaring as they come blasting down my street. All the neighbors will know immediately whose house is ablaze.

"I always knew that girl would set her house on fire," Mrs. Willows will tell the news crew, shaking her head.

"It's a terrible tragedy," the fire chief will say, "but it's an excellent opportunity to remind people about the importance of fire safety."

"Thank goodness the fire didn't reach my beautiful palace at the end of the street," Harley Laine will add, looking poised and perfect with the microphone in her hand.

What will Josh think if I burn his house down? I will never be able to look him in the eye again.

"Okay," Sue suddenly says, emerging from the kitchen, "back to counting."

Back to counting, just like that, when my home is possibly on fire? Does she not see the depth of this dilemma? She was the one who turned me on to the problem in the first place, with the biting of the lip and everything.

But what if the biting of the lip was for something else? Maybe it was for something she forgot in the kitchen. That's it!

When I started talking about cooking the turkey, she realized she had forgotten something in the kitchen. Whew! No house fire.

Well, there still could be a house fire.

No, I'm not going to think about it anymore.

"Hi, Maddie," I hear Mom's voice behind me. Turning, I see her standing there, wearing an apron and beaming at me.

"Mom," I reply stoically. "What are you doing over here? I thought you were prepping food."

"Yes, I am, but I thought I would come over and say hello. It would have been nice if you could have been assigned to food preparation, too."

"Well, I'm here to help as much as I can, and I probably wouldn't be very much help in that area. I'm sure you're doing a great job."

"Yes, we're doing fine. I had just hoped that you and I could volunteer together, that's all." Glancing over at her, I can't help but see her sad eyes. *Seriously, who are you and what have you done with my mother?*

"But we *are* volunteering together," I insist. "We wouldn't be able to talk much, anyway, since we're here to work."

"I guess you're right about that," she says dejectedly. For a moment I wonder what else to say, but suddenly her eyes brighten and a smile crosses her face.

"Look, Maddie," she whispers. "There's Harley Laine from Channel Six."

She's right—Harley just barged through the front door with her camera crew like she owns the place, and she's speaking into her microphone, although I can't hear what she's saying. She's pointing to the food preparation area. It's unfortunate that Mom didn't remain at her post, because she might have gotten her face on television.

"Do you think she'll come over here?" Mom whispers, grabbing my arm.

"I don't know, I hope not." Turning back to the cans of corn, I continue to stack them as I glance over at Audrey, who is amassing her own little pile. She has really impressed me today —

working hard and not complaining once. Maybe I don't give her enough credit.

"She's the prettiest news reporter, if you ask me," Mom continues. "She's my favorite of all of them, too. I've always wanted to see her in person. Do you think I'll get to meet her?" Trying to ignore her, I continue stacking.

"Over here, Kenny," I hear Harley order. "I think I see a familiar face."

Great—just what I need. Harley Laine is marching toward me and Mom is practically jumping up and down with excitement. Did Mom agree to come down here just in the hopes of meeting Harley Laine? Why did I have to invite her, anyway? I should have known there was something behind this nice, new demeanor.

"You're from Cooper Corporate Financial, right?" Harley confirms. "Madeline, wasn't it?"

"Yes, that's right," I reply calmly. "Madeline Heard."

"I'm her mom!" I hear from my right. Harley doesn't even bother to look at her.

"Could we get a few words?"

"Actually, I'd rather not."

"I could do an interview!" Mom chirps, while Harley continues to ignore her.

"Why don't you interview the staff here at the shelter?" I suggest. "They know more about what's going on than I do."

"We already have," Harley states, pointing to her cameraman. "I need to get the rest of the story, and this will just take a minute." She straightens her white blazer and fluffs her hair a little before holding the microphone in front of her face.

"Ready," I hear from behind the camera.

"Madeline Heard is the spokesperson for Cooper Corporate Financial, co-sponsor of the food drive," Harley croons into the microphone.

"Hold up," the cameraman says, tilting the camera to the side. "The old lady's in the shot."

"What? Ma'am, will you move, please?" Harley directs toward my mom. "You're in the camera line."

"I'm sorry," Mom mutters, stepping away a couple feet. She looks down at the ground in embarrassment.

That cameraman just called my mother an old lady. Who does he think he is, anyway? Besides, that Harley Laine might think she's pretty hot stuff, and it could turn out that meeting her was my mom's only reason for coming down here, but they can't treat people like dirt. Not just people, either—my mother.

"Okay, one more time," Harley huffs. "Madeline Heard from Cooper..."

"No, Harley, I decline an interview," I inform her, going back to stacking cans. I only manage to pick two or three up off the pile before she leans into me.

"Like I said, it will just take a minute, and then we'll be done here."

"And like I said, I decline."

Harley just stands and stares at me in disbelief. The cameraman has the camera at his side, looking at me with wide eyes. Neither one of them moves for a moment, standing there gaping in my direction. Audrey moves toward me just to my left, and I notice Sue looking at me from her station.

"You're refusing to talk to me?" Harley assesses, eyes narrowed and face slightly pink.

"Yes, I believe so," I reply cordially, stacking a few more cans. By now I am aware of an intense silence throughout the shelter. Everyone must be watching the drama.

"I...I don't know what to do, Harley," the cameraman states.

"Here's an idea," I offer. "Run a story about the shelter without looking for an angle. You've got enough footage for today."

"How dare you insinuate that I'm looking for an angle," Harley barks at me, now completely unaware of all the attention she's receiving. "I don't look for angles in my stories. Have you never seen me on the air? Do you have any idea how rude that is?"

"I'm honestly not that familiar with you," I tell her with a shrug, aware that my nonchalance is driving her crazy, but strangely feeling protective of my mother as she lurks just to my side.

"I'm the top reporter in this town. Number one most popular newscaster, in fact."

"Oh, come on now," I reply, looking into her face as I laugh quietly. "Why would Channel Six send the hottest reporter in town to a volunteer food drive?"

"Because I'm good with people," she rants. "No one else could possibly make these crummy little unimportant stories seem interesting. What would you know about it, anyway?" Whirling on her heel, she storms toward the door as her cameraman continues to stand in front of me, gaping with his mouth open like a fish. "Kenny!" she screams as she pushes the door open. He quickly jumps to attention and begins to jog after her.

"I'm so sorry, Sue," I whisper, but she just shrugs and waves her hand.

"Sounds like she needed it," she tells me with a laugh, going back to her cans. Shaking my head, I turn to go back to my own little pile.

"How could you do that, Maddie?" Mom hisses beside me, face red and hands on her hips.

"What, Mom?"

"How could you talk to Harley that way?"

"How? I was defending you. She and that cameraman insulted you. Did you miss that part?"

"Same old Maddie, always screwing things up," Mom mutters under her breath, pulling off her apron.

"What are you doing?" I wonder with a sigh, wishing she had chosen another setting to unveil this scene of hers.

"I can't work in these conditions!" she snaps at me. "I can't volunteer alongside someone who would insult another person like that."

"They're gone, so you don't have to worry about them insulting you," I insist, giving her a puzzled expression.

"I'm talking about you," she steams, throwing the apron at me. "You better shape up by tomorrow!" Just a few steps, and she disappears through the door.

Have I ever been more embarrassed in my life? Not likely. I'm the person responsible for co-sponsoring this food drive, and my mother just berated me in front of all the volunteers like a small child. Now they're all staring at me. Thinking quickly, I lift a can of vegetables above my head.

"Here's to all the people who are going to volunteer tomorrow," I announce. "Besides the obvious reason of performing a wonderful service for the community, I now understand why a person would want to avoid their own family on the holiday!"

A few snickers travel around the room, and then people slowly return to what they were doing. Sue smiles at me and pats my hand. Trying to calm my nerves, I stare at the floor for a brief moment before returning to my work.

"That was really something," Audrey whispers.

"Yeah, I know," I reply. "My mom is a trip sometimes."

"No, not your mom—Harley."

"Oh. Yeah, that was unfortunate."

"She pretty well announced what she thinks about the whole city, didn't she?" Audrey asks quietly.

Giving a slight smirk, I glance at her. "I guess so."

"Too bad her cameraman didn't film that, huh?"

"Yes, it's too bad," I agree with a laugh.

"Because I'm sure he would have gotten a much better video than I captured on my phone."

Around 5:00 p.m., Audrey and I leave the shelter side by side. When I begin to walk toward the Tahoe, she pauses for a moment and then walks silently in the other direction toward her own vehicle.

"I hope you have a happy Thanksgiving, Audrey," I wish aloud, to which she smiles sadly.

"We don't really do Thanksgiving."

"Well, at least you'll be able to spend the day with your mom and dad," I reply. She shakes her head and jabs the toe of her shoe into the gravel.

"Mom and Dad are in Jamaica," she says. "They left last night. It will just be me and the housekeeper."

"I'm sorry," I tell her, but she simply shrugs her shoulders.

"I'm used to it."

"What about Derrick?"

"He's with his family this weekend, out of state."

I can't believe I'm getting ready to say this.

"Why don't you come over to my house?"

"You don't have to do that," she insists, pulling her jacket tightly around her waist to keep out the chill.

"I know I don't, but you're welcome to come if you want. My crazy family will be there, but we'll have plenty of room."

Audrey looks down at the gravel for a moment as though she's a little embarrassed, and then brings her eyes up to meet mine. "Are you sure?"

"Of course I'm sure." While I'm waiting for her decision, I fumble with the keys in my pocket.

"Then I'll be there!" she replies, smiling. The sun comes from behind a cloud and hits her face, causing her to squint her eyes a bit. "Thank you, Maddie." She smiles warmly, and for a split second I'm afraid she's going to hug me, but she just turns and walks away.

Poor Audrey. She doesn't really have a family at all, just some people who happen to be her parents biologically, although they aren't available for her emotionally. They throw money at her and hope she'll leave them alone. I feel for her in a genuine, heartfelt way—probably more than both her parents combined.

"Maddie!" I hear my name being called across the parking lot. Turning, I see Sue rushing towards me with a big aluminum pan.

"What's the matter, Sue?"

She catches up to me and holds the pan out in front of her. "Here, this is for you." She begins to get goose bumps on her arms, which are bare past the sleeves of her T-shirt.

"What is it?"

"A turkey, fully cooked. If you warm it up tomorrow, it will taste like you took it right out of the oven."

"That's really nice of you, but I can't take this from the shelter."

"We've got plenty...there will be so much food left over. Please, take it." She shivers a little as the wind blows through again.

"But I've already got a turkey," I protest. "Can't you use this for someone else?"

"Please, Maddie," she begs, pressing her lips into a smile. "Just in case? Trust me on this one."

"Okay," I agree reluctantly, taking the pan from her hands. "Thank you."

"Thank you for all your help," she calls as she turns away. "Maybe we'll see you next year."

"I hope so!" I yell across the lot as I open the door to the Tahoe and slide the pan into the passenger seat.

Chapter Twenty-Seven

Oh my goodness!

Thank God for Sue.

Thank God, thank God, thank God.

I got home last night and my turkey was all burnt on the outside and almost frozen on the inside. Immediately I called Dina to complain about the horrible directions she gave me. I did exactly what you said, I told her, and thawed it for six hours and cooked for thirty-six hours. Well, I didn't exactly cook for thirty-six hours, because it looked horrible way before then.

"Oh, Maddie," Dina sighed, "you were supposed to thaw for thirty-six hours and cook for six."

Whoops. Tiny little error on my part. I must have reversed the directions when I wrote them down. This whole thing could have turned into a huge catastrophe if it hadn't been for Sue and that pan of turkey. I can only imagine what Mom would have said about not having any turkey at our Thanksgiving dinner, after our confrontation yesterday. *You better shape up by tomorrow.* What does that mean, exactly?

I'm only slightly stressed out about the dinner, because— I must confess—Hazel brought a lot of food. She insisted, and I didn't argue with her. I am in charge of the turkey (graciously provided by Sue), mashed potatoes (which were relatively easy to make, even for me), green beans and carrots (from a can – no one needs to know), and one dessert (cheesecake from a local bakery— believe me, no one wanted me to undertake that challenge). Hazel called me this morning and asked how I was coming with the turkey. If anyone else would have asked, I would have been offended; however, I know Hazel would never purposely insult me.

She was just making sure I had it under control, or she would have stepped in to help. That's very nice and motherly of her, in my opinion.

Dinner's in thirty, so I expect people to arrive any minute. Hazel and Tucker are already here, having arrived with practically a carload of food. I'm a little relieved, actually. Mom had told me before that she was bringing some food, but last night she called to tell me that she just didn't have time because she had volunteered all day. I didn't bother to mention that she stormed out before lunch time, as that is probably best left unsaid. Who knows what kind of mood she will be in today, and Brittany... Well, I hesitate to even speculate about her state of mind.

The doorbell rings, and I peek out the window. Audrey— so she did come after all. I didn't exactly expect her *not* to come, but I'm still a little surprised to see her here, at my own house. I mean, Josh's house. Now that she knows my address, she'll probably be here every night. Today's not the time to think about that, though.

"Hi," I say cheerfully as I open the door to her. She hurries in from the cold and pulls her scarf off her neck.

"Hi, Maddie," she adds with a big smile. "Thanks for inviting me. I didn't know if I should bring anything, so I stopped and got something at the bakery."

"That's nice of you," I reply, turning away from the foyer. "This is Hazel and her husband Tucker. They're Josh's parents. You remember me telling you about Josh, who owns the house?" She nods quickly. "And this is my...friend, Audrey."

"Very nice to meet you," Audrey states as I take her coat and hang it in the closet.

I quickly head toward the kitchen, and she follows close behind.

"Wow, did you do all this?" she wonders when she sees the huge spread of food on the counters.

"No, it was mostly Hazel. She's an excellent cook. If I cooked this meal, you might not want to eat it."

"Maddie, do you need any help in the kitchen?" Hazel calls. "I feel useless sitting out here."

"Sure, if you want to help."

Hazel is behind me before I know it, placing spoons on serving dishes and stirring some of the food she brought. I set the table a couple of hours ago, getting ahead of myself on timing. I figured it would take me all day to do the cooking, but with the limited number of things I wound up doing, it took no time at all. Now I feel like we're simply waiting until dinnertime, because there's really nothing else to be done.

I'm sure Hazel doesn't know what to do with herself either. She always thrives on being busy, so sitting and talking probably drives her crazy. She hadn't seemed overly enthused when I suggested having the dinner at our house, but of course she didn't refuse. She must have busied herself earlier with making the food, but now that she's here, she seems a little uncomfortable.

"So, how do you know Maddie?" Hazel questions Audrey, readjusting the rolls she brought in her basket.

"We work together." Audrey grins over at me.

"Yes," I chime in, somewhat afraid that Audrey is going to tell her we go shopping all day. "Audrey and I have been working together on all the special projects we've been doing recently."

"Really?" Hazel wonders, looking thoughtfully at Audrey. "It's so wonderful the things you've been doing lately to help the community. It's nice to see a company giving back to its neighbors."

"Thank you," Audrey states, standing a little straighter.

"Does your family live far away, that you're not with them on Thanksgiving?" Hazel continues. Audrey looks down from the corner of her eye, unsure what to say.

"Actually, Audrey's parents decided to use the vacation time to go on a little trip, so I invited her here instead." I attempt to give Audrey a reassuring smile.

"Well, it's certainly nice to have you with us," Hazel insists, going back to inspecting her dishes.

Audrey and I busy ourselves removing the plastic wrap from the food containers until I hear the doorbell again. While I'm

walking in the direction of the door, it suddenly flies open as Mom barges in.

"We're here!" she announces loudly. "I hope you don't mind, but we brought the Hubers."

The Hubers?! So it's not enough that you decide not to bring any food, but you also invite your own guests hoping that the food I have won't cover everyone. Very nice. And the Hubers?? It's like an official meeting of the Brittany fan club.

"Who are the Hubers?" Audrey whispers.

"The Hubers are my sister-in-law Brittany's parents."

Audrey nods her understanding as the house begins to bustle with activity.

"Hi, Maddie," Dad says, peeking around the corner. I smile at him only briefly before he disappears.

"Where did you get all this food, Maddie?" Mom grills me as she comes into the kitchen. "Did you buy it somewhere? I know you couldn't have made some of this."

So much for the inspirational vote of confidence.

"Actually, Hazel helped me out quite a bit," I explain, grinning at Hazel. Mom just makes a low noise in her throat and keeps inspecting all the dishes.

"We better eat soon. I'm starving," I overhear Brittany complain from the foyer.

"Are you comfortable, dear?" Mrs. Huber wonders. "Can I get you anything?"

"Something to drink," Brittany orders. "Why is it so hot in here? I can't breathe!"

"I need something for Brittany to drink right away," Mrs. Huber declares as she comes into the kitchen.

"Take whatever you need," I offer, pointing to the refrigerator before I take in the scene. Mom is poking about the food, Mrs. Huber's head is in the refrigerator, Hazel is stirring her gravy, and Audrey and I are hanging back in stupefied silence.

"I think everything's ready, Maddie," Hazel whispers, "if you want to go ahead and get started."

Hazel can tell the natives are getting restless. Well, not all the natives—basically one in particular, who never ceases to complain no matter where she is or what she's doing. I help transfer some dishes to the table and put the finishing touches on the ones that need it while Mrs. Huber hurriedly takes Brittany her drink.

"Who's the girl?" Mom asks, pointing at Audrey.

I get that you're upset with me, Mom, but you don't have to take it out on everyone else.

"This is my friend, Audrey," I explain. "She was at the food drive yesterday with me, remember?"

"How could I forget that fiasco?" she wonders, rolling her eyes. "I don't suppose you told Hazel what you did?"

"Oh, Maddie told me all about it," Hazel says, referring to the high number of donations and volunteering. Of course I didn't tell her about Harley. "It sounds like it was a fantastic success."

"I can't imagine what lies you've been telling, Maddie," Mom complains, turning and walking from the room. Hazel immediately shoots me a sympathetic smile. She knows all about Mom, and she's seen these kinds of scenes many times before.

"Can someone turn on a fan or something?" Brittany belts from the living room. "I'm practically dying in here."

"It is hot in here," Mrs. Huber agrees. "Why is it so hot in here?"

"For goodness sake, just open a window and stop complaining," Dad chimes in.

Thank you, Dad.

"The window's stuck," Mrs. Huber states. "The window's stuck. Why won't the window move? Somebody come here and fix this window."

"You have to unlock it first," I hear Lance tell her, and then I hear a whoosh as it rises into the air.

"Well, I was trying to unlock it," Mrs. Huber replies. "It must be broken. Brittany, dear, are you comfortable now?"

"I'm pregnant. I'm never comfortable."

"Mom," Marilyn interjects, "can we go outside for a minute?"

"Ask your dad. Can't you see I'm dying here?"

"Dad?"

"No, sweetheart, we're getting ready to eat."

"You better hurry, Maddie," Hazel hints. I agree—this is falling apart quickly.

"Dinner's ready!" I call. Shuffling can be heard as people begin to travel in my direction.

"Is it always this crazy?" Audrey whispers.

"Unfortunately, yes."

"You're going to have to open a window in there," Brittany demands. "If it's hot in one room it will be hot in the other."

"Why don't you just eat in here where it's more comfortable?" Lance suggests.

"No. Why should I have to miss out on the adult conversation just because I'm pregnant? I'm *having* a child, that doesn't mean I *am* one, Lance."

The level of restraint that I am showing in not hitting that lobbed softball is pretty impressive.

"Lance, why don't you push the recliner into the dining room for Brittany so she'll be comfortable?" Mrs. Huber suggests.

"No!" Lance replies. "If Brittany wants to sit in a recliner, she'll just have to stay put. I'm not dragging Maddie's furniture all over the house."

"Some of us are going to have to sit in here," Tucker speaks up. "Maddie wasn't expecting this many people, and not everyone will fit at the table."

"I can eat outside," Marilyn suggests.

"Me too!" little Jordan pipes up.

"You're not going outside," Lance states, "so drop it."

"Maddie set up a special table for you, so you won't have to sit with the adults." Lovely Tucker, defending me so heroically. No wonder Josh is so admirable—he has a great role model.

"I hope you set my place at the special table," Audrey jokes.

"Trust me, Audrey," I say with a laugh, "if I could have put *myself* at the special table, I would have."

"Tucker and I can sit in the other room," Hazel offers. "We don't mind."

"You don't have to do that," I tell her.

"That turkey looks good," Mom says, inspecting the table. "Hazel must have made it."

"Actually, Maddie provided the turkey," Hazel interjects.

"Humph!"

"Somebody needs to tell me everything that Maddie made," Brittany begins, waddling into the dining room, "so I don't accidentally make myself sick."

Nice—going to visit someone's house for the express purpose of eating dinner and then refusing to eat anything they prepared. Brittany and Mom have got to be in this thing together. It is "punish Maddie" day, simply because I ruined her celebrity sighting.

"Apparently she made the turkey," Mom states.

"She might have made this," Brittany says, pointing to one of Hazel's dishes. "It doesn't look very fancy."

"If you don't want to eat here, you know where the door is," I blurt, unable to contain my frustration.

"My goodness, Maddie," Mom chides. "What a gracious hostess you are."

"Maddie has invited us to her home," Dad comes to life, "and she has gone to a lot of trouble. The least you can do is be respectful." Diverting his attention from Mom, Dad offers me a hint of a smile. "Everything looks fantastic, sweetheart. You did a good job."

"Thanks, Dad," I manage through a lump in my throat.

"Well, I don't think—" Mom begins.

"That's enough," Dad mentions quietly, glancing at her. She shuts her mouth and crosses her arms over her chest.

"Maybe we should just say a blessing," Tucker suggests.

"I'm not playing that 'I'm thankful' game," Brittany whines.

"He wants to pray, Brittany," I tell her, "so be quiet a minute."

"Father, we come to You today with thanksgiving in our hearts for all the things You've done in our lives."

"Uh."

That must have been one of the kids. Can no one in this family be respectful of anyone?

"We trust You to feed our spirits, and we pray that You will use this food we are receiving to nourish our bodies as well. Please bless Maddie for her hospitality as she has graciously welcomed all of us into her home."

"Ohhhhh."

What the...?

"And we thank You for this food, which was lovingly prepared by the family You gave us to love. We are eternally grateful for all Your blessings."

"Ohhhhh."

Are you kidding me?

"Amen."

"Amen," a couple people repeat.

Who was doing that? How unbelievably, unspeakably rude.

Lifting my head to look around, I don't see anything unusual. The kids are both standing nearby, but neither one of them is being glared at by the adults, and they don't have guilty looks on their faces.

"Ohhhhh," I hear again, and look over to see Brittany clutching her abdomen. Her mom has noticed her by this time and has rushed to her side.

"What is it, Brittany?" she asks frantically. "Are you in pain, dear? Should I call the ambulance?"

"We're not calling any ambulance," Lance states matter-of-factly.

"Well, what is it, dear? Is it the baby?" Mrs. Huber wonders again.

"I...I don't know exactly," Brittany replies, rubbing her hands across her belly. "Something feels so strange."

"Have you eaten any of the food?" Mom interjects.

There it is: *Maddie has finally done it, after all these years. She has poisoned us all. We knew it would happen. Same old Maddie—always messing things up.*

"She hasn't eaten anything, Mom," Lance lectures. "We just walked in here."

"Ohhhhh."

"It's the baby!" cries Mrs. Huber. "It must be time. I'm taking you to the hospital."

"Maybe that's a good idea," Brittany whimpers.

"Well, if you're going, I'm going too!" Mom declares, heading toward the closet to get her coat. Dad shakes his head and looks up at the ceiling.

Brittany slowly rises from her chair, places her hands on the small of her back, and pushes her protruding stomach out as far as it will go. Mrs. Huber grabs her arm and slowly helps her toward the door, while Mom is quick to return and grab Brittany's other arm so she won't be left out.

"Aren't you coming?" Mom barks, shooting an accusing look at Dad.

"No," he tells her calmly, sitting down at the table.

"Well, how am I supposed to get to the hospital, then?" Mom cries, holding up Brittany's progress.

"Ride with the Hubers," Dad suggests. Mom makes a low noise in her throat and begins to shuffle along once again.

"We should hurry," Brittany urges. "The pain is unbearable."

"Oh my goodness," Mrs. Huber groans.

"Lance!" Brittany belts. "Get a move on."

"The hospital is ten minutes away," Lance answers. "I wouldn't exactly say you're in a life or death situation here. Why don't you wait a few minutes and at least time your contractions before we waste a trip? I mean, it is Thanksgiving, after all."

"I'm dying here, Mama," Brittany cries. "Please help me."

"Lance, how can you be so unfeeling?" Mrs. Huber rebukes. "Can't you see she's in pain? She's your wife, for heaven's sake."

"This is so ridiculous," Lance mutters under his breath, going to grab his coat.

"Do we have to go?" Marilyn wonders.

"Of course you do!" Brittany orders. Marilyn and Jordan stomp toward the front door.

"Russell!" Mom shouts at Dad. "This isn't funny anymore. Come on!"

"I told you, woman, I'm not going."

"Well, what are you going to do if the baby is born and you aren't there?" she asks, hands on her hips.

"I'll come see the baby after I eat," Dad says nonchalantly.

"Is there anything we can do?" Hazel wonders.

"No, you should stay and enjoy your Thanksgiving," Mom reasons. "You made all that food for Maddie's dinner, and it shouldn't go to waste."

Those of us who remain watch in shocked silence as the group makes their way out the door and into the driveway, leaving only Dad and Tucker around the table, with Hazel and Audrey joining me in the kitchen. Mom is the last one to button her coat and head out the door, stopping just outside to pull it closed.

"We've got to go, Maddie," she offers as an afterthought. "Brittany's having the baby."

Of course she is. Who would have expected anything less?

"You're a peach, Mad, you know that?"

The call from Josh comes through about two hours after everyone left his house, finding me lounging lazily on the couch, reading my third Camdyn Taylor/C.W. Oliver novel.

"Why exactly am I a peach?"

"You involved my parents in your Thanksgiving," he states quietly. "You made them feel like part of your family. I couldn't be more proud of you."

"Your parents obviously didn't give you the entire story." Gazing at the wall in front of me, I will my heart to start beating normally. Now that I know internally that I have feelings for Josh, I'm constantly nervous that he will somehow draw the information out of me.

"Yeah, they gave me the entire story—the bad, the ugly, and the rude. Like I said, I couldn't be more proud of you."

"Thank you," I mutter, finding it hard to come up with anything to say.

"You seem kind of quiet tonight."

"Probably exhausted," I joke, giving a slight laugh.

"How are things going with your tennis instructor?"

Pulling at a string at the hem of my T-shirt, I twist my mouth to the side momentarily. "As it turns out, he had a huge flaw—one that I couldn't look past."

"Of course," he says with a sigh. I can imagine him rolling his eyes at me in disgust.

"Well, don't be too disappointed in me, please, because I have sworn off dating for good."

"What?"

Rising to my feet, I cross to the window and glance out at the street, suddenly feeling very alone.

"If you were here, Josh..." I begin, but quickly stop talking.

"What? If I was there, what?"

"Nothing. You'd probably be watching football or something and completely ignoring me. Or I'd be stuck at my parents' house and ready to pull my hair out."

"Just for the record, I wouldn't ignore you, and I would gladly rescue you from any hair-pulling situations."

"I know," I acknowledge, tears suddenly filling my eyes. "I have things I need to do, so I better go."

"Oh, okay. Goodnight, Mad. And happy Thanksgiving." He sounds a little sad himself, probably because he has spent yet

another Thanksgiving without his family. And how insensitive am I that I didn't even consider that until this very moment?

"Happy Thanksgiving, Josh."

Chapter Twenty-Eight

I should have known better, really. You'd think after twenty-five years, I would have at least given it some thought before making the offer. Inviting Mom over for Thanksgiving dinner. What am I, a lunatic? The whole thing was destined for disaster from the beginning (from the moment I opened my big mouth, actually).

The funny thing is, as soon as the Brittany parade went out the door, everyone relaxed and we wound up having a very nice meal together. Dad seemed so relieved just to be out of their sight for a few minutes, and even Audrey appeared to enjoy herself. I couldn't have asked for a better Thanksgiving dinner—no drama, no yelling, and zero complaining. I can only imagine the horror that would have taken place had Brittany not made such a scene and decided to leave.

Oh, and I bet you're wondering about the baby. Turns out Brittany wasn't in labor after all. She had gas. What I would have given to see her face when the doctor gave her *that* tidbit of information.

Mom left a message on my voice mail yesterday. It was nothing like the messages she had been leaving before (in other words, the "I love Maddie" montage). This one was short and to the point.

"Maddie, this is your mother. We drew names for Christmas. I'll send yours in the mail." Click.

If I could just figure out some way to avoid the whole clan of them at Christmas time, maybe my life would be a lot less stressful. Let's see… I would have to find an excuse to sneak Dad out, because he would be miserable without me there. It's bad enough when there's two of us, but I can't imagine being poor Dad, the only sane one in the bunch. (There's always Lance, of course, but he is too closely linked with the madness to ever be able to escape.) It makes me so grateful to have Tucker and Hazel. If I didn't have a sane home to escape to, I would definitely have to move out of state. No ifs, ands, or buts about it.

"What do you think of this one, Maddie?" Audrey asks, pushing a black notebook in front of me. We are spending the morning at the florist, trying to decide on the arrangements for the wedding. The picture she placed in front of me shows the front of the church decorated exclusively with white blooms and green ivy.

"It's lovely," I reply, "but it doesn't exactly match your personality."

"I just thought it looks classy," she responds with a sigh.

"Classy is good, but we want a personal touch too, right?"

"Yeah," she mutters, pulling the book away from me and leafing through it again.

"Is something wrong?" I ask her. She shrugs her shoulders.

"I just wish Derrick was here," she states sadly.

"I'm sure he wouldn't be very happy about having to pick the flowers. Maybe he can help you choose the food or the music. Those seem like things a guy would be more interested in."

"I don't wish he was here, as in here at the florist. I just wish he was around, so I could talk to him."

"Isn't he back from Thanksgiving?" Sliding another notebook away from her and in front of me, I look at some simpler arrangements.

"He was back, but he's gone on a business trip now."

Derrick is gone practically all the time, from what Audrey says. Once they're married, she'll be spending a lot of time alone. Part of me wonders if she's really considered the ramifications of all his business travel.

"Well, maybe when he comes back to town we can try to get him involved a little bit," I suggest.

"That sounds good."

"In fact, why doesn't he help you pick the food? When we make the appointment, we'll make sure he's free as well."

Audrey nods her agreement and continues staring at the book in front of her, her finger stuck between pages as she keeps flipping back in a way that indicates that something has caught her interest.

"This is pretty," I say, holding my book in front of her. "You could make the roses the same as the colors you chose."

"Yes, it's pretty," she states uninterestedly, while I pull the book back in front of me.

Even though Audrey is much better than when I first met her, sometimes I wish she wasn't quite so moody. She really brings me down when she acts like this. I was beginning to become accustomed to her two distinct sides of giddiness and intense sadness. Giddy I could handle, although sometimes it was a little too over-the-top. Intensely sad isn't exactly fun, but usually I can talk her through it. This new, third mood—sort of melancholy without going over the edge into complete sadness—is difficult to understand. There's nothing I would like more than to say the right words and have her perk up a bit, but I can't seem to find them.

"What about this?" I wonder, showing her another picture. "The tulips look classy, but you could get them in the colors you like." She just resolutely nods her head. "What is that you have your finger on?"

"Hmm? Oh, nothing."

"Come on, Audrey, let me see it."

"It's just something I thought was nice, but it won't work."

"It won't hurt anything to let me see it, though."

"See?" she says as she relents and opens the book. "It's just way too—"

"I love it. I think it's great."

"Really?"

"Yes, really." The picture is of Gerber daisies, very bright and vivid. Audrey's colors could be easily incorporated. They're bold and cheerful, and they match the spirit of what a wedding is supposed to be. In my opinion, they're wonderful.

"You don't think it's too bright?" she questions.

"I think it's perfect. You made an excellent choice."

Audrey sits back in her chair, admiring the picture with a smile. Maybe that was a good start to bringing her out of her melancholy, but I think I have another idea.

We pull into the parking lot at around 1:00 in the afternoon. Audrey has been a little leery ever since we left the florist, wondering what I'm going to make her do. My response is that she should trust me, but she still seems a little anxious, even though she should know by now that I only have her best interests at heart.

"Beautiful Vision Day Spa?" she blurts. "That's where you're taking me?"

"That's right."

"What are you going to do, make me get a massage?"

"Something like that." I open the door to the Tahoe and head toward the day spa with Audrey following close behind.

"It smells funny in here," she comments.

"It smells like a camping trip," I inform her. Not that I would know, because I've never been camping. My mother would have never done such a thing, but if I was to imagine what camping smelled like, it would be the scent of pine trees and rain hitting the dust.

"Hi, can I help you?" a young woman with a sleek ponytail wonders as she emerges from a side door.

"We're here to see Tish," I state, and she tells us to follow her.

"Who's Tish?" Audrey whispers.

"A friend." We walk around the corner and into the salon, greeted by the sound of hair dryers and people chatting. Tish spots me from across the room and raises her hand in greeting.

"Hi, Maddie!" she calls. "How's it going?"

"Great! This is my friend, Audrey."

Tish is about five years older than me, with dark hair halfway down her back interspersed with streaks of green and blue and a little diamond stud in her nose. We've been friends for the last two or three years, after I came here once on a whim to get my hair trimmed. We hit it off and I've been coming here ever since.

"What are we doing today, ladies?" she asks, smiling at Audrey.

"Total makeover," I request, glancing at Audrey to gauge her reaction. She just blinks a couple times and looks at me quizzically. "She's getting married in a couple of months, and she needs to look absolutely perfect."

"Congratulations!" Tish gushes, pulling a cape from the wall. "So a total makeover—we're talking the works?"

"The works," I agree. "I'll leave her in your hands."

"You're leaving me?" Audrey squeaks.

"Don't worry, Tish is the greatest. You're going to love it."

"Well, what are you going to do?" Audrey wonders, worry evident in her voice.

"I think I might get that massage you mentioned," I inform her breezily, walking away and leaving her standing in the salon.

I snuck a quick peek at Audrey when I came back to the salon, but she was sitting there reading a magazine with tons of foils on her head. Tish caught my eye and asked if I wanted Audrey's makeup done, which of course was an affirmative. A total makeover

is a total makeover, and I am determined that she will leave here today a different person. Maybe a slightly more polished look will give her self-esteem a boost and will help her be a little more confident.

A total of three hours has passed when Audrey finally walks through the door, and I rise and drop my magazine onto a nearby chair.

"Audrey, is that you?" I ask teasingly, to which she responds by laughing. Her hair is now a lovely caramel-brown with subtle blonde highlights, and it looks sleek and polished. No more tousled dip-dyed mess. She will fit in with the most elegant guests at her wedding, and her makeup is perfectly applied. No rosy red cheeks or spider eyelashes.

"What do you think?" I question her.

She smiles and brings her hand up to gently touch her hair. "I love it!"

"As well you should," I inform her, standing proudly in front of me and looking comfortable in her own skin for the first time since I laid eyes upon her. "You look marvelous."

Chapter Twenty-Nine

It's Friday, and Audrey and I are sitting at a secluded table at the RK Steak and Grill. She is unbelievably excited, mainly because Derrick just got into town last night and agreed to meet us here for lunch to do a food tasting for the wedding. He hasn't seen Audrey since the big transformation, and I'm afraid she is going to burst with anticipation before he even arrives.

"What do you think he'll say?" she asks me for at least the fifth time. I glance up at her over my menu and smile.

"He'll say you look incredible."

She pretends to look at her menu for a moment, and then brings her eyes up and takes a breath. "But what—"

"Audrey, you asked me already. He'll be here in a minute, and then you'll find out for sure."

She forces her gaze to her menu and begins studying each item intently as I notice someone who looks like the picture she showed me walking around in front of the restaurant.

"Audrey, is that him?" I wonder, and she turns to look in the direction I indicate.

"Yes! Derrick, here we are!"

He slowly walks our way, pulling his cell phone out and looking at it once on the way over. He looks much like his picture—relatively fit, dark hair perfectly held in place, caramel-colored eyes.

"Hey," he says, pulling out his chair and sitting down. "I didn't recognize you with the hair."

Audrey smiles and reaches up to smooth her freshly brown tresses. "Do you like it?" she questions expectantly.

"Looks good," he mutters, not bothering to even glance in her direction. He picks up his menu and starts browsing through the selections.

That's the best you can do, Derrick? Shame on you.

"I'm Maddie, by the way," I interrupt his perusing.

"Yeah, nice to meet you," he states, jerking his eyes up to me. "Do we have to order something in particular, or just whatever we want?"

"You can order whatever you'd like. We're just looking for something that might be good for the wedding, but it's ultimately between you and Audrey what that food is going to be." He nods a few times and continues to look at the menu.

Derrick might be good looking, but he doesn't appear to have the best personality. I'm really wondering how he and Audrey met. They don't exactly seem like a compatible match, from the outside looking in.

We sit in awkward silence until the waiter comes to take our order.

"I think I'll have the lobster tail," Audrey begins, handing him her menu.

"Chicken with mushroom sauce," I add.

"Bring me the steak and shrimp," Derrick orders, "medium rare."

The instant the waiter disappears, I wonder what we're going to talk about. Audrey seems too nervous to bring much to the conversation, and Derrick appears to be extremely uninterested.

"So, Derrick," I begin, "Audrey tells me you're an investment banker?"

"Junior investment banker," he replies.

"You have to travel a lot with that job?" He shifts a little in his seat and places his right foot against his left knee as he leans back to make himself comfortable.

"You know, visiting clients and things, the normal business travel."

"A lot of your clients must be from far away," I casually mention, based on what Audrey has told me in the past.

"No, we deal mainly with local clientele."

"It's a wonder, then, that you have so many overnight trips."

"Well," he says, his eyes completely fixed on me, "you do what the job requires."

"Of course," I reply, taking a drink of my water. Audrey is simply sitting back, listening but not partaking in the conversation. "I'm curious, how did you two meet?"

"Work," Audrey states quickly. "Oh, not the job I have now, but at my old job. Derrick brought Paddy into the shelter to rehome him, and I wound up taking him home with me."

A bit stunned, I practically gape at Audrey. "You didn't tell me anything about a shelter."

"Didn't I? I worked at the animal shelter the entire time I was going to college. It wasn't until after I graduated that Dad insisted I get a real job at his company."

Wow, Audrey Cooper working at an animal shelter. I can imagine that driving Cooper out of his mind.

"Working at a shelter for free isn't a real job," Derrick complains, intensely scrutinizing my face.

"It's commendable," I offer, grinning at Audrey, suddenly with a newfound respect for her.

"So what do you do, Maddie?" Derrick asks, placing his elbow on the table and his chin on his hand.

"I'm Kent Cooper's assistant," I reply simply.

"So you work for Audrey's dad."

What is this, a job interview or something? This is supposed to be a casual lunch.

"How does Audrey do up there?" he continues. "Is she completely worthless?"

Audrey makes a noise that indicates she's offended, but he doesn't laugh or smile. "Derrick!" she exclaims. "I'm not worthless."

"Actually," I interject, "Audrey has helped me quite a bit lately with the charity projects we've worked on."

"Audrey's working for charity, or Audrey is a charity?" he wonders with a laugh, pausing to take a drink of his water.

"I've told you about the charity drives we've been doing," Audrey adds. He waves her off with his hand and continues to look at me.

"So, Derrick, do you have any ideas for the wedding?" I question, a bit uneasy about the direction of our conversation. "Audrey and I have been planning a lot, but it would be nice to have your input."

"Weddings are for ladies. I don't really care about it."

"Well, it's a big day for Audrey. She would probably like your input to make her decisions a little easier."

"If it's a big day for Audrey, then let Audrey make the decisions. It has nothing to do with me."

I really hope Derrick got up on the wrong side of the bed this morning, because if this is his permanent personality, he is horrible company.

"He does always say that," Audrey speaks up. "The wedding is for girls, and the honeymoon is for the man."

"So you're planning the honeymoon?" I wonder, glancing over at him. "Where are you going?"

"There won't be any honeymoon," he states simply, averting his eyes to the other diners in the restaurant.

"I thought you were going to ask about that," Audrey implores, and he shoots her a warning look.

"It's just not a possibility."

"Derrick has a business meeting the Monday after the wedding," Audrey explains to me. "I thought he was going to ask his boss if he could get out of it."

"The world doesn't revolve around you, Audrey. You'll just have to forget about a honeymoon for now."

The waiter returns with three salad plates, and no one speaks for a moment. It's difficult not to glance between Audrey and Derrick, wondering what weird circumstances would bring

these two people together. Audrey I can understand to a certain degree, because she doesn't have the greatest self-esteem and probably thinks she can't do any better, so she settles. Derrick, on the other hand… If he dislikes Audrey as much as he acts like he does, why is he even in this relationship?

"I think I'm going to the ladies' room," Audrey suddenly announces, standing up and walking away from the table.

"Audrey really looks great with her hair like that," I mention, not really expecting a comment but simply wanting Derrick to realize that he should have noticed.

"You can cut the crap," he says, picking at his salad.

"Excuse me?"

"Audrey told me she had this great new friend Maddie, and I have to admit I was skeptical. Audrey doesn't make friends. She's way too needy for that. Well, now that I've met you, the picture is crystal clear. You don't have to keep pretending to be her friend. I get it."

"Get what?" I ask angrily, placing my salad fork on the table.

"Look at you. People like you don't hang out with people like Audrey. Her dad made you be her friend—it's part of your job. He pays you to take her to places like this and get her hair done and pretend you like her. I get it, so you can drop the charade when she's not in the room."

"Audrey is a nice girl," I say quietly. "She deserves to have people in her life that care about her."

"Whatever."

This guy is exasperating. How dare he make such a judgment about me? He doesn't even know me.

"Well, if you don't mind me saying so, you're a very attractive woman," Derrick states, eyeing me suggestively. "Are you available?"

Am I…? Of all the nerve.

"Why are you with Audrey?" I confront him, almost ready to come across the table and ring his neck. As though he senses my emotions, he simply grins.

"Same reason you are, sweetheart: Daddy's money."

"Kent will never give you anything," I whisper. Derrick laughs and holds his fork suspended in the air.

"He's already given me plenty, and there will be a lot more where that came from."

"And Audrey?"

"What Audrey doesn't know won't hurt her. Look at her! That girl is desperate for attention. All I have to do is pat her on the head once in a while when I'm coming or going, and she'll be happy."

Audrey suddenly returns from the ladies' room, smiling at the sight of her fiancé eating lunch with her best friend, and I feel absolutely sick. Derrick may be the biggest jerk on the face of the earth, but he was right about me in one respect: Cooper definitely does pay me to be his daughter's friend. He might not have intended to do so, but that *is* the situation. I wouldn't be helping Audrey with the wedding had Cooper not ordered me to do so, and we wouldn't speak to each other at all if Cooper hadn't demanded that she work with me on the projects I've been coordinating.

"Here comes the food!" Audrey comments cheerfully as she sits down. Derrick uses the opportunity to wink at me before he looks over at Audrey.

What am I going to do? I can't *not* tell Audrey that her fiancé is only after her money, can I? Then again, how am I supposed to approach that kind of subject?

Hey, Audrey, by the way—Derrick is using you.

Oh, Audrey, in case you didn't know, Derrick is a pig.

Hi Audrey. Did I mention that your fiancé doesn't really love you?

I can't do it. I simply can't do it.

But I have to, don't I? If I don't, then that makes everything Derrick just said about me true. The only way to truly be Audrey's friend is to tell her this horrible thing that I absolutely do not want to tell her. What am I going to do?

Driving home from grocery shopping after work, I happen to see Derrick walking into one of the local clubs. I slow down as I'm passing, because I think my eyes might be playing tricks on me, but it's definitely Derrick. He told us over lunch that he was leaving on a two-day business trip. Apparently the trip was canceled. Funny that he didn't bother to tell his fiancée, who informed me at the day's end that she would be washing her dogs that evening.

A few blocks past the club, I pull the Tahoe into a vacant parking lot, screeching the tires. I didn't have the courage to tell Audrey about Derrick this afternoon, but I'm not going to let him get away with his lies. I'm going to that club, and I'm going to confront him face to face.

Just as soon as I back off of this curb.

The bouncer at the door doesn't look very friendly when I walk in. I stand on my tiptoes, searching for Derrick.

"ID, miss," the burly gentleman states.

"Oh, I'm not staying," I explain. "I'm just looking for someone."

"If you're inside the door, I need your ID," he says, speaking a little louder. I fumble through my purse for my driver's license and hand it to him. He waves me through, and I step forward into the pulsating, driving dance beat. There aren't very many people on the dance floor, but if I were to guess, I don't think Derrick is one for dancing the night away. He is probably here meeting someone, or at least trying to meet someone.

"Hi," a male voice behind me states. I ignore him and keep walking. I am *not* here to meet someone—simply to bust someone. I scan every table within my eyesight looking for Derrick, and finally see him sitting toward the back with his arm around a blonde. I know that is definitely not Audrey, because I was with her earlier, and her hair is still brown. Busted, buddy!

I march to the back, ignoring people staring at me. Halfway to Derrick's table, I stop and pull out my cellphone. It never hurts to have a little proof, does it? Snapping a quick picture, I drop my phone into my purse and tap Derrick on the shoulder. He looks up at me but doesn't bother removing his arm from the new girl.

"What are you doing here?" he asks, reaching for the beer bottle in front of him. I put my hand on the bottle and shove it just out of his reach.

"I suppose I could ask you the same thing," I say. "Who's the girl?"

"Who is that, Derrick?" the blonde questions, looking at me with wide eyes.

"Who am I?" I repeat with a laugh. "Who am I? Derrick is my brother, and his poor wife is sitting at home eight months pregnant. She asked me to go to the store to get her some milk, and guess whose car I see in the parking lot of this club!"

"You're married?" the blonde questions accusingly, pushing away from Derrick.

"Ash, let me explain…"

"You're a pig!" she exclaims as she walks away.

Derrick slowly picks up the bottle, laughing up at me. "What are you doing here?" He continues to grin at me over his drink.

"I just wanted to see what this out-of-town business you are on really amounted to," I reply, folding my arms across my chest.

"Maybe you just wanted me for yourself."

"I never have found a soft spot for lying, backstabbing, money-grubbing worms."

"Well, you certainly seem obsessed with me, for someone who doesn't care." He puts his drink on the table and leans back in his chair, coolly allowing his eyes to regard my entire form in a way that makes me feel like I need a shower.

"I do care," I inform him, "about Audrey. Here's the deal: either you tell her, or I will."

"You do what you need to do, sweetheart. Audrey won't believe you."

"We'll see about that," I say, spinning on my heel and heading for the door. What a horrible, impossible person! As soon as I get home, I'm sending him an e-mail with this picture from my phone. When he knows I have proof, he'll be forced to tell Audrey.

"Leaving so soon?" someone calls from one of the tables. I keep walking, completely focused on the door.

"Hey, Maddie!" I hear a voice behind me. Turning, I see Derrick coming after me.

Lousy scumbag – he's probably going to beg me not to tell Audrey. He'll plead with me to understand his plight, falling on his knees and asking for forgiveness.

"You dropped your wallet," he tells me, handing it over. "Have a nice evening."

Humph!

My cellphone begins to ring the instant I hit the door, and I fish it out of my purse and bring it quickly to my ear.

"Hello," I practically yell, placing one hand over my free ear to try to block out the noise as I step further from the building.

"Mad? Where are you?"

"Seedy bar chasing Derrick," I quickly tell Josh, glancing to make sure I won't be run down by any vehicles before I cross the street.

"Derrick, huh? Should have known your dating hiatus wouldn't last long."

"No, the hiatus is still in full swing. Derrick is Audrey's cheating fiancé. Not with me, in case you were wondering. Some poor blonde looking for love in all the wrong places." Stopping midstride in the parking lot, I ponder my poor word choice. "Again, not me. Just to clarify."

"You didn't need to clarify," Josh assures me with a teasing tone. "I knew that statement didn't apply to you. You're not blonde."

Ouch.

"Very funny, Mr. Mason. Why are you calling me on a Friday evening? Are you keeping tabs on me?"

"No, I just wanted to ask you a favor. I ordered gifts for Mom and Dad, and I was hoping you would keep them at the house and deliver them on Christmas."

"Yes, of course."

"Hey, baby!" a male voice calls across the parking lot.

"I have a Taser, and I will maim you!"

"Wow, you've gone all the way from dating hiatus to hostile territory."

Opening the door to the Tahoe, I slide into the driver's seat and then lock myself inside. "I don't really have a Taser. Maybe I should get one, though. Although I don't normally employ the habit of going to seedy bars."

"Remind me why you're chasing a man around a bar?"

"You know Audrey, Cooper's daughter, the one I'm planning the wedding for?"

"Of course, Maddie the wedding planner."

Yep, still sounds ridiculous.

"Well, her fiancé is only marrying her to try to get his hands on her dad's money. Add to that the fact that I caught him here tonight with another woman. Don't I owe it to her as a friend to tell her the truth?"

"As a friend? That truth is going to sting."

"More than waking up five years from now reeling from a divorce to a man who never cared about her and has taken half of everything she owns? What if they have kids?"

"You have to do the right thing," he surmises, clearing his throat. "Now, on to a more important question. Did you put up a Christmas tree?"

Smiling, I glance at myself in the rear view mirror. "I might have decorated a small tree in front of the picture window."

"How small?"

"Small, like eight and a half."

"Inches?" He sounds skeptical, with good reason.

"Feet. There may or may not be peacock feathers sticking out of the branches, and I also might have doused it with glitter."

"Leave it to you to celebrate the birth of Jesus with peacock feathers and glitter. Man, I wish I could see it. I'd give just about anything to be home this year."

"I'm sure it would be a disappointment," I add, sensing his melancholy mood.

"Being with you wouldn't be a disappointment." He paused and I felt my breath catch in my chest. "All of you, I mean. Mom and Dad. Do you remember a couple years ago when Jess and Levi were home, and Mom refused to put the star on the tree until everyone was there?"

"Of course I do. She included me in her 'everyone,' and you were all waiting for me when I showed up. Mom had just given me one of her famous 'why aren't you Brittany' speeches, and when I saw all of you saving your special moment, I turned into a basket case."

"We wanted you to put the star on the tree, Mad. Things just don't feel the same when you're not there."

"Because you need someone there to provide some comic relief?" I joke, shrugging off the sense of longing that's rising inside me.

"No, because you belong there. You're part of the Mason family just as though God designed it that way."

"So you could have two annoying sisters," I offer, gripping the steering wheel tightly, unable to force myself to start the engine.

"No. So I could have one annoying sister and one sweet Mad."

"Hey honey, where you going?" a gruff voice calls from the front of the Tahoe. "Party's inside."

Starting the engine, I rev it loudly and watch him jerk out of the way. Rolling my window down about an inch, I yell, "You better move! I have no idea how to drive this big old vehicle." The man scuttles out of the area as I inch forward.

"Nicely played," Josh assesses. "Sounds like you have your hands full. I'll send you my parents' gifts."

"You can count on me," I assure him right before he hangs up. "Always."

Chapter Thirty

It's been a week since the confrontation with Derrick. I thought for sure he would have made his move by now, but Audrey has continued to come in every day talking about her wedding. I don't know what could have gone wrong. I'm absolutely positive Derrick received the picture I sent by e-mail. What other proof do I need to make him come clean?

Even if he hasn't told Audrey, I just don't have the stomach to work on the wedding today. I've been keeping up with the charade all week, and I can't bear to look at her excited face one more time. When I think of all the money we've already spent on this wedding—the dress, the florist, the food—what's going to become of it all? And what about Audrey? The girl is finally starting to get a little self-esteem, and now this? I shudder to think about the meltdown she will have.

Instead, I'll work on my new project today. We've partnered with the fire department for their annual Christmas toy drive, and Cooper even voluntarily donated a large sum of money from the company. To say I was shocked would be the understatement of the century, but maybe he has seen the positive outcome of the work we've been doing lately. When the community begins to think you're a great company, only good things can follow, right?

We've been getting a lot of positive publicity lately, and Katie told me they were getting more applicants than usual for open positions. It makes sense, really—people want to work for a company that cares about the community. It logically follows that, if the company cares about strangers, it has to care even more about its employees. I'm not sure that's true about Cooper Corporate Financial, but perhaps it will be some day.

If I tell Audrey I'm working on the project today, surely she'll understand. There's nothing pressing that we need to deal with on the wedding, so if I can buy a little time until Derrick finally breaks the news, maybe we won't spend any more money needlessly on something that isn't going to happen.

Walking out of the door to my office, my eyes rest upon Dina's vacant desk. She's on vacation today, lucky woman. I would like to take some vacation time, but I'm sure Audrey would convince Cooper that she needs me too much to allow me to be gone. Just a little more time, and then maybe I can get away for a while.

"Audrey," I say, knocking on her door once before poking my head inside to find her sitting at her desk, reading one of those Hollywood gossip magazines. "Audrey, I think I'm going to work on the toy drive today, if you don't mind."

"That's fine," she states, not looking up. "I'm not sure I want you working on my wedding anymore, anyway."

"Is something wrong?" I ask, stepping inside the door. She flips another page of her magazine and continues to look down.

"Have you been e-mailing Derrick?"

E-mailing Derrick? Of course not! Only that one time, and that was just for the picture.

"I sent him one e-mail, about the wedding," I respond quietly, hoping no one is in the hallway to overhear our conversation. It *was* about the wedding—calling it off, to be precise.

"Well, you don't have to worry about pretending anymore," Audrey states, angrily flipping another page of her magazine. "I know about everything…how my dad pays you to pretend to be my friend, and how someone like you would never stoop to being friends with someone like me. I should have known all along. I guess I just hoped it wasn't true."

"That's *not* true, Audrey," I attempt. "Not one single word of it. I don't know who's telling you that, but they don't—"

"You know, it's one thing if you don't care about me, but do you have to try to steal my fiancé, too? You've got everything. Why do you want to ruin my life?"

"What are you talking about, stealing your fiancé? I want nothing to do with your fiancé. In fact, I—"

"Where were you last night, Maddie?" she interrupts, finally looking up at me with blazing eyes.

"Last night?" I mutter. "I was at home, of course."

"You weren't at Derrick's house?" she asks, eyes narrowing.

"Of course not!" Audrey reaches into her purse, pulls something out, and casually flips it toward me. I watch as it lands on the ground face down, and I bend to pick it up.

What? How did she...

"If you weren't at Derrick's house, tell me how that wound up on his coffee table."

My driver's license? I have no idea. Did he break into my house and steal it, or come into the office and take it? There's no other way he could have...

The club! That's it! He must have taken it out of my wallet before he returned it to me. I knew I didn't drop my wallet! He took it with the express purpose of stealing something that belonged to me. I was there to catch him in his lies, and he set me up. No wonder he hasn't bothered to break it off with Audrey. He thinks he has me cornered.

"Audrey, this is not what you think. Let me explain."

"Don't bother," she adds with a glare, returning to her magazine. "I'm not in a talking mood. Just go play Miss Important with your toy drive and leave me alone."

Backing out of Audrey's office, I close the door quietly. How could this have happened? All I was doing was trying to be a good friend, and the entire thing backfired in my face. Derrick's going to get away with it, too! Audrey's going to go right ahead with her wedding plans, believing that I tried to steal her fiancé, and they will be married in a few months. How long will he keep up the façade, until he finally breaks away and leaves Audrey

broken-hearted? Months? Years? Poor Audrey will never even see it coming.

Maybe I should talk to Cooper. Wait a second—what if she already told Cooper? What if Audrey showed him the driver's license this morning, and he believes I was at Derrick's house, too? He could be having the paperwork drawn up as we speak to have me terminated by lunch time. But then he wouldn't be able to have his tennis tournament. What is more important to Cooper, his daughter's happiness or his tennis revenge?

I don't want to know the answer to that question—it is sick, sick, sick.

Walking back into my office, I sit and stare at the cellphone on my desk. Nothing would have happened if I hadn't emailed that silly picture. Why did I have to do that in the first place? If I hadn't sent him the picture, he wouldn't have…

Wait a minute, though. He stole my license before he ever knew about the picture. He didn't know I had proof. He was going to set me up anyway, just for catching him in the act. He must really think he has a lot to lose, if he's willing to go to this much trouble to keep his act flowing smoothly. Who knows how much damage he's already done! I can't let him get away with it—I just can't!

Walking to the adjoining door in my office, I knock once before I push it open. Cooper is sitting at his monstrous desk with his glasses on, reading through some papers. He looks up as I open the door and pulls his glasses off his face, setting them down in front of him.

"Maddie," he says in surprise. "What is it?"

"There's something very important I want to talk to you about," I begin, attempting to sound normal. He motions for me to come forward. He doesn't look angry, so perhaps Audrey didn't tell him after all.

"It's about Audrey's fiancé," I state. "There's a problem with him."

"Audrey never mentioned any problem with Derrick," he counters, crossing his arms over his chest. Sitting down in one of the chairs, I take a deep breath.

"That's because she doesn't know."

"Well, what is it? I'm sure it's not something to be overly concerned about."

Pulling my phone out of my pocket, I drag up the picture of Derrick, holding it out for Cooper's inspection. He takes the phone and glances at it momentarily before returning it to me.

"What is that supposed to be?"

Come on, are you blind?

"That's Derrick with another woman."

"Well," Cooper sighs, leaning back in his chair and placing his hands behind his head, "that could have been perfectly innocent. She might have been a client or something. I'm sure it's nothing worth ruffling feathers about."

That's it? You don't care that I have photographic evidence of your one and only daughter's fiancé with another woman? You are the most callous, insensitive man on earth.

"But there's more, sir," I say, now becoming desperate for him to believe me. "He doesn't love Audrey."

Cooper laughs heartily and shakes his head. "Where would you come up with a crazy idea like that?"

"He told me, face to face. He's marrying Audrey for you."

"Why would he marry Audrey for me?" he asks with a smirk.

"For your money." There. I said it. Maybe that will provoke a reaction.

Cooper removes his hands from his head and sits up in his chair, placing his elbows on his desk and leaning towards me. The entire look of his face changes, and his eyes narrow as he stares at me. He's definitely not laughing anymore.

"Audrey can't touch my money."

"I told Derrick that he would never get your money."

"And what did he say?" Cooper wants to know, staring at me intently with blazing eyes. I'm not entirely certain whether he's angry with me or Derrick, but I hope for the best.

"He said that you've already given him plenty, and there will be a lot more where that came from."

Cooper sits silently for a minute, as though he's pondering the words, and then he leans back in his chair and smiles.

"Well, that's ridiculous," he states, shaking his head as though I'm a silly child. "I haven't given him any money."

Hasn't given him any money? Well, then what was Derrick talking about? I distinctly remember him saying that Cooper had given him plenty already. Plenty of what? Cars, houses, boats, clothing? What do I say now?

"You're absolutely certain you haven't given him anything?" I ask, feeling a bit foolish. "No money has changed hands? You have never given him a check, or cash, or anything of the sort?"

"Of course I haven't," he counters firmly. "The only money exchanges we have ever made were on some investments he made for me. He's an investment banker, you know. Occasionally we do business together."

Investments and business deals? Could that have been what he was referencing?

"Mr. Cooper, I am never going to mention this to you again. I only hope you will believe me enough to do your own research. Derrick told me specifically that you had given him a lot of money, and that he was marrying your daughter for the express purpose of obtaining more money from you. I don't pretend to know what he meant, but if the only money you gave him was through investments… Well, if I were you, I would do a little investigating to be sure they were sound."

Standing up, I walk toward the door, part of me wishing I had never broached the topic at all. What did I accomplish in the end? Audrey hates me. Cooper didn't take me seriously. Looks like my wedding planner days are over as quickly as they began.

"Maddie," Cooper calls as I'm about to shut the door. Pausing in the entryway, I return my eyes to his office. "I hope you didn't mention any of this nonsense to Audrey."

"I didn't," I say quietly.

"Good," he replies, placing his glasses on his face and going back to reading his papers.

Chapter Thirty-One

Brittany had her baby last night. Lance phoned a little while ago to tell me they had a girl, and she's very healthy, and her name is Abigail. He also apologized for not phoning sooner, and told me things have been pretty hectic.

Naturally, I forgive him—he is a new dad, after all. I'm sure his life is pretty insane right now, trying to take care of the other kids and serving Brittany's every need. The thing is, I can't believe nobody bothered to tell me that she was in the hospital or that she was in labor. Nobody even thought to call and tell me that I had a niece. It's almost as though they didn't want me there.

Actually, I'm positive they didn't want me there. They never do, really.

I am really dreading going over to Mom and Dad's on Christmas Eve. I'm not sure what kind of holiday spirit I can rouse over there, the way they have been acting toward me lately. (Well, not Dad. He's in my corner, at least.) And the gift exchange... I don't know whose idea it was to start those, but I am not happy. I got Mr. Huber. I know exactly nothing about Mr. Huber, so how am I to be expected to choose an appropriate gift?

The other day, I finally purchased a gift certificate for a few rounds of golf at a country club. Does Mr. Huber play golf? How on earth would I know? He looks like the type of guy who would play golf. I know he doesn't tinker around in his workshop like Dad. It was either that or a gift certificate to the tennis club, and that might have caused him to sprain or pull something. I certainly don't want that on my conscience.

When Mom called to tell me about Christmas, she was short and to the point. I didn't ask if she wanted me to bring anything. The way she and Brittany talked about the food I made at Thanksgiving, I seriously doubt anyone would eat anything I brought. I might not even stay for dinner. I do feel obligated to go to the gift exchange, though. If someone purchased a present for me, it would be really rude not to at least show up and exchange the gift.

I wonder who got my name. Probably Mr. Huber, who will get me a certificate to the tennis club, which would be a little funny, because Cooper has already paid for my membership. Well, at least it would be a nice gift, and I could re-gift it to someone who would appreciate it.

On a more positive note, people seem to be in good moods at the office today. In the elevator, one lady was humming Jingle Bells. Another woman had some kind of tinsel fixed in her hair. An older gentleman offered me some eggnog, which I turned down, of course. Never accept food or drinks from strangers—that's a pretty standard motto of mine.

Dina was also happy this morning, probably because we're going to have an extended weekend for the holiday. She gave me a gift box with hot chocolate and cinnamon sticks, which was really funny because I happened to get her the exact same thing. We must spend too much time together in the break room.

I also bought some fairly expensive lip gloss for Audrey from Tish at the spa. She told me it was supposed to plump up the lips or something like that. For what I paid, it should work some sort of miracle. I opened the door a crack this morning and slid it onto Audrey's desk.

"Merry Christmas, Audrey," I said, right before shutting the door. Since she hasn't spoken to me yet, I figured I wouldn't force her right before the holiday. When I came back to my office after using the restroom a little while later, the lip gloss was on the center of my desk.

I tried—I suppose that's all I can do.

Ding-dong.

Cooper must have some last-minute shopping that he forgot to do. Probably another gift for Audrey. She would die if she

knew I bought her Christmas presents. Sliding open the door between our offices, I mutter the obligatory phrase: "You rang?" Cooper gives me a tight smile and nods his head.

"Go ahead and come in, I want to talk to you for a minute."

He's not being his loud, boisterous self. Maybe he hasn't had his raw eggs yet this morning. Perhaps he's gearing up for the holiday, too.

"I thought a lot about what you told me the other day," he begins as I sit down, "about Derrick. I know it took a lot of courage to come in here and tell me those things, and I appreciate that."

"Thank you," I reply quietly.

"Well, I took your advice, and I had someone look into Derrick's investments. They were basically nonexistent. Exorbitant amounts of money spent on useless buildings that were worth way less than he expressed, and he's been skimming off the extra money for himself. Audrey just happened to be caught in the middle—the only way he could get his foot in the door, so to speak."

Poor Audrey. How could anyone do something so low?

"So, what happens now?" I wonder, rubbing my hands together in my lap.

He clears his throat and straightens in his chair. "Well, Derrick was arrested last night, so he can't do any more damage."

"But what about Audrey?" I can't imagine finding out her fiancé was using her to get to her father's money, and that he lied to her about everything—his intentions, his business trips, and his sources of income.

"Audrey doesn't know yet. Derrick had already told her he was out of town for the next two days, so I'm trying to figure out a way to tell her myself."

I sit there silently, staring at the floor and wishing I could help. If Audrey was speaking to me, maybe there would be something I could do. As it stands now, the only thing I can do is pray that she'll be alright.

"Well, not the happiest topic to start the holiday," Cooper states with a sigh, "but I thought you would want to know."

"Yes, thanks for telling me."

"You've done a lot for Audrey in the past few weeks. I don't know exactly what's happened, but her looks have improved a great deal. She's been a lot happier, too, or at least she had been before this fiasco. I want you to have this. Merry Christmas."

Cooper slides a Visa card across his desk toward me. I pick it up gingerly and hold it with both hands.

"Thank you," I reply quickly, and he chuckles to himself.

"It's not one of those with the endless limit, so don't get your hopes up. I didn't know what you would want, so that's one of those gift cards you can use anywhere."

"Well, like I said, thank you."

Leaning back in his chair, he sighs and shakes his head. "You know, Maddie, you get to the point where I am and there are always people trying to take advantage. I just wish Audrey hadn't gotten involved. And I wish we hadn't even started with this wedding mess. What all have you purchased to this point?"

"There were the dresses, and the food, and the flowers. Those deposits were nonrefundable, unfortunately. Luckily, we hadn't sent out the invitations yet."

"Yes, we were lucky with that one. Too bad all the other things will go to waste."

I sit there pondering the situation for a moment, with an idea forming in my brain.

"If I can figure out a way to use those things, are you on board?" I suggest, giving him a sly smile.

"Your ideas have been golden to this point," he says, giving me a wink. "Whatever you need, just make it work."

Headed to Mom and Dad's for the Christmas fiasco. Er, I mean feast. I am really looking forward to it, naturally. There's

nothing I would rather be doing right now, except perhaps having all my hairs pulled out by the roots, or walking across hot coals, or pressing red hot pokers against my bare skin. A girl can dream, right?

Maybe it won't be so bad. Brittany's not pregnant anymore, and she's got a beautiful new baby girl (or so I've been told), so she won't have anything to complain about. In fact, she should be downright cheerful. Mom and Mrs. Huber won't have anything to fuss over, either, except for cooing over the new baby. It could turn out okay, in the end.

As I pull into the driveway, however, I seriously consider throwing my gift at the house and running. One knock is all the warning I give them before I push open the door, and I'm nearly bowled over by Marilyn.

"Aunt Maddie!" she shouts, flinging herself against my waist. Jordan follows close behind.

"Where's my present?" he wonders, pulling at the gift in my hands.

"Uh-uh," I scold. "You'll have to wait for the gift exchange to see whether I got your name."

"The gift exchange is only for grown-ups, Maddie," Mom chides from the kitchen. "You were supposed to get gifts for the kids."

Great. Already I'm the bad aunt, simply because no one informed me of the rules.

"Here," I say, opening my purse and fishing through my wallet. "Sorry my gifts aren't wrapped." I hand each of them a fifty dollar bill.

"Cool!" they exclaim, almost in unison.

"Way to go, Maddie," Brittany proclaims from her chair in the corner. "Spoil them with cash, and then they won't like any of their other gifts."

I guess I was wrong—she can still find things to complain about.

Looking over to the corner of the couch, I spot Dad sitting next to Lance, who is holding the new baby. I quickly place my gift next to the tree and walk over to them.

"Hi, Dad," I say, kissing him quickly on the cheek. He looks slightly miserable. I believe he may be dreading this as much as I am. He can't escape and go out to his workshop with all the company.

"Hi, little Abby," I whisper, touching her tiny fingers.

"Abigail," Brittany growls from the recliner.

"Sorry," I whisper, directing my remarks to the baby and not Brittany. "Hello, Abigail." She wraps her little hand around my index finger and wiggles slightly in Lance's arms. As I watch, her face crinkles and she stretches her legs.

"Look, she's smiling!" I exclaim. Lance grins at me and then back down at the baby.

"She's got gas," Brittany states.

Must run in the family.

"Don't worry, Abigail," I tell her quietly. "I won't tell anyone."

"No," Brittany interjects. "I mean she's not smiling. She's making a face because she has gas."

"Well, I'll just go on thinking you're smiling," I continue to talk to the baby. "It's a lot sweeter than having gas. You are entirely too cute to have gas, anyway." Of course Abigail chooses this exact moment to let loose a noise that would have made me blush, had I done it myself, and a horrible odor begins to waft through the room.

"It's your turn, Lance," Brittany orders. He simply nods and gets up from the couch, taking Abigail into one of the bedrooms.

"Can we open presents now, Mom?" Jordan asks, standing at Brittany's feet and practically jumping up and down with excitement. "Aunt Maddie's finally here."

"Ask your grandma," Brittany directs. "I guess we wouldn't have had to wait for Maddie anyway, since all she brought was cash."

Keeping my mouth shut, I plop down on the floor next to Dad's feet, glancing over at Mr. Huber, who is sitting across from us on the love seat. He never says a word. Sometimes I wonder if he is one of those people who can sleep with his eyes open.

"How are you, Mr. Huber?" I ask.

He rouses a little and his head moves slightly. "Huh?"

"How are you?" I repeat.

He clears his throat and rocks a little in his seat. "Fine."

A man of few words. I'll let him go back to dozing.

"Grandma said we can open gifts!" Jordan exclaims, running back into the room. He makes a dash for the tree with Marilyn close at his heels.

I remember Christmas when I was little, how exciting it was. Of course, I usually spent a couple of days anticipating the marvelous toys I would receive, and then would be disappointed once the actual day was over. One year I wanted a simple bake oven, and instead I got a drawing kit. Those little ovens were too messy, Mom said. Turned out the gift she gave me was pretty messy, too, because my cousin Witt took my drawing kit and wrote all over the wall with it. I'm the one who got in trouble, even though he had written his own name, completely incriminating himself. I still haven't figured that one out.

Then there was the Christmas when I asked for a makeup case. I was too young for makeup, Mom said, so I didn't have any need for one. That was true enough, but a lot of girls at school were carrying around those cases, and I wanted a case, too. I wasn't going to put makeup in it, probably just pens and pencils and such, but I still wanted one. Imagine my surprise on Christmas morning when I opened my gift to find one of those sissy-wets-a-lot dolls. *You're growing up too fast,* Mom told me. *Sissy-wets-a-lot is a more appropriate gift for a girl your age.* You can't go back to junior high after Christmas break and tell your friends you got a sissy-wets-a-lot.

Oh, and I can't forget about that Christmas when Grandma and Grandpa came over. I was probably four or five. When I opened their gift, it was the most beautiful little snowsuit—pink with white fur around the hood. I remember holding it up against me and dancing around a bit, right before Mom snatched it from my hands. It wasn't an appropriate gift, she decided, and told Grandma and Grandpa they had to take it back with them. I remember her arguing with Grandma for quite a while. *What's wrong with it,* Grandma wanted to know. *This isn't Wisconsin,* Mom yelled. *It's just not practical in Kentucky.* In the end, it wound up snowing a lot that winter, and I had to use Lance's snowsuit, which was too big and had holes in both knees. I could have caught pneumonia.

Jordan kicks me in the shin as he runs by, bringing me quickly back to the present. Marilyn is buried somewhere beneath the tree, passing gifts to Jordan so he can sprint to deliver them around the room.

"Do you want to hold her?" I hear. I look up to see Lance standing above me with Abigail in his arms.

"Okay," I find myself saying, standing up to remove myself from Jordan's path. Wouldn't want little Abigail to be kicked in the head. After I lower myself next to Dad on the couch, Lance places the nearly weightless bundle in my arms.

Little Abigail, do you know what kind of world you're coming into? It's full of hurt and frustration and embarrassment. Of course, there are also some nice things, like you: still too tiny to be mean or rude or self-absorbed. Except you are probably completely self-absorbed, but rightfully so. You are still perfect in every way. Too bad you have to grow up someday and become an adult.

Abigail stretches her legs and kicks out of her blanket, and I take care to cover her back up. Her little hand reaches up as though she's searching for something, and I offer her my finger again. She wraps all of her fingers around mine and pulls her tiny arm back towards her chest.

"This one's for you!" Jordan exclaims, dropping a present on the couch next to me. Mrs. Huber and Mom make their way into the room from the kitchen, talking not much louder than a whisper, with Mom waving her hands as she speaks. After a second, Mom finishes gesturing and Mrs. Huber begins surveying the room.

"Where's the baby?" she asks, sounding frantic. "Where's the baby?"

"I have her," I reply, looking down.

Mrs. Huber hurries over to me and plucks the baby out of my arms. "Hello, pookums," she coos. "Did you miss Grammy?" She carries the baby over to Mr. Huber, who doesn't even seem to notice their presence.

"Can we open them now, Grandma, please?" Marilyn pleads while standing in front of the tree, which is completely bare underneath.

"Yes, yes, you can open them." Mom dismisses her with a wave of her hand right before she settles down in one of the arm chairs and yawns. I glance down at the gifts beside me, three of them, to be exact: one from Mom, another from Dad, and the third from...

Brittany. Who else?

"Who's this from?" Mr. Huber asks, holding up the gift I brought. It has my name on it, but apparently he doesn't care for reading.

"Looks like it's from Maddie," Mrs. Huber answers, taking it from him and shaking it gently. "It's not very big, whatever it is."

Mr. Huber takes the package back and slowly opens it, pulling the lid off the box and removing the gift certificate. He reads the card for what seems like ten minutes, and then calmly leans back on the love seat, holding it in his lap.

"Well, what is it?" Mrs. Huber wants to know.

"I have no idea," he states, not seeming to care.

She takes it from him and begins to read it over. "It's a gift certificate to play golf."

"To play golf? But what about my back?"

"Oh, wouldn't that be silly. You can't play any golf. It would kill you." She hands the certificate back to him and he continues to hold it in his lap, staring off at nothing.

Honestly, I don't think playing golf would *kill* him. He looks to be in pretty good physical shape. I know he uses the weed

eater on the lawn—I heard Mrs. Huber talking about it once. If he can use the weed eater, he can play golf. End of story.

Maybe she's worried that he will fall asleep on the golf course. He will be somewhere in the middle of the fairway, just standing there completely minding his own business, when someone behind him drives a ball straight toward the green. He won't see it coming, of course, because he will be sleeping with his eyes open. He'll just remain suspended there in his own little world when someone yells "fore" and the ball comes whizzing at his head, sinking into the back of his skull and killing him instantly.

Yes, that has to be it.

I hesitantly pick up Brittany's gift, fingering the paper. I'm not entirely sure that I want to open it. Brittany doesn't exactly hide her feelings for me, so I'm sure buying a Christmas gift for yours truly probably thrilled her to no end. I can almost see her rummaging through the bargain bins at the department store, trying to locate anything without a rip, tear, or stain. She finally finds something, but the tag says it's two dollars, and that seems like an awful lot to spend on someone you don't really care for, doesn't it? Maybe I'll get lucky and she will have sent Lance to get my present while she was pregnant.

I tear the paper from the corner and across the front of the box, and I pause in mid-rip with the gift on my lap. I can't bring myself to actually remove the entire thing from the paper, because then it will officially be mine. Other people might see it, and then I will have to acknowledge that, yes, this is my gift from Brittany. I will have to take it home and pretend that I like it, which I don't. I despise it. This is the rudest, most inconsiderate gift I have ever been given. She should have given me the golf certificate—at least *that* would have been trade-able. This is hostile and mean and tactless and very hurtful.

It's a video series…The Single Girl's Guide to Keeping a Man.

Disc 1: Making yourself more presentable. Disc 2: Appealing to the opposite sex. Disc 3…

I should wing it across the room and into the tree. This is a Christmas apostasy. If the wise men had brought such a disgrace to the baby Jesus, Mary would have told them to mount their camels and depart.

"You got your gift?" Brittany asks from her corner of the room. I look up to see her smiling brightly at me.

Yeah, I got your gift, you psychopath.

"You didn't even open the whole thing!" she chimes. "There's more to it."

More to it? Reluctantly, I pull the paper back further to reveal the back of a book. Turning it over, I see a very frumpy woman with her arms across her chest. *Dressing to Impress, a Makeover Guide.*

That's it. I'm going to leap across the room and attack her like a jungle tiger on one of those hopeless little antelopes you see on National Geographic.

"What do you think?" she asks, silly grin still plastered between her cheeks.

"Great," I mutter, really wishing I could go over there and wipe that silly smirk off her face. Even if I had a problem with my appearance, which I don't, what kind of inconsiderate person would give a gift announcing it to the entire room?

"What is it?" Mrs. Huber asks, lifting her chin to try to see the items I'm hiding.

"It's a book about dating," Brittany states nonchalantly, as though she has just given me a sweater or a pair of gloves. Dad's hand grabs firmly onto my knee, as though he senses the fact that I am seconds away from pouncing. He's holding me back so I don't go screaming across the room like a wild banshee, lashing my claws into her face.

"Oh, goodness," Mrs. Huber states, giving me a concerned look. "I didn't know we had that problem."

"*We* don't!" I say with clenched teeth, shoving the book into the couch cushions.

"It's nothing to be ashamed of, Maddie," Brittany says, pretending to be caring, which I certainly know by this time that she is *not*.

Dad decides to put his arm around my shoulders, and I give him a little smile to reassure him that I'm fine. I am a sophisticated, mature young woman, and I'm not going to fling myself across the room like a wild animal from the Amazon. I'll just do what every other sophisticated young woman would do in this situation—sit here despising her from afar.

I still have Mom and Dad's gifts, and they have to be better. I tear the paper from the one bearing Dad's name to reveal a clothing box. Inside is a pea green raincoat with a plaid lining. It's very pretty, and it looks like it will fit. Besides, it's not inconsiderate and definitely not humiliating. It is really sad that this is going to become a determining factor in whether or not I like a gift I receive. Is it useful? Is it humiliating? Is it cruel?

I set the raincoat down beside me and open the next gift, which I quickly realize is another book. Surely it can't be as bad as Brittany's, unless it's something like *Dealing with Being a Nobody* or *Coping with a Family Who Hates You*.

I realize as I finish unwrapping that none of my guesses are even close to correct. This book has a cover filled with various fruits and vegetables, and a blaring title in red letters: *Food and Nutrition: A Guide to Overcoming Addiction*.

Of course we had to go there again. I thought we were past this nonsense.

"What is that?" Mrs. Huber wants to know.

Why are you so nosy, lady? Open your own gifts!

"It's a food and nutrition guide," Mom states proudly. "It shows her how to eat properly."

"Hmm, that's funny!" Mrs. Huber assesses. "You don't look overweight to me. Why do you need a nutrition book?"

"Oh, I have an eating disorder, didn't you know?" I reply, looking over at Mom.

She puts one hand on her hip and gives me a warning look. "It's no good to be thin if you're not healthy," Mom says, looking to Mrs. Huber for approval.

"I'll bet that's why you're still single," Mrs. Huber announces. "Things like that upset the delicate balance, you know."

"You're probably right," I tell her, eyes wide. "Gosh, why haven't I thought of that before? I should kick the habit today— start by eating a lot of cake and pie, really pile the weight on."

"That sounds like binging, Maddie," Mom warns.

"Gosh, it does, doesn't it? You would think that I, of all people, would know that."

"You have an eating disorder?" Marilyn suddenly interjects, looking at me with concern.

"No, honey, I don't. I *definitely* don't."

"Good," she states. "That's not healthy."

"Tell me about it," I reply, shaking my head and rolling my eyes at my young niece.

"I hadn't noticed before, but now that you mention it, you do look rather sickly," Mrs. Huber decides. "You should try going to one of those dietary specialists, have them show you how to eat properly."

By this time I am seeing red and can barely control my temper. "I already eat properly, Mrs. Huber, and I feel good about myself, and that fact apparently bothers some of the people in this room who can't say the same."

"I beg your pardon!" Mrs. Huber exclaims, eyes wide and unblinking.

"She's right about that," Mr. Huber says quietly, coming out of his coma-like state for a brief moment.

"I just had a baby!" Brittany huffs, crossing her arms over her stomach.

"You have no right to say such a thing, Maddie," Mom complains, narrowing her eyes as she looks at me.

"You started it," Dad suddenly speaks up beside me. "Maybe you should try being nice once in a while, and this type of

thing wouldn't happen. You look fine to me, Maddie. I don't know what their problem is."

"Thank you, Dad," I say quietly. He smiles at me sadly as though we have a secret alliance in the family battleground.

"I just had a baby!" Brittany repeats. "It's not like your body springs back the second after you—"

"Be quiet, Brittany," Lance warns. She glances over at him and leans back a little further in her chair.

Glancing at the mess beside me, I pick up the clothing box, holding it gingerly in front of me. "Did you pick out the raincoat, Dad?" I wonder, and he nods. "Thank you. I love it."

"You're welcome," he says quietly. "Merry Christmas, honey."

"Merry Christmas."

Crossing to the door, I don't even glance back into the room.

"You forgot your gifts," Brittany pipes up.

"Unfortunately, I don't think I will ever forget them," I reply, beginning to pull the door shut.

"You're not even going to stay for dinner?" Mom asks.

"What's the point, if I'm just going to throw it up anyway?"

On Christmas morning, I awake alone and sit quietly, staring out at the bleak, dreary day. Tucker and Hazel have invited me over at noon, which leaves me with quite a bit of time to simply sit and ponder my thoughts. Sure, my family situation has been less than ideal at times in the past, but never to this point. Never to the point that I would rather sit alone on Christmas morning than be involved in the drama.

I've really never felt so isolated in my life.

Dad called about half an hour ago to wish me Merry Christmas. He told me he was sorry about yesterday, but I told him it wasn't his fault. I also told him I didn't know how he put up with her all the time, and he said that's what his workshop was for. We both laughed a little, and then I heard Mom yelling for him. He must have been hiding in the closet again, because it took her a minute to find him. When she finally did, it was like an inquisition.

"Who are you talking to in there?" she wanted to know.

"My daughter," he said.

"What does she want?"

"It's Christmas, and I wanted to call my daughter. Leave me alone, woman."

She slammed the door behind her and he chuckled a little. Poor Dad—he's going to have one great Christmas Day over there with her. I asked him if he wanted to meet me at Tucker and Hazel's, but he said he would probably just stay in the workshop all day.

Meanwhile, I am sitting on the couch, watching *It's a Wonderful Life* on television when my doorbell rings. Hurrying over to the door, I peek out to see Hazel waiting expectantly, so I fling the door open to her smiling face.

"Hazel? I'm sorry, I thought you said noon."

"Oh, I did say noon, Maddie. We still want you to come over, of course. We love having you at the house. It feels like having one of our own kids there, since Josh and Jess are so far away. I made the cinnamon bread you love, and we want you to put the final ornament on the tree, like the kids always did. I just thought you might want your gift now."

"You didn't have to give me a gift," I reply quietly, fighting back my emotion.

"It's not from me," she states simply, handing me the big square parchment. "Merry Christmas, sweetie. See you at noon."

She retreats from the porch, and I slowly let the door close in front of me, pushing it until it clicks into place. For some reason, I'm hesitant to open the package. Sitting down on the couch, I simply hold it in front of me, staring at the brown paper.

Finally, releasing a deep breath, I tear back the corner of the gift to reveal a wooden frame, and I gently pull a little farther, trying to inspect the gift without fully opening it. Once the paper is pulled away, I twist the frame around to look at the front of the picture, which is a Monet print with water lilies. I simply stare at the image for a moment, admiring it. Finally, I grab the paper and begin wadding it into a ball, pausing when I notice a white sheet taped against the brown. Pulling it free, I unfold it with trembling fingers.

Dear Mad,

Merry Christmas! Thanks for taking my place this year at Mom and Dad's, so they won't have to be alone. You're simply the best. The absolute best. I mean it. I miss you. I miss home.

I wish I was in Kentucky to hand you this gift myself. It reminds me of you—of how you see the world. You're always looking for perfection, and this is a pretty awesome piece of artwork. If you get close to it, though, you're gonna think that it's not so great. When you're close, really looking at it, it looks like a mess of mistakes. It looks like bunches of paint blobbed all over in no sort of order.

My wish for you this Christmas is that you don't focus on the paint so much that you miss the masterpiece. I'm thinking about you and wishing I was there. Please give my parents a hug from me.

Yours,

Josh

Allowing a tear to slide down my cheek, I glance over at Josh's picture staring at me. It's too much to think about, so I flip the TV to a channel playing nonstop Christmas music, intending to listen to the old standards as I get dressed. The words immediately pierce me.

Have yourself a merry little Christmas.
Let your heart be light.
Next year all our troubles will be out of sight.

Smiling to myself, I stare into Josh's eyes.

Next year. Next year, Josh will be here, won't he? My Josh. Maybe then I won't be able to notice the blobs of paint at all.

Chapter Thirty-Two

New year, fresh start, and a different outlook. I'm going to put everything that happened last year behind me, including the denied promotion, the plot for revenge, the thing with my mother, and the tiff with Audrey. None of those things are worth thinking about, really. Instead, I'm going to concentrate on all the wonderful things that are happening in my life. I have terrific friends, I'm healthy, and I get paid a rather large salary for doing practically nothing. What more could a girl want?

Besides the obvious man in her life, but that is on hold for the moment.

Speaking of Josh, I decided to leave the Monet print at home, hanging in the bedroom to remind me every morning that I wake up that there is beauty in the bigger picture. Also, it reminds me of the man I really want, which is a nice thought. I might be able to point out flaws in him, but it doesn't matter, because the big picture is pretty spectacular.

Here's hoping that someday soon I can convince him to feel the same way about me. No doubt I have flaws, and probably enough to fill a giant canvas, but I'm honestly at a point in my life where I'm okay with the bigger picture. That feels like a giant milestone for the New Year, and everybody else should take notice of that fact. Madeline Heard is perfectly happy with who she is, and she would like the entire world to bear witness.

In fact, I should print up a postcard and mail it to my mother.

In work-related news, Cooper's not here today; he went on a business trip about some investments he wants to make, presumably to make up for the fictitious ones he and Derrick partnered on. He's never really mentioned Derrick to me again, and I haven't bothered to ask. A man like Cooper is undoubtedly a little embarrassed at having been taken for a fool. Still, I'm sure he feels the same way I do—it's a new year, and things like that are better left in the past. I hope Audrey has been able to see things that way, too, but somehow I doubt it has been quite so easy on her.

Audrey hasn't worked with me at all since the day she stopped speaking to me. I've never approached the subject with Cooper, because if he wanted that to change, I figure he would have said so. For all I know, she might be reading magazines and talking on her cellphone, although I don't know who she would talk to now that Derrick is out of the picture. If she thought of me as her best friend, she must not have very many people who are close to her.

To be perfectly honest, I miss her a little.

Only a little, mind you. I actually feel free for the first time in a long time. Free to take a deep breath and concentrate on my own life for a change. No babysitting, no planning, and no being shadowed at everything I do. I am finally alone once again, and it feels nice.

A slight knock sounds on my door, and Dina pokes her upswept hair into my office.

"Busy?" she wonders, pulling her glasses off her face. I shake my head and she comes in, settling into the chair next to my desk. It may be a new year, but it's the same Dina—wool suit, beehive, red glasses, and the whole bit.

"Still getting the silent treatment, I suppose?" she asks, rubbing the bridge of her nose.

"Apparently." I wonder how much Dina really knows about what happened. I never really told her what went wrong, but she noticed last week that Audrey hadn't been coming around my office.

"I wouldn't worry about it," she says, placing her glasses on my desk. "Things have slowed down quite a bit, since the holidays are over."

"No more special projects," I state, "at least for a little while."

Except the "save the wedding fund" project I've schemed up with Cooper, but that's a secret.

"Any more news on the Project Cooper front? Still planning the revenge?"

No. That was so silly, wasn't it? I don't even know why I let those ideas formulate in my brain. Truth be told, after meeting Audrey, I've grown a little softer on the Coopers.

The mere fact that those thoughts just popped out of nowhere makes me wrinkle my nose.

"I don't think so," I admit with a sigh. "Besides, I have a feeling you'll have your office back soon."

"You know something I don't?" She places her elbow on my desk, and I smile as I shake my head.

"Probably not, but it can't last forever. The tennis match will be soon, and then he won't have any need for me up here. He'll find another place for me, and I'll be shipped downriver."

"Well, I'll be sorry for you if that happens," Dina assures me, a tight smile forming across her lips.

"Only for a second, and then you'll rejoice at being in the comfort of your old home." Dina and I both laugh briefly, and then she clears her throat.

"I'm not certain I want this office back, now that he's installed that idiotic doorbell. Honestly, I don't know how you put up with that nonsense."

"It is a little degrading, isn't it?" I ask with a giggle.

"Degrading? What does he think you are, a dog?"

"A puppy. A Labrador Retriever."

"Go on, doggie, fetch my slippers."

"Here puppy, bring me the newspaper."

"Don't doo-doo on the carpet, doggie!"

"I'll rub your nose in it!"

"It's really not funny," Dina blurts, suddenly sobering.

"No, it's not."

"Well, a little funny when he uses it on you, but it won't be if he uses it with me." She grins and picks up her glasses, standing up and smoothing her wool skirt.

"Get out of here!" I say quietly as she pulls the door shut behind her, pausing briefly to make certain I see the smile on her face. "I'm going to tell him you love it."

"Don't you dare!" she states through the closed door.

I wonder where Cooper will send me, when the time comes. He'll probably put me back in Marketing, working for Bill Davies. Well, Hamilton should know by now that I won't ever put up with *him* again, but I guess that would be an easy way to get rid of me, now that I think of it. Working for Cooper may be a little degrading and ridiculous, but at least he doesn't scream at me nonsensically.

Another knock sounds on my door—probably Dina coming back to get one last jab.

"What is it, Dina?" I ask. The door swings open, and there stands Audrey. "Oh! I thought you were Dina."

"Yeah, I get that a lot," she says dryly, remaining in the doorway.

"Are you looking for your dad?" I question, not sure of any other reason why she would be choosing this moment to break her silence.

She smirks and shakes her head. "No, he's out of town. I'm not that clueless. I just came to tell you that we won't be working together anymore. I'm going to be going downstairs for a while. Dad thinks I need to learn some management skills."

"Oh," I mutter. "Okay, then."

"There won't be any wedding, but I'm sure you know that," she goes on, still standing in the doorframe.

"Yeah, I saw something about Derrick's arrest on the news. I'm sorry, Audrey."

"Even though I'm not with Derrick anymore, that doesn't change what you did."

"You can't honestly still believe that I—"

"Why wouldn't I, Maddie?" she asks sarcastically. "Because you're my friend? You with your perfect body and perfect face and perfect life. Maddie Heard, who always knows just the right thing to say in every situation. I'm supposed to believe you would be

friends with me, Audrey Cooper? The girl who eats too much and drinks too much diet cola and doesn't have any skills or talents? Someone who's so naïve she can't even tell when her fiancé is using her to get to her father?"

First instinctual reaction—Audrey's perception of perfection is really skewed, if she's using that word to describe me.

"I don't think that, Audrey. Not at all."

"Of course you do, just like everyone else in this building." She turns on her heel and walks away, only leaving a trail of flipping and flopping as her shoes hit the floor. I hear the door to her office close, and I stand up and walk to the doorway. Dina is peering at me from her desk in the hall, where she obviously heard the whole conversation from beginning to end.

"Well, there you go," I say, grabbing the doorknob with a shrug. "The silent treatment has ended."

It is several hours later that same day when I walk into the bridal shop, pausing a moment to look at the gorgeous gown in the window. If you're willing to pay any price, you really can look like a queen on your big day. I cringe when I think about how much we paid for Audrey's gown, which is now going to sit on a shelf somewhere and gather dust. Perhaps she can use it someday, but who knows if she will? It might hold too many bad memories for her.

"Can I help you?" I hear a voice call from my right. I turn to see Jane, the saleswoman who helped us the day we were here trying on gowns. Her face brightens a little with recognition as she sees my face.

"Hi, Jane. I don't know if you remember, but I'm Maddie Heard."

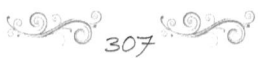

"Of course! I was so surprised when you called the other day to tell me that the Cooper wedding had been canceled."

"Yes, it was unfortunate, but these things happen," I offer, walking up to the counter.

"More than you know, really," Jane tells me. "People get so excited about the idea of getting married, a lot of them jump the gun and go buy everything right away. As time wears on, things just don't work out."

"Sounds like a lot of things in life," I say, opening my satchel and pulling out a few sheets of paper.

"Well, Maddie, unfortunately I cannot give you a refund, as I told you on the phone the other day."

"I'm aware of that. That's not why I'm here."

"Oh!" she exclaims, suddenly getting slightly friendlier. She walks to the counter and looks at the papers I've unveiled.

"I need a dress—"

"Well, you've come to the right place for that!" Jane interrupts, beaming at me.

"The thing is, I'm looking for something very specific. I know that no store is going to have it, and someone is going to have to make it for me. Is that something you would be interested in?"

"Possibly," she says, leaning her chin on her hand. "What type of dress are we talking about here?"

"What I'm thinking is the exact same style as Audrey's wedding gown. This one will be a rose color, and it will only fall to slightly below the knee."

"I'm with you so far," Jane states, writing down my instructions.

"This is where it gets a little tricky," I say, holding out one of the papers. "I'd like the back to resemble the butterflies floating along the back of this gown."

"The butterflies?" she asks, pulling her glasses onto her face and holding the picture close to her nose. "Ah, now I see! So you want the butterflies just like this, in white?"

"Actually, in a rose color, very similar to the dress."

"Very well," she states, making a few more notes on her paper. "Let's get your measurements, and we'll have something to go from."

"Oh, the dress isn't for me," I clarify. "It's for Audrey Cooper."

"Audrey Cooper?"

"You still have her measurements, right?" I ask, tucking my other papers away in my satchel. She begins flipping through a large file, humming to herself.

"Yes, here they are," she sings, pulling out a note card.

"So you can do the dress?" I question.

She nods and smiles at me. "We can do the dress," she replies. "It is going to be expensive to have it custom-created like this."

"I expected that," I state, throwing the satchel over my shoulder and digging through my purse. "This one isn't on the Cooper account, though. Here." Pulling my hand up, I offer the Visa card Cooper gave me for Christmas. "If this isn't enough, I'll cover it myself." She enters the card number into her computer and hands it back to me. With a slight sigh, I place it in a side pocket of my purse so I'll remember not to use it for anything else. As I start to walk toward the door, Jane quickly follows.

"When do you need it?" she wants to know.

"Same day as the wedding," I tell her, and she jots the note in her pad.

Flinging open the door, I step out into the cold wind, pulling my green raincoat a little tighter around my body. (It looks great on me, by the way. Dad has good taste.)

"Oh," I say, turning around right before the door closes, "if you have any questions, please call me. It's a surprise. Audrey doesn't know."

"It's a deal!" Jane beams, placing her pencil behind her ear.

I started feeling a little weird on my way back to the office from the bridal shop, but it really hit me when I was standing in the elevator. I don't know if it was the sheer motion, or the going and stopping, or the up and down movement, or the fact that I had eaten some questionable fish for lunch, but by the time I hit the top floor, I was completely nauseated. The instant the door opened, I headed for the restroom to collapse in a heap and let the sick feeling devour me.

Now that it's over, I feel slightly better, so I stand up and wash my face in the sink. Afterwards, I emerge from the restroom and walk towards my office, where Dina is standing patiently by my door. I remove the satchel from my shoulder and adjust the raincoat in my arms while Dina begins tapping her foot on the hardwood floor.

"Did something happen while I was gone?" I wonder, pushing the door open. She follows me into the office and pulls the door shut behind her.

"Do you care to tell me what's going on?" she questions, standing with her arms folded across her chest. I casually drop the satchel and raincoat onto a spare chair and turn to face her.

"What are you talking about?"

"The restroom. I heard you in there."

"I think I ate some bad fish," I say, "no big deal."

"Something else is going on," she replies, not backing down.

"Really, Dina, you're just going to have to spell it out, because I have no idea what you're talking about."

"Your mom called the other day, and I answered the phone. We had quite the conversation."

"What did you talk about?" I ask nonchalantly, pretending I don't know to what she's referring.

"Your bulimia," she asserts, looking back at the door as though someone might hear her.

Oh, good grief.

"Bulimia?"

"Yes, she told me all about it and asked me to keep an eye on you. I didn't believe it at first, but now that I've heard the evidence, I have no choice!"

Mom will not be happy until this nonsense has infiltrated every corner of my life.

"I'm not bulimic."

"Uh-huh," she says, nodding her head up and down. "She told me you would deny it. Maddie, you really need to seek some professional help here. Everyone's worried about you."

Blowing out my breath in a huff, I try to keep myself calm.

"Look, I'm not sure how to say this, but my mom can be a bit crazy. She's the one who started this whole misunderstanding."

"You shouldn't blame your mother for your own shortcomings," she says. "She told me about everything: how she tried to stage an intervention and you stormed out, how she tried to give you a nutrition guidebook and you wouldn't even take it with you—"

"I don't know how many times I have to say this: I am not bulimic."

"I know you won't admit it. Just know that I'm watching you."

"Thanks for that," I say, completely exasperated. She opens the door and pauses long enough to point to her eyes and then back to me while nodding her head in a knowing way.

I hope Cooper uses the bell when she moves back into the office.

I hope he makes her take his dirty shirts to the cleaners.

I even hope he makes her take his teeth to the dentist.

Cooper returned today, and he supposedly has something pressing for me to do this afternoon, so even though I'm still rather

out of sorts from the mild food poisoning I had yesterday, I pull myself to Cooper Corporate Financial. Knowing my luck, he probably wants his socks ironed or some other nonsense.

I step into the elevator and push the up arrow, and an elderly gentleman steps in right as the door is about to close. He pushes number 3 and stands back against the rail. After a few seconds, I am immersed in the scent of cigarette smoke and mild body odor. Forcing myself not to look at the man, I pull a tissue from my purse and fake having a runny nose, holding it in front of my face. It works pretty well to block the smell until the number 3 lights up and he exits the elevator. As soon as he's gone, I begin waving frantically because the stench is lingering.

The elevator surges upward, but stops abruptly on the number 4 as the door begins to open. A slightly chubby young man enters the elevator carrying a large, greasy bag of fast food.

"Hi," he states cheerfully, pressing the 5 button.

"Hi," I reply, removing the tissue for a split second. Immediately I wish I hadn't. The smell of something grease-drenched and fried wafts up at me, mingling with the previous smells left by Mr. 3rd Floor. I nearly gag and try to cover the sound by coughing, holding the tissue tightly against my nose.

"Cold?" he asks. "I just got over one myself. Hope you start feeling better."

I nod as the elevator reaches 5 and he exits through the open doors. The upward movement begins again, and my stomach lurches.

Exactly what would happen if a person vomited in the elevator? If they exited to tell someone, by the time they were back the elevator would be gone. They would probably just have to keep riding the elevator, telling everyone to stay away and to find a janitor.

Frankly, I don't want to think about it. The elevator finally reaches the top floor, and I make a beeline for the restroom, yanking on the door. Locked? No, it can't be! This is a dire circumstance, and I need in there.

My eyes drift to the men's room. The mere thought leaves me feeling even more nauseated than before, but I have no choice. I carefully check the door, which is unlocked, and enter as quietly as possible, making it just in time to close the door behind me.

A moment later, walking back into the hall, I'm met by one of the Vice Presidents who eyes me curiously as he sees the men's room door closing in my wake.

"Emergency," I explain, shrugging my shoulders. The door to the women's restroom swings open as I'm passing, and Dina emerges. She looks at me with knowing eyes and begins tapping that foot in a familiar rhythm.

"Not a word," I say, brushing past her and heading toward my office.

Chapter Thirty-Three

Two weeks have passed since the unfortunate food poisoning incident, and today Cooper asked me to go across town to get him a fish sandwich. It's about twenty degrees outside, and I still drove all the way back to the office with my windows down. The thought of having that fish smell trapped inside the Tahoe with me, when fish was what caused the poisoning in the first place...

Anyway, when I got back, I knew I couldn't ride up to the top floor with that fish in the elevator, so I'm currently taking the stairs. About three floors up, I start thinking about how easy it would be to go over the railing and plummet to my death. That begins a process of looking down as I climb, which leaves me very dizzy. Plopping down in the stairwell, I fight the wooziness. The fish sandwich is sitting next to me in a very taunting fashion, so I shove it to the other side of the step.

Remaining there silently for a moment, I place my head in my hands and wait for the dizziness to subside. After a brief period of time, a door bangs open directly above me, and someone begins whistling. Before I know it, one of the maintenance people is standing next to me on the stairs.

"You okay?" he inquires. "You didn't fall, did you?"

"No," I mutter. "Just taking a breather."

"Stairs aren't for sissies, huh?" he indicates with a laugh, walking over to the bag in the corner with Cooper's fish. "I hate it when people leave their trash in here. I'll just send it down for later." With that, I watch wordlessly as he drops the sandwich over the railing and it lands with a little thud on the ground below.

"You sure you're okay?" he wonders again before opening the door to the next floor. I manage to nod, able to think of nothing but that ridiculous fish sandwich that is now at the bottom of the stairwell, which means that I have to march back to the bottom to retrieve it.

On my way down to recover the sandwich, I try and try to think of a way to avoid trapping myself in a confined space with the fish.

After emerging from the stairwell into the lobby, I pick up the phone and dial Katie's number. I'm not sure what I expect her to do, but I know I need help.

"Katie?" I say when she picks up the phone. "It's Maddie. I'm in the lobby, and I need you to meet me down here."

"Something wrong?" she asks.

"No, nothing's wrong, I just need your help."

"I'm in the middle of something right now."

"Just hurry and get here as fast as you can."

I am aware by this time that the receptionist is glancing over at me every few seconds, most likely thinking I'm crazy, holding a greasy bag and muttering into the phone about needing help. Katie must believe something's wrong, too, because it only takes her about two minutes to find me.

"What is it, Maddie?" she asks, glancing at the brown paper bag in my hand.

"I need a favor," I begin, still not sure what to request.

"Okay, what do you need?"

"I'm going to go upstairs in the elevator," I mutter, pausing a second to think, "and then when it comes back down, I want you to come up with this bag."

Katie wrinkles her forehead and puts her hand on her hip, giving me a stern look.

"I'm not sure I want to be involved in this."

"In what?" I ask innocently. "Please tell me that you'll help me."

"What's in the bag?" she whispers. "It better not be drugs."

"Honestly, Katie, do you really think I would ask you to smuggle drugs?"

"No, but how do I know what Cooper would ask *you* to do?"

"Well, relax. It's not drugs. It's fish."

"Fish?"

"Fish. Now are you going to do it, or aren't you?"

Katie whips the bag out of my hand and points at the elevator.

"Go!" she orders. "I don't know why I let you talk me into these things."

I tell her thank you and step into the elevator, which lurches its way steadily upward to the top floor. Once there, I exit and stand silently in the corridor as I watch the lighted numbers go back down to 1. A couple people walk by while I'm standing there, but hopefully they assume that I am waiting to leave, instead of arriving. The numbers reverse their course and begin an upward climb, and I wait patiently.

"What are you doing?" Dina wonders behind me.

"Just waiting for the elevator," I explain at the exact moment the door opens to Katie holding the smelly bag of fish. Glancing over at Dina, I realize there is no way out of the situation, so I simply snatch the bag from Katie.

"Thank you!" I tell her as the door closes and Dina eyes me suspiciously. "It's for Cooper."

"Uh-huh," she blurts, walking away. I quickly deliver the sandwich to Cooper as requested, but I've only been in my office for about two minutes when the bell sounds overhead.

"You rang?" I ask as I open the door.

"Yes!" he barks. "This sandwich isn't like the last time. I want you to call them and ask them why."

"You want me to call the restaurant and ask why the sandwich is different from the last time?" I clarify, not quite believing that he's serious.

"Yes—call them. I want to know. Here, come get it."

He holds the paper bag out toward me, and even though I know I have to take it, my feet don't want to move. Ultimately, I force myself forward and take the bag from his hand.

What am I going to do with this sandwich? I definitely am not putting it in my trash can—I'll be sick for sure. I can't take it to the restroom, either, because I might have to go in there later, and I can't have the whole place reeking of fish. Where am I going to put this seafood, without having to get in the elevator and trap myself in the stale air with the pungent aroma?

Opening the door to my office, I step into the hallway, bag held out in front of me as far as it will reach. Dina remarks something about the sandwich being Cooper's sarcastically, and I nearly push the down button on the elevator, but then I pull my hand back. I know I would never make it.

Reluctantly, I turn to the door to the stairwell. It's a really long way down, but I don't have much choice. Pulling the door wide, I step into the cold, eerie silence. Taking a deep breath, I move down three steps before I stop to wait. The maintenance guy said he hated when people left their trash in here, right? But he also said that he would pick the fish up later, when he threw it to the bottom himself. It *is* the same fish, so technically it *is* the exact same trash, and he *did* say he would pick it up. Holding my hand over the railing, I let it go, watching the bag as it falls past two, three, four flights of stairs, ultimately catching on a step.

No! He'll know it's not the same trash if I leave it there!

I start to go down the steps to retrieve the bag when I hear a door open below me. Making a mad dash back to my floor, I feel a bit like a child afraid of being scolded as I bolt into the corridor.

Imagine all this trouble over a single fish sandwich, which Cooper didn't even wind up eating, and now I have to actually call the restaurant and ask them why it was different! *Different piece of fish,* they'll probably say. Still, there is no arguing with Cooper— when he wants something, he won't change his mind.

I casually walk back to my office, ignoring Dina's stare as I shut the door behind me, startling a bit as Cooper pokes his head in from the other side.

"Maddie," he states, "I'm thinking maybe I'll try something else. I want you to go over to Billy's and get me some oysters."

"Oysters?" I cannot believe my ears.

"Yes, oysters. A whole plate full of them, and hurry."

For a few seconds, I really consider going down to the Tahoe and driving all the way home, not bothering to look back.

"Miss Heard?" I hear the voice on the other end of the phone ask.

"Yes, this is Madeline Heard," I reply, scooting my chair closer to my desk.

"This is Shirley at the reception desk. A young man just brought a sandwich for Mr. Cooper."

Great. When I called to complain about the sandwich, the manager told me he would send over a new one. I told him that wasn't necessary, but he insisted.

"Can you just send him up with it?" I ask. I really don't feel like messing with any more smelly fish today.

"Sorry, but he's already gone. He just dropped it off and went on his way."

"Can someone down there bring it up?" I try again.

"I'm sorry, but I'm the only one here at the present."

"Okay," I mumble, hanging up the phone. Immediately I dial Katie's number, listening to the phone ring twice.

"This is Katie Green," she answers in a very professional tone.

"Katie, it's Maddie again."

"No."

"But you don't even know what I was going to—"

"I don't care what you ask me, Maddie, the answer is no," she insists more forcefully. "I delivered that stinky fish to you, and I didn't ask you any questions. Next you drew me downstairs for that pile of clams or whatever it was. I'm not doing any more of your dirty work."

"Please, Katie, just one last time."

Wow, I really do sound like a druggie.

"What are you doing, starting an aquarium up there or something? You should try to get some live examples, instead of stinky dead ones."

"I know," I groan. "I know it's stupid, okay? I wish I didn't even have to ask you."

"Then don't. Why don't you ask Audrey to help you? Your shadow will do whatever you say."

Because Audrey still hates me, that's why.

"She's...not here. Please, Katie."

"I can't, Maddie. I'm sorry."

Click.

Drat! Katie was my only good out for this situation. Now what am I going to do?

I reluctantly leave the comfort of my office, strolling casually past Dina and toward the elevator, pushing the button to head down a few floors. After only a few seconds, I sense a presence behind me.

"Going down?" I ask.

"Yes," Dina replies, standing next to me.

Perfect. An elevator ride full of awkward silence is just what the doctor ordered.

The door opens and I step inside, followed quickly by the bespectacled beehive. "I'm going down to the Accounting Department," she states, staring at the buttons on the wall. "Where might you be going?"

"Just running a quick errand," I mutter, turning away from her. The elevator jerks to a stop at the floor she chose. A quick moment later, I reach the bottom and step out to see the now familiar brown bag waiting for me, so I move casually to the desk and snatch the bag. The stairwell is clearly not my friend, but it appears to be my only option. I'm almost to the door when I hear some familiar humming. Turning, I see Greg from the mail room walking back from the reception area.

"Greg!" I call, waving the hand that is not holding the brown bag fish special.

He looks my way and smiles. "Maddie? Not used to seeing you down this way."

"No, I escaped," I joke. "Since I ran into you, I was wondering if you would do me a favor."

"Sure, I guess," he states, shifting a stack of papers in his arms. Greg has to be right out of high school, all tall and lanky with the long arms. If he ever had to lift anything heavy, he might snap in half.

"I need to take this bag up to my office, but I've got a couple of stops to make on the way, and it's just not very professional to carry it around with me. You understand, right?"

"I guess."

"So, since you're probably coming up in a few minutes anyway, I was wondering if you would drop it off on your way through."

"You want me to drop this bag off at your office," he repeats, totally taking the bait.

"Yes. You don't mind, do you?"

"It's not drugs, is it?" he whispers, glancing back at the receptionist.

Why do I keep getting that question? Do I look like a dealer or something?

"No, it's not drugs." Opening the bag, I let him look inside. "It's a fish sandwich, for Cooper."

"Gotcha," he says, grabbing the bag out of my hand. "No problem-o. I'll be up in a few minutes."

"Thanks so much," I tell him with a smile, heading back toward the elevator.

Problem solved! Three smelly seafood deliveries, and I didn't have to take any of them in the elevator with me. I would call that a very productive day. And yes, I'm aware of the sadness of that statement.

As soon as I make it back to my floor, I march past Dina and into my office, beginning to fiddle with some paperwork that

Cooper left on my desk. It's not very often that he gives me actual work to do, but today is the exception. If I didn't have to deal with all the errands and nonsense, it would probably last a good hour and a half. That's more than I do in some weeks, really, if you don't count all the extra tasks I create for myself.

Nearly twenty minutes later, I hear humming and the door to my office swings open.

"Your sandwich," Greg announces, handing me the brown bag.

"Thank you," I state as he continues his way down the hall. Ignoring the glare that I'm receiving from across the way, I immediately cross to the other side of my office and knock, opening the door to Cooper's office.

"What is it?" he wonders.

"They sent you a make-up sandwich," I tell him, delivering it to his desk. He nods and returns to what he's doing as I hurriedly leave the room. While I'm securing the interconnecting door between our offices, I notice that my door to the hallway is creeping ajar.

"Dina," I assess when I see her head poke around the door.

She steps into my office and shuts the door behind her, leaning against it with her arms folded across her chest. "Young lady, I think it's high time that you admit that you have a problem."

I fight the urge to laugh for a minute. It's quite the sight, Dina standing there in her blue wool suit, glasses toward the end of her nose, tapping her little high-heeled shoes on my carpet. She doesn't make an intimidating figure at all—sort of like when you pass one of those Chihuahuas that growls. Sure, it might attack you, but how much harm is it really going to do?

"There's no problem," I sigh. I'm getting really tired of this conversation topic. First I had to go through it constantly with Mom, and now I'm getting the same interrogations at the office. When is this garbage going to end?

"Normal people do not eat as much as you do," she goes on, foot still tapping.

"Don't eat as much... All I had for lunch was a fruit salad."

"You've had three food deliveries this afternoon."

"All for Cooper."

"I know as well as anyone that Mr. Cooper has a hearty appetite, but I have never seen the man eat three meals in one afternoon."

"That's because he didn't really *eat* all three meals. The first one was—"

"Oh, I'm sure you have an excellent excuse. You need help. Serious help. You're a very sick girl."

"Thank you for the observation," I mutter, sitting down and returning to my paperwork.

"Don't think I'm going to let this go so easily," she states, exiting the room.

Naturally, I'm sure I won't be that lucky.

Ding-dong.

I'm completely exhausted, seriously.

"You rang?" I ask at Cooper's door.

"The sandwich is better," he bellows, "but I can't eat it. I'm just not hungry. Here—take it with you."

The next morning, as I arrive on the top floor, Dina merely glances up for a second before she returns to her work. Normally I wouldn't find that odd, but the way she's been intensely watching me lately, it seems out of character. Not that it's a bad thing; quite the opposite, really. Maybe she will be leaving me alone for a little while and giving me some room to breathe.

I take a moment to listen to my voice mail messages—two about the revamped version of Project Cooper and one from Katie, who wanted to know if I needed a dead carp for my seafood museum. Before I get a chance to call her back and tell her she is decidedly unfunny, Cooper calls me into his office. I march across

his thick blue carpet, notepad in hand, ready to write down the next errand of the day. Instead, he motions for me to sit.

"Maddie," he begins with a sigh, "it has come to my attention that there might be a problem."

"Problem?" I manage. "What sort of problem?" Not a problem with Project Cooper, I hope. Everything has been going well to this point.

"A health issue."

Cooper's sick? He's probably got salmonella from eating all those raw eggs. Or, maybe it was that fish sandwich yesterday...the one he thought didn't taste right. Goodness knows I am aware of the problems *that* can cause.

"Okay," I mutter, unsure of how to respond.

"Health and wellness are very important to me. I'm sure you can understand."

"Of course."

The poor man is going to have a mental breakdown. He's so focused on his vitamins and supplements and all that business, and now he has a serious medical problem. I won't be surprised if he's driven into a deep depression, desperately needing someone to care for him at all times. I'm not sure his plastic wife will be up to the job.

"So I called some representatives for our health insurance company, and they highly recommend a local counselor—some woman named Ling."

So he does recognize the potential for his depression. He must, anyway, if he's considering going to a counselor. Wow, I can't imagine what that session would be like, delving into the mind of Kent Cooper. It could be a decade-long process.

"Anyway," he continues with a wave of the hand, "I went ahead and scheduled the appointment for next week. You will see this woman Ling at 2:00 on Thursday."

Huh? Maybe he doesn't realize that one doesn't send an assistant to their counseling appointment.

"Me?" I ask cautiously, not wanting to anger him.

"Yes, at 2:00 on Thursday."

"I'm sorry," I reply hesitantly. "I'm still not sure why you want *me* to go to the counseling."

"You expect someone to go in your place?" He gives me a very pointed look.

Yes—you! You're the one with the problem, apparently. Why should I have to go to your counseling session?

"This is just a little too confusing for me," I mutter, looking down at the floor. I'm slightly afraid that his mind is fuzzy, or he is in denial about the problem, but I don't know what to say.

"It's high time you get help for this problem," he insists, smacking the side of his hand against the desk for emphasis. "I can't have you unhealthy."

Me get help? I thought we were talking about Cooper. How did the tables turn so quickly?

"What problem are you referring to, sir?" I ask, looking earnestly into his face. The poor man really is severely, painfully confused.

"The eating disorder, what else? I know all about it."

Of course, the eating disorder. Dina. She has now earned a place in the fist-clench hall of fame. *Newman. Brittany. Cooper. Dina.* How dare she tell Cooper about that nonsense! If my mom hadn't invented that ridiculous garbage in the first place...

"This is all a big mistake," I explain. "I don't have an eating disorder."

"Maddie, you can't hide things forever. I know all about the vomiting, and the secrecy, and the food smuggling. Did you think no one would notice?"

Food smuggling, indeed. Those were his own fish sandwiches! Really, what am I supposed to say? Without a logical explanation for the fact that I have a weak stomach, I absolutely feel like I'm being backed into a corner. Any effective argument evading me for the moment, I manage to do nothing but sit here staring stupidly at Cooper behind his gigantic desk.

"So, you will go to the counseling on Thursday, and we'll get things back on track." He picks up some paperwork on his desk and begins perusing it, and I'm aware that he is giving me the signal

that we're finished. I somehow manage to pry my deflated body from the blue leather chair and make my way back to my office. How could one silly incorrect assumption have infiltrated this deeply into my life?

And what am I going to tell a counselor? I can only imagine how that session will go.

"You're Maddie?" she'll say. "My name is Ling. We're here today to talk about your bulimia."

"See, that's the thing," I'll reply. "I don't actually have bulimia."

"Uh-huh," she'll continue, nodding as she writes in her black notebook. "What's the problem then?"

"I don't have a problem." She'll flip out her little handheld recorder and begin talking quietly, her back turned toward me.

"The subject is hesitant to admit a problem," she'll report. "Looks like a clear-cut case of denial."

"Now wait a minute," I'll retort. "I'm not in denial."

"You deny having an eating disorder?"

"Yes."

"Then you are in denial." She will lean toward her recorder again. "Note—the subject is rather hostile when the issue of denial is approached. The damage must go deeper than previously believed."

"It's only denial when you have a problem," I'll try to explain, "but I don't have a problem, so it can't be denial. If I deny having a problem, that's because it's a fact. I. Do. Not. Have. A. Problem."

"The subject is openly antagonistic regarding the entire topic of denial," she'll tell the recorder. "Looks like this could take several sessions, possibly involving an entire team."

No good can come of this. Why does everyone have to keep messing up my life?

Walking to the door, I open it a crack. "Thanks a lot, Dina," I say just loud enough that she can hear. I notice her back tighten, but she keeps her head down.

After days of intense scrutiny, suddenly Dina literally can't manage to keep her eyes on me.

Chapter Thirty-Four

It would occur to me, if Cooper is really bothered by the idea of me throwing up, that he would not slurp his raw eggs in my presence. Also, that he would not bring me a tray full of dirty dishes with what appeared to be the remnants of salmon and creamed spinach. I can only imagine what the cafeteria thought when I called them to pick up the dishes. *That little diva can't even bring dirty dishes down here by herself. She has to call us up to the top floor in our hairnets like her servants to pick up the big dog's plates.*

Normally I would never do something like that, of course, but under the circumstances, I had no choice. Any possible instance where I might be grossed out is something I am avoiding like the plague, for obvious reasons.

I took a moment last night to call my mother and thank her for her part in my sordid office charade.

"Mom, it's Maddie," I stated.

"Oh," she replied. That's the welcome reception I get when I call my mother—Oh.

"Just thought I'd call and let you know what's going on at work," I said nonchalantly, wondering how she might respond.

"Really? Are you working on another special project that you want me to know about?"

As if I would invite her if I was.

"No, no, nothing like that."

"Then what is it?" she asked rather abruptly, as though the mere sound of my voice was interrupting her busy life.

"My boss has taken the liberty of making an appointment for me on Thursday, and I just wanted to thank you."

"Oh, well then," she said, voice brightening a little. "What kind of appointment?"

"An appointment with a counselor."

"A counselor? Like a career counselor or something?"

"No," I said pointedly. "I have an appointment with a counselor because my boss believes I have an eating disorder."

For a moment, I only hear silence on the other end of the line, and then a faint, "Oh."

"Don't you wonder why he would think that, Mom?"

"I don't know..." she muttered, pausing a moment. "Maybe because you're getting so skinny?"

"Care to take another guess?"

"I just don't know, honey. I don't know why he would think that."

"I don't either. You know, I've been thinking a lot about it, and the only person around me who would have told him that was my coworker, Dina. She wouldn't have any reason to think I have an eating disorder, though."

"Well, of course not," Mom said, her voice rising a little higher than normal. "How would she get such a notion?"

"I don't know anyone who would tell her such a thing," I lied, awaiting her response. No way can she talk her way out of this one.

"No...no," she mumbled.

"You've never talked to Dina, have you?"

"Well, now, I don't know. She might have answered the phone before when you weren't there. I can't remember all those peoples' names."

"No, I don't expect you to remember the names of everyone in my office. I would think, though, that once you have a lengthy conversation with someone, you would at least remember talking to them."

"And I'm sure I would."

"I would think you would remember telling them that you believe I'm bulimic and they should keep a watchful eye on me."

"Yes, of course I'd remember that."

"And yet you don't remember talking to Dina," I added, becoming exasperated with her game.

"No, I don't remember any Dina."

"I hope you realize I could get fired over this."

"Really?" she squeaked.

Well, no, I sincerely hope not, but she should have thought of that before she opened her big mouth!

"Yes, really. If that happens, you're the first person I'm coming to for money."

"Oh, but Maddie, I—"

"Gotta run, Mom!" I said, hanging up the phone.

Calling my mother only succeeded in making me angrier after phoning, which I instinctively knew would happen. I guess I just wanted her to know what kind of mess one little white lie could create. Not even a white lie, really, but more along the lines of an unfounded rumor. In any case, she started it, and now I'm doomed to go to counseling. If this mix-up continues, and the counselor really does give me a hard time, maybe I can convince her that Mom needs to go to the sessions with me, as the cause of my problems. I wonder how she would like that!

The date for Project Cooper is rapidly approaching, and so far I've managed to keep it tightly under wraps while organizing quite an event. Cooper has allowed me to ask a few other members of the staff for assistance, and they've been invaluable to me. I may consider myself brilliant at times, but I most definitely don't know everything.

Part of me wonders how Audrey is going to take the surprise. I don't know how she's doing right now, since I've only seen her in passing a couple of times, and I haven't had the chance to speak to her. Honestly, I'm not certain she would speak to me

anyway, since she still believes I did something to intentionally hurt her. Each time I ask Cooper about her, he insists she's fine, so it's a waste of time to even bother him.

Katie told me that Audrey trained in her department for a couple of days, just getting a feel for how everything worked. When I asked how she seemed to be doing, Katie said she wasn't overly friendly, but she didn't seem too depressed. Maybe she took things better than I thought she would, and it's doing her a world of good simply to be away from me. It would be a little depressing, after all, to have to sit all day and stare at the person who was recently planning your failed wedding. That would probably be enough to send any sane person into depression.

Picking up the phone, I dial the numbers I wrote down this morning to make the call I've been dreading all day. Not only am I expecting the conversation not to be pleasant, but truthfully, I am anticipating disaster. I am determined, however, to make Project Cooper a dazzling success, and this is an integral part of that mission.

"You have reached Channel Six Action News," a friendly voice states. "How may I direct your call?"

"Harley Laine, please," I request, clearing my throat. Part of me can't believe I'm doing this.

"May I say who's calling?" the voice asks.

"I'm a representative of Cooper Corporate Financial, and I have some information about a top-secret event that will be attended by the foremost members of the community. I thought she might be interested in the story."

"Thank you. One moment please."

Elevator music. You know, it's hard enough to sit on hold, but then they play that very soft easy-listening music that makes you sleepy almost immediately.

"Harley Laine," I hear her chirpy voice state into the receiver.

"Hi, Harley. I'm calling from Cooper Corporate Financial, and I have some information about a top-secret event that is going to take place on February 24th. Most of the important individuals

in the community will be there, and I thought you might want the scoop."

"Sounds interesting," she says. "Let me write down all the information. What did you say your name was?"

"Madeline," I reply.

"Madeline..."

"Heard."

"Your name sounds familiar. Have we met before?"

"Yes, a couple times." I hesitate, hoping nothing jogs her memory.

"Madeline from Cooper Corporate," she repeats with a slight laugh. "Yeah, I remember you."

Here it comes. She's going to rip me apart.

"Listen, I'm sorry about what happened at the shelter," I tell her. "The lady I was defending happens to be my mother, who is a huge fan of yours and was totally miffed at me afterwards."

"That about figures," she replies, growing silent for a second. "You live on my street, don't you? I've seen you jogging."

"Yeah."

This isn't what I expected. I have the video of her freaking out on my computer, where I'd downloaded it from Audrey's phone a long time ago. That's the card I was carrying in my hip pocket, in case she refused, but she seems like she's actually trying to be...nice?

"Well, sounds like you might have an interesting story. Tell me when and where, and I'll do my best."

Life has brought me downtown to a stuffy little waiting room where I'm about to see my new counselor, an individual Cooper only described as a woman named Ling. It's impossible not to feel ridiculous when you walk up to the counter and say you are

there to see Ling. Is that a first name? A last name? I wouldn't know, because I've been ambushed into coming here on completely false pretenses—sentenced and serving time without a verdict or any evidence. This is a completely unfair counseling incarceration.

"Maddie?" a middle-aged woman with long dark hair asks, standing partially in the doorway.

"Yes?"

"I'm Tania Ling. Why don't you step into my office?"

She doesn't look too awfully intimidating, but she probably takes on that mild demeanor so she can really get her clients to trust her before she lashes into them.

I follow Tania into her office, which looks like it was decorated in the early '80's. It is neat and tidy, but there's nothing modern about it. She lowers herself behind the desk, and I sit in a chair in front of her. The good news is, there is no couch, so hopefully she won't try to analyze me.

"I must say, Maddie, you're not at all what I pictured."

"Really?" I reply, afraid to ask what she pictured.

"You look really healthy," she states, her forehead creasing a bit.

"Thank you!" I exclaim, realizing a little too late that "healthy" is probably a polite way of saying I'm really not skinny enough to look anorexic. And why should I be offended by that, when I've been saying it myself all along? I do look *healthy*, after all.

"So, tell me a little about your eating disorder."

She doesn't pull out her notebook to write down my answers or anything. She simply folds her hands together on her desk, ready to listen.

"I don't have an eating disorder," I state. She shakes her head and looks toward her office door.

"I'm sorry," Tania says. "The lady who takes the appointments told me that you were coming in because you're bulimic. Our mistake, I guess. What are we really seeing you for, then?"

"That *is* why I'm here, actually."

"I'm confused." For a moment, I ponder explaining this misunderstanding to the lady before me.

"My boss made the appointment. He believes I'm bulimic."

"I see," she replies, nodding her head and beginning to twirl her thumbs around each other with her hands intertwined on top of her notebook. "Why does he believe that?"

"His secretary might have told him that." I wrinkle my nose a bit before realizing my action.

"Interesting," she states, lips curling into a smile. "And why does the secretary think you're bulimic?"

"My mother told her."

"And your mother?"

"She's just insane."

"I don't think calling your mother insane is going to help us come to any realistic conclusion here," Tania scolds. Of course, I knew she would go all counselor on me eventually.

"Okay, I guess the truth is that I lost some weight by exercising and eating right, and she came to her own conclusions."

Tania purses her lips and taps her finger on the desk a few times. "Why would your mother rather assume you were bulimic instead of physically fit?"

"Do you have all day?" I wonder, glancing at my watch.

She laughs softly and nods a couple times. "Okay, not a topic we'll delve into right now, then. This secretary, is she a friend of your mother's?"

"No, she just happened to pick up the phone once when my mother was calling me." If I could go back in time, I would pinpoint the exact moment of that phone call and would not have left my desk for any reason. Period.

"So your mother proceeded to tell her that you were bulimic, and the secretary just blindly believed her?"

"Not at first," I reply, trying to remember exactly how it happened. "She said that she didn't want to believe it, but then she started to see evidence."

"Evidence," Tania repeats, unclenching her hands and placing them in her lap. "What type of evidence?"

"Vomiting, mostly."

"Vomiting?"

"Perhaps a little strange behavior."

"Vomiting and strange behavior."

"Yes, I would say that's about it."

"Maddie," she begins, clearing her throat, "I've got to tell you—that does sound a little odd. How do you explain those things?"

"Well, initially it was food poisoning by a rotten fish sandwich. Then there was a guy on the elevator with BO… Then it was my boss ordering seafood over and over, which I simply couldn't place in an elevator with me, thus the strange behavior. I have a really weak stomach, and when I start thinking about things, or smelling things, it's my undoing. I kept trying to think of different ways to get his gross food to my office without actually accompanying it on the way. I know that probably sounds bizarre."

Tania starts laughing, and I just sit there uncomfortably. She surely thinks I'm a lunatic. She's going to call Cooper when I leave and recommend that he take me directly to a psychiatric ward or something. They're going to put me in a padded cell with one of those white coats on so my arms are tied behind my back.

"I'm sorry, Maddie. I think I get the picture."

"You do?" I ask quietly.

"Yes, I do. It's really unfortunate that your mom planted the seeds that led to this appointment, but I think you'll be just fine."

"What about my boss?"

"I'll tell you what…I'll write a letter for you right now that will help you clear up the issue."

Sitting patiently as she puts pen to paper, I'm thrilled that someone finally believes me about this idiotic nonsense, and I wonder what she's writing in that letter.

Dear Mr. Cooper,

You and your staff are completely paranoid. Please do not inflict any more of this baloney on Maddie Heard.

Ha, that would tell him, wouldn't it? Of course, I would be sure to make Dina a copy as well. Maybe they would think twice about ganging up on me if something like this ever came up again.

"There you go," Tania says, sliding the paper toward me. I pull it off the desk with my fingertips and grasp it in my hand.

"Thank you," I tell her as I stand up and head to the door, turning around after only a couple steps. "We're all done here, right?"

"We're finished," she agrees with a smile.

Heading back out into the waiting room, I pause briefly before leaving the building to read the letter she has written.

To Whom it May Concern:

Upon speaking in length with Madeline Heard, it is my opinion that she does not have an eating disorder. On the contrary, it would appear that Ms. Heard is in excellent health, with the exception of a slightly weak stomach. I could find no obvious reason to be concerned about her physical or emotional health at this time.

Sincerely,

Tania Ling

I couldn't wait to put my letter on Cooper's desk after the counseling session. I made a copy for Dina as well, and a copy for my mother, which I promptly mailed upon arriving home that same evening. Who knows if it will end her accusations, but at least she will have some written documentation that she is wrong, whether she chooses to admit it or not.

It feels so good to finally put this silliness behind me and concentrate on what is really important. The idea that the tennis match is looming in the near future is the only thing that should really concern me. Every time I try to wrap my brain around the aftermath of the match, I envision myself being sent to another

department within the company. He doesn't need an assistant, after all. He has Dina, who handles all his work for him. I'm nothing but a glorified errand girl who occasionally works on special projects, and I have to ask his permission to do that. He always has the same opinion—anything is fine, as long as it doesn't interfere with my tennis lessons.

In my worst nightmares, I imagine that he will send me back to the Marketing Department to work for Bill Davies. Bill will promptly make me a subordinate to Shelly, and then I will be her errand girl. If it's any consolation, running errands for Shelly would probably be preferable to running them for Cooper. She would probably have me do more interesting things than picking up fish sandwiches and finding socks of a very distinct color.

Plus, I'm sure she would never make me take her teeth to the dentist.

That's only the worst case scenario, though. There are lots of other departments to which he could send me. I'll be sitting in a little cubicle, bored out of my mind, anxiously watching the clock each day until it's time to go home. He might even place me somewhere where he knows I won't stay, hoping that I'll walk out one day and never come back.

At least I will have finished the party for Audrey before anything happens. My most sincere hope is that it will help her forget all the problems she's had the past couple of months, and that it will bring her family closer together. Besides, that girl really needs a boost in the self-esteem department, and I think this could help a great deal.

February 24th—for some reason, that feels very much like the culmination of everything…a real pivot point.

When the day comes, maybe I'll figure out why.

Chapter Thirty-Five

Believe it or not, Dina hasn't uttered a word about the letter from the counselor. Cooper hasn't mentioned it, either. You would think he might have given me an apology, after sending me across town to discuss a problem I didn't even have with a complete stranger, but no such request for forgiveness has ever been extended. I guess I didn't really expect it, knowing Cooper as I do, but it still would have been a nice gesture. Let's face it—the only reason he even cared whether or not I was unhealthy in the first place was that it would have interrupted his planned tennis thrashing.

Mom never mentioned the letter to me, either, come to think of it. Then again, she hasn't called since I sent it, so I'm not really surprised. If I did happen to bring it up, she would probably say it must have been lost in the mail. If she ever did admit to having received it, she would probably say that she doesn't know anyone named Tania Ling, and she could be a complete and total quack. I'm sure she would like to send me to a counselor of her own, but only after she went herself and briefed him or her on my numerous problems and issues.

Lance called a couple days ago to ask me a favor. I was a little surprised to hear his voice, because Brittany is usually the one who tries to keep contact with me. (I wasn't disappointed, though, just to make myself clear.) He told me that Marilyn and Jordan were both going to sleepovers on Valentine's Day, and asked if I would be willing to watch Abigail for a couple of hours. "I know you don't have any plans, since you're single," he explained.

My first reaction was to be offended, naturally, but then I realized he was right, and there was no use being insulted by the truth. I agreed to watch her, and I'm actually looking forward to it. I haven't heard from Brittany since Christmas, when I left her gifts stuffed in the cushions of Mom's couch. I'm still fairly incensed over that whole ordeal. Every time I think about it, I want to scream.

Valentine's Day stinks when you're single on the top floor of Cooper Corporate Financial. Everyone was feeling the love today, even Dina. It was like a day-long reminder that I am sad and alone.

So, as soon as I get home, I focus on decompressing. Here I am, sprawled out on the recliner, noisily chewing on a carrot, watching some documentary about sea life on television when the doorbell rings. I glance down at my sweatpants, T-shirt, and slippers, giving myself a once-over. I look like complete garbage, I know.

Walking over to the door, I peek out the window. Brittany? What is she doing here? And Lance, and…

Yeah, I completely forgot. Who knows why I agreed to do this in the first place. How could they be so inconsiderate, just imposing upon me on a holiday like I have nothing better to do?

Of course, Maddie's a loser, so she'll be home—let's take our kid to her house.

I know I'm being ridiculous, but sometimes it's helpful to have a little bit of a pity party.

"Hi," I say, opening the door. Brittany does a quick sweep of my clothing with her eyes before she steps in, Lance right behind her, baby carrier in hand.

"You look terrible," she states. "Are you sick?"

Yes, sick. That's a good excuse.

"Actually, yes, a little."

"Nothing contagious, I hope," she says, glancing over at Abigail.

"Just something I ate, probably," I reply, hastily thrusting the carrot into my pocket. "I'll completely understand if you don't feel comfortable leaving Abby here, though."

"We already made reservations," Lance tells me, glancing at Brittany.

"Yes, she'll be fine. You *can* take care of her, right?" Brittany stands in front of me, arms crossed, giving me an icy stare.

"Of course I can," I reply defiantly.

"Okay, we'll be on our way then," Brittany states. "The instructions are in the diaper bag. She just ate before we came, so she'll be fine for a while."

Lance places the handle to the baby carrier in my palm, and Brittany drops the diaper bag on the corner of the sofa.

"We should only be a couple of hours," Lance tells me, and I nod in response. They both walk to the door and quickly disappear. Standing in the middle of the room, I stare blankly at the empty doorway. Abigail stirs in her carrier, and I set it down and begin unbuckling the straps around her arms.

"Hi there, Abigail," I catch myself saying in hushed baby talk. "I'm Aunt Maddie, remember me? It's been a little while."

I finally manage to remove the straps and lift her into the air, and she snuggles into the crook of my arm. Her little eyes stare up into my face, and she makes a tiny O with her lips. Laughing, I stroke her cheek with my finger as my heart wells up with emotion.

She makes a little noise and then spits up down the front of my T-shirt, at which point I simply grab a cloth and wipe it off. "That's the kind of luck I have, Abigail. Just hanging around alone on Valentine's Day, getting puked on."

The doorbell rings again, and I cross to look through the blinds, seeing Hazel standing outside. Swinging the door open, I smile at her over Abigail's wiggling body.

"Oh, I didn't know you were babysitting," she says quickly.

"It's okay," I reply. "You want to come in?"

"Sure. I brought you dinner and a funny movie."

"Funny sounds good," I state, moving out of her way. She carries the food to the kitchen and then returns to where I'm standing in the living room, glancing at little Abigail.

"It's awfully nice of you to watch your niece."

"That's what happens when you're hopelessly single," I tell her with a wink. "Anyway, I wasn't being nice. I just couldn't think of an excuse."

She laughs as she sits on the couch. "So, Josh told me about the party you're having for Audrey. I just think it's wonderful what you're doing."

"Thank you," I mumble.

"I remember the day you came over after the preacher spoke about loving your enemies. Do you remember that? You said that it felt like he was talking to you."

"Yeah," I agree cautiously.

"Well, you must have really taken his words to heart. I bet you wouldn't have guessed then that you'd be throwing such a lavish party."

Not bothering to answer her, I stare blankly at a bare spot on the wall. I guess I haven't bothered to think about it at all since that day, really. What was it that Reverend Shell had said that Sunday, when he kept looking at me? *Watch for an opportunity*, or something or other. Could there be some reason that I was supposed to befriend Audrey and help her through a difficult time?

"And now here you are helping your sister-in-law, when she's been so difficult with you in the past," Hazel continues, smiling at me. "You must have taken the message to heart, sweetie."

"I'm just fumbling along," I insist. "Surely you know that."

"Hmm, no, I don't know that," she tells me quietly, patting me on the shoulder. "Josh said to tell you hello when you got home from whatever date you were on. I won't tell him you're babysitting."

Laughing, I shake my head. "I told Josh I've sworn off dating."

"He must not have believed you," she says with a smile. "You know, I think he was getting up at 5:30 in the morning, which is...9:30 here, right? Maybe you should tell him that he needs to believe you next time."

"You want me to call Josh," I surmise.

"Did I say that?" she wonders slyly. "Enjoy your dinner, and your little niece. I better get back home to Tucker. Tell Josh I said hi."

"Thank you, Hazel," I tell her as she reaches the door. "You are a silver lining in a sea of black clouds."

"So dramatic," she insists with a laugh. "Goodnight, honey."

She vanishes into the night, and I settle on the couch to watch the funny movie Hazel delivered. The dinner she brought consists of chicken enchiladas and chocolate covered strawberries. It's such an odd combination that I nearly laugh, but it's super sweet that she brought the food to me.

For her part, Abigail sleeps away while I watch the movie, like she's not even concerned about the fact that it's Valentine's Day and her aunt Maddie is spending it alone and dressed like a hobo.

When Lance and Brittany return to pick up Abigail, they are both rather quiet. Brittany doesn't throw any jabs at me, and they seem content enough that I didn't damage their daughter. The minute they are out the door, I pick up my cell phone and stare at the screen.

9:45. Calling Josh is second nature to me, but I feel rather nervous about it at the moment. I know the secret, and Hazel surely believes she knows something, after that inscription Camdyn Taylor wrote in my book. Sitting at home on Valentine's Day feels like admitting something, too, if only that I'm undesirable.

Nonetheless, I can't resist. Pushing the button next to his name, I wait.

"Mad," he whispers almost immediately. "Hang on, let me step out."

I won't ask him where he is—I usually don't, because he never wants to talk about it. He always insists that I try to make him feel like he's home instead.

"Okay. Are you taking a brief respite from your date?" he wants to know. "Who's the guy?"

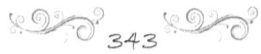

"Come on, Josh, don't be cruel. There is no date. I babysat Abigail, and then your mom brought me chicken enchiladas."

"Seriously?"

"Yes, your mom is an angel sent from heaven."

He doesn't say anything, and I wonder if he's talked to her since she left the house tonight. The mere thought makes me feel really uncomfortable.

"I spent Valentine's Day with a guy named Barker," he finally admits. "We watched *Top Gun*."

"I really hope it was romantic," I offer. "Abigail threw up on me, so there you go."

"Banner day for both of us, then," he surmises, chuckling quietly. "Listen, Mad, there's something I need to talk to you about. You got a sec?"

Stomach flipping nervously, I rise from the couch and start pacing. "Um, yeah. I called you, didn't I?"

"Yeah, I guess you did. I just... I'm not sure how to say this."

Instinctively, I stop moving. Josh is afraid to tell me something. It has to be one of two things: *Dearest Maddie, I love you with all my heart.* Or, conversely, *Jess told me you have the hots for me. Really, Mad? So gross.*

"Just spit it out," I plead, my voice sounding a bit strange.

"I don't want to make things difficult for you, but Mom and Dad will help if you need them to. They said they'd be happy to do anything."

"What are you talking about?" I wonder hesitantly.

"I need you to move out."

Oomph. It's like a sucker punch right to the gut.

"Are you serious?" I choke, coughing a bit as I feel myself deflating.

Happy Valentine's Day, Maddie. Get lost.

"I feel horrible even mentioning this to you, but Mom and Dad said you can move in with them."

"Move in with your parents, are you insane?" My heart constricts in my chest as I wrap my arm protectively across my abdomen.

"I'm trying to help you."

A tear escapes my left eye, hot and angry as it streams down my cheek. "Don't bother. I don't need your help. I'll be out by the end of the week."

"Don't be upset with me, Mad."

"Upset?" I balk. "Why would I be upset? You're doing me a favor, right? Now I can really get on with my life properly."

"What does that mean?"

"Happy Valentine's Day, Josh. I'll give your mother the key."

Pressing the end button, I fling the phone onto the couch. So much for expectations.

My new apartment has one bedroom, is tucked in Louisville safely away from the suburbs and Wonder Lane, and won't be available until March 1st. In other words, Josh has rendered me homeless. Oh, I could move in with his parents, he said, but how weird is that?

So, naturally, I ended up in the best possible situation.

That's right—I'm staring at the wall of my high school bedroom, which my mother has turned into some sort of scrapbook haven. My life is officially over.

Chapter Thirty-Six

Today I had to pick up Audrey's dress (which is beautiful, by the way) and deliver it to Cooper, since it's his job to make sure that she arrives at the appropriate place and time. I was a little wary of putting him in charge of such an important detail, but he has actually been somewhat helpful in making this happen. Maybe he really cares about making this a success, which would be a wonderful step in the right direction for Audrey.

Oh, and after the Visa, I only had to fork out $78.62, so not too bad.

I've also been busy setting things up for the big reveal…unpacking boxes, preparing shelving, and generally getting things ready. I didn't quite anticipate the level of work this little project was going to become, but it will all be worth it when Audrey realizes what her father has done for her. That is the moment I'm anxiously awaiting, simply to see the look on her face.

Ding-dong.

It's safe to say that I am very tired of this silly game.

"You rang?" I ask at the door.

"Yes, come in," Cooper demands. "I presume your tennis lesson went well today?"

"Yes," I reply, folding my hands together in front of me. Max and I coolly attempt to kill one another every week on the court without ever bringing up our little boyfriend misunderstanding.

"Max is quite impressed with your abilities. He thinks you could play in a match."

"Really?" I wonder, disliking the direction of the conversation. Any time Cooper calls the tennis club to check up on me, it means he is preparing his little scheme for beating his brother. I've never been crazy about the idea, but by this time I'm fairly resolved that I am not playing in any tennis match with Cooper. Period.

"We'll have to set up a match for you sometime, to see how well you compete."

No thanks. I'm one-hundred percent not interested.

"Oh, I meant to tell you," I say, "things are looking very favorable for Saturday. I think everything should be completely set up and ready to go."

Come on, Cooper—take the bait and change the subject.

"Very good," he replies. "I'm assuming everything will go as planned?"

"As long as you bring Audrey when scheduled, the event should be a success."

You will bring Audrey on time, right Cooper? You won't let her down on her big day?

"That should be no problem," he says with a wave of his hand. "It's under control."

"Why won't you tell me, Maddie?"

Jess has been on my case ever since my fallout with Josh. He's tried to call me a couple times, but I don't want to take his calls. What he did to me was so hurtful, I can't even think about it. Who kicks someone out on Valentine's Day? Especially a single person with zero love interests and baby puke on her shirt?

Besides, my heart might be slightly broken.

"I did tell you, Jess. I moved out. I have an apartment in Louisville. Everything's fine. End of story." I stumble over a pair of my shoes that are sticking out from underneath the bed. Trying to cram everything from my adult life into my little childhood bedroom is basically a disaster.

"Maddie, I hear the words you're saying, but your voice isn't telling me everything's fine. What's going on?"

"Nothing's going on," I insist. "I've got the big unveiling tonight for Audrey, and I'm trying to get ready."

"What are you wearing?" she wonders.

"I don't know. I got a new dress. It's blue."

"Snoozefest," she blurts. "Come on, what happened to my friend? Where's the play-by-play on your wardrobe choices? A rundown of the men that will be at this event? Come on, single lady! Give me some thrilling details."

"Okay, Jess, let's see, what can I tell you?" Something inside me threatens to boil over. "I don't really care what I wear tonight, because I have the distinct feeling that things are going to go south with my job, so I might as well be wearing yoga pants and flip flops. There are going to be no men at this event—none I want to be with, anyway. My apartment's not ready yet, so I'm living with my mother. Yes, you heard that correctly. When I went jogging last night, one of those Gardwin kids hit me in the head with a football." Abruptly stopping, I look over to the corner of the bedroom where the Monet print is sticking out of a box.

"Maddie, things aren't as bleak as all that," she says solemnly.

"Aren't they?"

"No, they're not. This isn't about your job, and it's not about your parents, or your clothes, or even that weird kid next door. Why don't you just tell him? I think if you did, you'd figure out really quickly that things aren't what they seem. Spoons don't go in the cat food, buddy. Just take his calls."

"I'll take your advice about spoons," I state, shaking my head. "The rest is ill-timed at best. I have to go, Jess. Kiss Isaiah for me, and tell him forks work better for cat food."

Sitting on my bed, I release a huge sigh as I look at that Monet. The thing with Josh, the tennis issue, my relationship with Mom, my job insecurities, my apartment woes… Those are a

whole lot of paint blobs, aren't they? Messy, ill-placed paint blobs threatening to obscure something that has the potential to be beautiful.

Still, the blobs aren't the focus, right? The blobs are part of the whole—a creation that is perfectly orchestrated on a large scale.

Maybe Hazel is right. Maybe all of this was for nothing but to put me in the right place at the right time, so I could watch for the opportunity to love my enemies. Like Reverend Shell said that day…when you pray about your enemies, you're not going to receive ammunition to use against them, but opportunities to love them.

I nearly laugh as I realize the truth with startling clarity: Being forced to have a job where I do nothing. Living with a parent who criticizes everything I do. Feeling betrayed by one of my best friends. Spending most of my time alone.

It's almost ironic, really, after all my criticism and judgmental thoughts.

I *am* Audrey Cooper.

"Is that what you're wearing?" Mom remarks as I step into the living room, adjusting the strap on the heel of my black slingbacks. Instinctively I glance down at the blue dress that skims narrowly over my hips, waiting for an insult.

"That was the plan," I state hesitantly.

"Come here," she requests, pulling off her apron and walking back to her bedroom. I reluctantly follow her down the hall as she steps into the closet. It's difficult for me not to slouch a bit. I haven't cried, because I want to look good for the party, but I really wanted to for a while. Really, really wanted to.

"Here," Mom finally tells me, jerking a black garment bag loose from the back of the closet.

"What's that?" I wonder, wrinkling my nose a bit as she unzips the protective lining.

"It's the dress I wore to my wedding rehearsal," she answers, "you know, back in the 1980's. When I was thinner."

I am terrified of what she's about to pull out of that bag. I'm picturing hot pink ruffles with a black leather jacket at the top, complete with legwarmers and studded heels. Instead, she pulls out a deep grey fitted dress, with one shoulder strap that disappears into a knot along the neckline.

"This was yours?" I gasp, reaching out to take it in my hands.

"Yes," she insists with a slight laugh. "I was practically perfect, too, once upon a time."

"You have to preface your comments with 'once upon a time' if you're going to invoke the words 'practically perfect' you know. Attaining that is an impossibility."

"Well, anyway, you should wear the dress. It deserves another moment in the spotlight."

"I'll try it," I assure her, stepping back towards my bedroom.

"Oh, and Maddie? Maybe tomorrow, when you go on your jog, I could start jogging with you? And maybe Brittany too—not tomorrow, but when she's ready?"

Imagining Mom trying to keep up with me on my jog is slightly humorous, but I don't laugh as I look at her expectant face. Now that I've reached the whole "loving my enemies" epiphany about Audrey, should I turn my focus to Mom and Brittany? The thought nearly makes me cringe, but I'm pretty sure I already know the answer.

"Sure, Mom. Sounds like fun."

I arrived at my destination when it was nearing 6:00 p.m., wearing Mom's dress and decidedly early. Since the event was scheduled for 7:00, I wanted to make sure there weren't going to be any hiccups that required attention. Everything appeared to be in order. The Gerber daisies Audrey chose for her wedding were set up along a trellis by the door, and the food smelled absolutely terrific. Everything looked simply perfect.

About fifteen minutes before the event begins, Katie finds her way to my side.

"You did all this?!" she exclaims, glancing around.

"Well, I had a lot of help, but...yeah, I guess so. Are you surprised?"

"Complete and utter shock," she mutters.

Katie makes small talk about the state of her job, but my nerves are racing and the butterflies are beginning to spin in my stomach as I wonder how Audrey will react. To be honest, I'm a little surprised that I feel this way. I didn't know I cared quite so much, but I really do want Audrey to be happy. Who would have ever believed that I would go to so much trouble for the girl who sat sullenly in her office that first day, primping and talking on her cell phone? The old Maddie was...well, I'll just admit it. I was too selfish to think about doing something like this for another person. It would appear that I really have progressed a little in the last few months.

"Madeline," I hear a familiar voice behind me. Turning around, I see Harley Laine standing there looking beautiful as usual, with no cameraman in sight.

"Harley," I state casually. "You're here."

"I said I would be. My cameraman is taking some shots of the crowd and getting some background. You didn't lie—the cream of the crop are here tonight."

"No, that was true." Harley and I glance at the people who are milling in and out, sampling the drinks and food. The event already looks like a success, even though Audrey and Cooper aren't scheduled to arrive for a few moments.

Harley makes her escape and I look to the front of the building, where I see Audrey emerging from the back of her father's car. The rose dress is shimmering in the street lights and the butterflies look like they're dancing in the breeze. I briefly wonder how Cooper convinced her to wear the dress and come along with him, but it doesn't matter. She's here now, and she is seeing the full effect of what her father has done for her.

For a moment, she almost looks skeptical. She stands on the sidewalk staring up at the sign in front of the building, assessing her surroundings. Cooper moves up behind her, placing his arm around her shoulders and speaking quietly to her. In the background, Mrs. Cooper stands silently in her expensive-looking white gown. Then, Audrey turns to her father, stares at his face for a moment, and throws her arms around his neck. He appears to be shocked momentarily, but he gently pats her back and allows her to hug him.

"She's happy, isn't she?" I whisper to myself. "Thank you, God, for unexpected glimpses of the masterpiece."

The little family enters the front door, and the room erupts into applause. Audrey beams next to her father, finally being the center of attention in the Cooper family. It's about time, in my humble opinion. I clap along quietly until the noise begins to die down and Cooper clears his throat.

"Thank you all so much for coming," he bellows, his loud voice completely filling the room. "This is a very big day for my family. Southbend Pet Resort may look like an upscale place to board your animal friends, but it's so much more. Through the generous donations of its paying clientele, it will also serve as a rescue facility for dogs that are difficult to place for adoption. Please help me in congratulating the director of the resort, my daughter, Audrey Cooper."

He pats Audrey on the hand, and she looks as though she is about to explode as people swarm the couple to offer warm wishes.

It's a strange feeling, knowing that a project I've been working on so diligently is complete and I'll be free to begin something new. What kind of future can I expect working with

Kent Cooper now? I suppose I could try to think of some other ideas to talk him into, but the whole thing seems like an ultimate dead end. I can't continue to be his errand girl, picking up his coffee and dry cleaning, performing personal chores and solely existing to make his life easier. It's so…unfulfilling.

"Maddie?" I hear a voice behind me speak up. Turning, I see Audrey, hands folded together in front of her. She has a smile on her face, but she looks a little uncomfortable speaking with me.

"Congratulations, Audrey," I tell her, and she nods hesitantly.

"Dad told me what you've done. I want to say thank you."

"Well, it was your dad, really. He was behind the whole thing."

"Dad would never think of this. Besides, he would have never given me this responsibility on my own."

"Maybe I *did* put a bug in his ear," I admit with a laugh. "He's had you going through the company learning leadership skills, right? I hope you do really well, Audrey."

"Me too," she states, glancing at her shoes. "I don't know how to be a friend, Maddie. You've proven yourself to be a good friend to me, and I'm sorry."

Staring at Audrey, humbly standing in front of me, I wonder why I ever thought I deserved better than her. Even though she's wealthy, she doesn't have a desirable life.

"It's okay, Audrey. The thing is, none of us really knows how to be a friend. I certainly don't consider myself an expert. We just do the best we can and hope everything turns out well in the end."

"Audrey Cooper?" a voice behind me asks, causing Audrey to look up and smile.

"Yes, that's me."

"We've got a few questions for you, if you don't mind," Harley tells her, coming into my line of vision. "That okay?" She glances at me, and I take a step backward, careful to be safely out of the line of sight. This is Audrey's big moment, after all, not mine.

"Good evening, this is Harley Laine reporting from Southbend Pet Resort, a new not-for-profit boarding facility that also serves as a pet rescue center. The resort's director is Audrey Cooper, and there is quite a party going on behind us for the big opening. Audrey, can you tell the people watching at home what they're witnessing here?"

Audrey glances nervously at me, and I attempt to smile reassuringly, but she continues to stand motionless in front of the camera, frozen like a Christmas Eve snowman. Harley sends me a visual plea for help, and I step up to Audrey's side.

"Harley, what I think you're witnessing is the culmination of a lifelong dream to rescue animals, assisted by this dedicated group of people who are donating to the cause for the betterment of our city. Audrey Cooper is uniquely gifted with a passion for this work, and is therefore donating her time to provide this asset to our community."

"And what should people do if they want to help?" Harley asks me, pointing the microphone at my face.

"There will be an open house all day Monday, so people can stop by and view the facility for themselves, look at the boarding options, maybe even adopt a pet. And, of course, there will be door prizes and refreshments, donated by Cooper Corporate Financial."

"Cooper Corporate Financial has been doing a lot of outreach in the community lately," Harley continues, looking at me pensively. "Is this a trend that we'll see continuing in the future?"

Smiling at that newswoman, I place my arm around Audrey. "I can't predict the future, or even tell you what tomorrow will bring, but I do know one thing: In life, you can remain stagnant and predictable, or you can learn and grow and become more than you thought possible. That means being less self-absorbed and learning to be a better friend. If a company can adopt that same mindset, imagine what Cooper Corporate Financial and other companies like them could be, when they choose to be good neighbors and friends to their fellow citizens."

"I can only imagine…" Harley states, turning to the camera. "There you have it—a veritable who's who from the local community turning out in force to support this new venture. Audrey, Maddie, thank you for your time."

"Thank you, Harley," I say as she drops the microphone and the cameraman tilts the camera toward the ground.

"Sure," she adds with a smile. "Maybe I'll see you jogging soon."

I allow myself to nod, even though I am perfectly aware that she will not be seeing me jog, since I am miles away from Wonder Lane.

"Your dad looks like he's waiting for you," I tell Audrey. "He's really proud of you."

"Maybe he will be, someday," she agrees. "Thank you, Maddie."

It's impossible not to smile as she walks away and Katie finds me once more.

"Got yourself on television again?" she teases.

"What's a girl to do?" I ask. "The camera loves me."

After Katie and I eat our share of steak and vegetable skewers, we stand to the side of the crowd and watch the festivities.

"Is Cooper always like that?" she wonders. I glance over to see Cooper and his wife next to the mayor. He is gesturing animatedly, and she is staring off into space as though this is the most boring party she's ever attended. It's amazing to me that they get along so well, since they seem to be such opposites.

"Yeah, he has basically one speed," I surmise.

"He's almost orange," she states calmly, causing me to laugh out loud. It's true—Cooper looks strangely orange tonight. Most likely he tried his hand at spray tanning this morning and had

a disastrous failure. Maybe that's why Mrs. Cooper is remaining a couple of feet behind him tonight…she's embarrassed at having to be seen with him.

"If you cross Ernie and Bert from *Sesame Street*, that would be Cooper," Katie whispers.

"Maybe we should call him Bernie," I offer with a giggle.

Katie coughs a couple times and puts her fist in front of her mouth to stifle a laugh. "Don't look now, but Bernie's coming this way."

She's correct—Cooper's heading in our direction and moving very quickly. For a moment I consider finding a place to hide, but I fear it's too late. He already has his eyes set on me, and scampering away doesn't appear to be an option. From behind me, Katie begins chanting: *Bernie, Bernie, Bernie.*

"Well, Maddie, who is your friend?" Cooper states, thrusting his hand out at Katie.

"Katie Green," she says, straightening up immediately. "Human Resources, sir."

"*That* Katie Green?" he wonders, looking at me with a smirk. "Kent Cooper. I hope you won't mind if I borrow Maddie for a moment. There are some people I would like to introduce to her."

"Absolutely," Katie replies, poking me in the back.

How I wish I could turn around and smack her, but Cooper is staring at me. Instead, I calmly smile and walk away, following Cooper into the crowd. It's difficult to keep sight of him as he weaves in and out through the throng of people, finally coming to a halt as he motions me forward.

"This is my brother, Brent," Cooper states, and I dutifully stick out my hand. Brent looks a little like Cooper (although he's not orange), but he does seem to be a little more on the physically fit side. If I were to guess, he could easily take Cooper in a tennis match.

"And this is his assistant, Kelli," Cooper continues, pointing at the young woman next to Brent. She's quite attractive, with hair the color of milk chocolate and light brown eyes, very thin and agile-looking. She has an air about her, however, that makes me believe that we would not be the best of friends.

"*Mrs.* Kelli Cooper," she says, holding her hand out limply in front of her. "I'm Brent's wife." Shaking her hand is like wrapping my palm around a dead fish in Cooper's seafood museum.

"Assistant, wife, it's such a long and confusing story," Cooper states, dismissing Kelli as though she's nothing. "This is *my* assistant, Madeline Heard."

"It's nice to meet you, Madeline," Brent says solemnly. "You deserve a medal of honor for putting up with my brother."

"My salary is fine, I suppose," I reply with a smile, "although I would accept a medal if it was offered." Brent chuckles at my remark, but Kelli rolls her eyes.

"I recognize you," she states. "You're the one I keep seeing in the paper doing those charity things."

"Yes, that's me," I agree. She lifts her chin a bit so she can look down her nose at me.

"Well, you look different in person."

It's impossible to tell whether that's good or bad, so I simply let it slide.

"Madeline is an avid tennis player," Cooper says, glancing over at me. "She's at the club every single week."

"Is that right?" Brent asks. "I wish I was that motivated. I'm lucky if I make it over a couple times a month. Kelli probably goes more than I do, but she enjoys it so much, and it's good exercise."

"That it is," I reply.

Cooper clears his throat and pushes a little closer into the middle of our circle. "I just had an idea," he states, pointing at Brent. "We should have a little match, the four of us. The two brothers and their assistants in a little friendly competition. Wouldn't that be a hoot?!"

You just had an idea? Really? Hmmm…

"I'm his wife, you halfwit," Kelli blurts. Brent immediately grabs her arm in a motion to quiet her.

"Are you sure that's a good idea, Kent?" Brent asks as he continues to restrain Kelli with his left hand. "The doctor said you

shouldn't participate in strenuous activity, with your heart the way it is."

"Exercise is good for the heart, Brent, haven't you heard that? You're not concerned about my health, though. Surely you're not afraid that we would beat you?"

Brent laughs quietly, releasing his hold on Kelli, who huffs a bit before she stares at the wall.

"I'm sure you're a terrific tennis player, Madeline, and you seem like a delightful young woman. I just don't feel that having a match would be appropriate right now."

"Admit it, Brent, you're afraid of a little friendly competition. You think we might have a chance of beating you, and you don't want to be humiliated. That's it, isn't it?" Cooper's face has turned into a new shade—sort of a burnt sienna. I've never seen him like this, so I don't know whether he's flushed or really angry.

"I'm not afraid, Kent, so drop it." Brent looks at me for a moment and gives a tight smile as though he's apologizing for his brother's behavior, and I widen my eyes briefly before staring at the floor.

"Then what is it? Why won't you give me the satisfaction of having one little tennis match against you and your assistant? What harm would it do?"

I look up just in time to see Kelli return her face to our group, inch toward Cooper, and look defiantly in his eyes. "I'm expecting, you tyrant," she informs him. "Brent and I are going to have a baby."

I *absolutely* did not see that coming.

Cooper stands back and drops his arms, looking at Brent with his mouth gaping open a tad. Instinctively I back up a few inches, although I'm not sure what I expect to happen. If this were a movie, it would be the scene where Cooper's head explodes and his body is left standing there, just a tuxedo with hands and shoes.

"You're…going to have a baby?" Cooper mutters, definitely quieter than I have ever heard him.

Brent nods and puts his arm around his little spitfire, drawing her closer. "That's right. We're going to have a child," Brent confirms.

I can't force myself to look at Cooper—no doubt this has completely deflated him. All these months of training me for the match, and now...

Well, it really is funny, isn't it? Here I was worrying about how I was going to get out of playing this dreadful match with Cooper, and it would have never happened anyway. Kelli is pregnant.

Ha! Kelli is pregnant!

I stifle the urge to laugh, biting my lower lip as I stand there silently looking at Brent and Kelli. They certainly do make an odd couple, but they have just made my day. My body wants to jump up and down and scream for joy, or perform a victory lap around the building, heels and all.

Cooper turns and stalks away, and I'm left alone in front of the strange couple.

"It was nice to meet you," I mumble, taking my leave. Cooper stops about halfway through the crowd and manages to find a barstool, where he slumps down and gazes out into the street through the glass front of the building. Remaining behind him a moment, I'm not sure if I should walk away.

"Monday morning," Cooper suddenly states, "I want you to go over to that electronics store across the street and get one of those new high-tech cellphones they've been advertising."

Cellphone—check.

"And then I want you to go to one of the department stores and find a white shirt with salmon stripes. Salmon...not pink. It's for my meeting on Thursday, so make sure they can have it tailored by then."

Salmon stripes—check.

"You might as well pick up one of those cinnamon buns on your way back, too."

Cinnamon... What am I doing?

"I'm sorry, sir, but isn't this getting old?" I manage to state, not even thinking about the consequences.

"Come again?" He glances up at me, allowing a wrinkle to form between his eyebrows.

Fighting to build courage, I press on. "You don't need an assistant, you have Dina. And there's no need for me to take tennis lessons anymore. Coming up with charity projects isn't a full-time job."

He grows pensive for a minute, and I'm fairly certain I've just managed to get myself fired.

"Well, I'm going to want you taking a lead on helping Audrey over here, naturally. And I'm not convinced that giving up the charity projects is worthwhile. I want you to keep heading those up. But the truth is, you're really not a great assistant."

Not a great assistant?! How can he say such a thing? I have been an incredible assistant.

"Not a great assistant?" I repeat doubtfully.

He wrinkles his nose a bit and shakes his head. "No. Come to think of it, you're definitely more of a Marketing Account Leader."

"I accept, sir!" I blurt, which causes him to laugh boisterously.

"Okay, Monday morning, I'll have Davies returned to his previous duties, and you can pack up your office, on one condition."

Half my salary? Return the tree frogs? Ugh, give back the Tahoe?

"What's the condition?" I wonder hesitantly.

He gives me a slight smile. "Once and for all, *stop* calling me sir."

Chapter Thirty-Seven

Thank goodness I didn't have the band canceled for Audrey's wedding, because I feel like dancing. Cloud dancing, to be exact. Top of the rainbow dancing. Instead, Katie and I settle for dancing the regular old way, in a group of people, throwing abandon to the wind. I stepped back from the blobs, and tonight I saw the Monet, and it's pretty awesome.

And now, I am slow dancing with some guy named Washington who works with Katie in HR. Is his first name Washington, or his last name? Who cares, really? I'm so in the zone, I don't even care that he smells slightly like Cooper's seafood museum. In fact, I'm mentally laughing at my own little joke when I feel a tap on my shoulder, and Washington releases my hand so I can turn.

It's really easy to be angry with someone from a distance, when there's just an abstract idea there and hurt feelings in the way. But when he taps you on the shoulder, and you turn around to find him standing there, muscles perfectly filled out beneath his black button-down shirt with the sleeves rolled up to his elbows, a couple inches taller than you in your heels, his gray-green eyes focused completely on you and you alone, the wall is melted really quickly.

"Josh," I breathe, nearly in disbelief. Saying more isn't necessary, because in this instant I'm simply happy that he's not half a world away. We're not separated by hours, or oceans, or phone lines. He's in front of me, in the flesh. Moving forward, I step into his embrace, and then I'm afraid to move...afraid that I'm imagining him here, and when I release him I will find that my arms are still being occupied by Washington from HR.

"I'm home," he says, his voice reverberating through his chest with a subtle vibration against my own. "Come with me? I need to talk to you."

Nodding, I stop to grab my coat as we head out the door. Katie isn't in my line of sight so I can tell her goodbye, but maybe she'll text me later and I can explain. I'm certain she would do the same thing, if the situations were reversed.

Josh opens the door to his black truck, which has been sitting at his parents' house for the past year, and I step up into the cab, noting the woodsy scent of his cologne. The minute he starts the truck, I force a deep breath and attempt to appear unaffected.

"When did you get home?" I ask cautiously.

"This morning."

I'm trying not to look at him, but it's extremely difficult.

"I had no idea," I admit, forcing my eyes to stay away from that face.

"Well, surprise," he states with little emotion. "I asked my parents not to say anything."

"So this is why you kicked me out?" I surmise, daring to turn my gaze to him again. He glances at me, lips lifting in a bit of a smirk.

"I like your dress." It's a blatant attempt to change the subject, but I suppose it works.

"It's my mother's," I tell him. "She wore it to her wedding rehearsal."

"You and your mom are back on speaking terms, then?" he wonders. Suddenly I'm hit with the fact that I haven't conversed with Josh in a week, and I feel extremely guilty for jumping to conclusions.

"Yeah, I'm sort of in her house right now, so some talking is required."

He looks at me pensively and sighs. "I'm really sorry. I had no idea you were staying with your parents until I had to call your dad to find you tonight. Move back into the house, okay? I'll stay with Mom and Dad. I would have never asked you to move in the first place, but I can't live in the same house with you. You know that, right?"

"I know," I tell him quickly. "You just came back from serving our country—I'm not kicking you out of your house. Besides, I have an apartment in the city that will be ready next week."

"So far away?"

I'm not sure how to respond, because a fifteen minute drive never seemed far before, but now the thought of being that distance from Wonder Lane is filling me with dread.

"You're not wearing your glasses," I casually insert, wanting to change the subject.

"No," he agrees, laughing quietly and glancing at the dash. "I was trying to look—"

"Like a different person," I offer, pulling his glasses off their resting spot on the dashboard. "Can you even see without them? Is that your plan, attempted vehicular murder by blurred vision?"

"I can see well enough," he insists, but he takes his glasses from my hand and pushes them onto his face. "Better?"

"Now you look like Josh," I tell him with a smile.

"And you look incredible. Sorry I didn't tell you that before."

We continue on, alternating between awkward small talk and even more uncomfortable silence, but I don't bother to ask him where we're going. The truth is, I'm not even paying attention. My mind is so focused on looking at him while not looking at him that I can't concentrate on anything.

When the tires begin crunching against gravel and I glance out the window, all I see is darkness, but I don't have time to think about it because Josh is already out of the truck. It's chilly in the night air as I step out and glance around, finally looking up.

"You brought me to the old water tower?" It's not really a question, but more of a statement, because I can see it rising above me.

"There comes a point where you can't keep seeing a wrong over and over without trying to fix it," he says cryptically, stepping

away from the truck. I take a couple faltering steps in the gravel with my heels, standing in front of the passenger front tire.

"I haven't been here since prom," I tell him.

"Me either." He returns to his truck and opens the door, rolling the windows down, which makes me wonder if he's gone slightly crazy during his time away. It's entirely too cold for that kind of action. Then, he punches some buttons on the radio and cranks the music up. A few bars manage to play before he walks away from the vehicle.

"Green Day?" I question accusingly. "You brought me out here to play the exact same song that was playing when Ricky Buchanan left me standing on the dance floor, waltzing away with Heather?"

"Yes." He crosses the gravel to stand in front of me, and then pauses to rub his fist against his forehead. "Ricky Buchanan left you standing there, and I said he didn't deserve you, but I was afraid to be honest with you that night."

"Honest about what?" I manage to whisper.

He smiles sadly as he looks into my eyes. "I knew Ricky wasn't the guy for you that night, just like I knew Ben wasn't the guy, or Vic, or Max, or any other guy that has crossed your path before or since, because I'm the guy, Mad. I'm the guy, and I'm sick of being your friend, because I don't want to be your friend."

"You don't want to be my friend," I repeat quietly.

"No. I want to be your everything."

My heart is pounding uncontrollably as I stare at his tense face.

"Josh, you are," I assure him. "You already are."

He shakes his head as he takes my hand in his. "How can you say that? You're always searching—"

"For horrible Josh substitutions," I insist, sliding my fingers through his until they're locked together. "I realized it the night I went out with Max. He brought me back to Wonder Lane, and I was trying to figure out what was wrong with him, when I suddenly realized... Well, I realized he wasn't you. I've been so stupid."

The words haven't completely left my mouth when he catches my lips with his, meeting my own partly open and relatively breathless. For a second I struggle to find my wits and balance, but then decide I simply don't care, allowing that mouth that has fascinated me for so long to possess my own in a moment that completely surpasses any expectations I held. With his free hand he circles my waist and draws me closer, forcing me to tilt my head up as he pulls his lips away, managing to draw my bottom lip with them for a split second. Allowing a shaky breath to escape, I gaze up into his eyes.

"I was in love with you the last time we were here, and I knew somewhere inside you loved me, too. Waiting for you to figure it out has been pretty brutal."

"What about the girls you dated? If you knew…"

"I was always trying to fill a Mad-shaped hole."

"Why didn't you say something?"

He continues to hold me close, not allowing any space between us. "I told you that love was patient and steadfast that night, and you said, 'You're such a great friend.' I told you I wasn't your friend, and you said, 'True. More like a brother, really.'"

"Josh—"

"I am not your brother, Madeline," he whispers with a short laugh.

"I know," I assure him, smiling into his handsome face. "If you kissed me like that then, I might have realized it a lot sooner. And don't call me Madeline."

He returns my grin with a smile that practically melts my heart. "Fine, Mad. Are you really mine at last? Am I free to love you?"

"Only if I'm allowed to love you back."

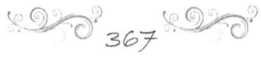

Sitting on the tailgate with a warm arm wrapped around my shoulders, I stare at the lights of Louisville that loom in front of us, barely noticing the cold. When I think about the countless times that I've been side by side with Josh, close enough to touch him, I could kick myself. My heart is pounding, a fluttering feeling is crawling through my stomach, and I can barely breathe. To think that I could find a man to love who is already one of my best friends…

Josh really knows me—embarrassing, horrible things about me. Things that I would have hidden from a prospective mate for years, and that would have caused me to flush with humiliation if my mother had brought them up in his presence. The man has seen me when I had the chickenpox, and witnessed several horrible home video productions that Jess and I dreamed into existence.

"Remember Jess and Levi's wedding, when we had to walk together down the aisle?" I ask, leaning into him a little further.

"Do I remember standing at the front of the church and watching you walk down the aisle toward me? Yeah, that's a pretty solid memory. Not sure I could uproot that one if I tried."

"I was really glad that it was you and me in the pictures together."

"I had big plans for that day," he says wistfully, causing me to pull back to look at his face. "I was going to tell you that night."

"What? That was four years ago!"

"You think I don't know that? Trust me, I've felt each day of every single one."

Allowing my eyebrows to slant together, I give him my best attempt at a glare. "So why didn't you tell me?"

"Because you caught the bouquet."

I consider extending the dirty look I've given him, but when a hint of a smile touches his lips and he rubs his knuckles against my cheek, any sarcasm dies instantly.

"What does catching the bouquet have to do with anything?"

"Nothing, by itself. After you caught the bouquet, though, you walked right up to Adam Hayes and asked him if he had any plans. The universe had spoken, you said."

"Please tell me you're making that up," I beg, biting the corner of my lip. With a solemn shake of his head, he wraps his fingers around the back of my neck.

"No. I wish I was. I just regrouped and started planning again, this time for Mom and Dad's Fourth of July picnic. You brought Brady Nichols with you, though."

"You can't blame that on me," I insist, lifting my eyebrows. "Brady had some beer in his truck, and when I informed him that he couldn't bring that inside, he left me there by myself."

Gazing at me with those gorgeous green eyes, Josh offers up a sideways smile. "Yeah, I sabotaged myself that time. When I saw Brady, I was a little miffed, so I called Cassidy Spencer. You were sitting there alone, and all I wanted was to go to you, but I couldn't get Cassidy off my arm the rest of the day. I tried, believe me. She probably thought I was crazy, calling her over to the house and then trying to get rid of her."

"I'm sorry," I offer, returning his grin. "I've certainly wasted a lot of your time, haven't I?"

"No," he says quickly, lowering his forehead to mine. "Loving you has never been a waste of my time."

His lips meet mine so slowly and effortlessly, it's as though they were drawn together. As the warmth of his kiss envelopes me, a sudden thought running through my mind forces a slight laugh to escape against his mouth.

"Do I want to know?" he wonders, pulling me against his chest.

"I was just thinking, maybe I should consider it a personal challenge to see if I can steam up your glasses. That might be kind of fun."

"Of course you would think of something like that," he complains, smoothing my hair away from my face. "But I'll be a willing participant, if you decide to give it a go."

"To be honest, I really miss Wonder Lane. I'm hoping to come visit now and then."

"Really? Because if I'm being honest, I think you're destined to be a permanent resident."

"I'll be around in the morning to help you pick up your vehicle," Josh tells me, smiling across the cab of the truck. We abandoned it when I left the party with him, and we never returned. Instead, we stayed at the water tower until well past midnight, telling each other all the things we've wanted to say for so long.

As it turns out, Josh has been planning this for a while. The reason he asked me to move was so he could date me properly, and then ask me to share his life with him, if things worked out. The way he smiled at me when he said that, I swear my knees went weak immediately. Of course things will work out, and one day...

Madeline Mason.

Too soon, right? Yeah, I know.

Josh places the truck in park, opens my door, and walks me to the front porch like a perfect gentleman. When he leans toward me, I do the same, meeting him midway in anxious anticipation of a kiss that sends butterflies into my stomach and flames shooting through my veins. Now that I've experienced the bliss of kissing Josh, I doubt anything will ever satisfy me again.

When we part, he brushes his thumb slowly across my bottom lip.

"My Josh," I whisper. "I love you."

"I know," he says, kissing the spot where his thumb just rested. "I love you, beautiful Mad. Goodnight."

"Goodnight," I repeat, hesitantly pulling my eyes away from him and stepping over the threshold into my parents' house.

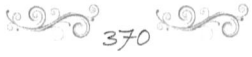

Still mentally sighing contentedly, I fumble through the dark, trying not to trip over Mom's rearranged furniture. When I finally manage to make it to the kitchen unscathed, the lights suddenly flip on overhead. Blinking against the instant brilliant exposure, I throw my hand up to block the glare.

"You're late," Mom states in a friendly tone. "I guess you must have had a good time."

"Josh is home," is all I can manage, and even at that I can't erase the ridiculous smile from my face.

"Oh, that's great news."

Wondering at her attitude, I reach down to slide off one of my heels as I tip precariously on the other. "You really didn't have to wait up for me."

She settles onto a bar stool as she looks over at me. "Oh, I know, but I wanted to make sure you had fun. Besides, your dad and I watched the news tonight, and we saw you on there with that Harley Laine."

"Harley Laine?" I repeat hesitantly.

"Yes, Harley Laine," she repeats, grinning at me like a Cheshire cat. "Are you two friends again?"

Chapter Thirty-Eight

The sun is shining brightly overhead on a Saturday in early summer as I stand on the porch on Wonder Lane and knock quietly on the very familiar door.

"No soliciting," I hear from behind the window, and then a grinning face peeks down at me. "Do you want to come in?"

"And break my 'no girls in the house' rule? I'm sorry, but I'll have to remain on the porch."

The door swings inward and my eyes rest on Josh, leaning against the doorframe with a completely beguiling smile. His crisp white shirt is unbuttoned at the collar, and he's holding a necktie in his hand. He's also wearing blue gym shorts.

"Your wedding attire is a bit casual, isn't it?"

"I've got a few minutes left," he insists, reaching for my hand and pulling me through the entryway. "I missed you like crazy." He leans down to plant a feathery kiss on my neck, and I can't stop the outward expression of my pleasure from showing on my face.

"It's been hours since I've seen you. Honestly, how did you make it overseas all that time?"

"I'd have never made it if you kissed me before I left," he says, wrapping his arms around my waist. "And look—just like that, you're in the house."

"Well, I never said I was good at following rules," I tell him with a smile. "Now, unless you're planning on going to the wedding wearing jogging shorts, I suggest you put your pants on, Joshua."

"The knot's not even tied and you're already bossing me around," he jokes, releasing me as he walks toward his bedroom.

Instinctively I glance down at the ring on my left hand, catching its sparkle in the light.

When I told my coworkers about the proposal, they said, "Wow, taking this fast, aren't you?"

The funny thing is, when we told Hazel and Tucker, their response was the opposite.

"It's about time," Hazel told us, tears filling her eyes.

As for Jess, she squealed during our long-distance phone call. "We're going to be sisters for real," she said. "Don't put the cracker back in the box after you licked it." I'm sure there was a real life lesson in there somewhere, but I'm fairly certain it wasn't meant for me.

"How was the race?" Josh yells from the bedroom right before he emerges into the hallway, wearing the requisite black pants with his tie in its proper place. His hair is finally getting longer and messy in the front again, just the way I like it.

"We didn't race, exactly, but they all finished the entire 5K. Mom made it to the end pretty easily. We had to coax Brittany through, but Audrey was determined enough that she pushed herself. I'm really proud of them."

"You should have let me come cheer you on," he says as his arms find their way around my waist again.

"You know I wanted you there, but Audrey is finally letting loose from her shell, and you would have made her self-conscious. She did try to get me to adopt three different dogs today. She's relentless!"

"Maybe when you're a permanent resident of Wonder Lane," he tells me with a wink. "I've got all sorts of plans."

"Tell me of these plans," I implore, staring up into those gray-green eyes. "What sort of elaborate details are included?"

"Nothing elaborate," he states, lowering his face until his lips are a whisper away. "Simply Mad."

About the Author

Christina Coryell is the Amazon bestselling author of The Camdyn Series. A resident of small-town southwest Missouri, where she lives with her husband and two children, she does most of her writing in unorthodox places and with lots of noise in the background. She is completely sane most of the time, but poor character development in novels drives her mad. As does stepping in water with socks on her feet.

She loves to hear from her readers and welcomes interaction on Facebook, Twitter, and by email at her website, www.christinacoryell.com.

Independent authors rely on your support. If you enjoyed Simply Mad, please consider telling a friend and writing a review.

A Few Words

Thank you so much to my family and friends who support me in this venture. I appreciate each and every one of you so much more than you know.

To Mike—thank you for the special Christmas gift that makes it much easier for me to write anywhere.

To Reinah and Truett, so many of my words are written while listening to you laugh or argue, and watching your joy over just being kids. Know all those times you asked, "Why are you staring at me?" It's because I love you, so you might as well get used to it.

Special thanks to Linda Meckem, for being my sounding board and sharing in my sometimes ridiculous excitement, and to my lovely author sister T.I. Lowe, for giving me insight into my blurting habits.

A huge pat on the back goes to my fantastic cover photographer, Kassi Hillhouse. You knocked it out of the park!

And an especially fun tidbit: My bestie version of Jess growing up was Tammy. Her niece is the cover model on this book. Rachel, thank you for agreeing to translate the Madeline in my mind to a form of reality. Working with you was lovely!

To those of you who enjoy my books, your kind words inspire me to keep going. Thank you for your support!

Most of all, thank you to God for taking me to places that I couldn't have imagined, and for blessing me beyond my wildest dreams. I can't wait to see what story unfolds next.

Coming Soon
Girls of Wonder Lane

Book 2
Harley Laine

Louisville's hottest reporter appears to have it all—a perfect job, great car, beautiful house, and designer clothes. She's poised to set herself up as the woman at the top, until a gruff old biker, a teenage girl, and the absolute wrong guy threaten to derail her plans.

Book 3
Alexis Jennings

Alexis has spent the past few years living someone else's life, but she's finally ready to make a fresh start. Outrunning her past might prove difficult, however, when Jake McAuliffe decides to follow her out of town.

And Don't Miss The Camdyn Series

Available Now:

A Reason to Run
A Reason to Be Alone
A Reason to Forget
For No Reason

Camdyn Taylor is a bestselling author hiding a bit of a secret—her identity. The victim of viral video proposal infamy, she heads out of town in the name of book research seeking a little anonymity. She never expects that a wrong turn could wind up not only changing her perspective, but possibly her entire life.

Equal parts romance, chick-lit, and women's fiction with a little history thrown in for good measure.

www.ingramcontent.com/pod-product-compliance
Lightning Source LLC
Chambersburg PA
CBHW030359180626
46812CB00005B/1854